dead souls

Morrígan Books

Available titles from Morrígan Books:

The Even
by T. A. Moore

How to Make Monsters
by Gary McMahon

Voices
Edited by Mark S. Deniz & Amanda Pillar

Grants Pass
Edited by Jennifer Brozek & Amanda Pillar

Coming soon from Morrígan Books:

The Phantom Queen Awakes
Edited by Mark S. Deniz & Amanda Pillar

dedication

For Audrey Kitara
for making my soul anything but.

Mark would like to thank:

Reece Notley for just about everything; Sharon Ring, Brad C. Hodson, Pete Kempshall, Sharon Kennedy, Kym MacFarlane, and Michael Bailey for your tireless proofreading work; Etina Deniz, for constant support and ideas; Nikki Phillips for some lovely cover art that we were unable to use, due to a change in direction; Amanda Pillar, always there when most needed and Greg Ballam for all the support I could ever need.

dead souls

Edited by Mark S. Deniz

Published by Morrígan Books
Östra Promenaden 43,
602 29 Norrköping, Sweden

www.Morríganbooks.com

ISBN 978-91-977605-8-4

Cover art by Reece Notley ©2009
First Published September 2009
The moral rights of the authors have been asserted.
All stories are original to this collection unless otherwise stated in the acknowledgements.

table of contents

introduction

Within these pages, you will find a man so affected by the horrors he witnessed at war, he believes another is guiding his actions; a small boy with enough malevolence to shake a young girl to her very core; a tattoo artist with a hidden agenda. You will read about a future not as bright as we might have imagined or hoped; a puppet show with a damning message; a new twist on the theory of Beethoven's *Immortal Beloved*; Adolf Hitler in a new guise, and something terrible that approaches us in the desert. All this, plus many, many more, tales of darkness and human suffering.

Dead Souls is a re-imagining of a previous book, forced into a new life, which began with the title before moving on to the cover and extra tales.

Trying to come up with a new title for a book that was about to be *reborn* was a little difficult, to say the least, but fell into place when I was having a day of nostalgia, going through my CD collection. Although it has been suggested on forums and in mails that the title has come from a certain Russian classic, I actually decided on the name whilst listening to one of my Joy Division albums. Granted, they may have taken their track's name from said book but that is by the by. I was reading one of the selected stories at the time, and it was a clear representation of my concept of *Dead Souls*. All of a sudden another story fit the concept, and then another, and it very soon became evident that everything I had for the book fell easily into this category, and the book could not have any other name.

Now, I had an interesting book and title but it needed something extra, something that would make it stand out in the world of dark independent press. I began contacting authors I admire: Ramsey Campbell, Gary McMahon, Kaaron Warren,

Robert Hood, Stephanie Campisi, amongst others, to write something for me. Some sent me whole new material, others offered reprints of previously published, yet fantastic stories, all of which I felt matched the theme.

The theme was further exemplified by Reece Notley's current cover and, in my opinion, this is the best Morrigan Books cover we have to date. It showed that all of us involved in the *Dead Souls* concept were starting to get to grips with the new theme of the book. The theme I most wanted to examine was that of human nature through short stories about people, people who do terrible things. These things could be of their own motivation, guided by others or, in some cases, forced by some malevolent entity.

Finally, slotting the stories in place and getting some thoughtful comments from an excellent team of proofreaders (who I am sincerely hoping will work with me again), made me see what it is we have produced — a book that stands very comfortably with the other titles at Morrigan Books. *Dead Souls* was a challenge which not only taught me a lot about how the industry works, on many levels, but also showed me what I had only suspected I was capable of.

If you, like me, hark back to the days of Stoker and Poe, and like your horror psychological and thought-provoking, then you are going to love this collection. And if you love it half as much as I do, then my work is done.

Mark S. Deniz
August 2009

genesis

the collector

Bernie Mojzes

It's not all death, here on this hill, now that the battle has moved on.

Not yet.

The crows and vultures aren't waiting, though. The winter has been harsh and long, and the wolves and foxes have been loathe to leave them their share. They make the best of unexpected fortune: vultures tear flesh from bone while the crows feast on the softer tissue, so recently exposed that it still steams in the snow. Neither discriminates between living and dead, so long as the meal is too weak to be a threat.

One old crow refrains. Perched on a rocky outcropping, she surveys the carnage with a glittering eye as she tries to compose her ruffled feathers (the efforts do little to coax the errant feathers into place). Of the dozens of bodies strewn across the rocky slope, perhaps half still show signs of life. Some scream or cry, others hiss or curse through pain-clenched teeth. Yet others lay still, blessedly unconscious as the blood pools and freezes around them. So many stories, all come to a common end.

Some of the stories she knows; she's seen them birth and grow, watched these tales through the twists and turns of marriage, work, and secret lovers. She's even written some of the chapters herself. Other stories are mysteries. The end is clear — is always clear — but how these men with their strangely rounded speech, their festive and plumed uniforms, and their finely forged steel came to be here, to die on this hill with those they came to kill, those are stories that will forever be lost.

All stories have a beginning, and all stories come to an end. (*All but a few*, her inner bird caws.) And she is a collector of stories. She watches them develop with greedy eyes, and when they come to a close, she takes them home and places them with the others, fitting them together like nesting dolls.

But what use is an ending when the beginning is lost?

There are curses reserved for so wasteful a *God*. The crow contemplates them.

Further up the hill, torches are touched to thatch, and the village begins to burn. The fighting has turned to slaughter, and the slaughter to rape and slave-taking. The crow is there as well, watching from atop an aspen tree.

But there is one particular drama that she finds most compelling.

His name is Zoran, and he waves his broken spear at an overeager vulture that stretches its neck toward the entrails that spill between his fingers. She knows this man, dragged him bloodborn into life, cutting him from his mother's broken body while she was still warm, bedded him sixteen years later, at the turning of spring. Later still, she mid-wifed both his daughter and his son, now almost old enough to bed as well.

In the village, Zoran's wife and daughter are dragged screaming from a burning house. On the hillside, his son, Javor, lies on his back, laboured breath bubbling pink from his mouth and chest, only a few spear-lengths away from his father. Beside his body sits the Byzantine soldier who put the sword through Javor's chest. The Byzantine is pale, panicked to nervous immobility, hands clutching the spear that Javor pushed through his gut. He mouths silent curses as he tries to coax movement from his legs. The Byzantine is perhaps less lucky than the villager; the spear has severed his spine, but not the artery, and his ultimate fate is paralysis and an agonizingly long death of sepsis.

The Byzantine is hardly older than the boy.

Zoran shoves his intestines back inside his belly as best he can and wraps a strip torn from a dead soldier's tunic around his gut to hold himself together. Then, using the broken spear for support, he drags himself to his son's side. The Byzantine sees him approaching and seems to get a hold of himself. Javor is oblivious of everything but his own pain.

"I'm sorry," Zoran tells his son. He washes the blood and shit from his hands in a snow drift before he touches the boy's face. "I'm here now."

"Papa?" The boy reaches weakly. His eyes are unfocused, glazed. "Papa, did we win? Is Danica safe?"

In the story of this boy's life, just yesterday, Danica, the miller's daughter, kissed him on the cheek at the market. She had watched him for months, and he, her. And perhaps they'd have married. And perhaps in a year or two they'd have had children of their own. Or perhaps not. The crow sees little point in speculation. Might-have-beens won't line the nest.

In the village, Danica drags a paring knife, concealed in her hair, across the throat of a soldier as he mounts her, and is rewarded with a quick death on the blades of his companions.

The Byzantine boy dying on the mountainside looks at the child he's killed, and at the child's father. "Yes," he lies, his tongue stumbling over the Slavic words, "Yes, you have won. I am your prisoner."

"Thank Perun," the boy gasps. He grips his father's hand weakly. "Papa? Tell Danica I love her."

Then he gurgles and gasps. This story is drawing to a close, but perhaps not quickly enough; the boy is drowning in his own blood. He draws quick, pain-filled gasps through clenched teeth. "Make it stop!" The hissed demand is almost inaudible.

His father draws a knife and presses it against his son's throat. There's no saving the child, not from this wound. Only from a lingering and painful death. His hand trembles.

"Wait," the soldier says, laying a hand on Zoran's to stay him. "No father should have to do this. Let this be my burden."

Zoran looks at his son, then nods and lets the Byzantine take the blade from him. These hands do not shake. It is quick.

Javor shudders once as the blood sprays, and then is still.

The Byzantine soldier hands the knife to Zoran.

3

His end isn't as quick as Javor's, but it's quicker than he'd expected. The knife burns in his chest, sliding between ribs and into his heart. "Thank you," he says, and when Zoran pulls the blade, the blood flows freely, and he slumps over the dead boy.

As this private drama comes to a close, the old crow takes flight and lands on the dead soldier's shoulder.

"Why?" she asks, her voice harsh.

Zoran swallows, still staring at the blade. "He helped my son. Could I have done anything else?"

"Why?" the crow asks again.

"He killed my son. Could I have done anything else?" Zoran lets himself slump to the ground. There's little enough left in him, and nothing left to keep him here.

She rests his head on her knees, strokes his hair with cool fingers, and he recognizes her: his first lover. She had been tender and demanding and loving and beautiful and cruel. She had taken him for her own use and left him. Twenty winters have passed, more or less. She hasn't changed a bit.

"You've come back."

"I've always been here," she says. She puts her fingers to his lips. "Always have been. And always will be."

"Who are you?"

"Don't you already know?" She smiles sadly, and examines his wound. "Perhaps I could heal this." She stares into his eyes. Her long black hair shrouds his face. "If you could have one wish, what would it be? Would you like to live?"

He laughs, bitter. "My son is dead. My wife and daughter also, or worse. My village is destroyed. Everyone is dead. What is there to live for?"

"I can't answer that."

"What would I wish? I would wish my wife and daughter safe. I would wish my son walking again. I would wish the damned Empire and its accursed god driven from this land. Can you give me that?"

"All that?" Her face is grim. "Yes. But there are costs. Are you sure this is what you want?"

"Yes."

"Very well."

The old woman gets stiffly to her feet. She pushes at her wiry grey hair (the efforts do little to coax the errant strands into place), and clicks her fingers.

There's a sound of something galloping, hopping — something massive — and soon a small hut comes into view, running blindly on chicken legs up the hill. Zoran has difficulty focusing on it; it is made of wood, of twisted twigs, or of human bones and candy. It is perhaps all these things, and none of them. One of the legs helps the old woman up to the door. A great clatter spills from the hut: the sounds of a kitchen before a wedding, or a funeral. And before long the witch returns, carrying a wooden bowl and spoon.

Baba Yaga scoops a spoonful of steaming liquid from the bowl and presses it into Javor's unresponsive mouth. Then she rolls the Byzantine boy off Javor's body and feeds a spoonful to him as well. She makes her way around the battlefield, ministering to the dead.

Javor moves. He sits up, then pushes himself to his feet.

"Javor!" cries Zoran. "My beautiful son! You're alive!"

Javor doesn't respond. He looks around for a weapon, and, finding one, walks over to one of the injured Byzantine soldiers left on the hillside and cuts his throat. Something is wrong. His movements aren't blind, or purposeless. If anything, they are nothing but purpose: he slays one wounded Byzantine after another, until they are all dead, and nothing distracts him from this task.

And then Zoran realises that although his son is walking, he isn't breathing.

"What have you done?" Zoran drags himself toward the witch. "What have you done to my son?"

"I've done what you asked," Baba Yaga says. "Your son walks. He and the others will save your wife and daughter. They will drive the army of the Christ-god from this land until the flesh falls from their bones and their bones turn to dust." She scoops up her skirts to get down on bony knees, straddling his hips, kissing him passionately on the lips. He shudders and recoils.

One by one, the dead rise and arm themselves. Then they join Javor and march toward the burning village.

"Don't worry," she says. "You'll get to join your son soon enough. But there is yet time enough for you to thank me properly."

She is young and beautiful as she pulls her dress over her head, pert breasts high on her chest. She is old, toothless, the hairy mole on her lip tickling his nose as she presses her lips against his. The rounded belly of a woman in her middle years presses against his wound; her hips are wide with childbirth.

She is maiden, mother, crone. She is birth, and life, and death. She is all ages at once.

Up the hill in the direction of the village, the screaming has resumed. They are the cries of men this time, however. Not of women.

But they are nothing compared to Zoran's whimper as the eternal witch takes the only thing he has left.

When he is spent, she ruffles her feathers and lets them smooth (the efforts do little to coax the errant feathers into place). Then she cocks her head to stare with one glittering black eye into his. His eyes are green, laced with a hint of hazel. She's always loved his eyes.

They taste as good as they look.

licwiglunga
T.A. Moore

Gudrid ducked her head and trudged on: an old woman wearing a nun's habit over men's trews and boots. She was exhausted, old bones aching and the air like splinters in her lungs, freezing on the fur of her cloak, but she couldn't stop. If she stopped she would die; winter could kill quicker than a knife, especially here.

Nor could she return to the comfort of her convent, where her sisters would press warm mead on her and send for her thralls to attend her, not with the Lawspeaker's geas still on her shoulders.

He had come to her in church — Lawspeaker Orm — and knelt to her, although there was no humility to him. Somehow he had learnt that she had been tutored by a spae-wife as a girl.

"The daughter of Volgang is dead," he said. "Beyla, who would have been my bride. She sickened of the wasting fever and Hel took her only two days ago. She was the heart-beat in my chest, the breath in my lungs. Bring her back to me."

She had refused. It was an unchristian thing he was asking and she was a Christian woman who had made pilgrimage to Rome and seen the Holy Father there. Orm claimed allegiance to the Church, though he still wore Thor's Hammer strung around his neck. What he asked should never have been asked.

The second time he came he brought a chest with him that near foundered the thralls who carried it. Inside was the wealth of a year's trade: wine, grapes, furs turned to gold, and gems. He pledged to give it to the church if only she would help him.

"The daughter of Volgang is dead," he said. "Beyla, who would have sat by my side in judgement. Hel took her four days ago. She was the blood in my veins, the light in my eyes. Bring her back to me."

Gudrid offered him her prayers and refused him for a second time: her heart heavy with fear of what would come next.

Like Odin pursuing Rinda, Orm returned for a third time. This time he did not beg, nor did he ask. He came with armed men and threats against both the convent and Gudrid's family.

"The daughter of Volgang is dead," he said. "Beyla, who would have mothered my son. Hel took her only six days ago. She was the speech on my tongue, the song in my ears. Bring her back to me, or I send all who give you joy to join her."

Unchristian or no, Gudrid had no choice but to accede to his demands.

He gave until the first day of the Cuckoo month before blood would be shed.

It was not a generous allocation of time. Only six days; the same length of time that Beyla had been in Hel's realm.

So Gudrid laboured across the brittle waste. Her footsteps filled with mist that then froze, hiding any trace of her passing.

Things moved in the mist. Huge shapes that moved so silently they might have been ghosts. In this place, perhaps they were.

The snow turned to icy pebbles under her feet: wide, flat stones that tilted and slid under her weight. She could hear the sea nearby, shushing over the shore. It sounded like distant voices whispering something she couldn't make out. Something dark. Prayer rose to Gudrid's lips, the words she would speak to dispel evil in the convent, but she did not let them escape the tip of her tongue. Those words had no power here. So she held her peace and saved her voice for later.

Stone turned to bone underfoot. It cracked and splintered under her weight. Despite the cold, the smell was foul, and it would only get worse. The sucked clean bones grew fat with cold, waxen flesh and wound with thick, uncombed hair. They moaned in their hollow voices when she stood on them and begged her to have a care of where she stood. Some of the dead wore faces she knew.

Gudrid turned her eyes away and kept walking. There was nothing she could do for them, nothing anyone could do for them, now.

A dark shape appeared through the mist, so vast that it hurt the eye to look at it. It was the root of the World Tree; it plunged down through the mist, from somewhere unimaginably far above, and burrowed into the sere, salted earth. For a famn around the earth was covered with every sort of beast that crawled on its belly: vipers and asps and nightcrawlers. In the middle of them, triple-wound around the tree: the Niddhog.

His great, grey bulk was wide around as a longship's beam and his flesh had grown around the root, anchoring him in place. Beneath him Hvergelmir, the wellspring, spilled out of the ground, a seething torrent of water laced with needles of ice. The cold of it was so intense that it cracked and blackened Niddhog's scales and withered the flesh beneath, leaving raw, weeping blisters along his flanks. If it pained Niddhog he did not show it, nor did it slow his ceaseless gnawing at Yggdrasil. Corruption spread from his bite, leaving a wet, rotting wound on the tree. It was from there the stench that fouled the air emanated, not from the corpses.

Gudrid's will failed and she stopped.

One of the corpses opened its blind, milky eyes and stared up at her.

"Turn back now," it said. The words drifted from between still, grey lips. "No-one but the dead will know your courage failed."

Spite planted Gudrid's foot firmly in the corpse's face when she stepped forward. Its nose cracked and its lips split under her weight. No blood flowed.

"I'm to listen to you about courage?" she asked. "If you had died a hero you would be drinking from Freya's golden cup, not lying here."

The truth in her words bit deeper than the serpent's fangs and the corpse's keening wail followed Gudrid across the shore of corpses — towards Yggdrasil's root.

She had to pass Niddhog to get there, close enough that she could have touched his scarred, wounded side if she had any reason to do such a thing. Splinters festered in his lips and bloody gums, studded between the worn stumps of his fangs. Her heart thundered so loud in her chest she could hardly breathe and her ribs ached. Though there was no point to her terror. She was far too small a morsel for Niddhog to concern himself with. The great, frost-blind eye didn't even roll to acknowledge her passing.

Gudrid found shelter behind a twist of root and sat down. The chill of the hard earth made her hips ache. She ignored it and pulled a wax-cloth wrapped package from her cloak, snapping the frost-brittle string with her fingers. The cloth fell open, revealing a wedge of cheese, a wizened winter apple and one of Sister Hilde's sugar-glazed sweet tarts. Gudrid's departure had been hurried but she was too seasoned a traveller to leave without provisions.

The bread and cheese she ate ravenously, tearing off chunks with her teeth and using a dampened finger to pick up crumbs from her lap. A draft of water, from a tributary and not the frosted well-spring itself, quenched her thirst well enough; although it was still cold enough to make her teeth hurt and her bowels clench. The apple and the sweet-tart she left sitting on the ground, covered by the waxed cloth.

Cold and exhaustion lulled her to sleep, shivering there under the tree.

It was the sound of ice breaking that roused her, and just in time. The cold had sunk into her bones, frosting the marrow, and slowed her blood. Her sleep had been within moments of becoming eternal.

Gudrid coughed and spat, blood mixed with the sputum that hit the snow, and struggled to her feet. They didn't hurt anymore: it wasn't a good sign. Gudrid gathered up the remaining food and brushed the ice off it.

A woman stood by the tree. She was white. Not just pale but white, like snow or swans: her hair, spilling unbound to her knees; her skin, flawless as mapping linen and the light tunic she wore in defiance of the elements. She went unshod in the snow. Water was frozen on her legs from where she'd forded the river. She carried a pot on one hip, her arm crooked protectively around it. It was full with thick white mud. The woman scooped it out, water dripping between her fingers and smeared it over the wounded, rotting parts of the tree.

A squirrel, red-furred and twitching his tail, watched from high in the branches.

Gudrid hugged herself, pinning cold fingers in her armpits, and waited.

The woman scraped the last of the mud from the bottom of the pot. It was barely enough to cover her fingers. She wiped it over the tree, covering every spot of discolouration that she could reach.

"Skuld," Gudrid said. Her voice sounded like it had gone unused for centuries instead of hours. She stopped and cleared her throat, seeking some moisture. The tall, white woman turned to look at her with a stern, heavy face that had no kindness in it. "Skuld, will you break bread with me?"

She held the food out, cradled in the half-frozen cloth. It looked a poor feast to offer to one who even the gods stepped warily around. Skuld contemplated the food and then raised her gaze to Gudrid. Under those pale, cool eyes, that offered neither condemnation nor compassion, Gudrid felt the years stripped from her face. Until she was, once again, that tall, strong girl who'd added her voice to the spae-wife's song and called down the future.

"Gudrid," Skuld said, walking over to her. Gudrid was not small, but the Jotun's daughter towered over her. "Gudrid Thorbjarnardottir. Is it the bread that is flesh of your White Christ that you offer me?"

"No. It's a tart baked by Sister Hilde." The corner of Gudrid's lips twitched into a wry smile. "Who would be equal parts

11

delighted and horrified to know that it had passed your lips. She is Christian now, but the old ways still have influence. Especially in times of trouble, people turn back to you then."

"Yes." Skuld took the tart and considered it curiously. "They do. But why should we listen? I know what is to come, Gudrid Thorbjarnardottir. I see your convent and the bloodline that passes from you to your son, Snorri, and to his children in turn. You lead the people away from my worship. "

Gudrid gestured around her, the sweep of her fingers indicating the slowly rotting corpses, the long-suffering Yggdrasil and Niddhog and his children.

"I lead my people away from this," she said fiercely. The air caught in her throat and she had to stop to cough again. Cold sweat filmed her forehead when she finished. She wiped it away on her sleeve. "Not from you, Skuld of the Norns. You need no worship and ask for no sacrifice. You are Necessity, and if the coming of the White Christ is part of that necessity then you will not stand in His way."

"Perhaps," Skuld said. It seemed impossible, arrogant to even think it, but she seemed weary. "It does not mean I have to like it."

Gudrid bent a creaky old knee and knelt amidst the snow and bodies.

"I sang for you once," she said. "In honour of that, aid me. For my mother, who loved you, aid me."

In the silence that followed her plea all Gudrid could hear was the sound of Skuld's breathing. She had not known the gods breathed like men.

"There will be a price," Skuld said finally.

"Anything."

"Do not speak so rashly," Skuld warned. "This is a price you will not want to pay, Gudrid Thorbjarnardottir. It will be a sacrifice."

Gudrid closed her eyes and thought of her son and her grand-children and the lineage of light that Skuld herself had once promised.

"Anything," she repeated.

A few pastry crumbs dropped to the ground in front of Gudrid. She looked up as Skuld finished the last of the treat and licked her fingers clean of mud and honey.

"Thank you," she said.

Skuld regarded her much as she had the tart — with distant curiosity. The ages were in her eyes.

"That is the last time you will say that to me," she said. "Say what it is it you want of me, Gudrid Thorbjarnardottir?"

"Beyla Volnursdottir," Gudrid said. "She died of plague six days ago."

"No," Skuld said, turning away.

The flat refusal rocked Gudrid. She hurried after Skuld, struggling to keep up with the Norn's long, tireless stride.

"No?" she said. "But you said you would help me."

"She did not die of the plague," Skuld said. She stopped suddenly and Gudrid stumbled to stop next to her, struggling to keep her footing. Skuld pointed. "This is where her resting place is — with the unhonoured and the secret slain. You should busy yourself more with your people, anchorite. They act behind your back."

The shell of a half-built ship stood in front of them, hauled up onto the beach. The keel and stem were already finished and the mast was raised. An unfinished square sail lay pegged out on the beach and barrels and bales, tarred and tightly wrapped against the weather, were stacked back behind the high-tide mark.

Gudrid's breath caught in her throat. "It looks half-finished."

"It is," Skuld said. "In just a few millennia the final plank will be sealed in place and the sail raised, ready to leave harbour."

Skuld said millennia like it was no time at all. To her it wasn't.

"And Beyla?"

Skuld pointed again, this time to the mouth of a cave.

"In there," she said, "where they harvest the materials for the ship."

Materials: nails for the wood and hair for the sail. Gudrid turned her mind from that fact.

"Can I get her back?" she asked.

Skuld dropped her hand back to her side and raised one snow-white shoulder in a shrug.

"You must ask the master of the ship," she said. "But I warn you, Gudrid Thorbjarnardottir, he will not surrender her lightly. The price will be all you can pay."

"And my children?" Gudrid asked. "My line?"

"Will burn brightly and be honoured."

Skuld left her standing there, by the edge of the cold, grey sea. The great, scaled sides of a serpent breached the surface, water running down its sides, and then disappeared again. It took all the will that had brought Gudrid this far to get her to take that first step towards the black, ominous mouth of the cave.

A tunnel, the floor worn smooth as glass, led into the earth. Gudrid followed it down, slipping and sliding as it grew steeper, tearing her gloves and skinning her hands. It grew warmer as she descended, until she was sweating under her clothes. She stripped off her cloak and bloody gloves, bundling them up inside each other.

In the distance there was the sound of bellows wheezing and the crackling roar of a fire. It sounded like a blacksmith's forge and a red glow beckoned Gudrid forwards, into a vaulted cave that would have put to shame the greatest hall in Midgard. The ceiling disappeared into the mists that sunk down through the earth; ropes of gold and gems grew from the walls and spilled to the ground in thick, tangled vines and statues of stern, incomparable beauty lined the walls with weapons in hand.

In the midst of all that glory was a filthy, blood-stained stone altar with a thin, wiry man bound to it with chains twice as thick around as his legs. He was filthy, caked with blood and dirt, and his chest was an oozing mass of sores and blisters from the venom that dripped from the snake caged over his body. A haggard woman stood next to him, swaying with exhaustion, with a bowl held up to catch the drops of poison.

A trickle of urine ran down Gudrid's thigh as her guts weakened from terror. The weight of awe threatened to stop her heart.

To tap into the old knowledge, to walk between the worlds, was unchristian and to bring back the dead was arrogance beyond words — but this was beyond that. This would damn her soul and even for her son, her grandchildren, she couldn't bring herself to say the words that would send her to hell.

In the end she didn't have to.

Loki turned his head to the side and caught her gaze with a bright, green eye. Despite the filth and the marks of suffering etched deeply on his face, he was more beautiful than the statues that lined his hall. When he smiled it felt like the sun had rose for the first time after a long winter.

"Gudrid Thorbjarnardottir," he said, his voice coaxing and cozening. "Welcome to my hall. Do you not bow to me?"

Without any command from her will Gudrid felt her legs start to fold. She tried to stiffen them, but the weight of Loki's regard was too much for her to bear. Her knees cracked hard against the ground. She crossed herself and closed her eyes to pray.

"Oh no," Loki said cheerfully. "None of that, now. Not here."

The words of the prayer went away. All of them. Even the names she used to pray too — the old names of the old gods. The only name left was his. All Gudrid had to cling to was the knowledge that there had been other names, once.

"Better," he said. The chains rattled as he made himself as comfortable as he could get here. His wife, his keeper, didn't react. All her attention was focused on the slowly filling bowl she held cradled in her hands. "Now. What is it you would ask of me, Gudrid Thorbjarnardottir?"

Gudrid swallowed and licked her dry lips. The words she needed hid in her brain, as if they were frightened of this chained, damned god too. It had been easier to speak to the Norn. Not because she was lesser, but because she had made no effort to overawe.

"One of the dead, one who falls under your purview, I need you to release her to me."

Loki raised his eyebrows.

"One of my dead?" he said. His voice danced with light mockery. "Oh, I fear I could never do that. What would I use to build my ship then?"

Gudrid looked up at him and then dropped her gaze back to her hands. She pressed her fingers into her thighs until it hurt.

"Only one of the dead," she said. "Just one."

Loki laughed. The sound was unexpected enough to make his wife flinch and spill the tiniest spot of poison on his seared chest. It sizzled on his skin and shattered his smug composure. He screamed and jerked against his bonds, wrenching his body from side to side. The earth moved with him.

Rocks and dirt fell from the unseen ceiling, bouncing from the statues and chipping their beautiful forms, and Gudrid cowered on the ground. She pressed her hands to her ears, trying to block out a god's screams, and tired to pray again. The words were still gone, leaving her bereft.

It seemed an eternity till Loki's agonies eased and he returned to sanity. He cursed his wife in bitter tones, voicing insults that would have driven any mortal woman to slit his throat in his sleep once her blushes allowed her. The weary Sigyn didn't seem to even hear the biting words. Her world was the bowl and the snake and the poison. Once Loki wore out his spleen on her, he turned his attention back to Gudrid.

"Every corpse that comes to me lends its substance to the ship," Loki said. The silver charm of his voice had turned to rust and sand. "Every corpse brings Ragnarok one breath closer, one breath closer to my freedom from this torment, and you think I will surrender one to you? What could you possibly offer me to make that one breath of extra torment worthwhile?"

There was contempt in his voice. He didn't expect her to have an answer; nor did Gudrid, until she remembered Skuld walking her down the shore and pointing to the Ship of Nails. The oldest of the Norns did nothing without intent.

Gudrid closed her eyes. The names were gone and even the words to shape them seemed hazy. There were other words, though. Words so old they belonged to no language, and were beyond even Loki's power to touch. They rose to the surface of her mind and pricked on the tip of her tongue.

She gave them a voice. The last time she had sung the weirdsong, she had been young and strong and her voice had been beautiful. Now it was tired and cracked, breaking in the wrong places and without the breath to hold the notes long enough.

Still, the weird's power was not in its beauty.

Power gathered close under the notes.

The horrible wheezing efforts of Loki's burn-scarred lungs eased and the newest wound on his bare chest crusted over. There were limits to the weird-song's power. Gudrid was only a spae-wife, half-taught and out of practice, and Loki's curse had been crafted by Mimir and laid by Odin, himself. The chains chafed and the poison dripped. All it could muster was a moment of ease. Loki closed his eyes and sighed.

Tears burned Gudrid's eyes. She forced the words past stiff lips.

"One moment less of pain, Trickster," she said. "My gift to you. Give me Beyla and you can have my soul in her place."

There was silence. Gudrid didn't know if he was surprised by her offer, or just her effrontery.

"And what good would your soul do me, old woman?" Loki asked eventually. "A wizened spae-wife. Even if I send you back, you'll most likely end up here as my thrall. Or do you think that the Lawspeaker will give you a decent burial?"

The contempt stung but he had given himself away. Loki, the Trickster, knew why she was here. That he bothered to hear her out at all meant that her offer had some measure of temptation for him.

"Who will navigate for you?" she asked hoarsely. "When the ship is cast loose and you take the wheel. Who will plot the course and read the stars, who will keep the log book and mind the stores? I have crossed the world, from one side to the other and back again. I have been to the land of the Skraelings and the home of the White Christ. Give me Beyla and I will be your steerswoman on Ragnarok, your thrall until then. Is that not worth a breath of pain?"

Loki pondered the offer in silence. In an odd, almost human gesture, he worried his lip as he thought.

"Very well," he said. "I will take your trade."

He shifted on the stone altar and lifted one arm as far as the chain would allow, pointing to the corner of the cave. A small, twisted creature, sallow skinned and lank haired, shuffled into the cave, dragging a shorn, waxen girl behind it. It led the girl over to Gudrid.

"Of course," Loki said, his voice bright again. "I made no promises as to the state of the girl."

The girl stood on bloodied feet and stared blankly at Gudrid. Her mouth was slack, drooling, and someone had drawn a second, raw-red mouth across her throat.

"Beyla. Beyla Volgangsdottir?"

Something stirred in the depths of those vague, milky eyes and the wet lips moved.

"So I was called," she said.

"Go," Loki said. "Go before the bowl o'erspills. GO!"

The honey-coloured poison trembled at the lip of the bowl, ready to pour over Loki's chest. One more drop, perhaps two, and it would overflow.

Gudrid caught Beyla's hand and dragged the stoic Beyla along behind her, fleeing up the runnel. They were near the top when Loki's screams echoed after them and the world wrenched with his agonies .

The two women, one alive and one not, stumbled out onto the shore. Gudrid was gasping for breath and doubled over a stitch that felt like a knife in her ribs. Beyla just stood, hands lax by her side. Eventually, Gudrid straightened up and took Beyla's clammy hand. She led her away over the shore, back towards

Midgard. Beyla's bare feet, nails torn from their beds for the ship, left bloody prints on the stones.

Clad in a fresh habit, her bloodied hands and frostbitten feet anointed with salve and bandaged, Gudrid sat in the Lawspeaker's budir, under the shadow of the Law Rock. Beyla, clad in a modest, high-necked gown with long sleeves, sat next to her. A close-fitting snood covered her shorn, torn scalp.

The morning was near gone by the time Orm came striding down from the Law Rock, gold glittering on his arms and chest and sword slung at his hip. His guards walked close by him. One of them, a giant of a man with an evil turn to his mouth, blanched and reached for his sword when he saw Beyla. For her part, the dead girl smiled for the first time since she'd left Nieflheim. It was not pleasant

"Greetings to you, Gudrid," Orm greeted her, as effusively as if she was an old friend. His smile slipped a little when he turned to Beyla, but only one who was watching close would notice. "And to you, Beyla. My heart is glad that you have recovered from your illness."

He drew Beyla to her feet and kissed her cheek, shuddering at the texture of her skin and the odd smell of her. Then he dismissed his guards and led the two women into his tent. A flask of mead sat on his table, waiting for him. He poured a goblet for himself and drank thirstily, swilling the honey-sweetness around his mouth.

Gudrid was too heart-sore and weary to even muster hate.

"I have upheld my end of the deal, Lawspeaker," she said. "Now, you swear to leave me and mine in peace?"

Orm spat the mouthful of mead onto the floor. He wiped his mouth on his sleeve and nodded.

"Aye." Then he pointed a warning finger at her face. "For as long as you hold your tongue on this, Gudrid."

Gudrid bent her head in stiff acknowledgement. She started to leave but stopped.

"Why," she said. "You killed her. Why coerce me to return to her?"

Orm shrugged and tossed back the rest of the mead. He walked over to his chair and sat down, his long legs stretched out over the furs.

"I could protest my innocence, but I doubt it would fool you," he said. "It was an accident."

"You slit her throat by accident?" Gudrid asked.

Orm smiled and looked down, like a child caught lying about a trifle. It chilled Gudrid. She might have bargained her soul away, but she doubted that Orm had ever possessed one.

"Things got out of hand," Orm said. "She was not eager to wed me; I forcefully pressed my suit and...went too far. If her father was to throw his wealth behind my latest trading venture, I needed her back."

Gudrid shook her head tiredly.

"For money, then?" she said

"Do you think I care what you think of me, old woman?" Orm asked. "Take yourself back to your convent and wait to die. You've done what I asked of you."

Gudrid nodded and drew her hood up over her head. The shadow fell down over her face and she peered out of it.

"That I have," she said. "And I paid dearly enough for it. So, Orm Lawspeaker, treasure your wife; she will be your bride; she will sit in judgement by your side and she will bear your son. And she will never be parted from you...not even by death. Nor will she share you with another or ever leave you, even for a moment. She bears you no love, Orm, but she will be loyal."

For the first time Orm's easy confidence faltered. His looked past Gudrid to Beyla as the dead girl started to disrobe, revealing her torn fingers, slashed throat and soft, dead flesh. Horror dawned in his eyes and his hand sought out the cross at his throat.

"Gudrid," he said. "Abbess. Send her back. In the name of Christ, send her back."

"He doesn't listen to me anymore," Gudrid said. "Nor you, I would think. Try not to scream, Orm. I doubt the guards would understand."

She left the tent and headed out of the camp, ignoring any offers of shelter that were made. She had a long way to walk: back to the shore of bone and death; back to the dead man's boat.

Orm didn't scream while she was in earshot.

the blind man

Carole Johnstone

The boys barely looked his way at all as they sorted the herring and hung out the nets. Donald noticed perhaps as many as a dozen new holes, and big ones at that. Towards one end of the drift even the tarred warp rope had snapped, buckling the train. Breaking its back. They wouldn't be going out again that night. Maybe not even the night after.

The boys knew that well enough; they were likely torn between frustration at their enduring misfortune, and relief that they would not soon be suffering another cold and stormy pitch black of night aboard their skipper's decrepit clinker. The catch was meagre, and boys they were — on land and the water. Donald's own faithful were all long gone: to the Moray Firth or the shipyards of the capital, though Donald held too healthy a terror for the Poor House to follow in their footsteps.

None of their callow replacements had the wit to realise that Donald had saved them from a slow death in the pits, or a slave wage on the saltpans. There were too many people now starving in the old villages all along the northeast coast. People whose families had fished and crofted there for generations. And the coastline had become studded with clay thatched huts, packed to the rafters with feckless Highlanders, who starved all the quicker and spread their diseases.

Donald turned back to the harbour, watching his battered skaffie where she sat low in the lee of the sea wall beyond Brora Bridge. He claimed perhaps a dozen of the fattest herring for his own, fishing them out of the barrels while ignoring his crew and their mutinous scowls.

"Get the rest tae the curing yard by sun-up. I don't want tae be hearing about them spoiling because ye were too busy sousing *yourselves* in the Bannockburn."

Off they went, west along the shoreline, just as another gust of icy wet wind pushed them backwards against their not so heavy loads. The gust carried with it weightier evidence of their discontent: muttered forecasts that they would doubtless be finished in the yard long before sun-up, and braver threats of defection to the vast Herring Busses and their favoured tonnage bounties. Donald was not overly concerned; even should a few of them fall foul of the fishery officers and find themselves signing on a dotted line, they would be back again soon enough. If not one of them could stomach a single night of inshore drifting, a couple of weeks at sea would likely finish them completely.

"And get back here when ye're done! Those nets won't fix theirselves."

Once they had disappeared beyond the harbour wall, Donald climbed up from the quayside on too weary legs. The late September wind coming off the North Sea still slapped against his face, lifting the hair from his scalp and filling his lungs with the briny taste of ocean. He struggled around the headland, looking to the empty sand beach below with a heavy heart; hearing the far off call to the bell-pit north of the river, its winches and water-powered pumps stretching wide above the grey swathe of village like a hungry raven.

He supposed that he was no more entitled to indulge his ill will towards the coal mine than he was to the vast salt pans that now stretched as far south as Easter Ross and Cromarty: from Kintradwell Broch to the mouth of the Dornoch Firth. His son had worked at the mine for nigh on two months now, and had survived no less than two cave-ins and three floodings; while Donald's own dwindling livelihood relied upon both the salt recovered from the ocean and the distilleries fuelled by Uaran's rich seams.

They were not the source of his malaise; his wretched decline in fortune. Nor was the culprit to be found in his sullen crew, battered boat, the bloody Fishery Board or the North Sea's temper. It was people — always people. Great, swelling, lumbering masses expelled from the low peaks, high moorland and small lochans of the Flow Country, and spewed onto the coast like herring worm and fish guts.

As he climbed the last few steps towards the narrow row of white-painted cottages that ran close to the shoreline, he fought as hard against an early assault of smurry as he did the hopeless fury that was ever now his constant companion. His too-empty creel banged hard against his thigh. The sun winked over the Clynelish in the east, where brown moor cambered inland away from grassy cliff. Before them, Brora's bell tower stood against the grey-gold skyline like a mournful sentinel.

He dropped to his knees just shy of the old Pictish cairn of the *Caledonii*, setting his creel upon the stone. "May Manannán of the Sea bless my catch and humble burden," he whispered close to the ground, though there was likely no-one else around to witness his heresy; most of the newcomers imagined themselves to be still in the hills and rarely rose before dawn. "May He have pity upon my fortune and send the Tuatha against all those who seek my ruin."

There was a familiar gloom above the thatched roof of his cottage, he could see it now: a rank, dark shadow that neither his prayer nor the miserable dawn looked ready to banish. Before he even opened the door, he knew that the cottage was still in darkness. He knew that the hearth would not be lit and his breakfast would not be cooked. *It* had happened again, and he had not the strength this time to stomach it.

Once inside, he wrenched open the shutters like a man possessed. He tossed his meagre catch into one of the salt barrels, and wasted too much flint in getting the peat alight in its damp recess. The air was frigid and stale with old smoke. The thickly cut turf had come away from a corner of the sea-facing wall, as if something had sought to burrow out in the night, exposing a leavening of rough stones through which more of that late September wind screamed.

On the other side of the curtain, he could hear stuttering crying that could too easily lapse into the keening wail that kept him awake most nights. Even when he was out at sea. Putting down his fury a second time was too difficult.

"Isobel! Get out here, woman. Where is yer husband's bloody breakfast? Where is his fire?"

She took too long to obey; worse than that, she then no more than loitered by the soiled curtain, twisting it between her fingers and offering no amends.

"Get out here, woman!"

Her hair was a tangled shroud that hid her face. Behind her, the sobs grew higher and uglier in pitch.

"It came again, Donald."

Donald was still better disposed towards anger than fear. "Aye? *I* spent a night close tae being battered against the Laoghal Rocks, and was rewarded by less than ten barrels of herring and the cliping of my crew. Yet yer troubles were the harder tae endure? Yer troubles see me starving and cold in my own hame?"

She came out from behind the curtain then, but still she did not venture near to him. Picking up an oil lamp, she kneeled down by the revived fire, leaning too close. Donald could smell the singeing of her hair over the low stench of peat before she stood again. Still she faced the fire, and Donald found that he was too glad.

"Do you want me tae warm some stew?"

"Aye, I want ye tae warm some bloody stew, woman! And I don't want tae hear another word about—"

The sobs beyond the curtain began their wail in the instant that his wife turned around, the lamplight exposing the wide white of her eyes framed by old crusts of blood. Deep scores ran from her temples to chin, and her frightened grimace exposed another new gap in her teeth. When he glanced down at the fresher blood on her skirts, she gathered the stiff material in her fists and clamped shut her mouth. There were raised and

26

blistering welts at her wrists and blooming stabs of purple inside her elbows and forearms. Still, she wouldn't look at him.

"Jesus, Isobel!" His gaze suddenly found the curtain again as a bird started battering wings against his ribcage. "Nancy? Is Nancy—"

For one moment there might have flashed some anger in those wide, red-framed eyes. "Nancy is fine, Donald. She slept through again. Though Moira—"

He had already stumbled past the curtain and into the ben beyond before hearing his wife reassurances. Nancy — *his* Nancy — was curled up on her side, close to the still sleeping bairn. He recognised the unhurried rise and fall of her slumbering breath. And finally released his own. The bird inside his chest calmed through more pleasant swoops and flutters.

Moira he remembered as an afterthought. She was not in the bed. Close to the piles of broken net and new hemp on the far side of the small room, his older daughter shivered and still bayed, her bony knees drawn up to her chest, blood pooling around her feet.

"Haud yer wheesht, Moira! Isobel! Get this child cleaned up." He stumbled in his haste to retreat, winning another barely-disguised glare from his wife in the process. As he caught her eye, the smell of his warming stew made him feel queasier still. "Shut her up, Isobel. We will not talk of this. Not again."

Isobel set down her lamp. "Aye we will, Donald. This time we will."

Donald was in the end spared that ordeal by another that was far more insistent. Awoken from an ill-easy slumber by a battering at his door, he stumbled towards the threshold, his weary mind no match for his ever present caution. Nothing good had knocked at his door in more than two years.

The Countess' factor stood just shy of the muddy dip ahead of the entrance. He wore a non-descript plaid, belted and held at the shoulder by the Sunderland brooch. His face was as grim as the weather that beat down upon his bonnet-less head. Donald's heart sank even before he glimpsed the men that loitered close to the bluff's summit.

"Mr Sellar, what can I do for you today, Sir?"

Patrick Sellar's mouth tightened into a grimacing smile. "Mr MacKay. I have heard that the North Sea has not been your friend of late." His thin lips stretched whiter. "Perhaps that explains why my officers are yet to take receipt of your rent?"

Donald pulled on a cloak and stepped outside. His fury was too quick and he fought to drown it down beneath the surface. A weasel Sellar might have been, but he was a weasel with the ear of both the Countess and the Duke; a weasel who had turned out thousands from their highland homes — burning them out when all else failed — and stealing a large portion of the parishes of Farr and Kildonan into his own hands while he was about it. Sellar could be his ruin before either the North Sea or his cursed family.

"Ye and yer masters will have my rent soon enough, Sellar."

"Soon enough is not soon enough, fisherman," Sellar grinned, eyeing the banned colours under Donald's cloak. "What else can you barter?"

Donald drew the cloak tighter over his tartan. "None."

"Young Murray has much praised the talents of your youngest daughter, MacKay." He threw a glance towards the sniggers of his men behind. "An eager servant is always welcomed in the House of Stafford."

Donald heard his wife move into the doorway in the instant before he lunged for the factor. Her shriek found him faster than Sellar's own or the angered shouts of his men. "Ye'll not have her, ye rank son of a Lowland bastard."

Only after Donald found himself pinned fast against his own house by more than half a dozen grim-faced sub-factors did Sellar move to grasp him tight around his throat. Donald could vaguely hear the protestations of his roused neighbours.

"Then give me the other, MacKay. I've heard she's bonny enough."

Donald's relief was predictably short lived. Isobel's cry was too loud and carping. When he nodded once, Sellar's men let him go, and Donald turned back for the entrance of his home in unsteady steps. Isobel had cleaned her face he saw, but ugly swellings already claimed much of her cheekbones and jaw. Her eyes had become wide and grasping once more.

"Bring her out, Isobel."

The desperation that commonly found her pleading for his sympathy upon every recent return from the sea now sought him out in a low moan and easy tears. "No, Donald. Please, no."

"Bring her out, Isobel."

She flew at him then, her fingers clawed and bloody, her curses more wicked. He pushed her back into the gloom of their home. "Isobel! I've not the money tae pay the bastard. Do you want the Black Watch tae come for us in our beds?"

"Not Moira, Donald." Isobel dropped to her knees, letting go her hold upon the crusted blood on her skirts. "Please, Donald, not Moira. She has suffered en—"

Despite the jeers outside, Donald sunk also to his knees. He cupped his wife's face in calloused hands and kissed her swollen mouth. "If evil is truly in this house, Bel, be grateful that Moira can be spared from it. If ever ye loved me, bring her out."

He kissed her again, but this time she flinched from it and he met only dry matted hair. He choked down a sob. "Bring her out."

Donald could still hear his child's screams many hours after the day had gone and the vocal batter of night called him back to the shore. He pulled the short net over his shoulder and picked up his creel, eyeing his clumsy repair of the turf wall with something close to disgust.

Isobel crouched close to the now roaring fire. She had not looked his way for all of the day. Not even when he had sent Donnie to the pit had she so obviously punished him.

When he opened the door, an icy gale swept away their silence. "Keep the door barred, Isobel. Let none in until I return."

Her laughter was too harsh. "Aye, husband. I'll let none in. Much good that will do."

A pervasive pain that Donald could not place found him stumbling over the threshold and into the stormy night beyond. "Don't mither me, woman! Always I have done only my best to protect—"

Isobel's shadow reached across their floor of moor-rushes and damp earth. "The Reverend Murray is tae visit us after ye have gone. He will—"

Donald again felt the keen point of incrimination at his throat. "The Reverend Father sits at the Countess' table, Isobel! The Reverend *bloody* Murray numbers among those who extort frae us our meagre lands and monies, while celebrating the vengeance of Heaven and eternal damnation upon any of us who dare to resist!"

"The Reverend bloody Murray will bless our house and drive out its demon!" Isobel shrieked. "I care none for land auctions and the Highlanders' persecution. While *my* nights are still plagued by shadowed rape and torture, I hardly even care that the Sutherland Clearances and Herring Busses have thus far cost me both a son and a daughter!"

Isobel's curses followed him onto the rain-logged road. When he looked back, her hair flew about and above her face as if she were an old Lunan witch. "And a husband!"

He ran until she had disappeared from sight and until only the smoke from the hearth was visible above the muddy slopes. Her ragged whisper still found him beyond the headland, where many feet below, his crew loaded their repaired nets onto his skaffie in silence. He could go back; he had done it time enough before. He could send out the boys, while he went back home. He dismissed his resumed tears to the North Sea wind, and climbed down to the shoreline.

As soon as they had cleared the lee of the harbour, he gave himself up to the lure of the sea completely. He was too tired. Too tired of it all.

When they returned just before another dawn, the coast was a fiery red haze beneath the jagged shadows of the Dornoch Moor and Brora Links. Donald made himself look northeast towards the recently built Helmsdale and Gower. There, all manner of ousted Highland farmer sought to eek out an ignorant existence, sucking dry the coastal lands and their resources where Cheviots and Blackface Lintons had usurped their own.

Donald hated them. Hated them more than greedy lairds and their corrupt factors; perhaps even more than the rank black shadow that ever plagued his own home, his children, his wife. If he *was* truly cursed, then impotence and the shared company of despair was no comfort at all. He had never seen the monster that blighted his house; he had only witnessed the bloody mess and ruined walls that it left behind in its sated wake.

Many months before, when their son had only just received his summons to the pit and had not yet answered it, Isobel had found Donald crouched by the stuttering hearth in the death of night. Then her face had borne only the beginnings of the persecution that was soon to find her; only the long and drawn worry of every east coast mother and wife. Yet It had been between them even then. She had long cried of It in dreams and in muttered distraction. It had grown far bolder since.

"There is an evil in this house, Donald. I feel It in the walls and in my dreams. I feel It even in the children. It is waiting. Just waiting."

Donald had perhaps rolled his eyes; certainly he had given little quarter to her wifely histrionics.

"The evil in this house is *not* born of noblemen or driven-out clansmen," she had whispered angrily as he had bowed closer to the fire.

Then he had been too consumed by fear, too overwhelmed by the sheer numbers that were fleeing to the coast from the highlands of Sutherland, to think upon anything else. "Ye say that only because ye were once a bloody MacKenzie before I made you my wife."

There had been no sobbing then either; no stiff red blood upon his wife's skirts.

"The crofters talk of fired villages and the illegal dispossession of the swain, Bell. Those that come down frae the hills are naught but our enemy. They are parasites that seek to steal our lives and drown us the quicker."

Isobel had reached out a hand to his face that first night, had reached out a hand to stroke his cheek and press a finger to his lips. Her eyes had not been wild or wide, but the tears in them had brimmed and almost fell. "The evil in this house is not born of nobleman or highlander," she had again whispered. "Ye bring it back frae the water, Donald. It finds ye in the drift and it follows ye home. And I live in fear that one day it will choose never to leave."

After dispatching his complaining crew once more towards the curing yard beyond the Strath, Donald climbed the bluff from the harbour and headed for home. Again the rising sun winked over the Clynelish in the east, throwing the old bell tower into long shadow. Donald did not stop at the old Pictish cairn, did not even glance at it. Before he reached his home, he threw his empty creel back toward the shore with a cry. The dark shadow still squatted above his home regardless. And Donald prayed to none. Not anymore.

This time he heard the wailing before he stepped over the threshold. This time it found and revived the bird in his chest far quicker than the dark emptiness of the *but* and its stone cold hearth.

"Nancy?" He raced towards the ben upon feet that had forgotten their weariness. Only when his daughter flew at him from the shadows did he falter, buckling as she threw herself upon him, her sobs almost drowning out that dreadful keening howl beyond the curtain.

"The bairn, Daddy! They took the bairn!"

Donald fought for a decent hold upon her, dragging her down to the reed floor and pulling her close until he could feel Nancy's own bird kicking out at his own. His voice was too weak. "The bairn?"

"They took him!" she shrieked again. "The Black Watch took him, and the factor threw him into the Brua-a Marsh."

For the first time since her birth, Donald pushed Nancy from him with a scream. He crawled towards the curtain in wretched sobs. The heather thatch over his head dropped lower its malignant shadow. All the time, Donald whispered his promises, his empty retribution to the hills and moorland high above. their home.

When his wife drew back the curtain, he tried and failed to regain his feet. She had tied her hair back from her face and had changed both her gown and her apron. Where there had before been bloody cuts and swollen welts, there remained only yellowing bruises. Her smile was too serene.

"Isobel?"

She looked down at him as the north wind whistled through his ill-repaired breaches. Her smile exposed too many missing teeth. "The evil is in the water, Donald. It finds ye in the drift and ever it follows ye home."

The bird died fast in Donald's chest even as he still struggled to rise. "God I am tired, Bell. I am tired of it all."

His wife's beatific smile implied that she hardly cared. She pressed a fisted hand to her breast. "I need to feed the wean."

In the instant that she turned her back again upon him, she drew the knife across her throat, so that her sin might not touch either him or Nancy. Instead it sprayed dark crimson across the curtain and what little was yet exposed of the ben. Nancy's shrieks drowned out his own. But only for a moment.

The sunrise was too brilliant a witness to his and Nancy's lumbering progress down to the shore. Lazy arcs of wisplike clouds, stretched so thin across the sky that they were almost transparent, drew the eye stubbornly away to the east: heralding the autumn yellow sun as it rose above the horizon. Hues of angry purple, mauve and indigo spread across those skies like bruises, framed by spans of golden light that undulated slowly, shiftless and resolute in their evasion of both cloud and cliff.

They set Isobel down upon the shale close to the harbour, and Donald left Nancy by her lifeless mother only for the time it took to release the skaffie from its mooring post. Before he turned back, he glanced once towards the misty moorland above the cliffs. The shadow still hung there, low above the headland and the home that they had left.

Another shadow suddenly moved out of the first, reaching towards them on mournful and crooked wings. Its feathers were hoar frost and wild thistle, its wingspan greater than ten feet across. As it soared towards the breakwater, the sea eagle's black throat caught the rising sun and glowed like shot-silk. Donald hid another sob as he returned to the shore and helped Nancy carry her mother to the boat.

When they were at least a mile out to sea, the silent raptor returned, following their progress as the sun rose above the Clynelish. Donald tried to smile for Nancy, and she tried to smile back. This morning there was no rain, no hail, no battering crosswind to drive them back toward the shore.

Once Brora had become little more than an ill-defined shape to portside, Donald dipped the sail and swallowed two fingers of scotch. Nancy looked to him and not to her dead mother as they both heaved Isobel over the curved stem and dropped her into the sea. Its eager waves lapped her scarred and still battered face before cold shadows drew her down into their depths. While Nancy sobbed, Donald watched his wife's white, wide eyes as they left him and dwindled into only memory.

The sun had climbed high above the horizon, and Donald had taken another few fingers of scotch before he found his courage again. Bent close to the stem, Nancy still sobbed, and Donald twisted around her bony shoulders, pulling her onto his lap as he had done so many times when she had been a child. The sea eagle gave only one mournful cry before heading out into the open ocean.

"There's no hiding frae them, Nancy," he whispered to her hair, while his shoulder grew damp with her tears. "They've had it all frae me. All of it." He drew back from the embrace, his gaze taking in the tarred hull and warped timbers of his boat before returning to his daughter. "This is all that I have left tae me."

Her fine fair hair slapped at his face and when he cupped her face in his hands, her cheeks were feverishly hot. He saw that she didn't understand even then. And was glad.

"I'll not give them ye, Nancy. Never ye."

He had already closed his hands around her throat and begun squeezing before she realised. Even then, it was still a few seconds more before she began to fight. Donald closed his eyes as she kicked and struggled against his will. His salvation. He thought of the thousands of herring that had ever swum into his nets; of how long and hard their bodies quivered and fought against the mesh trapped under their gills. Suffering should never have to be so relentlessly borne — not if the battle was always lost. With more strength than he had possessed in many, many years, Donald snapped his daughter's neck in two.

It was only many hours later, when he had finally determined to throw Nancy overboard to join her mother that Donald began to feel doubt creep in. He tried not to look at his daughter at all as he hefted her onto the roll and balanced her there: too afraid to let her go and too afraid to hold her with him.

When finally he dropped her down, Nancy sunk like a stone. Donald's sobs were now more for himself than for her. Only when a shadow moved suddenly beneath the water, did Donald abandon his grief and remember his doubt.

His dead wife came for him in a vengeful rush: her hair wild and fanned around her bloated face like kelp, her fingers wrinkled and clawed as if in spasm. She drew ever closer, reaching out of those vertiginous depths, her mouth wide and whispering too close to his ear.

"The evil does not come from the water, Donald."

Donald's horror found another home. "Ye told me *It* did!"

From her watery grave, Isobel smiled wide and long. The gaps between her teeth became blurred caverns as she turned her head back and forth. "It is in you, Donald. Always you brought it back from the water. But it was only ever in you."

"Ye told me it did!" Donald screamed, stumbling back from the edge as Isobel, not this time looking like an old Lunan witch, but like the demon Tuatha Himself, swam up towards him — *for him* — her fury an ugly mask of wet earth and spent blood. Donald fell backward against the skaffie and hunkered down in its hull. He looked down at his old and calloused hands. "Ye told me it did," he whispered.

Donald's hands had grown steadier as he turned the yard and tacked the lugsail. He pulled on the halyard and gathered his nets. As the sun winked behind darker coastal clouds, the sea eagle returned, its wings catching the same wind as Donald's old skaffie, a fat mackerel clasped between its claws.

Upon the distant horizon, the vast convoy of Herring Busses lumbered into view, heading finally for home. High above the grey swathe of Brora village, the bell-pit sounded its mournful call. The new villages of Gower and Helmsdale were no more than distant squat shadows in the northeast. Donald cast his nets and buoys, and tied the warp to his stern.

And waited for the drift.

dry places
Tom English

When the unclean spirit is gone out of a man,
it walketh through dry places, seeking rest, and findeth none.
Matthew 12:43

With the ferocity of a wounded animal when it is cornered, he rushed from the desecrated tomb, shaking his gnarled fists and screaming obscenities at the small group of men. He was completely naked except for the broken chains hanging from his bleeding wrists and ankles. His emaciated frame was lacerated with numerous wounds that had become infected by the dried gore and excrement encrusting his body. Here in the country of the Gerasenes, east of the Sea of Galilee, this madman had become infamous for terrorising the townspeople. Oftentimes his violence made it impossible for travellers to pass along the road leading into the city. At other times he had been observed tearing clumps of hair from his scalp or ripping open his flesh with jagged stones. Several attempts had been made to restrain the man, but as attested to by his broken chains, all of them had failed.

Flies buzzed about in the baking Mediterranean heat, alighting and feeding upon the lunatic's festering wounds. Several of the men covered their mouths as the stench of pestilence greeted them. Most of them shrank back from the confrontation now imminent between this filthy wretch and the leader of their tiny group, a rather unimposing figure whose expression appeared to be a mixture of slight annoyance and weariness. One of the men, however, the one called Cephas, moved much closer to his leader, but was careful to stand behind him, as though this would afford a certain degree of protection from the crazed brute running toward them.

"Master," he said quietly but hurriedly, "we are not safe here. This man is possessed...by a demon."

When his master gave no response, Cephas quickly added, "He sleeps here among the tombs." Then, as if to clarify his statement: "He has lain with the dead."

The demoniac continued to close in on the tiny group. Then suddenly, as though he had struck some invisible barrier, he stopped abruptly in his tracks. He dropped to his knees just a few short paces from the men and began to curse them.

The leader of the group studied him. "Tell me your name," he said firmly.

The man flopped to the ground, thrashing about like a fish tossed upon dry land. He gurgled something inarticulate, then cried hoarsely between foam-covered lips: "We are Legion, for we are many!"

Two swineherds, bringing their stock to market by way of the Gerasa road, stopped to watch the spectacle unfolding at the edge of their town. They stared in confusion as the demoniac squirmed in the dust while hissing:

"*We* know who you are, Son of God. Why do you torment us? We have departed the land of Jacob — why do you seek us here, in the land of the unclean?"

Cephas stepped back, but his master simply frowned at the man writhing upon the ground. "Be silent, Legion," he said. "Depart from the man at once!"

For a brief moment the man convulsed like one in the throws of an epileptic seizure. Then slowly his body began to relax, and an expression of serenity brightened his grimy features.

No sooner had this happened than a new disturbance broke out, this one to the alarm of the two herdsmen. The swine, which until then had been drowsing peacefully at the roadside, began to squeal, frantically jostling and snapping at one another. Within moments they began charging up a low hill opposite the tombs, their wild movements so synchronous their motion appeared to be that of a single frenzied beast.

The two herdsmen ran after them, reaching the hilltop in time to see the frightened animals race down the other side, a hopelessly steep cliff that plunged to a swirling river. They watched helplessly as the pigs, unable to escape the momentum of their mad descent, hurled themselves into the churning water below. The frantic beasts sank to the bottom of the river, and a piercing squeal of terror rose out of the ravine. A ghastly shriek unlike that of anything earthbound.

Upon hearing this unnatural cry, the herdsmen fled to Gerasa. Within an hour they had returned, accompanied by the town's chief official. They found the man they had believed to be demon-possessed sitting outside the tombs, surrounded by a group clearly foreign to their region.

Addressing their leader in an antagonistic voice, the official said, "We cannot explain the strange feats you have accomplished here today, but these things are terrifying in our sight. Consequently, we demand that you leave our country at once."

As the tiny group of strangers departed, Cephas looked back and said, "Filthy creatures!" Whether he was referring to the swine or the townspeople, the chief official couldn't know for certain.

Neither could he know that down in the ravine, a silvery slick had begun to form on the surface of the river. It glistened under the noon sun as it floated toward the far bank, but when it reached dry land it seemed to dissipate in a heat shimmer. This ribbon of distorted light wavered momentarily above the riverbank, before moving off into the east, in the direction of the Syrian Desert.

The man surveying the eastern horizon turned and remarked to his companion, "Halfway there, Mateo, and still I have misgivings about this journey."

Mateo returned the map to the pouch on his belt and said, "Perhaps you should address them to the Papal legate upon our return."

"We are living in a new and enlightened age, brother; secret missions across the desert belong to the past — as relics of the Crusades...and we should thank God for that."

"Times change, Renato, but in all the generations since Jerusalem fell, the hearts of men have not."

"It is not men, but the perils of the desert that concern me. Or have you so quickly forgotten that we began our journey as a circle of seven. How many do you number today?"

"Do not count them as dead so soon," Mateo said irritably. "We may yet find them."

"Two men do not disappear in the heart of a sandstorm and then return. They were swept away, surely, or covered over with sand until they choked."

"These men were no less than yourself: priests, yes, but warriors also; and all of us trained to overcome such obstacles. I would not be surprised to see Gaetano and Uberto come walking into camp tonight."

Renato pointed to a twisting column of sand slowly meandering across the dunes. "We have company."

"A dust devil," Mateo said.

"Come," Renato said, turning back, "we are at greater risk up here."

The two men made their way down the ridge, their boots kicking up tiny clouds of dust with each hasty step. In the distance the funnel of sand was doing a slow dance across the dunes, bending and weaving. It seemed to perfectly parallel their return to the tiny group awaiting them below: three priests who were trying to calm the seven Arabian horses now tugging at their reigns.

"You are being followed," Eusebio said in a gleeful tone, pointing across the dunes at the dust devil.

"I see no occasion for mirth." Mateo said, taking the reigns of his restless sabino. "Nor do the horses, apparently. Have they more sense than we?"

"Well, perhaps they have less *intelligence*," Eusebio answered softly, for he realised that Mateo blamed himself for the loss of their missing companions; and that despite his hollow words of optimism, Mateo had given up hope of finding them. What Eusebio couldn't comprehend, though, was how a man so nominal in the faith as Mateo could attain such a high position in their order. True, many noblemen had pledged huge annuities to obtain membership and higher rank, but none of them had risen to "Master" — not until this Castilian Count turned his back on his title and lands to wear the purple mantle of the Brotherhood of the Holy Veil; not until Mateo the warrior-priest left behind a wife and children to lead the Pope's secret service.

Eusebio pondered this, and other things, as he rode behind Mateo. Half a league across the dunes there were now three dust devils churning up the sand. Their dirty plumes rose up against the blistering sun hanging in the western sky. The wilderness of the desert had a history of weird phenomena, much of it purely physical, caused by the extreme heat and wind. Thirsty travellers continued to see water where there was none. This, of course, was simply the refraction of light through ribbons of heated air. But there were plenty of other, more severe, meteorological disturbances: violent electrical storms that repeatedly struck the desert floor, but delivered little or no rain; the bone-dry, insufferably hot *sirocco* that blew from the north, sucking the water out of whatever stood before it; wind-whipped sand that could scour away the exposed flesh of any man or beast not fortunate enough to find shelter. And ultimately, there were the sandstorms, like the one that had swallowed Gaetano and Uberto — massive walls of grit that could tower over a mile above the earth, rolling, like ocean waves, across the desert, able to flatten dunes and anything else.

Eusebio shuddered and looked back at the slanting funnels of sand continuing to snake along the horizon.

The desert was home to other, less explainable phenomena as well; a traditional environment for supernatural occurrences, where men who'd come to face their inner demons found themselves face to face with devils far more real. Eusebio thought of Moses, plagued by Azazel for forty years in the wilderness of Sinai; of his Saviour, who for forty days fasted and resisted Satan in the desert; of Saint Anthony, who had been tormented by an endless legion of evil spirits. Natural terrors, he decided, paled in comparison to such unnatural things.

"Finally the dust is settling," said Ludovico, who was riding next to Eusebio. "I have watched these desert whirlwinds persist for hours...tower a thousand feet into the sky...move across several miles of open terrain. These were not so high, by far. Nor particularly wide." Both men watched as the last of the grey columns collapsed behind a distant dune. "Who could imagine so much life resides in a grain of sand?"

The Veil party rode on for another hour before stopping to eat and sleep. They pitched a small, low-ceilinged tent not far from a shallow *wadi*, long dried up. Sitting cross-legged in the tent, one of the brothers, Ignacio, played on a lute.

"I hope you devote as much time to swordsmanship," Mateo said, as he sat sharpening the edge of his Damascus blade.

Ignacio nodded. "Almost as much time as I devote to the study of the Holy Scriptures."

Mateo stared sullenly at the honed steel.

"You mustn't blame yourself for the loss of Uberto and Gaetano," Ignacio said. "It was preordained by our Lord."

Mateo smirked. "God no longer concerns himself with the affairs of men, Ignacio. Why should he?"

"Tell me, Mateo," Eusebio said. "If you've so little faith in God, why did you join the order in the first place?"

"I believe in what the Church is trying to accomplish," he replied. "I've sacrificed far more than most, in order to further its cause. Must I embrace all its doctrines as well?"

"Your exploits as a warrior are legendary, Mateo," Eusebio said. "We could not ask for a more experienced leader. But what can possibly prompt such zeal? How can an unbeliever hope to do the will of God?"

"I believe," Mateo said defensively, "though differently now, and perhaps less than I once did." He hefted the sword. "But what is more real? The steel of this weapon, which I can see and touch — or an invisible God? I'm sorry, Eusebio, but I put more faith in this sword and my ability to wield it."

"That's precisely the problem with the Church in Rome," Renato said. "Too many leaders with too little faith! They attempt to accomplish in the flesh what God alone desires to accomplish in the Spirit."

Ignacio put aside the lute and stood up. "I will see if Ludovico requires help tending the horses."

"My dear brother," Renato continued, "we cannot hope to change the ways of kings and kingdoms until God changes the hearts of men. The Church cannot accomplish this. Only God."

"The Church in Rome may not be perfect," Mateo said, "but it is God's instrument on earth."

"His sword, you mean?" Renato said hotly. "To cut down all who oppose it? Heaven have mercy on your soul, brother. Have you so easily forgotten the atrocities committed during the Crusades? How we set fire to the Synagogue in Jerusalem — with men, women and children in it? Was our Saviour not Jewish?"

"Those were unfortunate consequences, I admit," Mateo said.

"And how many Saracens are buried beneath these sands?" Renato asked.

Mateo stood and sheathed his sword. "Far fewer than those who died defending the Faith," he said. "Saracen hordes beheaded thousands of Christians...*and* Jews. *I* don't forget, Renato. I don't forget."

Eusebeo stood also. "The unbearable heat of the day has affected us all," he said. "We should be resting while it is cool."

Ignacio rushed into the tent. "Ludovico is gone," he said, breathing heavily, "and something is wrong with the horses!"

Eusebio grabbed a torch, and the four men hurried out into the darkness. The desert night was almost impenetrably black.

"The fire's gone out!" Mateo said as he passed the mound of glowing embers.

"Ludovico!" Ignacio called out. But there was no reply from the dunes — and no sound in the camp except the strange, subdued whimpering of the horses.

"No moonlight," Renato said.

"There," Eusebio said, pointing to a dull crescent hanging low above the dunes.

The horses shifted nervously in their tethers. Mateo placed his hand on the neck of his sabino. "This horse is wet," he said. "Bring the torch here."

"It is blood," Renato said, running his hand along the flank of his own horse.

"Do you see any wounds?" Eusebio asked.

"Several," Mateo said. "No...not wounds. They are covered with sores!"

"More like patches of raw flesh!" Renato replied. "Where the devil is Ludovico?"

Ignacio took the torch from Renato. "I shall find him," he said, and then hurried toward the dunes.

"Come back here!" Mateo yelled, but Ignacio's torch had already become a pinpoint of light in the distance.

"I doubt Ludovico had anything to do with this," Eusebio said.

Renato nodded slowly. "The wounds *could* be sand abrasions."

"Sand must be driven by powerful winds to do this," Mateo said. "The last two days have been dead calm. Besides, the horses were fine when we left them."

"Why do we stand here in the dark?" Eusebio said. "I'll get another torch."

Mateo knelt before the heap of faintly glowing embers that less than an hour before had been blazing cheerfully. "No wonder the fire is out," he said. "Someone has kicked sand over the coals."

He stirred the ashes back to life, and then piled on additional pieces of charcoal.

Together the three men bathed the horses' wounds, using water they could scarcely spare. Afterward they applied a medicinal ointment made of crushed Balsam roots.

"I doubt this will be enough," Renato said.

Mateo wiped his hands. "It will have to be."

"These horses need proper attention," Renato said. "We should turn back."

"No, we finish what we started. We deliver both the signet and the document as planned."

Renato sighed. "I'll take the first watch. I would rather stay out here with the horses, anyway."

"I will keep you company," Eusebio said.

Mateo shrugged. "I will relieve you both soon," he said, then walked back to the tent.

Renato sat heavily in the sand. "There goes a stubborn one. He will lead us all through the flames of perdition." He picked up a handful of sand and let it pour through his fingers. What are we doing here, Eusebio? We risk our lives over a piece of paper and a king's bauble!"

"Which may very well prevent another war," Eusebio added.

"Possibly. Assuming we get there."

"You have always had misgivings about this mission, Renato."

"I felt it was cursed from the beginning," he said bitterly. "Out here in the desert like latter-day Crusaders. No, my brother, I have no taste for clandestine meetings in the wilderness."

"I, too, have grown quite uneasy during this expedition," Eusebio said. "I still cannot believe that Uberto and Gaetano are gone. And to so suddenly vanish from our midst, as though swallowed up like Jonah in the belly of some great leviathan." He stared broodingly at the burning coals. "This thing with the horses...I've heard legends of a desert creature the Arabs call Palis. It licks the wounds of men and animals; it feeds on their blood."

"A bloodsucking demon, Eusebio?"

"There are *many* things that inhabit the desert, Renato. Strange things we have yet to explain."

"Well, if ever a place were suited for such things, it is surely here. Think of the blood that was spilled across those dunes, the inhumanities that were perpetrated. The desert harbours far more than Arabian folk legends, Eusebio. It covers all our guilt as well."

Renato poked at the fire. "Don't tell your stories to Mateo. He will laugh at you," he said. "Here he comes now."

"So soon, Mateo?" Eusebio called. "You cannot have slept much."

The dark figure coming toward them gave no reply. It moved slowly, dragging its feet with difficulty.

"Mateo? Dear Lord!" Renato cried, jumping to his feet. He tried to reach the staggering man but was too late. The poor soul fell face down in the sand.

Eusebio knelt and turned the man over. "I think it's Ignacio!" He touched the man's face. It was sticky. "Mateo!" he yelled.

"I am here!" Mateo answered, running from the tent. "Pull him closer to the firelight!"

Eusebio gasped. "What happened to his face?"

"What happened, Ignacio?" Mateo asked. "Who did this?"

"The skin is gone," Renato said in disbelief. "Scoured completely off his face."

Mateo shook the wounded man roughly. "Ignacio! Tell us what happened?"

"He is dying," Eusebio said. "Leave him be."

Ignacio tried to speak and began coughing.

"Give him water," Mateo said. "Ignacio, did you see Ludovico out there?"

Ignacio swallowed hard. "Some...thing," he said. "Behind... the dunes." He coughed again. "Coming. This way. Not like us."

"Nomads?" Renato asked.

"Not like us..." he replied.

For a few seconds Ignacio struggled to breathe, before growing still in the arms of Eusebio, who gently laid him back upon the sand and then crossed himself. Renato, too, made the sign.

"Saracens," Mateo said. He stood up and scanned the curtain of blackness obscuring everything beyond the tiny circle of firelight. "Renato, put out the fire," he said. "Someone is out there...behind the dunes. Someone followed us here."

Renato flung several handfuls of sand across the flames, plunging the four men into almost total darkness. "Moon's behind the dunes. All we have is starlight."

"Who could have known our route?" Eusebio asked. "Or the timing of our journey?"

Mateo touched the hilt of his sword. "Perhaps we had a spy among us."

"One of us?" Renato asked in disbelief.

"One of our missing brothers," Mateo suggested. "Gaetano or Uberto. Maybe both. And what became of Ludovico?"

"Ignacio's face — none of our brothers could inflict such monstrous wounds!" Renato said.

"Nor do men simply walk off into the desert without horses," Eusebio added.

An unnatural hush had fallen across the desert floor. To the east, the dunes were barely discernible in the darkness. The night air, though cool, lay heavy with the anticipation of the impending encounter. Mateo could feel it.

"Check your swords!" he said. "Perhaps our brothers were met by someone *with* horses."

"Gaetano and Uberto disappeared in the middle of a duststorm," Eusebio replied. "Hardly a place for a rendezvous."

"And Ludovico?"

"The night is like pitch!" Renato said. "How far could anyone go?"

"Cut the ropes and drop the tent poles," Mateo ordered.

Even as Eusebio acted, he said with vehemence, "Whatever did this to Ignacio is not human, Mateo."

"What are you saying?"

A bright flash illuminated the dunes on the eastern horizon, and a low rumbling rolled across the sky. A few seconds later came another, brighter flash, followed by a loud clap of thunder.

"I don't like the looks of *that*," Renato said. "We are too exposed here. These electrical storms can be extremely violent."

"This whole thing is Satanic," Eusebio said. "First we lose Gaetano and Uberto; you yourself said they should have survived the sandstorm. Then Ludovico. Now Ignacio. And what about the horses? What could cause such things?"

"Does the Church not have enough enemies without dredging up fanciful ones, Eusebio?"

"Mateo, listen to me, please! Whatever is out there ... is not human! Perhaps not even of this world."

"What, then?"

A brilliant flash lit the sky, and for a brief moment Eusebio could read the scepticism in Mateo's face.

"I believe it's supernatural," Eusebio yelled above the thunder.

"The Devil? Demons?" Mateo exclaimed. "Then you had better gather up your faith *and* your sword, because here they come!" He pointed across the horizon, but neither Renato nor Eusebio could see anything.

A lightning strike behind the dunes cast the desert floor in an unnatural blue light. It lasted barely a second, but it was time enough for the men to see several silhouettes approaching from the east.

"These are men," Mateo shouted. "Not the powers of Darkness; not the ghosts of the Saracen dead come back to haunt us! If you do not—"

A deafening burst of thunder drowned out the rest of Mateo's words. Behind him, the horses, rearing and crying in blind terror, snapped their tethers. They stampeded past Mateo, who narrowly avoided being trampled by one.

"You are stiff-necked, Mateo," Eusebio said. "Your unbelief in these things may doom us all!"

"My personal convictions are not on trial here," he replied.

For a scant second, the night was torn open by a dazzling burst of energy, revealing a dark shape crouching near Eusebio. Renato had no time for his eyes to readjust to the blue-blackness. He ran in the direction of the invisible enemy, its transient image flickering in his confused mind. Had he seen the glint of a scimitar, the peak-domed helmet of a twelfth-century Saracen warrior? He swung blindly and repeatedly until his sword sank into something firm.

Another fleeting blaze of light...but now he could see nothing apart from the continual sea of sand rolling away toward to the dunes. Between the crashes of thunder he could hear the battle cries of his brothers, both of them chopping wildly at the darkness.

Eusebio had cut down three of the marauders in the gloom, but he had yet to get a good look at what he was fighting. Whatever they were, they were solid enough to fall before the blade. But how many more were out there? How long could he continue to fight in the darkness?

He gripped the sweaty hilt of his sword, poised to swing, straining his ears to interpret the shufflings in the sand around him. Atop the dunes, three lightning strikes in swift succession revealed a huge shape looming over him. He felt the sudden pressure of its lunge, and then the wetness of his internals being poured out.

Renato shrieked in terror. He had seen Eusebio being torn apart...as well as what had done it. *Grey. Malformed. A filthy corpse leaking sand onto the desert floor.* "Not like us," he raved. "Not like us!"

He stood fixed for a moment, shaking, before charging in the direction of the attacker. Before he was halfway there something knocked him to his feet. He rolled over in the sand and tried to fend it off with his upraised sword, but the arm that brandished the blade was severed at the elbow. His mouth sprung open in pain, but a deafening peel of thunder obliterated the scream.

Renato felt himself weighed down by intense pressure, sinking into a dry abyss with the sand pouring in after him...burying his nose and mouth. He struggled for air before allowing the darkness to overtake him.

"Renato," Mateo called in a hushed tone. "Eusebio. Are you there?"

A massive discharge of electrical energy shot into the desert floor not far from Mateo. *Too* close, he thought, staggering through a field of red and purple spots.

He had lost count of the number of invaders he had destroyed. He knew that at first light he'd find the desert floor littered with their bodies. Were they Saracens? And was that the last of them?

No. Something was moving toward him. He could feel it drawing closer. He raised his sword, tightly gripped in both hands. He took a slow, deep breath and held it until he thought his chest would burst open.

When it came out of the darkness he swung at it so hard the exertion forced all the wind from his lungs. The thing made a heavy thump as it fell to the sand. He couldn't make it out, but whatever it was, he had cut it in two at mid-thorax.

The sky overhead flickered brightly several times. Mateo turned about, scanning the area for several hundred paces in every direction. To his relief, nothing moved out there now. To his shock, the desert floor was *not* littered with dead bodies. He could see three, at most, not far from him.

Abruptly, he was knocked to his feet by a powerful blast that threw the world into a white haze. He tried to stand, but he was overcome by a wave of dizziness making him drop again. He wiped the sand from his face and realised his forehead was bleeding.

Above him the electrically-charged sky continued to flare. Mateo could feel the static building in the air, and he dropped to his stomach. He did not want to die this way...waiting to be roasted to death while cowering in the dirt. He lifted his head and swallowed hard. Not a pleasant or even an honourable way to die.

Two seconds later came another jarring blast, not as close this time, but close enough to send electric ants scurrying down his arms and legs. The sensation was followed by a bitter chill washing over his body, for during the dazzling illumination of the second lightning strike, he had seen something rising up from the sand; something far removed from the world of men: a huge dark mass, as wide as it was tall, lumbering across the desert toward him.

Despite the darkness, Mateo knew it was coming for him; and each time an electrical discharge starkly illuminated the landscape, the thing was nearer. He caught himself praying aloud to be struck by lightning, for the thought of being electrocuted suddenly became far more appealing when compared to waiting for this unknown terror. Unexpectedly, he remembered something he'd read long ago, but dimly, as though from another life; something about a God constantly tested by his people in the desert: *They have displeased me by their unbelief, so they shall become spoil and plunder for their enemies.*

Swift on the heels of this vague memory came a sorrowful realisation — and with realisation came resignation. He was to die this night, he thought bitterly. Here in the wilderness. Did it matter now whether he would be electrocuted in the storm, or torn apart by an unseen horror — one which had probably existed in the desert for centuries?

A brilliant burst of energy, a half a league away, silhouetted the hideous creature closing in upon him. Mateo dropped his face into the sand and covered his head with his hands. Another electrical discharge exploded just feet away from him, releasing a deafening concussion and bringing an abrupt end to his thoughts.

Human knowledge has always been limited to what can be measured with the physical senses, to what man can define by his intellect, thought Mateo as he hurriedly buried his fallen comrades. It had taken him at least an hour after the storm dissipated to recover his shattered wits, but the moment he had, he had begun scooping a shallow grave out of the sand. Time, he knew, was not on his side, so he was relieved to finish the task before the first rays of sunlight broke across the dunes.

He packed up only the things most crucial to his survival. His chances of making it out of the desert on foot were marginal, at best, but if he didn't travel light he'd have no chance at all.

And who would believe his tale? Certainly not the sober council awaiting him in Rome. *No*, he thought, *there will be a long inquisition upon my return. It will not be easy.*

He picked up his sword and approached the crystalline monolith rising from the sand; a grotesque monument to the hellish thing that had been stalking them. Whatever it had been, it wasn't human. Not Saracen; not anything even remotely natural. There were far too many extremities, for one thing — and where there should have been a head, there was only a dense cluster of appendages. Even hunched over, it stood more than eight feet tall.

Had it been a demon taking shape in the dust? He couldn't be sure. Whatever it had been, it was now only a misshapen mound of sand fused to glass by a bolt of lightning striking the desert floor.

He avoided touching it. Something about the slickness of its milky surface repulsed him. And beneath its cloudy shell there were dark patches of shadow stirring.

Mateo kicked it with the heel of his boot, toppling the translucent mass to the desert floor. The glazed surface crumbled. Inside, it was still mostly packed sand. For a moment he considered removing a chunk of the dark glass. Perhaps one of the broken appendages. Such a bizarre souvenir might be sufficient evidence to acquit him with even the greatest of scoffers in Rome.

Men will always seek after proof of the things they cannot see or understand; the bizarre and unexplainable things existing just outside the realm of the possible, or the probable. But such proof often comes at a terrible price.

Mateo sheathed his sword and turned away from the monstrosity. Civilization and sanity lay many leagues beyond the horizon, and the day would soon be growing hot. He picked up his food and water and contemplated his impossible walk across the dunes. *Who could know for certain,* he mused. Perhaps he would find one of the lost horses.

He began walking in the general direction of Damascus, leaving behind him the toppled monolith to be covered up by the windblown sand; to be reclaimed by the desert.

begin with water

Sharon Irwin

The man wanted her, but he still haggled over her price for most of the morning, sometimes pretending to lose interest and walk away only to return and push his dirty fingers under the few pieces of clothing she had been allowed and make crude comments about her beauty. Finally, spitting and slapping hands and shoulders, he had agreed with the slavers on her worth. The amount was pitiful. She watched them pour the coins from one purse into another and turned her face away from the insult, swirling around, taking in all the faces, every detail of the marketplace.

Since she had been stolen from the pool, she had been forced to breathe the stench of death riding the wind and settling into the grains of sand and the fabric of her clothing. Here in the marketplace it was particularly cloying. The bazaar was only a withered husk of its former vigour. The food stalls were few and widely spaced. They promised to be small islands of nourishment in a sea of sand, but closer inspection showed they had only wizened fruit, shrivelled roots, and rancid meat to offer. The open bags of grain were contaminated with rodent droppings and the dried up shells of dead insects. The breath from the traders and their beasts smelled as if their lungs were lined with excrement. They held perfumed cloths to their faces. Scented rags hung off every tent post. Spice burners also competed with the stench, but even they smelled wrong — as if there was nothing pure to burn anymore.

The man she had been sold to was hung with thick jelly-like fat beneath his robes. She felt it when he rubbed up against her. She felt a rush of nausea at the thought of how much of this rotting food it took to sustain his girth.

He leered at her as she pirouetted in a slow circle.

"Not half right in the head, is she?" he said.

"What does it matter?" said the slave-master. "All women are trouble." She came to a halt facing him and regarded him in silence. His lie hung on the still air, adding to the stench of the decaying world. *Did this slaver even know he lied*? she wondered. Was there some part of him that longed to acknowledge the truth, to speak it, to sing it? He could not suffer her stare. Turning away from her, he rotated a finger near his head to indicate her madness. Then he brought his hand down to clasp it to his belly, his features stiffening into a mask of denial and fear of the unknown disease gnawing at his insides. She knew he had been feeling sick since he had captured her. She had seen the darkness spreading beneath his eyes, the hollows in his cheeks growing deeper every day. She knew what was wrong with him, knew how he could be healed — but also knew he would listen to nothing she said. Yet, she decided to make the offer now, before it was too late and he was beyond her assistance.

She plucked the pale violet flower caught in her sandal strap and stretched out her hand indicating he should take it. The flower should have been dead by now but at night she allowed the dew that beaded on her skin to feed it. In that way she had kept it alive since the pool. The desert had ceased offering up its beauty in flowers a long time ago.

The slaver gave the flower scant respect. He rumpled up his forehead in a mockery of confusion and flicked the flower out of her hand with the side of his. It swirled up into the air and descended to get lost in the muddle of donkeys and camels, traders and slaves.

"Come on." The fat man who had bought her thumped his elbow into her back, disturbing her concentration. She moved to retrieve the flower, to return it to the safety of her person, but he slid his hand down her arm and onto her wrist. Then he dragged her after him. Anger, white and furious, raged within her; an urge to throw herself upon him and bite and claw until his blood flowed into the dry sand. She swallowed it down, placing a hand upon her stomach, taking comfort in the act, calming herself.

"Hush now," she whispered. "Not yet." Her new owner, thinking she was talking to herself, laughed with delight at the craziness of his new slave.

He brought her to the women's quarters. Forty of his wives and concubines lived there. Bound to him alone, they were fretful-eyed and anxious, their minds bent under the weight of a thousand petty squabbles. At first they all hated her. They could only see her violet eyes, her straight nose and clear skin, her beauty eclipsing theirs like the Sun chasing the stars before it. But then they came to realise how much comfort she carried in her slender frame. They came to her and sat at her feet, their faces buried in her lap and their shoulders heaving with sorrow while she stroked their hair until their tears stopped. All the women cried. They cried when they first arrived and cried when they aged and were sent away to die. They cried at the pain of childbirth and when the futures of their children were taken from them. And when these women laughed there was no joy in it. She hated the sound of their laughter and the way they laughed at what should have broken their hearts in pieces.

They asked for her name but she wouldn't tell them. She would only laugh when they pressed her. She shook her head so her long black hair waved and danced as if there were a breeze. They could not stand for her being nameless; it made them shiver, they complained, so they made one up. Alluna, because she was as beautiful as the Moon. She liked the name that was not her name. The women were insightful, which made it all the stranger that they allowed themselves to be bred like animals.

At night he sent only for her. The women were grateful she took their place in his bed. She would return tired and wasted, her back sore from the weight of him, her legs aching and her skin stinking from his mouth.

She would be as quiet as she could, but always someone would hear her footsteps and rise out of bed to greet her. There was no water to spare for washing, but they would dip cloths into perfumed oil and help to scrub at her skin until the scent of him was gone. Some would pour the oil directly into her hair, and cleanse every rib with careful fingers until she smelled only of women and perfume and despair. Sometimes they would cry, and their tears would wake the seeds, and she would have to hush them back to sleep. The women, thinking she was losing her mind, would cry all the harder for her, but Alluna hadn't failed to notice the relief on their faces as night after night she was hauled off to lie under him. No one cried for her then. They accepted it for her as her lot, as a woman's lot, a fate they did nothing to escape. The women's weakness and despair harmonized with the anger and hatred of the men. Alluna was weary of them all.

She made her decision. She was ready. Now she only waited for the Moon.

It was Ebouline who rose to greet her the night she decided it was time. Ebouline helped her wash, her eyes black in the day-bright Moon; eyes as deep and dark as the drying wells heralding their doom as she wiped the rag into the crevices of Alluna's skin. Something tore at Ebouline. Her head jerked oddly, once, twice, as if she fought the urge making her bend down and kiss Alluna on the cheek, and then lower, beneath her ear. Alluna leaned back and breathed in the scent of the woman, a scent so fragile it threatened to disperse on the wind and be no more. They all longed to touch her, the men and the women, to lean into her and wrap her around them. The women were gentle, their fingers tingling with reverence and timidity. The men thought they owned her and could take what they wanted. All were alike in that none of them asked Alluna what she wanted.

Alluna got to her feet, pushing away the kneeling Ebouline and padding away on bare feet, saying not a word.

I will not even say goodbye, she resolved as she returned to her room. Her womb was hurting. The Moon was calling to it, ripping it this way and then that in her abdomen. She moaned and turned with it, rolling with the pain. Finally the hurt became too much to lie still and she got out of bed and went to the window. The desert stretched outward as far as she could see — farther than it should. Rags dipped in scented oil fluttered from sills and rooftops. The world was dying though they tried to deny it, tried to mask the last breaths of its disease. Near where the animals were quartered a camel was down on the ground, bellowing in labour. Her belly rippled like a snake while men dragged the calf from her with ropes and curses. The calf's coat, when they pulled it clear, was as dry as the sand. It flopped lifeless beside its mother and the men whooped around it, beating its chest and puffing dirty breaths of air into its mouth. After a while the men became quieter and then walked away, leaving the beasts on the sand, the mother snuffling her dead while the gathering of flies over their heads grew denser.

A gust of wind managed to steal its way through the perfumed rags and deliver a breath of pure decay to her lungs. She coughed until she spat up blood. The hushed seeds, smelling it, stirred again.

This time she did not quieten them.

"Yes, now," she whispered. "Now at last."

The muscles of her belly contracted as the seeds awakened. She screamed with the pain of it, falling to her hands and knees and breathing in harsh pants.

After a moment the ache eased enough that she could crawl over to the wall and lean her sore back against it. She held her arms out in front of her to examine them. Her skin was shrivelling, pulling tightly back from her fingernails so they seemed elongated, gleaming like talons in the moonlight. Her veins bulged upwards through her drying skin. Alluna dropped her hands back down, hating the look of them. The seeds were sucking her dry. She felt blood at the side of her mouth where her screams had torn her cracked lips.

59

Loud footsteps sounded outside the room. She knew the guards were coming to investigate. The women would never have dared to make so much noise. They entered her room and found her, bent and bleeding, shivering against the wall, her arms clasped around her belly. Fearful that the man's most treasured slave would die and they would have to answer for it, they hauled her to her feet and dragged her to him, letting her fall on the ground before him.

She moaned on the rug, gripping her belly. He extended one foot to push away a fold of her skirt where it had flowed towards him.

"The slave-driver had something wrong with him as well," he said. He looked down at his own vast stomach swelling beneath his robes and then back at Alluna writhing on the ground.

"Take her away," he said, stepping back from her. "Get her away from me!"

Once again the guards grabbed her beneath the arms, heedless to her further cries of pain. They pushed her into the nearest room, closing the door and locking it behind them. She knew from the way they scurried away, wiping their hands against the sides of their legs, they would not be back. Alluna looked around. She had never been here before. Hunting trophies and weapons lined the walls. A low table surrounded by cushions sat in the centre of the room. She dragged herself over there and placed one of the cushions beneath her knees and another beneath her head. Then she lay back, exhausted, as the seeds continued their work. Her eyes stung as the seeds stole water from them. Her skin tightened. Cracks appeared not only at the sides of her mouth but beneath her arms, at the back of her knees, and between her fingers and toes. She hacked and coughed, twisting on the ground, her throat torn apart by her spasms until it seemed the air she breathed in passed to her lungs over a bed of knives. .

The door to her room opened and a slight figure entered. Ebouline.

Alluna froze, hushing the seeds even though they protested. Despite herself, Alluna couldn't help but be intrigued by Ebouline's action, by the risks she had taken to be there.

The woman crossed the distance between them to kneel down and place her hand on Alluna's forehead.

"Oh Alluna," she said. "What has he done to you?"

Alluna smiled at her, blood trickling from the corners of her mouth. She felt a pang of remorse for what she was about to do. Another bout of coughing racked her, forcing her to try and sit up. Ebouline held her, placing one hand on her back and intertwining the fingers of the other with hers, not minding the blood or the dry skin or the ropey veins. Alluna felt her trying to push comfort across her skin, the weakest hint of it. It surprised her.

The coughing passed. Ebouline helped her to lie back down. She ran her fingertips across Alluna's bloody lips.

"You're so thirsty?" she asked.

The two women looked at each other. Ebouline's eyes betrayed her fear for Alluna. The women were allowed only half a jug a day. By now, this late in the night, everyone would have drunk theirs. There would be no more until the morning. A guard stood over the well. There was no way to get any.

Alluna didn't answer, unable to speak through her shredded throat. Ebouline placed a finger into her mouth and felt her gums.

"They're dry as dust," she said. "You're dying of thirst. I can't let him kill you."

A thought struck Alluna. One last test. She forced her throat to speak even though it was her own blood lubricating the chords.

"What can we do?" she said. "We have no water. A soldier guards the well."

Ebouline pushed the hair away from her eyes.

"The sentry is old and often sleeps. I can creep up on him and steal some."

Alluna leaned back.

"And what if he wakes? He will have you killed."

Ebouline pulled her veil across her face to demonstrate. "I am young and fast. If he wakes, I will run, and he will never know who disturbed him."

"And what if he wakes before you can fetch me water?"

The women were silent. The threat of Alluna's death hung between them.

Alluna pointed to the wall. A knife, as long as an arm, curved and vicious, a line of moonlight dancing upon the blade, hung there.

"See. You could take that."

Ebouline looked at the knife. Then she crossed the room and took it down from the wall, holding it in front of her so Alluna could see the reflection of the woman's eyes in the blade. Then Ebouline walked out of the room, the knife held in a firm grip at her side.

"I'll get a jug and return to you," she said as she left.

Alluna played no further part in the test, but when Ebouline returned with blood on the knife, she knew it had been a true one. Ebouline dropped the knife on the floor and knelt to offer Alluna water from the jug she held with trembling fingers.

"Are you sorry you killed him?" Alluna asked.

Ebouline shook her head no. "They would have let you die," she said.

Alluna smiled and pulled Ebouline close to kiss her on the forehead.

"Go now," she said. "You have healed me. You have saved a life tonight."

Before Ebouline left she paused and looked at the animal heads lining the walls. One, a male ortex with long curling horns, was of particular interest to her. At last, shaking her head as if chiding herself for being foolish, Ebouline tore her eyes away from the heads and, smiling at Alluna, she left, locking the door as she had found it.

Alluna was certain now she had made the right decision. Ebouline had sensed something. The ortex was newly killed, and so its spirit still clung to its flesh, denying its death.

"Come," Alluna said to it.

The ortex came forward, torn between a fear of abandoning its post and a desire to do Alluna's will.

"I am the last of my kind," it said. "I cannot die. I must stay alive for them all. I must stay alive or there will be no more ortex." It bleated in its despair.

"*Sshh*, ortex," she said. "I harvested your seed. Don't you remember?"

She allowed him to retrieve the memory of the time he had played with a young female ortex, and the joy he had in finding her because he had been convinced all the females had died, and his despair when she had disappeared before their young had been birthed.

"Your young will be born," she promised him. "Now take your rest. You have done well."

Her voice reassured him and the ortex at last consented to abandon his lonely vigil by his own grave.

Then Alluna spoke aloud the name of each seed. All this time and she had not lost a single one. All had their place, the hard-shelled and the many legged, the swimmers in the sea, those that lived in the breeze, the poisonous and the timid, the toothed and the clawed, the rooted living. All would be given their second chance. Even the one who had forced them all to this beginning again, the one she had this night vowed to destroy forever.

Man.

Close to her womb, the last seed of the man cowered, certain it too would be destroyed as the others if its kind had been, but Alluna turned aside the tide of anger that would have fallen upon it, and she allowed it to enter.

"So that Ebouline's kind may try again," she said as the last of the seeds completed its journey to her womb.

In the morning the guards returned, expecting to find her dead. Instead they saw she was huge with child. They called the man and when he saw her, he sent at once for his brothers and his uncles so they could praise his fruitfulness.

They arrived with jugs full of wine and brandy, ready for a celebration. They pushed Alluna's dress up and spread her legs, staring upwards into her cavity, hungry for what would emerge, hungry for something else to own.

She released her baby upon them. It poured out of her in a flood that drowned the men and the camels, the women, the creatures of the deserts and the plants.

And the waters kept rising until they covered the whole world. Alluna swam in the currents, the knife in her hand, striking at any remaining living thing until the waters flowed red and warm with blood.

Then she rested, floating on the waves, cradling the child on her stomach. It cried in confusion as all infants do, wanting to know its name, needing to know its story.

"Sshh," she said. "Do not fear. I remembered it for you. In time you will remember everything."

in the name
Robert Holt

Just before sunrise, three girls were led to the altar where they quietly sat and waited. Addu was the youngest, having just entered womanhood with the coming of the moon, but the other two were not much older. Addu, glad to be the youngest, knew she would be last.

Her hands fidgeted, knees bounced, and heart pounded in anticipation. The binds that held her wrists together were made from a thorn bush, and the sharp points dug deeper into flesh every time she moved. It was excruciating, but she refused to cry. She promised her father that no tears would be shed and all pain would be endured quietly and with dignity.

The priest, a bare-chested man with a braided beard, pointed to the three and said something in a language Addu had never learned, a Babylonian dialect of some sort. She picked out only the name Marduk from the speech. Marduk was the reason for her presence. She closed her eyes and thought of when he had turned the sky dark over her home village and blessed them with rain, beautiful rain in the middle of the dry season. That was three years ago and the last time Addu saw rain. Tiamat had opened her foul maw and exhaled her deadly breath on the town killing the crops, animals, and many people, including Addu's mother. This led her father to the decision that Addu would be the one to save the village. It had been the happiest day of her life.

Now, with thorns digging into her wrists, she cursed the day but would not cry. She would go fulfil her promise with honour.

The priest came for the first girl, grabbed a handful of hair, and lifted her onto unsteady legs. The crowd cheered enthusiastically as she begged in Egyptian. Addu repressed laughter as the poor fool evoked the name of Horus. 'Your petty gods can't penetrate Marduk's temple,' Addu thought. The brutish priest slapped the Egyptian, and she fell to the ground. Chants from the crowd grew in intensity, drowning out her continued pleas and prayers. Addu did not know the chant but joyfully joined in.

The priest took a blade from his robe, and the chant broke away into deafening screams of approval. Addu watched mesmerized as the showman circled behind his intended victim. His long, bony fingers wrapped into the girl's black hair and yanked upwards, stretching her neck. She screamed and squirmed but could not get away. He placed the inwardly curved blade against her throat. Addu looked away as a sickening feeling rose inside her, but then she thought of Marduk and returned her gaze to the scene being performed in his honour. The blade, crude and dull, did not slice the fragile skin as much as sawed through it. The Egyptian's scream drowned in a gurgle that sent blood splashing from her mouth and smearing her fine Egyptian makeup. Addu smiled.

The body went limp, and the priest struggled to get his blade between the bones of the spine. Once he did, he held the head up for the crowd, which once more roared with approval. He signalled at two men who began pulling on chains to reveal a hot glow of a roaring fire behind the altar. He said a few more words and tossed the head into the flames. Then the body was lifted by the two assistants and was fed into the furnace. The stench made Addu hold her breath in revulsion.

The next offering was trying so hard to break her bindings that a pool of blood was forming beneath her. Addu watched as the grinning priest grabbed the bloody hands and pulled her into the centre of the altar. He danced around her, laughing and speaking his strange words. This girl was a Babylonian, for she knew the tongue that mocked her and replied with venomous gumption. The blade cut the retort short by entering into her open mouth and ripping out the side of her cheek. She did not try to speak again but continued to scream. The bare-chested, blood-drenched priest sawed open the girl's stomach and seized her innards. Addu had thought nothing could smell worse than the Egyptian's flesh burning, but exposed insides were far worse.

It was over quickly, and the disembowelled body was tossed to the flames. The priest turned toward Addu and stuck his tongue out in a taunting gesture. Addu did not know what torments awaited her, but she decided that if her fate was to be the same as the Egyptian girl's, then she wanted her hair to remain pristine and untouched when her head was displayed for the crowd. Before he stepped towards her, she rose to her feet, walked across the altar, and dropped to her knees before the executioner. She stretched her neck as far as possible and lifted her dress to reveal her stomach, giving him the choice of targets.

The crowd fell silent. Addu looked up into the priest's confused eyes and forced herself to smile. There was a clanking sound, and she lowered her head to see what it was. The knife had fallen from his hand. She looked up to meet his wide eyes again. Not understanding, she leaned forward, picked up the knife, and placed it back into his hand, but he stepped away and let the blade fall again.

A chant began in the crowd, not bloodthirsty but a peaceful one. Addu choked back her tears and tried to interpret the situation. Was she being rejected as a sacrifice?

The priest stepped forward with unease, placed his hands delicately in her armpits, and encouraged her to stand. He picked up the blade, and Addu smiled. He put it between her hands and cut the bindings, then motioned to the furnace. Addu pointed and asked if she was to go in there. Someone translated for the priest, who nodded and escorted Addu to the furnace by the tips of her fingers. She lifted the end of her dress and stepped into the flames.

Beneath her, the inferno turned from orange to blue. The two corpses continued to sizzle and pop, but she did not burn. The wide-eyed priest tried to reach his hand toward her but pulled away as his skin blistered.

Addu stepped out of the furnace and onto the altar. The crowd kowtowed at the sight. The blood splattered, sadistic executioner bent down and kissed her bare feet. At the feast in her honour, she was adorned as Marduk in the flesh, the forty-seventh name.

The next day they sacrificed three children to her, and Addu wept.

when they come to murder me

Bill Ward

Upon this baldric of tough hide hung my sword all these short, glorious years. With it now I hang myself; suspended from this stone like a pillar. I will not lie down in death. In the time after me, when this age is naught but mist and memory, they will carve upon this rock and not know why. They will say it is for another who died young — another who knew his fate and tasted it with his every breath. They will confuse us, though I am the monster and he the meek. I know they will confuse us in the same way I know that this moment of dying is only a kind of end. Only a kind.

With the third cast I was struck, here below the rib. The red and grey ropes of my belly slipped out with the wound upon the chariot floor and I gathered them back into me. Loeg watched as I did so with eyes like willow water, no life in them. He too died for me.

I smile because fate has decreed I die a man and not, as was always the chance, the god-spawned monster. Can you know how many I've killed? I slew the sons of Nechtan as easily as you draw breath; their heads a gory display upon my chariot. Whole flocks of swans I brought down with my stones, and stags...stags I outran on the hoof, their necks I broke with an action of the fingers. And that was but the first day of my manhood. So hot did I become in the doing of this, the green of the earth was blackened at my passage, and three barrels of cool water did I burst and render steam before those around me no longer feared death at my hand. All this was done to win the love of a girl.

My heat, I believe it to be the heat of the sun. My father is the sun, I know now.

To refuse a poet and singer of songs a gift is to know shame. Would I, who put my head willingly upon the block that it might be struck from my shoulders, accept such shame? Or, like the king who plucked forth his own eye in accordance with the bard's request, should I do as they ask and damn the cost? When my enemies gathered round me, the anger of Medb hovering over them like the ash cloud of a ruined Dun, three times they asked me for my spear, and three times I agreed to their demands.

Loeg, you were more loyal than I deserved, for you loved me despite my greatness.

The Grey of Macha, peerless among your breed, may you die in peace.

The third cast was for me.

In a future time you will say I did not leap the wall of Dun Forgall, you will say I could not have broken the wheel-poles of a hundred chariots over my knee, or part whole fields of foemen from their heads with a snicker-snack of my sword, as weeds before the scythe. I see the hordes of Medb even now come upon us. While all Ulster's manhood groaned in sickness and pain I alone held the field and a thousand thousand men I slew with each hand — their bodies made into mountains of red ruin and rot, their heads spitted upon poles and driven into the earth. Day after day I held the ford against their champions, and only despair undid me.

In my life, I've lived with death at each hand. My friends I've slain.

My son, slain at my hand — when I lick my fingers at the feast I taste his blood.

You'll not see me weep; I chose this short, bright prelude to my end. Let others weep.

They have come to murder me as I stand — *stand*! — at the stone. There, there, there...in all directions they close upon me, their knives sharp, their eyes hungry. The foul sons of Calatin, brothers to those I've killed. My hand is weak.

Then a grey wind, a storm, and dying Macha kicks and bites at them, his hot blood spinning in the air as he spends it in my service. He, too, can be a monster and I laugh to see him kill so well.

They will say of me that I changed when the heat of battle came upon me, that I twisted and grew, that bloody mist surrounded me and light swirled about my head. It is true. It was my father's gift to me.

I thought the gift made me great — and it did — but greater still was the choice I made. The choice I am making. Confuse not fate, confuse not *geas*, with lack of choice — long before I ate of my namesake I looked upon this death and rejoiced in its coming.

Perhaps that is why they will confuse me with that other; the humble men in their cold stone rooms writing of gods and heroes while wolves out of the north batter at their door.

But that is so far away from now. And you are farther still.

Fergia's death was more painful than this; his death I regret the most.

I regret also killing the hound.

But now they come again, and the Grey I do not see. Come fate, come fame, come glory. They will take my head, and my hand, but with my back upon this stone I stand. I will not lie down. I die not as half a god, but fully half a man.

The Raven lights upon me, I feel its sharp grip. I go — having chosen. You will know my name; long after my father is forgot, you will know my name.

once upon
a time

the unbedreamed
Christopher Johnstone

He walked the high hills under marbled skies, yet seemed to see none of it. He did not look at the boulders like knotty fists, his eyes never went to the heather or the mosses. Not once did he look into the distance, to gaze at the changeful Atlantic. Although the wind was cold, he did not shiver. Although the gleds cried like ragged eagles, he did not stop and listen. There were grey shadows on the irises of his eyes.

Dughall was hunting hares near Garleffin Fell and he already had three of them bloody and gutted on his belt. It would mean dinner tonight, and pelts to sell, but he did not feel happy to have them. He did not feel sad either. He did not, in truth, feel anything. When a shiver passed through a thick scrub of gorse, he stopped and eyed it, but he did not back away. When the grey muzzle poked out, when the black eyes shone and flashed, he did not feel fear.

The wolf was a half-starved thing, bone-thin and mean with hunger. It circled Dughall, and the man watched it, and wondered abstractedly if there were more, or if this were a straggler from its pack. Dughall slipped an arrow out and eased it into the cradle of his bow.

The wolf growled once, feverish, then came at him. Dughall's arrow went wide. There was no time for another, so he threw the bow aside, and plucked out his gutting knife.

It was strange. Even as the wolf knocked him over, even as it snapped at his face, he felt nothing. They rolled in the heather, man and wolf, like some monster, half-made and ill-made. They seemed to be one thing, full of self-hate... only... only... Dughall thought... he had no hate... no fear... just cold awareness.

The wolf twisted its head closer and dug its teeth into Dughall's shoulder. The pain was distant. They writhed together. Dughall stabbed the wolf — once — twice — again. They were both red and sticky now. Their blood mingled. They were one creature truly. And together they tumbled down the slope, then slid, then tumbled some more. Teeth found a way to Dughall's throat. He remembered, distantly, that he ought to scream or pray or something... and then... and then there was nothing... just a sickening sense of falling.

Was this death?

Dughall could still feel the wolf all over him. He could still smell its wet-dog reek. They seemed to twist together in mid-air, then they slammed into something very cold and hard.

He lay a long time in shadows, gasping, and not quite conscious, listening to the Devil singing. When his sense came swimming back, Dughall got up on one elbow and looked at the dead wolf. It would be a valuable pelt, he thought, but couldn't summon anything more. Up above, a gash of grey light tore through an enclosing blackness. He could see clouds passing, and now and then the wings of a gled. He was in a hole. A tunnel to hell, perhaps, for Dughall could still hear the Devil singing.

He stood, shakily, and looked about for his knife, which he found buried up to the end of its bone haft in the carcass. The wolf must have broken his fall, and the creature's back was shattered, the left side of its skull also a mess. He skinned it without haste or care, bundled the fur and tied it up on his back.

All the while, the Devil sang unseen in the dark.

There did not seem to be any way out of the hole, certainly he couldn't climb back up — the walls were loose dirt and dead roots. There was another hole, though, one that was smaller and went deeper into the side of the hill. It was from this hole that came the uncanny voice, still carolling away.

Dughall crouched down, he sniffed the air of the tunnel, shrugged, and crawled inside.

He must have crawled for a hundred paces, two hundred, more, before seeing at last the sallow light of a candle. Now he went more carefully, creeping as quiet as he could, barely breathing... though not from fear, rather it was an abstracted sort of prudence.

Dimly he began to realise that this was all wrong. Why was there no fear left in him? It seemed wrong. *He* seemed wrong.

He edged to the end of the tunnel and peered into the candle light. It was, he supposed, some sort of workshop. The walls were lined with rough-cut stone, and the floor with reed mats and rugs. There was a burnt-out fire in the room, a bowl of embers, over which was a pot, and over the pot was the strangest fellow that Dughall had ever seen. He was a misbegotten thing, humpbacked, and stooped. His face had a bulbous nose and nostrils full of wiry hairs. His ears were huge and waxy and drooping. Though the hunched man's clothing nearly reached the ground, Dughall could see that the poor fellow's feet were malformed too, and it seemed that perhaps they looked more like the feet of a crow, or pointed backwards, though he couldn't be sure.

All the while, as Dughall watched, the bent man sang and worked over the pot. So far, Dughall had not been noticed, and he planned to keep it this way. He could see another opening not more than a few feet away — it was curtained with rotten sacking and the material swayed in a gentle breeze — surely, thought Dughall, a sign pointing to the way out. But as Dughall was about to sneak along the wall and vanish through the door, the misshapen man did a strange thing. He stopped stirring the pot, and picked up a full sack from the floor. When the man upturned the sack and emptied it into the pot, there tumbled out all manner of airy shapes and bubbles of colour. Rich and beautiful things went into the pot with a plop and a hiss. Beautiful phantoms were swallowed up and gone. Darker things too, small stormy nightmares, and grey and hopeless colours and then...Dughall couldn't quite understand what he was seeing...

He saw a shape and in it was a field full of flowers and in the field was Iseabel, who he had fancied for some years, but lately...

lately he had stopped loving her so much... then he had stopped loving her at all... and now he barely remembered her — they passed each other in the village sometimes and looked at one another with grey-shadowed eyes — but there she was, in such a beautiful field and in the same field, standing beside her and looking so happy, was Dughall. The image fell into the pot and was devoured by the boiling liquid.

It was a dream, he realised, one of his dreams — a dream he didn't remember, but a dream he recognized all the same.

The wee man worked away steadily, pouring dreams into the pot. When he turned his back, Dughall took the opportunity to creep to the door and then he was through.

Dughall walked a way down the slope. He stood and watched the clouds sculpt and resculpt. A gentle rain crawled slow towards him, wetted him, then rippled away like the cave's rotten curtain. Dughall let the rainwater trickle on his face, he tasted salt that had beaded on his lip... He looked again at the sky. Two gleds glided overhead, crying out, hunting for voles or mice.

He was alive.

He remembered.

That one small taste of a dream forgotten, it was enough to remind him that he was alive.

That night Dughall did not sleep. He ate his bannock and black sausage — as he always did — he put out his wisp lantern — as he always did — he went to bed and pulled his wool quilt up to his chin. But he did not sleep. Instead he put his gutting knife under his pillow, and waited. Darkness gathered in the room. He watched as a few fingers of moonlight snailed across the floor and walls.

The moonshine moved, the hours passed.

Dughall was still wide awake when a noise disturbed the night. He kept still now and watched. The shutters of one window opened, and a bolt of moonlight spilled into the room. Haloed in the light was a small, misshapen thing — the hunchback. It crept into the room, carrying in one hand a strangely shaped candlestick with five dim flames on five grey tallows. This odd stick was left on the window-sill, then, while singing softly to himself, he unravelled something like a fisherman's net, but silver-bright and gossamer. With net in hand, the man came to the bed-side, and then he cast the net into the air as if fishing for salmon, but instead of falling gently to cover Dughall, the net drifted over him, wafting as if the air were water.

Dughall had seen enough through his half-cracked eyes. He moved as quick as a wild-cat, snatching the knife out from under his pillow, then jumping at the wee man before the creature had a chance to do so much as shriek.

Dughall got a firm hold of him.

"What mickle is this?" said Dughall, "What are you doing here in my house? For I thinks ye're stealing my dreams."

"Get off me." The wee man squirmed, but his wizened bones were too weak. "Let me go."

"No." Dughall stretched the fingers of one hand almost the whole way around the man's throat and dragged him into the hearth-room, where a bundle of cord was lying ready. The wee man struggled as Dughall tied him up. He screamed, then wept, then begged. "I'll give you great treasures, if you'll let me go."

"No."

"Gold and silver. Fine carbuncles and rubies."

"No."

"Power. I promise power, wine, fine riches and women."

"No."

Satisfied that the knots were tight, Dughall plopped the wee man against a wall, and pulled up a stool. He sat down, glared and played with his knife for a time. "So, ye're been stealing our dreams."

Neither of them said a thing more. Time passed. Dughall eyed the wee man, and the wee man glared back. Dughall considered trying to make him talk, but striking a bound man is a cowardly thing and probably against the church too, he thought. He decided to ask Father Seumas later. He grew bored waiting for the man to say something more, remembered the man's feet, and so lifted up the tunic's long hem. The feet were more disfigured than he remembered. They were so malformed that they did not ever look human, more like the feet of a bird.

"Ye're not a man at all, are you?"

The wee man glowered but said nothing.

When the grey of morning began to paint the air, the wee man started to look nervous. The sun rose, and the wee man started to fidget and chew his fat lower lip. "Lad, if you'll just be letting me go, I'm sure we can come to some arrangement that would be beneficial for—"

"No."

"But aren't you tired? Wouldna you like to sleep?"

"My eyes feel like pissholes in a sandy beach. But I'm gonna keep awake, and I'm going to be watching you 'til you tell me why you're stealing our dreams. It's the whole of Linfern village, isn't it. And probably Dalquhairn town too. Everyone's been dullard and grey for months now."

Sun trickled through the still-open window and made a puddle on the floor, and slowly, Dughall realised, the wee man's attention was increasingly focused on the light. As the puddle of light crept closer to the wee man's feet, he looked first frightened, then terrified.

"You're worried about the sun?"

"Aye, you're a sharp one. State the bloody obvious. Cretin."

Dughall yawned. "Fine. I won't move you then."

"No, no, I didn't mean it. Please...I dunna like it." "Don't like what?"

"When the sun gets me. I hates it. It's terrible. I hates it. I hates it."

"But if you hates it, then it sounds as if it doesn't kill you, aye? It's not like you'd be some sort of troldey-creature that'd be turned to stone. Why should I move you, then?"

"But I *hates* it!"

"Tell me about the dreams."

The wee man gurgled, unhappy.

Dughall leaned closer. "Tell me about the dreams."

"Arrg!" He spoke rapidly. "Eideard, Thegn of Dalquhairn is secretly a warlock. Eleven-month ago, he worked a hex on me and bound me to serve him. Each night I goes out and I thieve dreams for him. I brew them into a fine broth, and on the tax-day each month, I gives him the potive, so as he can drink it. He chuggles down all the dreams of all the commoners and work-a-day louts, and as a consequence, he is fitter and finer, for he is full of dreams. And all his serfs, all of them are kept dull and obedient, cause they have no dreams, not any more. Right. That's all of it. Now, move me away from the sun."

"The Thegn of Dalquahairn is a warlock?"

"Aye. That's the truth. Now, move me. Somewhere nice and shady. Under the bed, perhaps?"

"What happens when you get caught by the sun? Do you turn into a stone? Go mad? Is it painful?"

"No, it's not painful. It's just...well, it's embarrassing. Move me!"

"Look, you wee pillock, I'm being very civil and you're just being impolite. Mark me, I'm only asking out of being curious, and it'll be least another half-hour before the sun reaches your toes and—" But as Dughall was speaking he began absently waving his arms about. He still had his gutting knife in one hand and without realizing what he was doing, the blade slipped into the sunlight, caught it, and threw a flicker of light into the face of the wee man.

"Arrghur." The wee man struggled against the ropes. "You idiot. You creatin. Fool. Moronic, rock-headed...arguurhur..."

It spread across the man's skin like wind ruffling the waters of Linfern Loch...first it was a greenish tinge, then his flesh became even more warty and pocked than it already was. He began to shrink. Soon he was too small for the ropes to hold him, and Dughall, alert now, jumped to his feet. Soon, the wee man was too small for his clothing, and he disappeared within the greasy folds of linen. Something stirred within the tunic, and a tiny green face popped out. Dughall jumped on it and caught it before it had a chance to hop away.

Dughall cupped it in two hands and squinted. "You've gone and turned into a puddock."

"Ribbet", said the puddock, accusingly.

Dughall dropped the little creature into an iron cooking pot and weighed a lid onto it with a stone from outside. Then he lay down and slept, and for the first time in eleven months he dreamed, and he knew happiness and hope, and a nightmare or two as well, but that was alright, because he had other dreams that were happy and more.

When he awoke it was late afternoon. The puddock was still in the pot, which was good, though it still looked mean and angry, which he supposed wasn't so good. It would be an hour or so until the sun set, which was when Dughall presumed that the wee man would turn back into himself. At least, so he hoped. He used the time to cook some dinner, then set out two plates on the table. He found a full bottle of whiskey, and put this on the table with two mugs as well. It was as the sun was turning red and the sky was darkening, that frantic noises began to come from the cooking pot. Dughall removed the lid and upturned the puddock onto a stool, where it sat, looking miserable.

The change back was as quick as the previous transformation. In a blink, the puddock was gone and a bone-thin and naked man, all malformed and gangly, was sitting on the stool, a snarl on his face.

"If you expect me to sit at yer table and have a chum-chummy dinner with you, then yer a stupider, more dunderheaded..."

Dughall began cutting off a hank of bannock. "The sausage and white pudding are hot, and the whiskey's from a good year. And yer not going anywhere. I'm bigger and faster and nastier, I wager. Now put some clothes on."

They ate in silence. The wee man stared at Dughall and Dughall eyed the wee man.

"What's your name?" said Dughall, eventually.

"Not telling. It'd give you power over me, wouldna it? It's how that bastard, Eideard, got me. He found out my name."

"What do I call you then? How about Puddock?"

"You're a hate-worthy cretin."

Whereas Dughall sipped his whiskey, the wee man gulped it. Each time the mug was emptied, Dughall obligingly refilled it.

"You know," said the wee man, after the fifth mug. "You're not shuch a bad host really. I mean you threaten me with a knife, then you go and tie me up, and let me get all sunlightified, but ashide from that, you're not shuch a bad host." He swayed a little, and Dughall refilled his mug.

After the seventh mug, the wee man was singing merrily, after the ninth he was snoring. Dughall fetched the silver net, which was still lying on the floor where it'd been dropped. It was slippery to the touch, and cold. He went back to the hearth room and looked down on the sleeping Puddock. Now, how had the wee man done it...?

As Dughall cast the net and dragged it through the air above the wee man, he considered what he was planning, and it thrilled him. It made his heart skip. It made his pulse run. He felt alive. Really and truly *alive*. He'd owned his own dreams again, for the first time in months, and though it had just been a few hours, just a few dreams, it was enough to spark the rebuilding of his heart and mind and soul.

The wee man's dreams were dark and nasty. Dughall saw them flicker and move, as the net caught them, and was able to study them still more carefully as he emptied the net into a spare coal-sack. Mostly, the dreams concerned the many and various ways that Eideard, Thegn of Dalquhairn, might die horribly. There were one or two dreams about Dughall too, but these he discarded, onto the floor where they flopped about before dissolving away to nothing. He only wanted the dreams concerning Eideard.

When he was finished, Dughall considered letting Puddock sleep unfettered, but decided it was too much of a risk. He tied up the wee man's hands and tethered the end of the cord to a beam. Pudduck was so drunk that he barely stirred.

Then, Dughall went to bed. He lay awake for a while longer than he wanted, thinking things over. There were still three nights until tax-day. Would it be enough?

"It's not enough." The Puddock spoke suddenly, so that Dughall started.

"Sorry?"

"It's not enough, is it? The Thegn will be expecting a full bottle of potive and yer've only got three night's worth of dreams from one soul."

Dughall said nothing. It was the morning of tax day, and Puddock was sitting at the table, untied now. He seemed to have enjoyed the free food and whiskey, and had stopped trying to run off at every opportunity on the second day. Dughall had moved the table so that it sat always in shadow.

"I know what yer've been doing. Collecting my dreams when I'm asleep. I know cause I feel better. Lighter."

Dughall considered this. "I thought you'd feel worse. Grey and stretched thin, like rained-out clouds. Like how I felt."

Puddock sighed. "No. Yer dreams are mostly good — but my kind know only nasty dreams. My dreams, they weigh me down. Yers free you."

"I see."

"Use whiskey."

"Hm?"

"Whiskey is a sort of false dream." Puddock leaned closer and sniffed the bottle that was full of the dark and churning stuff of his own nightmares. "It can be used to water down dreams, and Eideard will never know. I've done it a couple times when I came up a bit short at the end of the month."

"Will it kill him, your dreams?"

"Probably not."

"It will be bad for him, though, won't it?"

"Aye, in a manner of speaking."

"Thank you." Dughall took one of the many bottles of whiskey he'd bought over the last couple days, and poured it into the dreams. He then gathered Puddock's rotten old cloak around his shoulders and pulled down the hood. By hunching himself up and stooping he was able to make himself something approaching the size of the wee man.

Puddock watched all of this with an unimpressed air. "You need to hobble more. When you go into the castle ask to see the 'Thegn's Librarian'. He has no librarian, it's a sort of password. He'll expect you to grovel and fawn a lot, so do it. Make your voice more wheezy. You'll not be safe until he's got all of that stuff down his gullet. Oh, and take the net too. You'll want it."

"Why?"

"Just take it and go. You'll know when it's wanted."

Dughall didn't have time to argue. He tied the net to his belt. "Thank you."

"Idiot. I'm not telling this to you for your own good sake. If you fail, that bastard Eideard will think I've betrayed him. He'll cast a hex and summon me, and there'll be long hours of torturing and hot irons and sharp needling things." His head drooped a little. "Long hours."

"Thank you," said Dughall, again.

A sigh. "You're welcome."

As Dughall left, the wee man said, "and, good luck," before pouring himself another cup of whiskey.

Dughall decided to keep up his disguise from the moment he left the door, so it took him almost all morning to limp from his village on the shores of Linfern Loch, to Dalquhairn town. With the hood pulled so low, he could barely see the people moving around him, let alone the high walls and timbers of Thegn Eideard's fortress.

The guards at the keep did not seem suspicious, perhaps they recognized the sight and smell of the old cloak. When Dughall asked for The Librarian, one of the men nodded and said, "You know the way."

"I gots lost last time," said Dughall, in a weak voice. Then, as an afterthought he added. "I hates it, getting lost."

He couldn't see, but he thought the men were probably sneering or rolling their eyes at one-another, given the span of silence that followed. "Right," said one of them, eventually, and he accompanied Dughall down a series of corridors to a large black door. "Here you are then. Don't get lost on the way out." The guard walked off.

Dughall checked to make sure his gutting knife was good and loose in its sheaf. He wasn't stupid, and he wasn't sure this was going to work. It was best to keep the knife handy. Then, tentatively, he knocked on the door.

A voice came from within, muffled, "It's about time."

Dughall pushed the door open. He entered what seemed to be a luxuriant room, judging from the richness of the rugs and the richness of scented smoke and good food smells. He dared not raise his face. Falling to his knees, Dughall held the bottle out, and made some small noises that he hoped were suitably pathetic.

Within a moment, the bottle was snatched from his hands.

"You're getting fat," said the voice, gruff and rumbling. It was Thegn Eideard. Dughall recognized his voice from the monthly Proclaiment, when disputes and felonies were adjudged. "If you've been skiving off to feed your face, I'll have you skinned alive and thrown in a pit of lampreys." A pause. "And I've been noticing that some of my servants have been uppity these last few days. It's *almost* like they're remembering their free will. One *might* even think that they have a few dreams of their own again...you wouldn't know anything about that, would you, you ugly little toad? You wouldn't have been taking a holiday, would you?"

"No, my glorious Thegn. It is perhaps something to do with a passing movement of the stars. A temporary change, no doubt." Dughall had long ago noticed that travelling cunning-men and soothsayers blamed a lot on the stars, which seemed unfair to him, as the stars didn't do much other than sit in the sky and twinkle. Still, the explanation seemed to assuage Eideard.

Dughall listened to the sound of liquid going down a throat. There was a pause, then a sniff. "Tastes different." But then the glugging drinking continued. For a time there was quiet.

"You can go now."

Dughall got up to leave.

"Wait!"

He froze.

"Turn around. Face me."

He turned, slowly.

"Next time, do *try* to harvest some sweeter dreams. That lot was bitter and...and..." Thegn Eideard made a choking noise. "You...you...you can't have...I spellbound you..." He gasped. "Poison...*poison!*"

Dughall gave up the pretence. He threw back the cloak and stood up straight. His knife was in his hand too, but he didn't need it. Eideard was staggering. He grabbed hold of the edge of a table, slipped and fell to the floor. "Poison!"

While Eideard writhed on the floor, Dughall glanced around. It was a room full of richess and treasures, but on second glance it was also a room full of strange and frightening things. There was a human skull on the Thegn's desk, and what looked like a human skin stretched on the wall like a rug. Bones and roots and other tools of witchcraft lay piled on shelves, demoniac symbols splodged the walls, and what Dughall took to be a circle of magic was marked out on the floor in the red-brown of old blood.

Thegn Eideard had stopped moving now. He lay still, gasping, his eyes wide open. Dughall approached him cautiously, then crouched over the lord. Dark dreams chased over the surface of the man's eyes. Would he be trapped forever in the nightmare web of Puddock's dreams? Would he live over and over again the many and varied horrid deaths that Puddock had dreamed up for him? Dughall was wondering it if would be kinder to just slit the Thegn's throat when he noticed that there was a change occurring.

He saw it first in the face. The cheeks that had been full and ruddy, were now sunken. His bristly beard was growing lank and thin. Then the whole of his body changed, contorted, shrank. It was when Dughall heard the bones of the lord's feet popping and snapping as they twisted into malformed lumps, that he was certain.

"I see."

Dughall unhooked the silver net from his belt and threw it onto the still unconscious lord. "You'll always have the means to capture your own dreams and escape the nightmares for a while. You'll have the means to give those dreams to someone else, too, but how does a man catch his own dreams, even if he owns the right sort of net? You can't. And I wager you'll never trust another to do it."

Before he left, Dughall collected everything that looked like it might be a tool of the unhallowed arts and threw them all into the fire that was roaring in the hearth. He didn't want Thegn Eideard to have any of his black arts handy when he awoke.

As Dughall was throwing the last skin-bound book onto the fire, Thegn Eideard began to stir and groan. It seemed the dreams were wearing off. It was time to leave, before the Thegn woke up enough to properly fix an image of Dughall's face in his head. There was no point in tempting revenge.

The guards gave Dughall no trouble on the way out of the fortress, and he took off the cloak as soon as he was safely outside the town walls. He walked home with it under his arm, enjoying the sunshine, listening to the blackbirds singing their own stories from the trees.

"It's done," said Dughall, as he pushed open the door. "You knew, didn't you? You knew what would happen to—"

Slumped at the table was the blue-grey corpse of a stranger...an old man. His hair was a white halo and his skin was so wrinkled it looked like scrunched up leather. He was ancient, but human. Cupped in one hand was a mug of whiskey and on his face was a smile.

goldenthread

Elizabeth Barrette

Something wakes me from my slumber. The emptiness in my heart is an ache I remember all too well. The air of the cavern stirs around me. It smells of brimstone. I hear the clink and crunch of coins underfoot. Dust rises and swirls.

At last you move into the field of my vision. Your armour glitters in the sunbeams that fall through chinks in the stone. You kneel beside me, pull off your helm and set it on the carpet. Ah, of course you are handsome. Your hair is black, I see, your eyes as well. Your fingers follow the threads of red and blue beneath your knees.

I stand before you, naked. I know what you see — my golden hair, my sapphire eyes, my ivory skin. I would be strange to you regardless, even if you had not found me like this.

What are you doing here, beauty, you ask of me?

I do not reply.

You touch me. The heat of your flesh seems to burn. I clear my throat. Dust, cobwebs — you brush away my resistance, just like that. Your fingertips pluck my heartstrings. I vibrate. I can no longer remain silent. I cannot sing, so I must speak.

My voice emerges, creaky with grief and disuse, but still sweet as a girl's. Startled, you jerk away — I fall silent — but soon you compel me to begin again.

I suppose I should begin at the beginning. I was born in Chakor, the land of the moon-loving birds. Perhaps you have heard of it. Then again, perhaps not. My parents bore only two children, my elder sister and me. They named us Nishikiran and

Haimikiran, that is, Ebonthread and Goldenthread. She was as dark as I am fair, her hair as curled as mine is straight.

When we had grown old enough to turn the heads of men, our mother sent for the matchmaker, and the matchmaker sent a man. His name was Dayit. He came to marry my sister. He courted Nishikiran with silks and sweet pastries and jewels. Yet his eyes went to me whenever I passed by, and I could not resist. My heart lay itself at his feet like a flower.

Nishikiran noticed, although we never did anything improper. One day she called to me ... Come, sister, walk along the river with me. It was freezing but I went. I thought she wanted to talk about her wedding. I still remember the twelve yards of silk that our mother bought for her, as red and blue as this rug.

Instead, my sister pushed me into the Ganja. I could not swim. Nishikiran knew this. I cried and called out to her. I beat at the water with my hands, kicked at it with my feet. My sister stood watching as the current carried me away. Soon the water closed over my head. I drowned. Nishikiran had killed me.

But it did not end there. No, no. That would be too easy, too simple. That would be too sane.

Did you know that the soul takes a while to roll free of the body? Have you heard that it can take hours to find a new place on the Wheel? No? Ah, but you should. You are a hero; you may need to know such things.

Before the sun quite closed the door of the day, I was found. A musician had gone to purify himself in the sacred waters. He pulled my body from the icy river. I heard him weeping over me, muffled as if from a great distance. I thought it very foolish, for he did not know me. It would have been decent for him to build a pyre and send my ashes on their way. He did not.

Instead, he cut the bones from my body and the hair from my head. He took gold from the ground and golden wood from a tree. He took the ivory of an elephant. From the wood and bone he made a harp, tall and fair, its front-post the figure of a woman with sapphires for eyes, its pins and inlays of ivory and gold. He strung it with the fine strands that had given me my name — and he called the harp Goldenthread, though he had never heard it said. Perhaps he was a mystic.

Certainly he was a wizard, for he cast a spell on the harp that bound my soul to the musical instrument. Never again need I take my turn on the Wheel, he said.

The first time he touched my heartstrings, I thought I would die. It was as it is with you — I could not keep silent — the voice poured out of me like a river. I had a beautiful voice in my youth. I do not blush to say that even now. My family said that I sang like a moonbird. So I sang to him what had happened to me, and he wept afresh, his fingers trembling on the strings.

He carried me up the river. I did not want to go. I did not want to dishonour my family. I would have begged him to stay away, but I could not speak unless he played along. The musician went to my father's house. It was quite a fine house, with tiles all around the door, and sandalwood screens in the receiving room. I had loved it once.

My mother and father sat in their stuffed chairs. My sister and her soon-to-be husband sat beside them. They looked at me without recognition. The musician they greeted with polite welcome.

His name was Sarang, he said, and he wanted to play a song for them.

Then he began to touch me. Oh, I longed to stay silent, but I could not! The music swelled inside me and I had to release it or burst.

I see my mother, dear as dear;
I see my father, never fear.

I see my sweetheart, one last time,
Who does not know his own bride's crime.

I see my sister, in her gown,
Who pushed me in and watched me drown.

Then it was done. The song sung, the tale told; my family knew at last what had happened to me. They must have believed it an accident before.

Now there will be justice, Sarang said.

Yes, my father said, justice for a foul sorcerer who came among them with lies and curses!

I think he was simply too surprised to respond, my poor musician. Steel flashed as my father drew his talwar, the curving sword soon buried in Sarang's belly. I fell to the floor. Blood soaked into the carpet. I could see it from where I lay. My sapphire eyes pointed that way. I watched Sarang die. There was no one to make a musical instrument out of him.

Dayit reached for me. I do not know if he meant good or ill by it.

My mother snatched me away from him. She ran to the door and yanked it open. Then she hurled me out into the snow. Something broke in me. It broke before ever I hit the hard cobbles of the street. Perhaps it was my heart. Perhaps it was only part of the spell.

I have not been able to sing since. What good would it do? I lost all that I ever cared about — my beloved Dayit, my family, my family's honour, even the well-meaning if improper Sarang.

Some merchant took me from the street. When he plucked my strings, I whispered to him in my broken voice. I spoke of my pain. He put me in his wagon. Quickly he threw a bolt of silk on top of me. I do not think he wanted to hear me any more than I wanted to be heard.

Not long after that, I heard screams. The wagon smashed apart. I found myself lying in blood again. This time I did not even know whose. The dragon picked over the goods quite delicately. She purred when she discovered me. Then she carried me to her lair.

All of that happened a hundred years ago.

So you see, young hero, I do not need to be rescued. I am lost, and it is better this way. I have my carpet to sit upon. I have the quiet. I wish no harm to the dragon you came to slay. Leave her in peace — she will only rouse if you try to *take* something. Go back the way you came. There is nothing for you here.

What can you do for me, you ask? Lift your hand from my strings. Walk away and leave me here. Let me sleep.

Just let me sleep, and let me never wake.

when the cloak falls

Catherine J. Gardner

Ghosts of ancient trees lingered. As if the feet of fallen giants, gnarled roots poked out of the earth waiting to trip the unwary. Sunniva knew, with a simple breath from the west wind, that the charcoal branches would disintegrate to dust. Tristan lay among them, fragile. He wore a coat torn from the back of a sheep's corpse, had washed his face in its blood.

She snapped off a strip of burnt wood and crushed it between her fingers. More than one man caused this, and those men were trying to destroy something other than forest. Whatever the lords muttered among themselves, whichever way the wind blew their swords, she knew. There was more to this. The farmers of Bedburg whispered the same as they removed the ravaged corpses of sheep and goats from their land. Some whispered of her grandfather and crossed themselves. And they were wrong.

"Brother." Her voice was soft. "Come out, brother, and do not be afraid."

Tristan dug his fingernails into the earth and attempted to stare out of bloodshot eyes glazed by lunacy.

"I know you did not do this." She looked across the path trodden, through the weave of trees. They were coming. "And some of them know as well, but they remember grandfather. That is why we must go."

The magistrate and townsfolk had pinned their grandfather to the wheel and tortured him. Of course, he *was* a bad man.

Sunniva wrapped her grey cloak about her thin bones — knew she faded in this landscape, merged, as if waiting for the wind to blow her out of life.

A growl bubbled in her brother's throat and he rocked forward. Branches shattered beneath her step, and their dust lifted and settled on her slippers. Sunniva curved her palm over her mouth, stifling her cough. Tristan shook his head and brayed backwards, kicking his heels and trying to grip onto the dusty earth.

Crack!

The sound reverberated through the forest and tore bark from the trees, thinning out the landscape.

"They are coming," she urged, and knew his madness did not understand. "We must leave. We must go."

Her voice served only to force him further back, deeper into the forest. If he turned, they were lost.

Light blurred against the fog of dead trees. Blood pumped fast and hard through her veins, and she felt her heart swell as it swallowed and refused to release. She pulled the hood of her cloak tight around her flame-red hair, afraid it would prove a beacon.

"Tristan." She urged his name, yet guessed he did not recognize it. "Oh where has your mind fled?"

"Children of Stubbe!" a gruff voice called out from the mist. "Plague of Bedburg…"

The lights shimmered closer. There was no place to hide in this dead world. She turned. She fled. Faded into the forest; a grey phantom with the whole of Germania chasing her. Tears ran down her cheeks, her hand too wary to wipe them away. The further she weaved through the trees, the more distant the world became. As if she were never a part of it. This was something fashioned from nightmare. A sequence of images that would end when she broke through the fever.

Though her flight should have found an abrupt end at the river, Sunniva walked on. Her cloak billowed and swelled. The swirl tugged at her legs as waterweeds threatened to entwine and pull her under. Her feet slipped as a tortured cry crept through the forest and shattered branches. A sudden slosh and splatter of the lake startled her. She was not alone. Sunniva turned and, at the sight of the black beast, stumbled back.

The world morphed and became a muted grey with indistinguishable swirls of black as she sank. Water bubbled as it rushed between her lips, proved her enemy as her hands and legs batted against its pull. The black beast, a terrible, terrifying steed, pushed its nose through the water and pressed hard against her stomach.

Sunniva gave up her fight.

If a horse can manage such a thing, then this horse smiled. Though washed away by the current, tears flowed from Sunniva's dying eyes. She wondered where her mind would flee to when death claimed her.

Relief as the water-horse ceased its press. Water poured down her face as she shot up, back into the ash-thick air. She lurched forward, spewed water and clutched her stomach. Hooves broke her left ankle as the creature turned and kicked out against something as big and nasty as itself and red mist rose from her foot. Sunniva attempted to pull herself away from the fight of sleek black skin and grey fur. She struggled out of her cloak, and cared not that her red hair stood bright against the washed-out world.

The horse-beast fell with a splash that washed onto the bank. The grey thing that had won looked down at her with curiosity. With its left paw, it picked her up. Its muzzle rubbed against her sodden skin. It stood as a man, and yet was every bit the animal it appeared.

"What are you?" she coughed.

It answered with a bite.

Tristan lay as if dead. Sheep's blood mingled with his own, his mind already severed from reality. She thought of pressing the wound on her arm to his mouth, but she knew he already carried the disease. Her fiery hair fell across her brother's pale skin as she pressed her ear to his chest and listened to the steady thump, thump, thump.

"We are to wait for the bright Moon." She ran her hand through his hair as the glaze of madness persisted. "And then we can walk amongst them. Then we can frighten them from our world, as they did you from theirs.

the price of peace

Anna M. Lowther

Ernst moaned and rubbed his head, noting the blood that came away with his hand. A bright ray of sunlight pierced the dark interior of the Panzer, streaming down through the hatch, which should have been shut. Ernst looked around and shook his head in disbelief.

Gone! All gone. He strained for a memory, and at last it swam into his consciousness. The ice storm had been heavy, worse than predicted, and they had somehow been separated from the rest of the 4th Division. Visibility had been zero, but the tank should have been able to roll over anything in its path.

He shielded his eyes and looked up at the hatch. The door was open, but the edge was misshapen and he could see a massive ice-rimmed tree lying across the front of the tank. A blast of wind sent clots of snow down the open hatch, and he winced as it struck his face.

Ernst pulled himself to his feet, fell backward and vomited a mix of blood and bile on the cold steel floor. He looked down and groaned; his left leg ballooned over his boot and the shockwave of pain told him it was broken.

Where are my men? I'll send them to the camps for this! He pulled a rifle off the wall rack and using it as a crutch, stood again. He leaned against the ladder, summoning the strength to pull himself up when he heard movement outside the tank.

Ah, so they were just securing the area. He sighed and looked up the hatch ready to be pulled free of the wreckage when he heard voices speaking, not German, but instead Russian.

Before he could react, two arms grabbed him by the shoulders, pulled him upward and cast him on the ground. His arms were pinned, denying him access to his Luger and the knife hidden in his boot. He turned his head and saw three shallow depressions in the snow, laced with blood. He pictured his little sister lying in the snow, flapping her arms and legs to make snow angels. Whoever made these angels had bleeding wings.

He strained to see the soldiers holding him down, but the sunlight reflecting off the snow rendered him blind. He heard the rustle of a long coat and a stooped man stepped to Ernst's shoulder, blocking the light.

Ernst expected a Russian officer, yet this was merely an elderly peasant. He struggled against the restraining arms.

"Was is los? Du bist? Wo sind meine Manner?" Ernst barked in a voice that demanded the respect due an officer.

The old man chuckled. His German was rough around the edges, but sufficient for Ernst to understand. "All in due time, Kommandant. You will join your men soon enough. As for us, we are Protectors of Witterstadt. Perhaps you will indulge an old man and listen to his tale, da?"

Ernst thrust upward, felt something in his chest grate and threw up again. Collapsing back into the snow, he glared at the peasant.

"It seems I need to rest a bit and am in no position to stop your chatter."

The old man clapped his hands. "Very good, then. We have a chair ready for you where you may rest."

Ernst was lifted to his feet and carried through a copse of trees. In the centre of a small clearing stood a high-backed chair built from snow and coated in a thick layer of ice. It rose about a foot above the ground, as if it sat on a hillock.

No longer facing directly into the sun, Ernst was able to clearly see his captors as they bound him to the chair. The three men were stoop-shouldered and their faces were wizened and ruddy. Their hair and beards were long and white as the snow; their eyebrows were bushy white mice crawling across their foreheads. Arthritis twisted their hands into grotesque mockeries of youth.

Panic tickled the edges of Ernst's mind. *How could such old men restrain me?* He struggled against the thick rope that held him. The cold of the ice seeped through his uniform, numbing his legs and buttocks. Blood dripped from his forehead and fell to the snow at his feet, spreading like rose petals scattered at a wedding.

The first old man pulled a flask from his coat and held it to Ernst's lips. The vodka was bitter and Ernst choked then sighed as the alcohol spread fire through his veins.

The old man nodded to his companions and they slipped back into the trees. He took a seat on a stump across from Ernst and took a long swallow from the flask.

"Allow me to introduce myself. I am Gregor, Chief Protector of Witterstadt. Since you are a, shall we say, captive audience, I will tell you a tale most old and beautiful. It is the story of the Snow Maiden."

Ernst coughed and spit a clot of blood toward the old man. "The Snow Maiden? You want to waste my time with children's fairy tales? Don't bother, for I already know it. The old man and woman, so desperate for a child build a girl of snow. She falls in love and when the young man returns her ardour her heart grows warm and she becomes real. Oh so sweet and touching."

Ernst coughed again and nodded at the flask. Gregor tilted it so that Ernst could take another swallow. Ernst shook his head and drops of blood flew across the snow.

"Look, old man! Do you not see my blood? Why speak of warmth and love today? This is war. Kill me and be done with it. I am not afraid to die." Ernst gritted his teeth and glared.

"But, young man, you are mistaken. My tale is not the one you know, though it is the one most often spread beyond our village. Had you not become separated from the other tanks, you would never have heard the true story. That should be some comfort to you, da?" Gregor's lip turned up at one corner.

Ernst barked a hoarse laugh. "Some comfort, indeed. Tell your tale if you must. I grow tired."

Gregor pulled out a pipe and lit it, puffing as he began. "The beginning of the tale is correct. Once in times long forgotten, here in the hidden village of Witterstadt lived a couple that longed for a child but were never blessed with one. One long, bitter winter they built a snow maiden and dressed it in the things the woman had made for the child that never came."

Gregor paused to sip from the flask. "The story goes that they prayed to God for a real child, but the truth goes far deeper. They prayed to God, for years and years but their home remained empty. By the time they built the snow maiden they prayed to anyone that might hear, and at last someone heard and answered."

A cloud passed over the sun, darkening the sky. Ernst shivered from more than just the cold seeping through his damp wool. "So who was it that heard their prayers, then?"

"An ancient power, with a name you could not speak with human lips. The maiden came to life the very night she was created, and her beauty was cold and terrible. She was a cruel young woman, but so intoxicating to behold that every man fell under her spell."

Gregor's eyes clouded over as he stared into the distance. "Witterstadt was a happy village then, ruled by a kind Boyar. He had a sweet and innocent daughter, Katerinka, who was betrothed to the son of a Romanian Boyar."

Ernst grunted. "Let me guess, he dallied with the Snow Maiden?"

Gregor waggled his finger. "Patience, young one. When the time for the marriage came and the young man arrived in Witterstadt, our Boyar ordered the old ones to lock their daughter away. By this time the village was quite divided with the women calling the Snow Maiden a demoness and the men protesting her purity and innocence."

Gregor looked past Ernst's head and lifted his hand. Ernst tried to turn to see what was behind, but the back of the ice chair was too high. He cursed beneath his breath and waited for Gregor to continue.

"Once happy marriages were torn with discord. Wives accused husbands of lusting after the Maiden and in turn the husbands beat their wives for their jealousy. The village priest decided that the maiden should be dealt with beyond the time for Katerinka's wedding." Gregor dumped his pipe and refilled the bowl.

Ernst heard the snow crunch behind his chair. He tilted his head and listened and caught the sound of heavy breathing.

Gregor smiled and taking a deep breath, resumed his story. "The old couple waited until their miracle daughter went to bed and bolted her door from the outside. The women of the village threw a brace over the window shutter and stood guard so that no man might let the maiden out. The priest stood beneath the window and recited a ritual to seal the demon within the room. She could not come out unless set free by a willing hand."

The wind began to blow, carrying whirls of snow about the clearing. Gregor brushed the flakes from his beard, puffed his pipe and continued on.

"The next day Katerinka was wed, and the Snow Maiden beat upon her door begging her adoptive parents to set her free. The old man and woman wept to hear their beloved daughter so distressed and promised to open the door as soon as Katerinka and her groom were safely away to their new home in Romania."

The snow began to fall in a heavy curtain of white. Unable to brush it away, Ernst shivered as it blanketed his thighs.

Gregor nodded his head and lifted his face to the storm. "The wind hears my tale and answers. That day so long ago, a blizzard settled over Witterstadt and prevented the departure of the newlyweds. For a fortnight they waited for a break in the storm. Meanwhile, the Snow Maiden wailed and beat upon her door pleading for release. She cried out to her mother that without the snow she would die, and a trickle of water seeped beneath the door."

The sky began to colour with the setting of the sun. The blowing snow glinted copper red as it fell. Gregor closed his eyes and spoke. "The old man left, for he could not bear the sound of her cries. The old woman sat outside the bedroom door and wept, her voice in sorrowful harmony with the Maiden's. At last the morning dawned when no snow fell. Wanting to surprise his bride before they set off, the groom slipped out of bed and wandered into the village seeking some harbinger of spring."

Ernst could no longer feel his fingertips nor his toes. Squirming, he asked, "Is there a point to all this?"

Gregor chuckled. "Indeed, and you will understand all when the tale is done. As the young groom neared the cabin where the Snow Maiden languished, she sensed his approach and began to sing. Her song was low and mournful and he was compelled to follow the sound. As he drew near she pierced her finger and let the blood seep under the windowsill. The drops were icy blue and where they fell in the snow a pale cerulean flower blossomed."

Ernst felt dizzy and his chin sagged to his chest. His eyes watered and the fluid froze at the tips of his lashes. He blinked and squinted, then shook his head trying to clear both his thoughts and his eyes. *Where did those flowers come from? How can there be flowers atop the snow?*

Gregor waved his hand and the other old men returned to stand beside him. "The Boyar's son picked the flowers, and the Maiden stopped singing. He begged her to continue the song, but she refused until she could see his face. She pleaded with him to set her free, and he tore at the shutters until the noise awoke the villagers. They ran to the house and tried to stop him, but he had pulled one corner loose."

The wind rose again and carried a sad and haunting song around Ernst's head. He lifted his chin and tried to pinpoint the source of the sound, but it seemed to come from everywhere at once. Gregor stood and the three old men moved to stand in front of Ernst.

"The Snow Maiden poured herself liquid through the gap and rose reborn from the snowdrift below. Her face was terrifying, filled with a grotesque blend of rage and beauty. The priest faced her and ordered her back from whence she came, but she laughed and mocked him."

Ernst felt the chair lurch, looked down and saw the snow slide away from his feet. The chair did not sit on a hillock as he had thought, but rather on a raised turntable. It was rotating into the west, where the sky was bleeding over the snow. He dropped his head and closed his eyes.

Gregor reached out and slapped Ernst on the cheek. "No sleeping yet, my friend. The tale is almost told. The priest held the Snow Maiden back, though for how long was uncertain. The village men bowed at her feet while the women shrieked in rage and cursed her power to enthral. At last Katerinka reached her groom and brushed her lips across his own."

The chair lurched a few inches more toward the setting sun. Ernst retched and spat out a clot of bile. The haunting song filled his ears as the cold sapped his strength. The blood from his wounds froze in rivulets down his face.

"As a sleeper awakens, the groom shook off the Snow Maiden's spell. He offered to strike a bargain with her. If she would release Witterstadt and restore peace to the village, he vowed the village would honour her with annual tributes."

The chair took another lurch, now forty-five degrees from its original position. Ernst let his head fall forward again and the edges of his vision grew dark.

Gregor slapped Ernst once more, and a thin trickle of blood ran down his chin as he snapped awake.

"The Snow Maiden stiffened her back and grew taller than anyone in the crowd. A dark red halo of light surrounded her, and no one could bear to look directly at her face. Her words are remembered and told from one generation to the next in Witterstadt. I repeat them now as I learned them from my father and he from his father for countless years."

Gregor laced his hands behind his back, and his companions snapped to attention. "Foolish humans! You have amused me with your impudence and therefore I will accept the bargain, though on my terms. I will claim one sacrifice now, of my choosing. Each year hence, on the anniversary of this day you are to build a snow maiden to host my spirit. Seek out and bring to me those who have a heart for battle, those who do not shy from spilling innocent blood. If the sacrifice pleases me, your pitiful village will remain safely frozen until the next year. It shall be forever winter, cold and dark, the price you pay for peace."

Gregor relaxed his stance and sighed. "Then the Snow Maiden seized the priest, pursed her lips and blew across his face. Thick frost clogged his nostrils, while his eyes were fixed open and iced over. She plunged her fingers into his chest and withdrew his heart; it beat but once and stopped dead in her hand. She lifted it to her lips and bit into it slowly and sensuously as a lover takes a strawberry from another's mouth. His blood stained her lips, and yet no one looked away."

The chair took another lurch and Ernst saw before him a snowman. A childlike creation of three balls of snow, largest on the bottom, it looked harmless. His vision swam into clearer focus and he noticed this was not a snowman, but had smaller mounds of snow in strategic places lending a feminine physique.

Gregor clapped Ernst on the shoulder. "How fortunate for us that you brought the front to Witterstadt. After all these years it has become hard to find a warlike spirit, as no one wants to become the sacrifice. Your comrades perished before we could finish the maiden, but I think you will suffice."

The song grew stronger and the snow maid began to quake. Fissures formed in the hard-packed snow and a deep red glow burst forth through the cracks. Gregor snatched a handful of Ernst's hair and jerked his head upright as the most beautiful woman he'd ever seen emerged from the snow.

She smiled at Ernst and he felt warmth return to his fingers and toes, or at least they were tingling now. He felt the bindings fall from his wrists and ankles and somehow stood pain-free on his broken leg. He held out his arms and took a faltering step toward the woman, entranced by her beauty and the song that resonated in his soul.

She pulled him into her arms, breathed across his face and ripped his heart from his chest. She held it aloft and it took three slow beats before it stopped forever. Ernst collapsed on the snow, a look of wonder and peace on his face.

Gregor and his companions stood unable to look away as the Snow Maiden consumed her tribute. She stepped over Ernst's corpse and patted Gregor on the cheek.

The sun dropped from sight as a frigid wind swept the clearing driving needles of snow into the old men's eyes. When they opened them, the clearing was dark and the Snow Maiden was gone. They carried the body away and burned it, and returned to their homes, sure of another year of peace now that the price had been paid.

your duty to your lord

James R. Stratton

Otsu slid out of her futon nestled among baskets of vegetables in the kitchen of Jiro's noodle shop and stole to the lake to wash in the pre-dawn shadows, creeping cautious as a kitten sneaking past wild dogs. The Spring after her parents died, she'd stumbled into a pack of boys while running an errand for her employer. They'd groped her and said disgusting things.

"We want a woman for sex, not babies," the biggest one had said. "You'll be ready next year." They'd shoved her into a ditch and walked away laughing.

Otsu thanked the gods over and over that day that she was small for her age. Ever since, she had slipped to the outskirts of Isida township, wafting through the shadows like a ghost, trembling at every noise. She carried her father's tanto now, but couldn't imagine what she'd do with it if she was attacked again.

She was hurrying back to the noodle shop, damp from the lake, her spare kimono wet and bundled up after being rinsed out, when the noise of the street crowd died away. The tradesmen and townsfolk parted before shouting horsemen wearing silk hitotare jackets embroidered with Lord Ieyshu's family crest. Otsu stepped back against the tea shop wall, staring at fierce samurai, then gulped when the troop halted opposite her with a rousing "Hai!". A tall man with coal-black hair and fierce eyes sat astride a giant gelding, its white coat glowing in the sunlight. The warrior wore spotless hakama trousers and a hitotare jacket embroidered with gold thread.

This must be Lord Ieyshu.

Without thinking, she darted over and clutched his trouser leg, her head barely reaching his boot as she stared up wide-eyed. She had no idea what she thought she was doing. Pain exploded in her side as a footman kicked her, shouting, "What do you think you are doing, little bird? Are you a spy? Or an assassin?"

The soldier jerked her away by the hair and slapped her. "Eh? Nothing to say? Well, we shall see!" He yanked her kimono open so that she was exposed naked and shouted when the tanto fell out. "Just as I thought! An assassin! I wager the blade is poisoned as well!" He threw Otsu down and jerked the blade from its short scabbard. Grinning, he held the blade against her throat. "Shall we find out? Or do you wish to confess?"

"Hold, Honzo!" Lord Ieyshu leaned over, glaring. "She is a child. Let her up." He stared at Otsu as she sat up, pulling her kimono closed, red-faced. "Well girl, what have you to say? It is a crime to approach me without leave. Especially with a weapon!"

Otsu shook as tears streamed down her face. She was panting so hard she couldn't speak. The townsfolk lining the street stood staring, grim-faced. Across the road she spotted Jiro standing in the doorway of the noodle shop, watching wide-eyed and open-mouthed. When their eyes met, he reared back, shook his head and ran into the kitchen.

Otsu took a deep breath. Jiro was a good man. He had given her a place to stay after the fire, and gave her two meals a day. In return, she played her bamboo flute, the shinobue, and swept up. But when she complained about the boys, he only clucked and shook his head.

Otsu sighed and straightened her shoulders. Kneeling, she bowed until her forehead brushed the dirt. "I am sorry, Lord. I meant no disrespect. I have been alone since my parents died. You remind me of my father. The short sword was his. I carry it for protection."

Lord Ieyshu sighed and held out his hand. The footman slapped the unsheathed sword into it. The Diamyo turned the blade in the sunlight, his face twisting with surprise. He then examined Otsu. His gaze paused on her silk kimono, her freshly scrubbed face, and the shinobue tied across her back.

"Well, the blade isn't poisoned, and is certainly the work of Masamane Jetetsu. This should be part of a matched set, tanto and katana. Do you have the long sword? And who was your father? I have searched for a Masamane sword for my collection for years." He gazed again at the blade, gleaming in the sun.

"My father was Saito Toshiro, a samurai in your service until he was injured in battle. I have the katana in a safe place. The two blades have been in my family for generations."

Lord Ieyshu nodded, sheathed the blade and thrust the short-sword into his sash. "Fetch her things, especially the katana," he said to the footman. "Bring her."

He swung off his horse and strode away.

Otsu knelt on the tatami mat squeezing her shinobue so hard her hands shook. Lord Ieyshu sat on the dais examining the swords, nodding and smiling.

"You've taken good care of these. Where did you learn to oil and polish blades?"

"My father always cleaned and oiled them, even after he was injured. I watched. He was proud of them. Many times he said they would pass to me and mine once I married a samurai." Her gaze dropped to the mat. "But he died."

Lord Ieyshu set the blades on the tatami mat, gestured for her to play her flute, then turned to a small shrine behind him. As she played soft, wailing music, he offered sake and burnt incense to his ancestors. Inside the shrine was a scroll wrapped in embroidered silk. Her father had such a scroll, his family history dating back centuries, lost in the fire. After bowing and praying, Lord Ieyshu turned back to her.

"You play beautifully, Otsu-san. Did your mother teach you?"

Otsu nodded.

Lord Ieyshu gestured and she handed him the bamboo flute. "This isn't an old instrument! The bamboo is fresh! Did you make this?"

Otsu nodded again. "My mother taught me. It is not nearly as nice as hers." Otsu drew a shuddering breath. "It was the best I could make."

Lord Ieyshu tugged at his moustache and nodded. "My chief steward made inquiries in town and confirmed your circumstances. You have no family here in Omi Province?"

"No, I have no one. My parents never spoke of other family. Their parents died before I was born, and I have never met any relatives."

"So how will you live? There is no one to look after you?" When she did not respond, he blew a puff of air from his lips and frowned. "I can't abide that. Your father was injured in my service. I owe him a debt. Would you be willing join my personal staff? I've needed a new maid since Yami married. Your duties would be simple, just running errands for me, playing that wonderful music for me when I am in the mood, really just taking care of little things I need every day." He handed her back the shinobue and smiled. "Well?"

Otsu gulped. *He is offering me a home! A place to sleep and eat and bathe and live.* Her gaze drifted to the matched swords on the mat. *A trade? Is that what this is?*

"And my father's swords?"

He laughed. "You need not worry. They are yours, an heirloom of your house. But for now I will keep the katana in my strong-house. A matched set of Masamane blades would fetch a handful of gold in Osaka, with no questions asked. You are fortunate you never showed these to anyone else. There are some who would slit your throat for them." He handed back the short sword. "Carry this if you like, but keep it out of sight."

Smiling, Otsu bowed, clutching the tanto tight.

She soon surprised Lord Ieyshu with her courtly skills. Her mother had taught Otsu flower arranging, the tea ceremony, calligraphy and poetry writing, as well as the flute. She became indispensable. By New Year's Day, Lord Ieyshu allowed no one else to wait on him. She served his meals, sat in on his meetings to keep notes and draft letters, and looked after his clothes and quarters. Many nights she slept on a quilt outside his door in case he needed her. When he visited other daimyo, she rode ahead with his samurai to arrange his quarters and meals.

Most important for Otsu, Lord Ieyshu never showed her any disrespect, treating her with courtesy and modesty. Indeed, when one samurai, drunk on sake, tried to force himself on her, Lord Ieyshu came running with sword drawn. Red-faced and seething, he wanted to behead the fool on the spot until Otsu interceded.

And then, on one of Lord Ieyshu's frequent trips to the Capital, she met Rikya. He was a young samurai in Lord Ieyshu's service. After that day, she and Rikya rode side-by-side on trips. The following spring, he proposed marriage. Lord Ieyshu himself sat with young Rikya and negotiated the contract, paid her dowry, and personally planned the wedding. When Otsu's son was born, Lord Ieyshu hosted the naming banquet and insisted on holding the baby throughout the meal.

Her life was full. She spent most of her time with Lord Ieyshu, but she and Rikya had a small house on the grounds. She had no higher hopes for herself, Rikya and her son than to be in Lord Ieyshu's service.

Otsu jerked upright on her futon, waking Rikya as she did. "What is wrong?" he mumbled.

"Fire! I smell smoke! Something is burning!" Her gaze darted around the room, but everything was fine. The baby was sleeping in a basket in the corner. A lamp flickering in the hallway showed everything was in order. As Otsu sat up, the iron clang of an alarm resounded across the compound.

Otsu snatched up her tanto and ran into the hall. Her maid, Yuki, scurried to her.

"Otsu-san, it is terrible! The main house is on fire! Is it an attack? What should we do?"

Otsu grabbed the young woman by the shoulders. "Calm down! We are safe here. Look after my baby. I am going to see what I can do." Behind her Rikya shouted, but she ignored him.

Please, not like last time! Not like my parents! Lord Ieyshu must be safe...

Hiking up her thin yukata, she sprinted barefoot across the compound towards the orange glow of the blaze, short-sword drawn. Samurai ran from all directions shouting, many carrying buckets. She heard Lord Ieyshu's voice and found him surrounded by his guard in the main courtyard.

"I must go back in! You dragged me out before I could get my things. The family scroll! My swords! The proclamation from the Emperor! I must save them!" The chief steward stood in front of Lord Ieyshu with a dozen samurai.

"Please, Lord," the steward said as he bowed over and over. "Calm yourself. We will do what we can. We had no choice, the fire was too close. If you died, we would be lost, leaderless and homeless. Think of your servants, your samurai. We all depend on you."

Slowly, gently, the steward took Lord Ieyshu's hand and drew him away from the conflagration. The Daimyo jerked free and stood clenched-fisted, trembling.

Otsu stepped around the grim-faced samurai and bowed. "Come along, Sire. There's nothing for you to do. The risk is much too great."

"But my things! I have to save the scroll at least. It recites my family history back five centuries. It is my duty as the head of the Watanabe clan to save that. My father entrusted it to me when I became the head of the family — and his father before him into the mists of time."

Otsu drew a shuddering breath and faced the blazing building. She could see that only the front sections of the main house were ablaze. But even as she watched, the wood and paper walls along the far side flashed into flames.

"I will get the scroll," she muttered without thinking. "Yes, I will get it," she said louder. She nodded to the samurai. "Get him to safety. This might be part of a sneak attack. Hurry!" The samurai huddled into a tight knot around Lord Ieyshu and pulled him away as he shouted.

Otsu stared at the conflagration, trembling as she considered what to do. *But how can I refuse? I owe him everything.* She tied her yukata robe tight and tucked her tanto inside, then ran to the rear of the blazing building as sparks popped and crackled around her, singeing her hair. But at the back of the palace all was quiet, the fire still confined to the front. *I can get in and out if I am quick.* She ran through the garden behind Lord Ieyshu's rooms and pushed open the soji screen.

The roar of flames whooshed as the wind whistled overhead. In the flickering light, the hall looked quiet; normal. But in Lord Ieyshu's residence, in the heart of the palace, everything was chaos. Smoke filled the hall, causing Otsu to hack and wheeze. The shoji screens to various rooms hung open, revealing clothing and futons tossed aside as the occupants fled. Twice she tripped over loaded trays, the bowls and flasks scattered across the mats, dropped as servants ran. Near Lord Ieyshu's quarters, the smoke glowed a lurid red.

She darted in and slammed the shoji screen shut. The paper walls glowed from the flames outside, revealing the scroll nestled on its altar. As she darted across the room, there was a roar, and the floor shook.

The house is collapsing!

She snatched up the scroll and turned to the doorway. Flames danced behind the shoji screen casting wild shadows, and the heavy paper blackened and smoked.

Otsu knelt before the family shrine with the scroll. *After all he's done for me, I'm going to fail him.* Tears burned as she stared at the heirloom. *No, I won't have it!* To think was to act. She drew her tanto and held it up. *At least I can try.*

She opened her robe, staring at the unsheathed blade. Her skin crawled as she pressed the razor edge against her stomach, her hand shaking so hard she almost dropped the blade. Behind her the paper walls crackled as flames flared through.

"No!" she shouted and pushed the blade in. The heat of the flames was nothing compared to the fire in her gut. She gasped open-mouthed, and dragged the line of fire across her middle. Panting and moaning, she jerked out the blade and dropped it.

"For you, Lord." She took up the scroll in her fist and pushed it into the wound. The room brightened as flames licked across the ceiling. Despite the heat, she felt cold. As her robe smoked, darkness flowed in from the edges of her vision as she fell over. *I didn't fail!*

Lord Ieyshu knelt in the quarters of his summer home in the mountains where he normally stayed once the heat of summer was upon the plains. He bowed to the family shrine and held up the Watanabe family scroll. It was blotched with stains, but otherwise whole.

"Father, forgive me for the condition of the scroll, but I will not have it cleaned. They are marks of honour. She deserves our thanks. I have added the name of Saito Otsu to the list of members of the Watanabe clan. I should have adopted her while she still lived, but I have corrected that mistake. She has a son, Matsu, who will be my grandson and heir."

With care, he set the bloodstained scroll into its niche.

the beast
within

mercy hathaway is a witch

Ken Goldman

*"Sleeping or waking, we hear not the airy footsteps of
the strange things that almost happen."*

Nathaniel Hawthorne — Twice-Told Tales (1837)

The sight of the handsome couple wandering off together toward
the blackest part of the forest might have raised eyebrows back in
the town despite the excellent reputation of the soon-to-be-wed
gentleman. A hardworking physician's son who would someday
assume his father's practice, Jonathan Browne attended The North
Church each Sunday and had captured the heart of Amelia
Worthington, Boston colony's finest specimen of both Christian
upbringing and womanly charm.

But today the young man chaperoned not Amelia but her
comely dark-haired seamstress. They travelled a lonely wooded
path, far from Boston's muddy roads from which they had set foot
an hour earlier. The two did not walk side by side as lovers might;
instead, in a most uncommon fashion, the woman led while her
fellow traveller trailed in silence several paces behind. After a
tiresome tramping along the forest's twisted and untravelled
paths, the gentleman could keep his silence no longer.

"You requested that I attend you to this place, Mercy Hathaway, and I have done so. What is of such import that we have traversed half of New England in search of?"

Despite young Browne's irritation his voice managed to fall short of reproach. Still, the raven-haired girl remained silent.

"Mistress Hathaway, nightfall is near. You must know my fiancé expects me this very moment, and there are those in the village who will talk. What do you entreat that you must ask it within this dark wood?"

"I desire nothing of you, Jonathan," the seamstress insisted. "Nothing you choose not to give freely, that is. Besides, we are almost there."

The girl turned from him before Browne might discover her amusement, for in all of Boston town there seemed none more likely than he to misjudge the power of a woman's enticement.

"You speak with such displeasure, Jonathan. Is my sin that I desire a gentleman's company to my most secret of places? When have you set eyes upon a part of the forest so abundant with wildflower? I wish only to share this place with you."

Browne responded with an awkward grin. Mercy's words flattered him, although concerning the womanly emotions that lay hidden behind such words he understood little.

"Yes, this wood is unquestionably enchanting compared to the muddy tow paths of Boston, Mistress Hathaway. But you must agree that the hour is late. I shall try remembering by which paths we came so that I may return some later time."

"You could not find it, Jonathan," Mercy teased. "Not if you searched for a thousand years. But I shall be happy to bring you here any time you wish. You need only ask."

Browne placed his hand upon the woman's shoulder, but there was little warmth in his touch.

"And shall I bring my bride as well?"

The smile faded from the girl's lips.

"This place is a secret, Jonathan. Mine, and now yours."

"Then never will I return here. I am sorry, but you know I must not join you here again. It would not seem fitting." If the young man's words were meant to have bite, then Mercy Hathaway matched him tooth for tooth with words of her own.

"You flatter yourself in your assumption that you know me, Jonathan Browne. Do you really believe I have no understanding of what is fitting? I assure you that what I regard as fitting has little to do with what other people think!"

The two walked on in utter silence. The path they travelled could hardly be called a path at all, and fallen tree limbs impeded their progress practically every step of the way. Dappled sunlight winked through the evergreens and cinnamon ferns made plush by late summer rains. The place had its enchantments, enough of them to soften the heart of any man.

"Forgive me. I never meant to suggest that you would ever...that your intentions could be anything less than honourable, Mistress Hath—" She stopped his words with a finger to his lips. Their eyes met for a moment longer than seemed necessary.

"Mercy."

"What?"

"You may call me Mercy, Jonathan."

"Well, Mercy, then. You must know that I never intended to offend…"

"—Hush…" she interrupted, cupping her hand delicately behind her ear with a dramatic flourish worthy of the stage. "Do you hear what I hear?"

The sound of cascading water nearby, a torrent of it, filled the forest, as if its immediate appearance from nowhere resulted from the girl's suggesting it was there.

"A waterfall?" he asked, glad for the diversion from unpleasant matters. "I swear I heard nothing, or I would have certainly been curious to see it."

"So strange that these surroundings have not captured very much of your attention," Mercy suggested with conspicuous innuendo. Her air of whimsy did not elude the young man's notice. She leaned closer with such measured deliberation Jonathan pulled away.

The young physician studied the roundness of the girl's cheeks and the fullness of her lips. Every proper instinct he owned shouted that he must not kiss Mercy Hathaway, but his desire proved another matter. Perhaps if he envisioned her differently, if he concocted a large brown wart on the bridge of her nose, teeth gone to rot, aged skin shrivelled and festering with boils, gave to her a dozen misshapen features common among Boston hags, perhaps if he could envision her thus, *then* desire would fade.

It was idiocy to try. Mercy Hathaway appeared far too magnificent a specimen of ripening womanhood. As she stood motionless before him Jonathan could not help himself. He touched her face while his heart fluttered like a hundred windmills and the voice within him stirred.

[Can you speak words of love to her, Jonathan Browne? And can you speak these same words you have whispered so often to your Amelia? Once you embrace this seamstress, shall you tomorrow speak similar words of love to your betrothed?]

"You have bewitched me, Mercy Hathaway," he told her as her cheek brushed his. "There can be no other explanation for what I feel this moment."

Her lips went to young Browne's ear. She whispered close to it.

"Speak not words of what you feel, Jonathan. Show me."

Now a thousand voices whispered to his brain, and each uttered that he should flee this woman before the next moment passed.

Jonathan ignored them.

Taking Mercy into his arms he carried her towards the sound of the cascading waters, setting her in the glade alongside the rushing falls. Unravelling the cumbersome frock she wore with little of the studied grace he usually displayed, Jonathan placed one hand flat on the girl's breast in the unschooled manner of a curious child reaching out to touch a mysterious object. The girl let escape a little squeal of pleasure. Encouraged, Jonathan reached to remove the flimsy blouse she wore.

Her hand stopped him, and for one terrible moment Browne almost fell to his knees to beg the young woman's forgiveness for his audacity. To his surprise, Mercy tore open his shirt and kneaded his chest with her long fingers. She undressed herself for him and stood without so much as a blush, her naked flesh like burnt gold in the fading sunlight.

"I promised to bring you to my most secret of places, Jonathan Browne. And so I have." Guiding his hand she set it firmly between her thighs, permitting his fingers to explore the warm moistness inside her.

Mercy broke free laughing like a school girl. Jonathan first watched, then rushed to follow her beneath the waterfall while dropping articles of his clothing along his path. The cascade turned Mercy's silken flesh to soft cream, and he hungrily tasted her mouth like a ravenous animal. He could not receive enough water-soaked kisses from the woman. Mercy's guttural moans became shrieks as he explored skin turned slippery smooth by the cascade. Upon a large flat stone he pressed against her. A hot rush churned within, and were he able, he would have climbed inside the woman's skin. Together they shared a baptism intended to eternally wash clean all memory of Amelia Worthington.

Eternity proved short-lived. It lasted not one hour.

As Jonathan lay upon the dry grass he grew pale with the realization of what he had done. Unable to breathe, he muttered as if Mercy Hathaway rested somewhere other than upon his bare chest.

"My God, I have yielded to temptation! What atrocity have I committed toward Him and the woman who is to be my wife?"

Browne's entire body shook as the demons inside him took full possession, yet all the while Mercy seemed to battle none of her own.

"We have committed no wrong here, Jonathan. Would God not allow that you and I have merely satisfied a hunger we have shared since first we exchanged glances? Not all acts require His consecration to be acceptable to Him. Where, then, is the sin?"

The woman spoke with such assuredness her words might have becalmed Browne's internal mayhem had they come from anyone other than she. Instead, her companion in sin almost sickened himself with bitter laughter.

"A consecration from God, you say? For this? Tell me instead we have received approbation from the devil himself! Say we have together consigned our souls to eternal hell! God has abandoned this black forest, and with it, the both of us!"

Browne turned himself abruptly from Mercy Hathaway with his soul on fire. Although desiring no sleep, his exhaustion left him without choice. But complete repose immediately yielded to the rabid dreaming of a conscience heavily burdened with newly found shame.

Time lay still within the forest as a crescent moon drifted behind ghost driven clouds. An indistinct consortium of voices interrupted Jonathan Browne's sleep, a cacophony whose volume he could not isolate from the wild ramblings inside his head. The strange music awakened him, if the pandemonium within the forest could be called music. The aberrant strains seemed more of a chant, the tumult resonating throughout the sycamores.

Rising with a start Jonathan discovered Mercy Hathaway no longer by his side. The woman's absence brought his apprehension to a boil. Stumbling in the darkness he followed the cluster of voices to a small clearing. As he peered through a thick mesh of shrubbery Jonathan's jaw dropped like an unhinged latch.

Many were gathered around a crackling fire, perhaps two dozen male and female shapes. Some undulated grotesquely with hands poking the air in an exhibition no sane man would call dancing. Every soul among them was naked.

"Hoof and horn, hoof and horn,
All that dies shall be reborn!
Corn and grain, corn and grain,

All that falls shall rise again!"

"Demons...witches...and in our midst!" Jonathan muttered, bringing his hand to his mouth for fear he might be heard. A realization struck him like buckshot. Could these same shadowy denizens be citizens of Boston town to whom he nodded his good mornings?

Impossible to tell...Too terrible even to consider...

"She changes everything she touches,

And everything she touches changes!

Changes...Touches

Touches...Changes..."

He could not see their faces clearly amid such deceptions of darkness and light. Instead his mind sketched images of hags and wretched beings too abhorrent to reveal their warted hideousness in the light of day. He conjured creatures so old and deformed as to prove unworthy of any human reaction excepting disgust.

Another image issued from his mind's eye and hammered his brain until it would not fade. He pictured Mercy Hathaway among these fiends with the surging fire flame dancing upon her naked breasts, her flesh glistening as it did beneath the waterfall. The more fervently he wished his thoughts of her gone, the more intensely he tasted Mercy's lips a hundred times over.

[Give yourself to me, Jonathan Browne! Give to me everything that you are, and join us now and forever!]

During one misguided moment he had permitted his soul to become twisted like a child's mold of clay by the charms of this woman. He would not make that mistake again. If he succeeded in detecting Mercy Hathaway among this coven of fiends, she could burn in hell before he gave her another thought.

The ceremony turned suddenly solemn, and the revellers formed a circle around a large robed figure. He alone now delivered the chant.

"Come we all from the horned one, And to him we shall return.

Like a spark of fire, Rising to the heavens,

To him we shall return..."

Someone carried a squirming horned creature into the circle's centre. Its brays indicated a kicking live goat, and the poor brute shrieked as the throng surrounded the animal. The robed silhouetted figure raised a butcher's knife above his head while another lifted the animal for all to see.

The circle tightened. The coven, chanting, drew nearer.

"...and to him we shall return..."

The goat's wails lasted for only a moment before thick gurgles replaced them. The shadowed man was cutting the animal's throat, his knife continuing to slash at it even after the creature's whining ended. Dripping with blood and held high, the head had been hacked completely off. The incessant chanting grew louder as the blood soaked vessel passed from hand to hand. Each among the gathering drank its sopping gore directly from the skull.

Jonathan strove to keep his revulsion silent. He determined not to remain another moment and stumbled through the darkness searching for any sign of the seamstress. Beneath the dull moon the forest's shadows went unseen, and every obstacle proved treacherous. He struck his forehead upon a hanging bough and toppled face first to the ground. A fire storm of colours exploded inside his brain, then turned quickly to black.

Browne's fevered insensibility seemed neither sleep nor stupor. The sinister images reinvented themselves in muddled dreams, and there they remained murmuring into the night.

...Everything she touches changes...touches...changes...

And then, another voice, softer and more familiar.

...We have committed no wrong here, Jonathan...

...No wrong...no wrong...

...Where is the sin, Jonathan...? Where is the sin...?

When he awakened his head throbbed. Browne had no idea how much time had passed, but morning could not be more than a few hours away.

Shaking off sleep Jonathan felt uncertain he had witnessed the outlandish revelry at all. Mercy slept alongside him as before. Perhaps he had suffered frenzied dreams, the creations of a mind fevered with wrong-doing and shame. Running his fingers through hair matted with sweat he discovered a small lump near his scalp. He shivered with cold but resisted moving closer to the woman, having had his fill of the seamstress' enchantments.

He waited until the sliver of moon drifted into a small patch of open sky, enough to illuminate the girl's milky flesh. Jonathan saw her face clearly for only a moment, but it was enough to make him gag. Plum coloured stains smeared Mercy Hathaway's mouth and chin. Thick streaks of goats blood sopped down the girl's neck.

"Not a dream," he muttered. "Damn all witches to hell! Not a dream at all..."

Browne took to his feet. He could ill afford awaiting daylight to stumble his way back to Boston. Becoming lost within these sycamores seemed a small peril compared to spending another moment in the company of the treacherous seductress who had passed her midnight hours engorging herself with blood. The devil alone knew what further sinning the woman had devised.

He chose a measured and steady escape, not wishing to crack his skull upon another unseen bough. The shrieks of bull frogs and night crickets caused Jonathan to investigate behind him with every step he took forward, and he cared little where his journey carried him. Only one thing concerned him; he had to leave this place and its witchcraft behind him.

He floundered for over an hour through utter blackness. It seemed daylight never had visited this forest. If dawn ever arrived, only then would he find his way free of this *Godforsaken* maze of wood.

Godforsaken...

Was ever a word more appropriate? Dark sycamores suffocated him from every side. Satan himself could not have uncovered a place more suitable for his minions. In this black forest did it matter how much distance he put between himself and Mercy Hathaway? She had already done her worst, and he had bartered his soul for a few moments beneath a waterfall with the raven haired witch. Could he ever again greet Amelia Worthington at her father's door, then seat himself at her table to say grace and enjoy a meal? How could he return to his home pretending nothing had happened? He was a man lost beyond all hope and redemption, as lost as any of those who drank blood beneath a pale slice of the moon...

"*No! You shall not have Jonathan Browne's soul! I am lost only in finding my way from this forest. I have not lost my way to heaven!*"

His voice returned to him in ghostly mimicry that resonated among the tall pines.

>*...lost my way...my way...my way...*
>*...to heaven...heaven...heaven...*

Startled, Jonathan spun on his heels like a trapped animal.

"Only my echo...only my own pitiful voice, lost and alone. Dear God, I have lost my way, and am I about to lose my mind as well?"

His answer came to him from the sycamores.

"*Jonathan...! Jonathan Browne...!*"

...Browne...Browne...Browne...

He had gone mad in this forest. He felt certain of that now. His only hope was that death would come before someone discovered him blithering to himself like an imbecile, screaming back to the voices inside his head that called to him from the wind, voices that knew his name and would call to him again and again until the last fragment of his sanity disappeared.

"*Jonathan Browne! Where are you...?*

The reverberations surrounded him and were moving closer! There was nowhere to run!

"*Jonathan!! We heard you shout your name!*"

"*We were so very worried! Where are you?*"

This last voice belonged to a woman! There was something familiar about it. He knew these people!

"Amelia? Is that you?"

"Jonathan, yes! We searched this entire night for you! Keep shouting! We'll find you!"

"Oh, thank God! Thank God! You seem so near! I am here! I am here!"

The thick sedges behind him parted, and with torch in hand, Jonathan's woman stood before him covered with grime and thorns. She rushed into the arms of her fiancé before he could utter a syllable.

"You're safe! Oh, Jonathan, I was so very worried! When I heard you had gone off so close to dark with Mercy Hathaway — and when you had not returned — I was fearful some harm had befallen you."

Others with torches entered the path. Jonathan recognized Reverend Habersham and the new church minister, Edmund Porter and much of his congregation, along with several hunting companions. Also there was Peter Farnsworth who practiced law in England, even old Mrs. Hutchinson who sold vegetables in the market square with her humpbacked husband. More entered behind them. It seemed Amelia had brought with her a search party consisting of half the town.

"I feel so ashamed, Amelia — so ashamed for what pain I must have caused you. But how in this dense forest were you able to find me?"

The question seemed to confuse his woman, and she looked towards Reverend Habersham for an answer. The old minister whispered something to Porter. The younger clergyman nodded and stepped forward.

"You say you spent the night here in the forest with Mistress Mercy Hathaway, the young seamstress who lives alone in the cottage by the edge of this forest?" Edmund Porter asked.

Suddenly Jonathan felt as if he were on trial.

"If others say that I did so, I see no reason to deny it," he answered. He was not able to look at Amelia.

Porter turned to the lawyer, Farnsworth, to speak. The whole matter had an air of officiousness made even worse by the young Englishman's cold and direct question.

"Jonathan Browne, will you come with us? There is something I believe you should see before morning. It is only a short distance."

Amelia took hold of Browne's hand and held it close to her. He looked into her eyes with complete bewilderment, turning to those who suddenly acted his accusers.

"Come with you? To where?"

"You must go with the ministers and the others, Jonathan," Amelia urged. "I shall remain by your side, I promise you."

Browne walked with her and the others, noting the gathering of townspeople following close behind. Moments later the sound of a rushing waterfall stopped him in his tracks. In his escape earlier, the darkness must have confused him and he had come full circle. He was back where he had started!

Mercy Hathaway slept undisturbed exactly where Jonathan had left her, not far from the cascading waters of the falls. The seamstress had covered herself completely with her long frock against the night chill, but her bare legs extended beyond the garment. Seeing them, Jonathan's face went crimson with shame. Amelia did not look at the woman, but she held the hand of her fiancé more tightly than before. Despite the bitter chill his brow glistened with sweat. He spoke to the church elder like a man at confession.

"Reverend Habersham, I make no excuse for myself. But you must know the truth about this wanton seamstress, and I will swear to it. Mercy Hathaway brought me to this spot so that I could witness those with whom she consorts. She wanted me to join them, I am certain of it. They killed a goat this night, and drank its blood! I saw them! And I saw her face smeared with it!"

The two priests exchanged glances with the townspeople. Amelia took Jonathan by the arm before he might say more.

"They found Mercy Hathaway like this, Jonathan," she told him. "The Reverend and the others, when they were looking for you. They did not want me to see her, but I insisted on coming."

"*Found? Found her...?*"

Reverend Habersham put a hand on the young man's shoulder. "Mercy Hathaway's throat has been cut, Jonathan. Probably here where she slept. Do you know anything of this matter?"

"*Dead? Mercy Hathaway is dead?*"

Any additional words Browne might have added withered upon his tongue. The night's events exploded into fragments, and no matter how many ways he pieced them together he arrived at the same conclusion.

"*Witchery and that accursed ritual of blood...*"

"What?

Pulling himself from Amelia, Jonathan turned towards the others. The townspeople whispered to one another never taking their eyes from him.

"*Satan's fiends are responsible! Can't you see that? The demons and the witches did this! They placed the woman's mutilated corpse alongside me while I slept. They knew I watched them! My dear God, was the blood on Mercy Hathaway's face her own?*"

Amelia tugged at Jonathan's arm, but already his rants had revealed too much.

"Then you saw blood on this girl?" Farnsworth asked in the manner of a magistrate gathering evidence. The attorney indicated the frock that completely covered Mercy Hathaway's face. "Did you see a knife?"

"*What —?*"

"A knife, Jonathan. Did you see who killed Mercy Hathaway?"

"I told you I saw her face blood smeared, and I thought — that is, I believed — *I have already told you who killed her!*"

Farnsworth looked toward the clergymen.

"Demons and witches, you say?" Habersham asked.

"*Yes! Yes!*"

"And Mercy Hathaway? A witch?"

"Yes! *Perhaps...I don't know!*"

The Reverend scratched the smaller of his two chins.

"You say demons and witches killed the woman because the seamstress herself was a witch? I see no logic here, Jonathan. Do you?"

Browne had entangled himself within a maze more mired with traps than the forest itself.

"Do fiends from hell require reason for what they do?" Jonathan asked.

The English attorney had a ready answer as if the two faced one another in a chamber of law.

"Fiends may not require reason for their actions, Jonathan Browne. However, men do."

"Murderer!" old Mrs. Hutchinson cried out. "A fiend himself who speaks of fiends!"

"I say we hang the man tonight!" her husband shouted.

Amelia tried to step between the crowd and Jonathan.

"This forest is no courthouse. And none here are my Jonathan's jurors!" The elderly Reverend held her back, and Amelia shouted, "Jonathan, you must listen to me! Say nothing more, only listen! There is a way out for you! You must believe me, there is a way out!"

The humpbacked Mr. Hutchinson would hear none of it. "There is no way out for a man whose guilt bleeds through every pore as does the blood from that butchered girl's cut throat!"

"*Hang him! Hang him now!*" another hollered, and several others took up the chant.

"*Hang the murderer!*"

"*Let him see the corpse of his victim as he chokes!*"

"*Death to him! Death to Jonathan Browne!*"

Some threw their torches to the ground to create a bonfire. Others formed a tightening circle around Jonathan. Amelia shouted back to the unruly throng with a rage Browne had never seen his woman display before.

"You know not this man I love! Jonathan Browne fears God! He is not one who changes into a murderer in a single night simply because he has been enchanted by a young whore! My Jonathan is as steadfast as the constellations, as unshakable in his beliefs as the most holy of men!"

Amelia Worthington turned to her fiancé. Her mouth curled into an unlikely grin. Suddenly others were laughing. The amusement became shared among the entire gathering, and some nearly fell into seizures.

"So tell me, my most dearest love. Are you not such a man?"

In a night signatured with incomprehensible occurrences, Jonathan witnessed yet another. Here stood his Amelia speaking to this diverse assemblage as if lecturing from the Reverend Habersham's pulpit.

"And does not such a man's cherished Christian beliefs exceed the insignificance of a hundred Mercy Hathaways and those whose souls prove all but worthless to Him we serve?" Approaching the man who would be her husband, she took his hand. "I told you there is a way out, Jonathan. And so there is. Do you wish to be saved, my love? Shall you enter His kingdom this very night?"

Amelia's face took on the countenance of those Jonathan had seen only in his most horrific of dreams. Her skin bubbled, then split like a badly sewn garment. The girl's porcelain teeth turned yellow and cracked while a wart the size of a pea sprouted on her chin. All the while Amelia Worthington's grin remained. She took her lover's hand and placed it on her breast whose flesh now had the insubstantial feel of a decaying old woman's. Reverend Habersham stepped forward in dark robes. He chanted the words first. The others quickly joined in.

"She changes everything she touches,
And everything she touches changes..."

Jonathan pulled himself from this creature who no longer resembled the Amelia he knew. He wanted to scream, to run as far as his legs might take him. But there were too many surrounding him, too many who would never allow him to leave this forest alive. He knew tomorrow each would tell the story of the well-regarded Jonathan Browne, who had taken a beguiling young seamstress into the woods, had his way with her, then became so deranged with shame he cut the poor girl's throat. The townsfolk would explain how they had, together, meted out justice swiftly and avenged the man's detestable act on the spot. With so many villagers already here, who in Boston would question any of this?

"Join us, Jonathan," the Amelia-thing muttered. "Join us tonight."

Old Reverend Habersham, his face suddenly gone to rot, kneeled over the corpse of Mercy Hathaway. In one motion he plucked away the frock that covered her remains. The seamstress's throat still sopped thick crimson gobs, although much of the blood on her face had clotted and dried to dusty cakes. Habersham lifted the body while Amelia approached. The humpbacked Mr. Hutchinson produced a long butcher's knife and handed it to the woman. She held the glittering blade close to her, addressing the dead girl to her face.

"Poor Mercy Hathaway, thinking it was your own inclination to practice your seductions on my beloved, foolishly believing you had cast a spell of your own to bring him to this place. Rarely have I enjoyed the cutting of a throat so much as I did yours. But my work is merely half finished..."

Jonathan could only watch as Amelia plunged the blade deeply into the murdered girl's thin neck, hacking away at flesh and bone until she had severed the head entirely.

"None here shall cry for Mercy, Jonathan! But you and I will drink to her sins!"

She held the skull for the others to see as if displaying a trophy she had taken pride in winning, swilling the blood from its leaking neck with none of the delicate mannerisms of a woman. Thin crimson streaks veined Amelia's warted chin and she wiped it with the back of her hand in grotesque parody of a bar wench. With the firelight in her eyes she turned to her bewildered lover.

"Drink and join us, Jonathan."

The clergymen repeated her words. Every member of the assembly added voice to the chant, and already the pockmarked Mrs. Hutchinson had removed her clothes.

"Drink and join us...Drink and join us..."

Jonathan Browne could not explain it...

His disgust had passed in a heartbeat. These unholy creatures no longer revolted him. Even the hag who had once called herself his fiancé, even *she* seemed strangely appealing. There was no explaining any of this.

[...touches...changes...touches...]

He felt a sensation even more strange...

Something within him thirsted. He could not understand why, but there was no denying the craving. Watching Amelia taste Mercy Hathaway's blood directly from the woman's severed head as if she were imbibing from a bowl of fruit punch, not even this seemed loathsome. It did not seem even remotely unnatural.

He stepped forward.

"Well, then, where is the sin?" he asked of Amelia, and his woman could not restrain her toothless smile.

Jonathan held out his hands to receive his drink.

immortal beloved

Lisa Kessler

As I pen these words, I am sitting in my room, my flesh stone cold and without colour. Melina's feverish pounding of the *Moonlight Sonata* is beginning to wear on me. I have given my word to my dear friend Marcus to keep her safe but I fear she knows that I am weakening. She begs me with each sounding of the grandfather clock to give her the Dark Gift. I have never met a mortal who yearns so deeply for immortality. If she only understood what it was she longed for, then she would know it for the curse it truly is.

I am beginning to believe Melina derives pleasure from tormenting me with her warm, intoxicating mortality, teasing me with her scent. Each time the piano goes silent, she is touching me, offering herself to me as if I were the only man she had ever known. I have no desire to make another vampire, to damn another person to an eternal existence such as mine. But I am so greatly tempted by her, and I am infuriated with myself for my own weakness. Her future is for Marcus to decide, not me. I gave my word she would be safe while he was away.

But I didn't know her then. Didn't know that she played the damned piano...the *Moonlight Sonata* of all pieces...She plays Beethoven's masterpiece with a flawless, insane brilliance and a feverish intensity that makes my blood race through my ancient veins with a fiery passion that leaves me dizzy at times.

She is in danger with me, I know this, and yet, I cannot keep her away from me. And now the melody is playing again, the third movement with all of its agitated fire. She plays the piece just as he did, making me feel sensations that I haven't experienced for nearly two hundred years, not since the night I heard Beethoven begin his work on the *Moonlight Sonata*.

He was thirty years old, the night his frenzied melodies first attracted my attention. I was walking the streets of Vienna late at night. All of the homes were dark and quiet, save for one. I could hear a mortal man's crazed ranting, followed by the most intricate, complex, and passionate piano melodies, unlike anything I had heard since the death of young Wolfgang Amadeus Mozart.

Intrigued, I followed the sound and quickly located its source. In the upper room of a modest home, I saw flickering candlelight illuminating through the window, and in the shadows cast against the walls; I saw the form of what seemed to be a mad man.

Silently willing my body into the air, I peered through the upper window. Inside I found two pianos, and a wild-eyed man sitting on the floor between them. The legs of the pianos sawn off, leaving the huge instruments to rest on the floor as he banged fiercely at the keys only to follow the action with hurried scribbling of musical notations on crumpled parchment.

I remember that night as if it were yesterday, hovering in the darkness for hours watching this mortal genius at work. I found his thoughts were as scattered as his hair when I attempted to read them. He was a paradox, his mind full of passion and anger, while his heart was full of love and divinely inspired music, or so he believed. I watched him each night for a week as he spent countless hours composing his *Moonlight Sonata*, until I could no longer stand to observe him from a distance. I needed to know him. I wanted to understand him.

I was intrigued with the genius that was Ludwig Van Beethoven even though we had never met, but that was soon to change. I arranged to meet the man I had been secretly watching, explaining that I was a wealthy Lord who admired his musical genius. He welcomed me into his home, and I was shocked to find that my mortal companion was completely deaf. I soon learned that was the reason for the pianos resting on the floor. He explained to me that he could *feel* the music through the vibrations in the floor while sitting between them.

I remember finding myself awe-struck at his accomplishments. How could a man write such difficult, intricate, and emotional music without being able to hear a single note?

Being a vampire made it possible for me to send my voice past his deaf ears, directly into his mind, which frightened him at first, but eventually he came to welcome my silent voice. When he was with me, he was no longer a prisoner of silence. And how happy I was to set him free.

When I finally revealed my true nature to him, he surprised me again. He never questioned the truth of my existence, and did not turn away in fear. Instead, he became even more fascinated, wanting to know about past civilizations that had long since died. He even went so far as to ask me if I had ever seen the face of God. His undying faith inspired me. I had never known such a man, who could love his Creator in spite of the tremendous loss he suffered when his hearing was taken from him.

Many nights we spent debating why God would have inspired him to a life of music only to steal away his ability to hear it. He never had an answer except that God's will be done. He was furious over his loss, but he never allowed it to take away the music that he loved.

Days turned to weeks, and weeks into months, when I began to realise that I loved the crazed mortal composer. His music spoke to me in ways that words could not, and his fiery passionate spirit ignited my immortal heart with a new zeal for life.

After a few years, I could see that my beloved Beethoven's health was beginning to fail. I could hear it in his fluttering erratic heartbeat, and I began to worry for him each sunrise when I laid to rest. Would my friend still be alive when I awoke?

Human life is such a fragile gift...I begged him to accept immortality, to drink of my blood and live forever, but of course he would not. He was still devoted to his *God*. He was convinced, regardless of what I told him to the contrary, that his music was a divine gift from heaven. If he were to become a vampire, he was certain that he would be cursed and lose his music forever. Without it, he saw no reason for living.

I respected his wishes and was lucky enough to enjoy his company for nearly twenty years. During that time, he composed some of the most brilliant music I have ever heard. His ninth symphony still moves me to tears.

Over our twenty-year relationship, there were periods of time when I was called away, but even then we kept in touch through letters, wonderful letters, that expressed a love we could never discuss face to face. For what we felt for one another in our hearts, was forbidden by his God. So we buried our true feelings from the world as well as ourselves. I had no choice. I loved him too much to do otherwise.

He was beginning his tenth symphony when his liver began to fail. He continued to refuse my offer of immortality. It was relentlessly painful for me to stand by and watch him suffer. During our last night together, I cradled my beloved friend, kindred spirit, and love of my soul, holding him close to my heart. And although he could barely whisper, his mind spoke clearly as I read his thoughts. But what he told me was not what I wanted to hear.

He asked me to leave him.

I shook my head, refusing to move, but he begged me to go, to remember him as the man he was and not the invalid he had become. Tearfully he asked me to never forget him. I wept with him, and vowed to honour his wishes. I spoke into his mind of my undying love for him, promising to remember the *Moonlight Sonata* that brought us together twenty years before.

He drew me close and very tenderly kissed my lips. It was the first and last time that our lips ever met to bond us for a brief moment as we allowed our secret adoration for one another to surface beyond our hearts. I met his eyes as he whispered, "Ever thine, ever mine, ever ours...My Immortal Beloved..."

And now Melina sits in my home, playing my beloved Beethoven's feverish melody on the piano. Igniting his memory in my heart and mind. His florid *Moonlight Sonata* once again filling my ears and burning into my soul. She is driving me to madness.

For nearly two hundred years there has been speculation about the identity of Beethoven's secret love, his "Immortal Beloved" from his letters. Never would anyone guess that his love still walked this earth; that the immortal love he described was an ancient vampire. Never would they guess that his Immortal Beloved still missed him.

Damn that woman! Will she never stop her infernal playing? She no longer calls to me with her voice, but with her music. I cannot stand the pain and temptation his memory kindles inside of me. Perhaps she knows this.

My beloved Beethoven would have approved of her interpretation of his masterpiece. She plays his *Moonlight Sonata* with the same combination of blind anger and carnal passion that he had in his soul when he composed the piece nearly two hundred years ago. She knows his fury and his pain. But Melina is teetering on the brink of insanity; I can see it in her eyes. And her playing is no longer coming from notes on a page, but a masterpiece written in her heart. There is a striking difference when music comes from the soul rather than the page, no matter how tortured that soul might be.

I cannot stand to hide away in my room any longer. I must go listen, and pray that listening is all that I do. Her music is hypnotising me, wrapping me in her spell and I am helpless to resist.

Standing in the doorway, watching her play, I cannot help but wonder if it is really Melina that I hear? The longer I listen to the piano sing, the more I see my beloved Beethoven, sitting on the floor of his upper room with candles flickering around him.

This is madness! Surely his spirit cannot live again inside of this tormented mortal woman's body...But what if I am wrong? What if he lives again inside of her? Perhaps that is the reason behind her insistent playing. Could my Beethoven be calling me through his music to save him and free his soul?

Her heartbeat is pounding in my ears; I hear it and I wonder if it might be his. The scent of her mortal blood tempts me, calls to me, until I can no longer fight my thirst.

The piano bench crashes onto the floor, as I pull my beloved back from the piano keys and sink my fangs deep into the fount of blood hidden inside of her throat. I drink deeply, my ancient flesh warming as I quickly take Melina's life, for sadly this is not my beloved composer. I know this now. And now it is too late.

The body in my arms does not hold Beethoven's spirit. This is simply a tortured, angry young woman on the edge of madness, and I am about to give her eternal life. Her eyes are dead as her lips search blindly for the open vein in my wrist.

It would be best to let her go, to just let her die. But I gave my word to my only friend left in this world that she would be safe in my care. Am I such a monster to kill her after promising to give her sanctuary? I must let her drink, but in my heart I know that even immortality will not save this one from death. Her mind is not strong enough to face an endless eternity of dark evenings, but she will not perish this night. I have learned over the centuries that a friend is more precious than gold. Marcus is my friend, and he loves her.

Melina is pulling at my veins now. Drinking deeply of the eternal life in my blood with a voracious appetite. My decision has been made. She will be a vampire.

I watch her open her eyes, the madness is still burning deep within them as she stares at me with a twisted grin. What have I done? But I already know of my horrible mistake. And all that I can offer my dear friend, Marcus, is a silent prayer. Forgive me…Please forgive me.

subito piano
Lisa Kessler

Pianissimo...Hauntingly soft

I cannot escape her music. Hidden behind the closed door of my room, I still hear her playing. How could Peter make the same mistake again? He swore he would never make another immortal. Perhaps our kind are doomed to repeat their errors throughout eternity. The blood enables us to live forever, but our hearts are still those of impetuous human beings. Sadly, eternal life and preternatural ability does not grant us wisdom.

I hear Melina's fingers floating over the ivory keys, making the piano sing with glorious melodies that used to bring me such joy. Now they stab at my heart mercilessly. Music used to be my passion, my first love. I played the lute, and...I sang. Perhaps it was her music that first attracted me to Melina...Perhaps.

Now her playing brings me pain. Peter stole her mortality before she could experience the magic that her mortal life could have held. She was barely eighteen! She was angry, rebellious, depressed and underneath it all, so naive.

For years the piano was her sole friend. Her family paraded her across the country, through countless cities to perform. She never experienced life, and now she is locked in the clutches of an eternity of numbness. She is a child of the night now, neither dead nor alive in the mortal sense of the word. Trapped somewhere in-between. Peter stole her from the beautiful sunlight that might have healed her tortured soul, and his decision wounds me each time I see her face, her cold inhuman eyes.

She will never experience an afternoon kiss in the hot summer rain, walking on the beach watching as the sun sets over the water, or making love under the stars. Did he know my precious Melina was still a virgin when he drank from her veins? All of the simple human pleasures, the memories of life that our kind cling to through the centuries, Melina never experienced, and now she never will. Instead of yearning for pleasures of the flesh, now she will crave blood. I am left wondering if she will grow to hate me for entrusting her to Peter's care that fateful night.

He promised me she would be safe with him.

Mezzo-Piano...the melody grows with intensity

I watch her playing the piano, and I see pieces of myself, of an impossible puzzle. When we first met, she had recently lost her parents in a car accident. I found her in a bar brandishing her false identification, and inside of her mind I saw her new guardian's abuse, her own uncle beating her to make her perform, to play the piano. In that instant, I was taken back to the Rome of centuries ago, when I was still a mortal boy. When I lost my family.

I was taken, stolen from my home, and sold by my captors to sing for the church, as many boys were in my day. Our angelic voices soon became our curse when the priests castrated boys to keep their voices from changing into the low-pitched voices of men. Our bodies would be forever disfigured in order to keep our songs pure like those of angels. But Peter saved me from that fate.

Who would save Melina?

When I reached into her thoughts that first night we met, I felt her fear, and I understood her pain. The darkness that consumed her mind was so similar to my own when I was a mortal man. We talked, and began to meet in the dark corners of the bar nearly every night. The evening that she came in with a black eye, I paid her uncle a visit. After taking his life, I became her saviour just as Peter had been mine centuries before.

Mezzo-Forte...the passion in the notes builds

My chest tightens with emotions that I will never allow to surface. How can I stop her feverish playing? Can anyone stop her now? I wanted so much more for her, and yet all she desired was the *Dark Gift*. She longed to live forever, to be strong like me, just as I had once yearned to be like Peter. But she didn't understand what she was asking...Does she understand now?

How did all of this come to pass? Peter denied me his blood until he was certain I was ready to face lifetimes of endless night; yet now, centuries later, he shared the *dark gift* with a young mortal girl in the passing of a single night? A child I asked him to protect and watch over in my absence.

I will probably never understand his decision. Melina isn't equipped to face eternity. Are any of us really? Was I prepared for the true burden of immortality?

Peter had been my friend in the outside world, the world beyond the expansive church walls. For months, he secretly took me under his wing, teaching me to read, discussing philosophy and art. He told me stories about other parts of the world and I became an enraptured student.

All the while, I sang.

The chorus master groomed me for my future within the church. "You have the voice of an angel, Marcus," he would say. "Your music must be preserved, not molested by the secular world."

But I didn't know the horror that would lie in store for me. I immersed myself in my studies, learning to read and write music, and under the cover of nightfall, I would secretly crawl out of my window to meet my mysterious tutor outside the church walls.

Peter and I talked together for hours, and then I would sing songs just for him. Not the sacred Latin songs of the church, but secular songs in my native Italian tongue, songs of love and longing, of young lovers and moonlight. How I loved to sing.

But I gave up my music when I gave up my mortality to Peter. Each time I hear Melina playing her feverish melodies, I remember the night when the priests bound me while I slept and took me to the secret chamber. I awoke, and fought to break free, my screams muffled by a tight gag in my mouth. I was only thirteen, barely more than a boy myself, trying to fight off four grown men who stripped me naked and tied me down to a table.

All for the love of God and music.

Forte...the music reverberates with power

That was the night I sang my last song...Peter broke through the window just as the priest raised the blade. Hot blood sprayed across my shivering body, and the sounds of the priests' screams pierced my ears. The knife missed its mark and cut deep into my thigh, sending searing pain through my entire body. Peter scooped me into his arms, and carried me out into the night, saving me from a life without passion.

I sang for him that night, a pain-filled cry to heaven. Dies Irae for my precious family I would never see again, for the other boys in the church who would not be saved as I was, and for the happiness that I would never know again. Dies Irae for the darkness I would embrace years later when I took Peter's blood. Dies Irae, Day of Anger...

My music was silenced forever.

Her playing is louder now. I can feel the vibrations in the floor beneath my feet. How can a child who is so completely lost in darkness play with such fiery passion? How I wish I could make her stop!

I remember the night I gave up my mortal life. I sat in Peter's chamber, weeping like a babe. I had opened my mind to him and welcomed him into my life. I had thought myself to be a man, but I was still a child. I thought I understood what I would be giving up. I wanted eternity with Peter. I wanted to be powerful and live without fear of death. No one would ever harm me again, and I would never be at another man's mercy.

It wasn't until I watched my newly-made Melina playing that I understood what I had lost. I gave up music, and love, and family. I never enjoyed the rush of infatuation or the pain of heartbreak. I ran to the arms of immortality to hide from life. I realise now that those precious mortal years can shape an entire millennia. I have been forever searching for someone or something to believe in, to cling to for balance. Always yearning for the family I lost, and the one I never had. Without it, the endless nights on this earth become pure chaos and darkness. When I look at Melina now, that is all I see...Darkness.

Decrescendo...the melody softens

Is she looking for something to believe in? What does she see? Will I be forced to care for her for all time? Will she ever stop playing the piano?

I can't bear to look upon her anymore. She is a reflection of me. A mirror that I do not wish to gaze upon. Now she too will never know independence, or the love of a man or mortal children. I wanted more for her than I had. I wanted to protect her from the *Dark Gift*, to fill her mortal life with light and love as mine had never been, and maybe through her, my own soul could be saved. But Peter misread my love for the girl...He made her one of us.

Already she is showing signs of madness, and I cannot help but wonder what eternity has in store for her. She won't stop playing, not even to feed. Only the sunlight ends the insane lustful passion she calls forth from the cold ivory keys of the baby grand piano. Will I have to sever her hands to stop her frenzied playing? Could I bring myself to take her hands? Is there any other way to save her...and myself?

Subito Piano...Suddenly silent...

Melina's pain-filled silent whisper echoes through my mind, *Help me, Marcus...Help me.*

the migrant
Michael Stone

On 18th December, 1918, a young Austrian by the name of Adolf Hitler disembarked from a train in Munich. Snow was falling from darkling skies, curling like ashes in bitter wintry draughts. It coated the stark framework of the steam sheds, glistened like sweat on the engine's black iron flanks.

Adolf stepped onto the platform, his nostrils flaring as he savoured the commingled scents of coal, dung and oil-laden steam. He thumbed the moustache that grew thickly on his cheeks. I thought he appeared calm and appraising, if a little dishevelled after his train journey.

He sauntered past me, the snow squeaking under his boots. He gave no indication of noticing that the snow at my feet was ugly with bloodstained phlegm.

I fell into step behind my quarry.

Presently he stopped outside a *gasthaus*, squares of sallow light leaking from its windows onto the slushy road. *Das Schwarz Wildschwein*. The Black Boar: a drinking hole popular with servicemen. Adolf hitched the rucksack higher on his shoulders, straightened his bonnet cap and ran his fingers through the close-cropped hair above his ears.

He shoved open the door and let the babble of deep male voices wash over him. A badly scarred pine counter ran the length of the opposite wall. Pewter steins hung by their handles from brass hooks. Yellow candlelight flickered on brown bottles. The smell of beer, stale sweat and fresh sawdust commingled with the blue-grey miasma of pipe-smoke. A single oil lamp struggled to penetrate the fug. Adolf Hitler placed a coin on the counter then selected a table near the fireplace.

I stood on the pavement outside and watched through fern-frosted glass and condensation as he struggled to remove his wet rucksack and greatcoat. A Christmas tree stood in one corner, decorated with spent cartridges and silver paper, the role of the fairy taken by a crude imitation of Wilhelm II, cruelly complete with a withered left arm.

Placing his cap on the table, Adolf sat down with his back to the fire and stretched his legs. He wasn't made to wait long; a wide-hipped serving-girl threaded skilfully through the clamour carrying a stein and a jug of beer.

I couldn't see what was said, but she laughed at some witticism he made. He took a sip of the cold beer and smacked his lips in appreciation.

My own mouth was a mass of painful sores. My feet were dead from the cold.

I entered the *gasthaus* and ordered myself a drink, although I knew I would be unable to taste it. I stood well back from the fire.

"Won't you join us?" a man at an adjacent table asked Adolf.

Adolf gave the speaker a cursory glance, registering the man's round florid face and gleaming high forehead.

"We were just about to start another game." The man shuffled a deck of cards with the jaunty air of a showman drumming up an audience.

"Room for another at the table," said one of his two companions. "Especially for a comrade back from the war."

Adolf declined and rooted the inside pocket of his greatcoat for a slim, finely etched cigarette case, opening it to reveal two dog-eared cigarettes. He selected the slightly longer one and lit it with a taper from the fire. I have never claimed to be a telepath, but I find I can often judge a man's thoughts by his facial expressions, eye movements, or by subtle changes in his posture. Adolf was thinking: *To welcome one of our boys back from the war? Some welcome.* We had returned from the Western Front to a Fatherland weighed down with disease, poverty and, worst of all, defeatism. Some welcome indeed. In that we were agreed. He settled back with his cigarette, the smoke purging the cold from his bones. He looked at ease. I would soon change that.

"It is very busy tonight," I said. The chair scraped noisily over the stone floor as I sat down at his table. Adolf closed his eyes, blanking my intrusion.

"I remember you, don't I?" I said.

He opened his eyes wearily to see me craning forward, scrutinising his face in the dim light. "You were a rider, taking messages to and from the Front. I am right, aren't I? Tch, my manners." I offered a grubby hand. "My name is Hubert."

"Adolf. You are quite right, I sometimes performed despatch rider duties." He shook my hand — I could see it made him uncomfortable — and moved his head slightly to allow some of the light from the fire to fall on my face. To his credit he suppressed a natural reaction to flinch. I admired him for it; many did not hide their disgust. My face was grim, I knew. Blood and discharge from my ruined lungs crusted in the creases of my lips. My eyes were yellow and crazed by small veins; the pupils looked like black flies trapped in amber.

"I was caught in a gas attack," I said.

"Ah." Adolf relaxed. "Me, too, and blinded. I have just come out of hospital. One eye is still worse than the other. A little fuzzy." He waggled a hand. "But it is improving."

"The Somme?"

He nodded, his expression bleak.

I raised my glass. "To fallen comrades."

"To fallen comrades."

I gasped as the spirits scorched a trail down my gullet. "So, you are a local man?"

"I come from Branau am Inn, Austria, but I was in Munich when the war broke out so I enlisted in the Bavarian infantry. The List Regiment," he said with obvious pride. "I shall be reporting to the adjutant after this drink."

A buxom *fraulein* placed a candle on a saucer in the centre of the table. I imagine I looked even more grotesque by its flickering light.

I said, "The army has dispensed with my services so I have no barracks to welcome me, but there is dry spot in some cellars not far from here. There are many of us ex-servicemen down there."

I removed a bullet from my breast pocket and slowly turned it in my fingers. It was squashed and misshapen from an impact, but easily recognisable by someone with Adolf's experience as an eight-millimetre round.

"A wartime keepsake?" he asked.

"More than that," I said, but before I could finish my sentence I was taken by a violent spasm. I coughed noisily and raised a rust-red handkerchief to my mouth. Mindless of my surroundings I had to retch and spit into the handkerchief to avoid choking on a blood clot. I folded away the piece of rag and gave myself a moment to recover. Spots floated before my eyes.

Adolf was looking with open distaste at my sleeve cuffs, which were slimed with the same discharge as my handkerchief.

Quietly, I began to tell him my story. "We were sent over the top three times in quick succession, each assault doomed to failure. The enemy's heavy artillery was fierce and unrelenting."

I was pinned down behind a dry-stone wall. It provided adequate cover, but the muzzle-flash of my *Muskete* at the interstices gave my position away. I was trapped like a rat cornered by terriers. Despite the numbing cold, I was sweating profusely.

I sniffed, then sniffed again. Tin. I could smell something like hot tin, a piercing tang over and above the cooling gun at my side. My eyes were starting to smart too. I blinked away a tear. Quelling the rising panic, I tugged the gas mask from its receptacle webbed to my chest and pulled the bulky hood over my head, taking care to replace my helmet afterwards. I made it just in time for a corrosive mist had billowed in on the breeze; a dirty, choking cloud of sour green.

I rolled onto my knees and made ready to run. I could see other figures beating hasty retreats, some with their protective masks on and some without, the latter flapping at themselves as though putting out flames. One soldier spun to let loose a grenade before continuing his sprint back to the relative safety of our trench.

Kicking hard, I left the cover of the wall and began to run. Bullets cracked the air like angry lead hornets, kicked up splinters of frosty mud. A grenade exploded behind me, giving me a moment's respite from the withering Allied riposte. The mask made my breathing laboured, a harsh scraping sound in my ears. I struggled to pick out obstacles as the glass eyepieces steamed over. I was terrified that any second would see me pitch headlong into a crater or be cut down by enemy fire.

Ahead, I could discern the grey, blurred outline of a comrade running pell-mell, his legs rising and falling like pistons, his heavy boots thudding on the packed earth.

I hit the ground hard. I struggled to rise but my legs weren't responding. There was a pain high in my belly. My eyes stung fiercely. I put a hand to the respirator box at my chest. There was a small neat hole in the casing, and my coat felt wet and sticky. My head snapped back as scalding gas flowed into my mouth and up my nose. My eyes burned as though they roved in orbits of hot ashes. Blisters erupted on the inside of my cheeks. Wave upon wave of hellfire flooded my body as delicate veins burst and membranes shrivelled. My nose trickled a warm coppery fluid into my mouth. I wept blood as the linings of my eyelids swelled and ruptured.

I retched, and bright red blood cannoned off the inside of the mask.

"I had been less than twenty metres from home." I rapped the bullet on the table in a steady rhythm. "This slug hit me here, high in the belly. The surgeon said I was fortunate the respirator box had prevented it from penetrating deeper and causing any real harm."

Adolf smiled his appreciation of the gallows humour. It was, he agreed, a game of chance. "A bullet passed clean through my sleeve during an attack on enemy lines, missing my arm entirely although I don't know how. Your whole life hinges on moments such as those. Our fates were in the lap of the gods."

"You said you were caught in a gas attack, too."

He shrugged. "There is nothing to tell. My unit was resting alongside the artillery, just behind the frontline trenches. A mustard gas shell detonated nearby and we got out of there fast, but not fast enough. Many of us were blinded. We placed our hands on the shoulders of the man in front and were led to safety." He shrugged again and took another sip of his beer. He turned at a tug on his sleeve.

"Look at them," said the first card-player. Adolf followed his gaze to where some newcomers were standing at the bar. Something indefinable — small nuances, their modes of dress — singled them out. An area had cleared around them.

"What of them?" asked Adolf in a reasonable tone.

"Jews. They only call themselves German when it suits them, when they want our money and our homes. But while we fought and died for the Fatherland they came hobbling home in their droves. Stones in their shoes, most likely. Pah!" The round faced man spat on the floor, the spit rolling in sawdust. "Jew boys, I hate them all, every last one of them. The knife takes more than their foreskin, it cuts off their balls too."

Adolf Hitler's jaws clenched. He looked as though he was about to argue with the man but turned away instead. The card player mumbled something inaudible and then returned to his game.

"Do not be troubled," I said. "One becomes immune."

His penetrating gaze roved over my face, trying to work out if I was a full-, half- or quarter-blood Jew.

"I spent much time among your people when I lived in Vienna as a student. I have served with them and, despite that oaf's assertion that they are all cowards, they were good men. In Vienna, before the War, things began to turn ugly and I fear now it will spread. The rampant anti-Semitism in that city always struck me as wrong. Righteous anger at politicians misdirected onto innocent people. I am a patriot. I wear my uniform with pride. I would lay down my life for my countryman, but nationalistic pride does not mean having to hate everyone else."

I felt crusty blood cracking on my lips. "Your sentiments bring you much credit, but I fear that you are in a minority. And also I am thinking you didn't tell me the full story, Herr Hitler."

"What do you mean?"

"The gas attack."

"The what?"

"The gas attack. You didn't tell me everything." I raised the squashed round and rotated it between finger and thumb. He understood. I saw it in his eyes.

He stood and grabbed his greatcoat, putting it on with jerky, uncoordinated movements. His knee bumped the table, causing beer to slop over the rim of the stein.

"Don't forget this." I passed him his cap.

Adolf snatched it up and hurried through the crowd of drinkers, heedless of the dirty looks as he barged them aside. He tugged the door open and staggered outside, gasping as the cold air hit him.

I wiped condensation from the window to watch him. Visibility was poor in the mist that had descended after the snow petered out, but I saw him run across the road. He surprised me by dashing in the opposite direction of the army barracks. His feet skated on the icy cobbles.

I picked his rucksack from under the table and went after him. I gambled on him cutting back to the army barracks once he had regained a cool head.

He had not lied to me about the gas attack on his unit, but he had omitted the truth. When Adolf was temporarily blinded, he had not acted calmly or with bravery. He had been commended for the coveted Iron Cross twice — he was no coward — but unable to see, his eyes and skin burning with the effects of mustard gas, he was temporarily unmanned. He unslung his *Steyr-Mannlicher* rifle and let loose with two shots before someone still in possession of their faculties disarmed and knocked him to the ground. Adolf endured the pressing weight of comrades as they piled on him, held his thrashing limbs until his fear spent itself. He was then dragged unceremoniously to his feet, had his hands placed on the shoulders of a fellow soldier equally blighted and ordered to keep his fool head down.

I had not picked his brain for this information. Have I not already explained I am not a telepath? But it had been surprisingly easy to discover who had opened fire after the order to cease firing during a retreat had been given.

Blind and in considerable pain, that march to safety would have been the longest night of his life. Over the ensuing nights, as he lay in a hospital bed, he would have wept with the fear of being permanently blind. Was the silence behind his bandaged eyes punctuated by those two reports from his rifle, his moment of cowardice? The first shot he had heard ricochet off stone, but the second...now he knew the second had winged away into the green mist to strike a fellow infantryman named Hubert.

I found Adolf staggering in an alleyway. The network of fizzing gas lamps did not extend far enough to dispel the swimming mist-wraiths around us. He pressed a hand to his side and leaned against a soot-stained wall, his ragged breath swirling in droplets of moisture. His sodden moustache hung limp.

He stiffened at the sound of my footsteps and peered myopically through the shifting grey curtain of fog. I imagine I looked quite daunting: a silhouetted figure in a long trench coat emerging from the mist. I carried his rucksack. It contained his Iron Cross and several paintings.

Adolf froze. I strode closer, ice-skinned puddles crunching under my heels until we were separated only by an arm's length.

My chest heaved. I could feel wet blood on my lips and chin. I wiped it off on my sleeve.

"You left without your rucksack. I thought you would want it." My words sounded as though they had been dredged up from a deep well. I knew my time was near.

Adolf swallowed, his dry throat clicking. "Thank you."

I watched impassively as Adolf put his arms through the straps of the rucksack and cinched them tight.

"I owe you an apology," he said. "I don't know what came over me. Perhaps I could have a word with someone about a room for you, or...I don't know. If I had anything to give you, I would. But I don't."

I nearly smiled. "Oh, I wouldn't say that." I took Adolf's unresisting hand and pulled him closer. "You have your body."

Adolf recoiled, his head smacking into the wall in his haste to get away. My head darted forward like a striking cobra. I had done this before. Many times. I pushed my sticky tongue between his lips. It skated over gritted teeth. I kneed him hard in the testicles so that his mouth sagged and let me in.

I made the exchange.

He tried hard to lever me off, but he would be feeling weak now. He would feel his strength dissipate as though every particle of his body was rushing away at impossible speed. I was experiencing the same thing myself. It is like being flipped inside out, as if your insides are being drawn through your navel, your brain tearing from its anchors, the inner ears and optic nerves detaching. The sensation is horrifying, especially the first time, but it is, paradoxically, without pain. I released him, his wheezing breath echoing in my ears.

Adolf stumbled, bereft of sensation; deaf and blind. His knees crumpled, his world spun and the flagstones struck him a vicious blow to the left temple.

While he slept, I absorbed his memories. Sifted, correlated and assimilated them.

He would dream. They always do.

The sunlight is blinding, the sky a burning copper bowl over a scorched earth. The heat buckles the ground beneath the watcher's feet. It scorches his nostrils and threatens to hammer him to his knees.

A crowd jostles and shoves at his back. He snarls and shoves back with his elbows, determined to keep his place at the roadside. Shielding his eyes, he squints into the dazzle and watches the ragged procession snaking its way up the rough track. It shimmers in the heat haze. Centurions — tall and lean in their horsehair-plumed helmets, their polished breastplates dulled by dust — jeer and goad their charge as he struggles under the weight of the coarse, unplaned timber.

The watcher sees the bent figure draw closer, close enough for the streaks of dried blood on the victim's face to become apparent, the cruel imitation of a crown on his head and the gouges on his shoulders and legs made by the whip. He is smaller than the watcher expected, this self-proclaimed Son of God, and darker; his skin burned nut-brown by the sun.

The watcher wants to whimper, but instead hostile foreign sounds spill from his throat, the sarcasm unmistakable. He extends a finger and jabs the air. The bent man pauses under his burden and establishes eye contact. And though he speaks quietly, and from a distance, every strange-sounding syllable rings like a bell.

The watcher falls to his knees as if physically struck, the superheated air drawing the moisture out of his lungs

Poor Adolf. I could see his chest burned with every breath as though he drew in flames, a fire not even the freezing fog could quell.

"Open your eyes, Herr Hitler. Come on."

He tried to move, but it took so much effort...it was easier to just let oneself liquefy and bleed into the cracks between the flagstones.

"Don't sham me, I know you are awake."

He gingerly opened one eye and gazed unfocused at my feet.

"That's better." My voice would be tauntingly familiar . I strode away, keeping my back to him. I wore his greatcoat and rucksack.

"*Thieving bastard!*" he whispered, and spat a string of pink and black mucus that roped his chin to the floor.

I executed a smart about-turn. The tip of the cigarette I smoked glowed in the darkness, illuminating my bushy moustache.

Adolf screwed shut his eyes, but not before I saw the panic in them.

"What did you see in the dream?" I asked. "Tell me."

Adolf's eyes swivelled to face me and looked with horror into his own face, for I wore more than just his clothes.

"Ach. You know who I am? What I am?"

Adolf was silent. His mother would have told him the legend of the Wandering Jew.

I squatted to look my victim squarely in the eye. "The Roman soldiers took Christ, they stripped and whipped him, humiliated him, were about to crucify him...Back then, I was simply Ahasue'rus the cobbler. I got caught up in the heat of the moment and I shouted, 'Faster, Jesus, faster!' I still don't understand why I did that; it was so out of character for me. The Son of God said he forgave me, but told me I would roam the earth until he comes among us again.

"I never saw him nailed up. A singular moment in human history, but I had retired to my workshop feeling curiously sick and exhausted. While they were nailing the Nazarene to a cross I was busy cutting leather to repair sandals."

Sparks bounced brightly off the cobbles as I discarded the end of Adolf's last cigarette. "So, then, I had become an eternal. But flesh ages, corrupts and decays. And it can be damaged." I gave him a pointed look. "However, I possess an instinct: I always know when I need to leave a shell and seek out a new one, like a hermit crab finding a new home. For without a shell, I would just be a lost soul, a blind and mewling, intangible thing cast upon the wind.

"I spent the first few centuries making myself a very rich man, bequeathing wealth from shell to shell. Then one day I gave it all to the Church. But God obviously recognised a bribe when He saw one and I remained here on Earth. I spent the next few lives in debauchery thinking, Why bother?

"I became a sheep. Some men become wolves, and others shepherds, but most are content to be sheep."

I squatted on my haunches beside the mortally wounded carcass of Hubert Schmitt, a shell of less than seven years. I felt no sentimental attachment to it.

"This country will rise like a phoenix from the ashes, and I shall be at its head. A wolf in the guise of a shepherd. There will be no weak leaders procrastinating, just a select cabinet of men who will crush all before them with an iron fist. I have observed people for two millennia, I know how to manipulate them; tell them what it is they want and then promise it to them. Give them words like bones to dogs. Words are power.

"You've seen all these disaffected young men, standing around in small knots on street corners. Revolution is in the air. They are waiting for someone to come along and guide them." I pinned a medal to my chest and patted it significantly. "A war hero, perhaps."

He opened his mouth to speak. Nothing came out. I squatted closer. He lifted a hand and beckoned weakly.

I knelt and put an ear to his lips. "It's no use," I said, "I cannot hear what you are saying."

His left arm shot out and clasped me behind the head. He dug his fingers into my neck and gripped tightly. I screeched in pain and surprise as Adolf brought our faces together in a passionate embrace, mouths mashing, tongues entwining. Then he fell back, panting, dark blood bubbling on his lips. His head struck the icy ground.

He must have known then that it was all over. Fingers of ice would be entering his belly; that welcome, numbing coldness that flowers in the chest.

Adolf's amber eyes stared into the milky opaqueness overhead, as though waiting for the enduring chill to overtake him.

I stood sharply and raised a foot to plant a kick, then lowered it and laughed. "My God, but you are a plucky fighter, Herr Hitler. No one has ever tried that before."

I recovered my composure, for he had shaken me.

"I was at a church service, and in the pulpit was a real fire and brimstone preacher as they say in that part of the world. He told his congregation that when they have children, that they were giving God a lever, a hostage, that no matter how much love and devotion they poured into that child its fate was in the hands of One higher. I saw it all then: you threaten someone through their children and you have a terrible power over their heart and soul. And what do I see all around me? Despised and feared wherever they settle? The Jews. The Children of God. Doomed as I to be strangers and migrants and outcasts, forever misplaced. *They* will be my hostages."

"You're mad," Adolf whispered.

"You think so? Maybe I am. But if so, the world is an asylum. I won't be short of volunteers to my cause."

"Burn in hell." Adolf's final breath rattled in his chest.

I nudged the corpse enviously, then looped the rucksack over one shoulder and began to trek back to the *gasthaus*. I knew I would find at least a handful of men there who would listen to my politics.

sandcrawlers

Robert Hood

The person responsible, the murderer, has his life ahead of him.
How he faces this life is something I cannot answer.
But he will always be hunted and haunted.

Mrs Elizabeth Schmidt,
Sydney Morning Herald, 16 January 1965

*

"I worked for him, you know." He leaned his balding head toward me and his prominent upper lip twisted at one side. "Askin. Back in the sixties."

"Yeah? Big deal, eh?"

"For a while there I was his main man."

The disco music was too loud, the beer too expensive, and this particular corpse stank of chain-smoking, month-old sweat and urine. He'd limped over and plopped himself next to me out of the blue, but I didn't want to move because where I was gave me a good view of Arnold Karroll, who was drinking his third gin and tonic at a table near the jukebox. His wife thought he was having an affair with "some tart" and wanted to know who it was. I hoped he was just drinking. Better for her and easier for me.

The bloke who'd sat at my table wanted to talk and ignored me when I told him to piss off. He pointed at a framed photograph hanging on the wall behind us. Despite myself I looked. It showed a tall, badly dressed dude — one-time proprietor of this place — shaking hands in a posed manner with the long-gone State Premier. There was a horse in the background.

An unclear pen scrawl read: "Best wishes to Tom, who could run a good race. Bob."

"Made some decent money back then," he went on. I sipped unenthusiastically at the beer, wishing I didn't have to involve myself in this. Surely I had better things to do. But Arnold Karroll's wife Lillian was an old friend who'd asked a favour — and offered a large fee for me to oblige her.

My unwelcome companion shifted on his bar-stool, fingers tapping out a rhythm on the table's Formica top. "S'pose you were into all that hippy stuff, eh? Spaced-out like the rest of them?"

I looked at him but said nothing. He took this as confirmation. He was, I guessed, considerably older than me; the bags under his eyes and the sallow grubbiness of his skin suggested he hadn't taken much care of himself over the years.

"While that lot was sniffin' doss sticks and sproutin' all that shit about peace and love, I had a good time with rake-off workin' for good ol" Bob on the rackets, collectin'. That's how he got in, you know? Sucked the cocks of the SP bookies. They were scared shitless the TAB'd be the end of 'em."

"Look, mate, I'm not much interested in political history. I'm busy."

He sneered. "Busy? Doin' what? Perving on that guy over there?" He took a big swig of his beer. "Why don't ya just make him an offer? He fucks cheap."

I stared at him.

"Sure," he said, "Amateur meat. Comes around here all the time."

Poor Lillian. Even news of some gay affair would've been hard enough on her; but Arnie was working the game. How would she handle that?

"Prefer pussy, meself," the drunk added. "Most of the time. Younger the better." Something about the tone he'd adopted made me glance into his eyes. They were looking past me, at Arnie, and for a moment a sense of recognition came over me, like a chill draught. I couldn't quite define it.

"Back then," he said, talking more to himself than to me, "I took the birds, any way I wanted. Just took 'em."

"That right?"

He grinned. A sort of self-satisfaction that was deep and cruel shimmered over his lips. I felt recognition again, this time more defined. "I was bad, back then," he said, pleased to be able to say so.

"Not anymore?"

He glanced across the bar as though he thought someone might be watching him. He smelt like misery. "Accident...put me outta the real game." He thumped against his leg. "Arsehole kid's fault. Then I got done by the cops in '78. Intimidation and robbery. Once you've been inside, they're on ya back, all the time." He grinned, mischievous. It looked silly on a face so wasted by failure. "Still a bit grubby," he whispered, "But I stay away from that stuff. The good stuff. Too old maybe."

"Or too scared."

His eyes bored into mine, indignant but knowing the truth of it. I saw the truth as well, cold and empty like a back street at three in the morning. It was a truth I'd lived with for nearly two decades.

January 1965. I was fifteen and looking greedily toward my sixteen birthday. Sixteen was a sort of landmark, I thought. A frontier.

It was a particularly hot summer. Fires in the National Park made sunset spectacular, if you were interested in sunsets. I wasn't. Life was girls, money and getting my own way. That's all.

Early Sunday afternoon, 10th January, and I guessed what my father was up to. Fussing about with his shoes and his summer coat, which he wore whenever he went out, no matter how hot it was. Counting and re-counting his money. Shoving it all out of sight whenever Mum wandered past, and trying to pretend he was reading the *Sun-Herald*.

"Cup of tea, Patrick?" Mum said at last.

"What?" he started. "Tea? No, no."

"Beer then?"

"No."

Then, without a pause, she said, "I wish you wouldn't, Patrick Crowe. It's not safe."

He dismissed her with a wave of his hand, dropping the pretence that he wasn't going anywhere. "The cops don't care."

"There was a raid the other day out at Lane Cove. I read about it in the paper. Don't tell me they don't care!"

"They get paid off, for Christ's sake. The blokes that run it pay dummies to get arrested. Never the players."

"It's wicked. What sort of example is this for Michael?"

"It's life, Pam, that's all."

He left at about two, walking down the street with his light coat and his hat and a look of predatory innocence on his face. I snuck out the back and followed him, catching up once we were out of sight of the house. "You can't come, boy," he said as I trotted up to him. He scratched at his balding head. "Won't be home till late."

"I want to go."

"Forget it. It's business."

"It's two-up," I said. "Don't bullshit me!"

He smacked me across the face. "Watch your mouth!"

"Why can't I go?"

"You're too young."

"I'm nearly sixteen."

"Isn't there something real grown-up you should be doing then?" he snorted.

He watched me head off home around the corner, then ducked away quickly; but I wasn't so easily put off. This was a matter of pride. "Bugger you!" I muttered at him, though he couldn't see or hear me, and ran to Kirrawee station in time to meet the train he'd catch at Gymea. He didn't notice me, but I watched him board the last carriage, as he always did.

When we got to Cronulla station, he got off and so did I. The wind was up, though the afternoon was still pretty warm, and it pushed across our path as Patrick walked northwards. It was quite a hike. Tailing him was easy, hinting of the endless surveillance jobs I'd take on in later years, most of which were much less exciting because by then the novelty had worn off. By the time we got to the edge of the reserve behind Wanda Sands, beyond the high school, I was feeling pretty cocky. He hadn't noticed he was being followed.

The two-up game was on a patch of compacted ground near a sandpit, along a winding path off Captain Cook Drive. Every now and then a car would come along the rough track and I'd have to jump off into the low miserable-looking scrub until it had passed. I lost sight of Patrick, but figured it didn't matter because the path would lead me right.

A big bloke in dark glasses appeared suddenly. He had a heavy tubular torch on his belt, hanging there like a bludgeon. That's probably what he used it for too. I wondered if he had a gun. His arms were crossed and his mouth was hardened. "What do you want?" he growled.

"A bit of the action," I replied cockily.

"Yeah?" His tight lips took a shot at grinning, though none of the rest of his face shifted at all. "The arcade's that way." He pointed back over my shoulder.

"The two-up, dick-brain."

I thought I was being tough. The big bloke's raised hand jerked down and forward and collected me backhand across my right temple. I fell over. Not so tough after all — just stupid.

"Sorry," he said, "Slipped. There's no two-up here, mate. You must be mistaking us for some bunch of crooks."

I picked myself up off the ground, protesting, trying to come up with a reason why he should let me past. "Get lost!" he snarled. His tone was so coldly threatening, I began to back off, wondering if I could work my way around him through the scrub. "Me and my mates'll be checking things out on and off," he said suddenly. "If we catch you in there, they'll be playing two-up with your balls!" He sounded like he meant it.

I moved backwards away from him until he was half-obscured behind the bushes. He was still watching me stonily. I gave him the finger, turned and ran head-on into an FJ Holden that was just bumping its way along the track. Its hood was suddenly there, shadow on the windscreen making the driver invisible — I leapt aside, tripping and rolling into spiky brown grass. The car stopped.

It was being driven by a young bloke, maybe twenty, maybe older. He had one of those gaunt faces that made it hard to tell. He stuck his head, scruffy blond hair and thick, pouting lips out the driver's window. "What the hell you doin', mate?" he said.

I looked up sourly from the scrub. "Getting a tan, what's it look like?"

"Wouldn't let you into the game, eh?"

"I got money," I said.

"Too young."

"Yeah? Well, bugger you!"

He was grinning as I dragged myself up. "Get in!" he said suddenly. I stared at him. "Damn it! Get in the bloody car!" It took me a moment to react, then I ducked around the other side and slipped in next to him. The interior smelt strange, as though chemicals had been spilt on the seat. I couldn't place what kind. "What's your name?" he said, grinding the gears.

"Mike," I answered. "Yours?"

He smiled. There was a cruel cynicism on his lips. "You can call me Dean."

"Like James Dean?"

"Yeah," he grinned, "Like James Dean."

The guard let us past, giving Dean a slight nod of recognition and me a wry smile. "They know you?"

He said nothing.

The game was already underway. About thirty blokes were crowded around a sort of clearing, yelling and swearing and jostling each other. There was an old shed to one side, mostly covered in bush and very temporary looking, with cars parked near it. Bits and pieces of rusting equipment were scattered here and there. I saw my old man and slumped down in the seat. Dean sneered. "Not getting spineless on me, are you?"

"I want to watch him," I muttered.

He stopped the car alongside some others. "Watch then. I got business to take care of."

Dean slipped out of the Holden and strode across to a group of men over in front of the shed — talking among themselves, gazing at the two-up occasionally, drinking from thin, dark bottles. One of them gave him something, something apart from a beer. It was a thick parcel; he held it up to his nose as though to savour its aroma, grinned and slapped the man on the back.

Dean was wiry and moved in a way that was sort of nervous. I was sure he wasn't nervous though; it was just his manner. I became increasingly convinced of this as the afternoon wore on and turned into night. He was sharp and in command of the situation, but pretty much wound up. I never saw him really relax. He lost his temper easily — at one point knocking the front teeth out of some bloke's mouth because the bloke accidentally shoved him. "Don't touch me, you faggot!" Dean roared, swinging his fist.

People chatted to him politely, though I could tell they didn't like it. But he was bagman for some big shot who had a stake in the game and they had to put up with him. Once he referred to his boss as "Robin Hood". "Hates gettin' called that," he said, laughing.

"Called what?"

"Robin Hood, you dick." Then he added, "Wants to be called *Robert*."

"What's his real name then?" I asked, sipping at a beer he'd given me, not caring, just making conversation.

"None of your bloody business!" He shot me a look that froze my guts.

By the time twilight was thickening, the number of players had thinned out, though a group of them kept going, tossing like their life depended on how the coins fell. Maybe it did. Dean told me something like £10,000 had swapped hands already that arvo — but the really big numbers would come later, he reckoned, around seven. A couple of lawyers would turn up then, he said, and a well-known second-hand car dealer from over Parramatta way. Sure enough, though cars left now and then, and blokes would wander off down the track and disappear along the road in the direction of Cronulla, other cars started arriving and soon the numbers picked up again. When it got dark, the whole lot of them went into the shed, where there were fans in the roof, lights and ringside seating.

"You ever play?" I asked Dean.

"You kidding," he said. "Think I'm a fool?"

Patrick had left long before this, still unaware that I'd been there with him. He was bewitched by the gambling, as he was by drinking, and I think he lost the lot — his money into the pockets of half a dozen other blokes, the contents of his stomach onto the sand. "Your old man's a pisspot, eh?" Dean had said, watching him from a distance, as he heaved and dribbled. "You take after him?"

"Sure," I'd replied, gesturing for another beer.

We drank a hell of a lot and why Dean kept giving it to me without making me pay I didn't know and I didn't choose to think about it either. I drank and watched the comings and goings, checking out an occasional punch-up when alcohol and loss turned some bloke sour, and sat in the dark talking to Dean, who in fact didn't talk much, but when he did was keen to gossip. "See him?" he said, indicating a suave-looking bloke in a nice suit, who had turned up late, played a few rounds and then spent the rest of the time talking to another bloke in a suit. Dean told me his name. It was sort of colourful. "You heard of him?"

"Sure," I said, not really clear about where I'd come across it. Probably in a newspaper. I thought he was some kind of crook — now, of course, I've been aware of his nefarious activities for decades.

"He's great," Dean whispered, with a husky envy. "Gets away with friggin' *everything*. I heard he throws these wild parties up his place at Palm Beach that'd make ya bloody dick drop off with the excitement. Naked women everywhere. Takes pictures while they fondle themselves. Whips 'em. That kind of shit. Wish he'd invite me over some time."

We fetched more beer and then a couple of bottles of scotch from a van that seemed to be the main source of supply, and drank ourselves silly, while the game went on inside and the night got fuzzier. By midnight I could hardly stand and Dean was trying to sing "you're sixteen, you're beautiful and you're mine" with obscene lyrics that never managed to make much sense. Finally I passed out in a sandy hollow next to a bush I was pissing on.

Sunlight was like needles being stuck in my eyeballs when I woke up next day. My head was throbbing, my throat was dry and felt like I was breathing in sand, and just about every part of me ached, from having lain across knots of grass all night, I guessed. I pushed myself up, squinting and groaning, then gave away the attempt because I couldn't get my balance and just fell sideways into the shade of a bush. Damn sun. Damn wind. Somewhere in the distance I could hear surf. Or maybe it was just the ringing in my ears.

I drifted out of consciousness and back again and this time, an angular face was leering down at me.

"God," I moaned, "What's the time?"

"About three."

"In the afternoon?"

"You slept in, baby." Dean squatted next to me. He was wearing the same cream-coloured slacks he'd had on last night, but now he was stripped to the waist. His hair was matted and damp, as though he'd been swimming, and he'd smeared his nose with white sun-cream. "Maybe you better pull ya daks up, eh?" He reached out and grabbed my dick and that was when I suddenly realised one of the reasons I'd had trouble getting up

171

earlier was that my trousers were around my ankles. His fingers squeezed.

"Hey, let go!" I yelled, shock driving away the pain in my head. "What're you doing?"

He grinned, squeezing harder. "You were enjoyin' this last night."

I pushed at him. "Frig off! What are you? Some sort of queer?"

Suddenly there was a knife in his hand — a half-inch, long-bladed one that had appeared from nowhere; the point pressed in under my jaw, piercing the skin. I pulled my head back, but he kept up the pressure and I felt blood running down my neck. He was still squeezing. "Be nice," he said, "or I'll rip it off and shove it down ya throat."

He grinned at the look of pain and horror that was skidding over my face; then he relaxed his grip and began stroking me instead. "Nice little John Thomas you've got there, Mikey." He kept my head back, the knife cutting into my skin, so I couldn't see what he was up to. I cringed in shock when I felt his tongue on my glans.

"Christ almighty!" I choked.

"More than a mouthful now, eh?" he said, and his thick lips went right around my dick, surrounding it with warm breath and moisture. In that position keeping the knife against my throat was difficult; I felt the pressure ease. As it did, I pulled back, grabbed his knife-hand and pushed him away, screaming at him. Bush tangled me up and I swore again. Suddenly his knife was pressed against my stomach. "Keep movin' around so much..." he whispered, "...and I might slip."

"Shit, Dean!" I said, and he laughed.

"That dick of yours ever been in anything warm, Mike? Other than your hand, that is?"

"Get stuffed!"

"Feisty little bastard, aren't you?"

Suddenly the blade disappeared. "Pull ya pants up," he said, moving back. "I got something better than my mouth to put ya dick in."

"Get away from me!"

"While you were sleeping like a baby, I went into Cronulla for some breakfast." He reached back. "Here." He tossed me a Wagon Wheel and a bag of Smiths Crisps.

I knocked them aside and squirmed about, trying to cover myself up. "I don't want anything from you, you friggin' pervert."

"Saw this bird I rather fancy," he said, smirking. Then he added, "She's got a friend."

I didn't care; all I wanted to do was get away from him. I stood and began to move backwards across the sand dunes. He watched me for a moment, his dark eyes cold and cruel. "Come on, Mike..." he said. "It was just a joke."

"Some joke!"

"I'll give you fifty quid if you stay! Told the chick you'd be here."

"Forget it! You're a goddamn lunatic."

He shrugged. "Lunatics can be fun," he said, but didn't come after me.

I was already on the platform of Cronulla station when I realised my wallet wasn't in my pocket. It was a new leather one, not full of money, but full of the only money I had — a couple of pounds. My initials were etched on it and everything. Halfway back to the reserve, I thought to wonder whether Dean had taken it. I wasn't at all sure I'd want to fight him about it.

Wind was blowing sand everywhere. My head had started aching again. It was what day? I tried to think. Oh, yeah. Monday. The beach was sparsely populated, because the weather had turned the surf choppy and the guards had closed it. All I wanted to do was go home — I felt pretty sick. But I made it along the track and headed out over the sandhills, searching for anything familiar, so I could find the spot where I'd spent the night. I wished I hadn't thrown away the Wagon Wheel. I was hungry.

Wanda was a bleak and miserable landscape that afternoon, wide and windswept — like a desert, if it hadn't been for the ocean surging like a grey mist on the far side of the hills. I pushed closer to the edge of the scrub, squinting against the sun and the wind, not finding what I was looking for, though there was plenty of other litter — scraps of newspaper, crushed wrappers, cigarette stubs, broken bottles, driftwood. Then, as I crested a sandhill covered in tea-trees, I saw some figures in the distance, off to my left. They were moving along the beach, right up from the water's edge. There were three of them. I couldn't make out details, but I just knew it was Dean and the two girls he reckoned he was going to meet.

I ducked back and flattened myself on the hidden side of the dune. Peering over the top, I watched them approach and then cut across in front of me, perhaps fifty feet away. They were nice-looking girls, it seemed, at least from that distance. I guessed they were about fifteen or sixteen, both medium height — shorter than Dean — and slim. Both had shoulder-length hair, tossed madly at the moment by the wind, framing childish, smiling faces. They might have been sisters, except one was dark and the other fair. The fair one was wearing a blue and white jumper and white shorts. The dark one was in a swimsuit, with a green shirt over it. Fair was talking animatedly, though Dean wasn't listening. The girls looked concerned. Dark kept looking back, like she'd forgotten something. I heard her say, "...thought I saw Wolfgang a while ago. Maybe we should go back. The kids..."

"Just a bit further," Dean said, and used his weight to pull them on.

These girls weren't tarts. I wondered what story Dean had used to get them to come with him — or what they'd do when they got to wherever they were going and it became clear what he wanted. Curiosity got the better of me. I slithered along the slope and followed just out of sight. The wind would cover the sounds of my movement.

"I'm going back," said one of the girls suddenly. The voice seemed close. I stopped and squirmed along the side of a rise covered in flailing grass tufts. The trio was about twenty yards away, down in a hollow.

"We should keep looking," said Dean. "I tell you I saw the kid around here someplace."

"Peter's ten," the fair one added, "They'll be all right. We told them to wait for us."

"Maybe we should check he hasn't come back by himself." Marianne glanced toward the top of the sandhill.

"What's wrong?" said Dean, with mock indignity. "Think I'm lying, do you?"

Dark ignored him. "We ought to go back, Chrissie. If he's still missing, we can get help."

Dean's face went dark and intense. I tensed along with him, but for different reasons, afraid.

"Okay," he said, "Okay. Here's the deal. I want Christine to stay. You, too, if you want. But Chrissie stays..."

Christine frowned at him. "What do you think...?"

He gestured to shut her up. "It'd be a shame to waste all this isolation."

Marianne backed further, dragging her friend. "You stay away from us. We'll call the police if you touch us."

"Touch you?" Dean laughed, a low, mirthless groan. Then, suddenly, before the girls could react, his right fist swung out and cracked into Marianne's face. She shrieked, stumbling to her knees. "I'll do more than touch you!"

In that moment of shock, Christine took a step away from him. She whimpered. Marianne was clutching at her face. Dean reached down, grabbed her shirt and tore it off her. She tried to get away from him, but he hit her again and ripped the top of her swimsuit down over her breast. She was screaming hysterically. He stood back, then kicked her in the stomach.

I'd leapt up by then and was stumbling down the sandhill, yelling for Dean to stop. This distracted him; he looked up and grinned. "I was wonderin' where you'd got to," he said.

"Leave them alone!" I skidded to a halt in front of him, getting between him and Marianne. Christine was looking at us in dazed indecision, torn between helping her friend and running. "What the hell do you think you're doing, Dean?"

"Hey," said Dean jovially, "I'm big-time, man. Boss'll be king in May. I can do what I want." With that he pulled his knife out of the sheath at his side and lunged at me. I fell backward and the blade tip scored lightly across my T-shirt, cutting it and drawing blood in a line down my chest. I struck at him, missed and lost my balance. The knife came at me; I kicked and suddenly felt intense pain in my right thigh. Blood splashed on the sand and I cried out. "Stay outta this!" Dean yelled, and kicked me hard in the face. I fell away, the wind turning black around me, sand spinning into sucking maelstroms of fractured light. Pain exploded in my head.

I wanted to yell "Run!" to Christine and maybe I did. I couldn't tell and can't remember. I tried to push myself up and backwards. Where was Dean? My eyes had gone funny — tight and out of focus. I crawled in the sand.

Someone screamed. It was a terrible cry, sizzling with pain and horror. I forced my eyes to focus and thought I saw Dean and Christine about twenty feet away, dancing. No, not dancing. His knife was gouging into her back for the second time, while he held her shoulder and pulled. She was jerking and shrieking; red spurts of blood got caught on the wind and spun out over the sand. Dean let her body drop; she was too weakened by shock and her wounds to get away, but she wasn't unconscious either. She was still screaming. Dean moved slightly to one side, picked up a piece of pipe or something that was lying there and went back toward her. I tried to get up, but my legs folded. Dean smashed the pipe down on the back of Christine's head and the screaming stopped.

The rest is a blur, though my mind played over it again and again for half a decade, and even now, more than twenty years on, it'll come back in dreams when I'm depressed or anxious. I've sorted the fractured impressions, the memories blurred by my own injuries and hysteria, until they fit into a sort of story — a fiction to give it form so it can be coped with; but I'm not confident of the truth. Maybe I don't want to be confident of the truth. It's not a secret of identity — I knew who the murderer was. But it is a secret. One that haunts me, sometimes making me violent, sometimes drawing out acts of irrational charity.

Dean dragged the bloody but docile body of Christine back across the sand. Sunlight caught on a chain bracelet she wore on her wrist, sparking like a warning. Marianne was moving, whimpering and moving, though I don't think there was much consciousness there. He dumped the corpse next to her, ignoring me, leaned and drew a hard stroke of the knife across her throat. Blood. Cries. She was still moving, even then, so he stabbed the blade into her chest. There was more blood, lots of it.

Both must have been dead, but it didn't stop him. He beat at them, first one, then the other, with his fists, muttering something, swearing. I couldn't hear. I was barely conscious. Perhaps I wasn't conscious at all. I don't know. I must have been crawling away, vaguely aware that he'd kill me too, when he was finished with the girls. It wasn't something I thought about, as such. I wasn't capable of thought. But my body knew and it wanted to get away. It crawled through the sand, trying to escape from the nightmare.

Yet all the time part of my mind must have been noting what Dean was up to, because images of it come, like ghouls from the darkness, eating at me in the night. I feel the tearing of their teeth, cringe in pain. Dean stripping the girls. Baring himself. Getting down on his knees in the sand. Crawling. Toward the corpses — one, then the other. Circling. Approaching. Making strange mewling noises. Lying over them. Crawling on them. Up, down on their dead flesh. Up, down. Paroxysms. Cries. Fondling them. Up, down. Crawling. Crawling.

...While I crawled through the sand away from him. How I managed it, I don't know. Perhaps the intensity of his homicidal passion was so great he simply forgot about me. Until it was too late. Maybe forever. Perhaps he remembered but figured there was nothing I could do. I didn't know who he was. I didn't know how to find him. Perhaps I simply became part of his memory of an orgy of violence. A confederate. Perhaps in his mind I was always, or never, with him.

There was a blank time when I knew nothing. I must have wandered through the scrub, maybe for hours. Made my way home. Eventually. No one noticed me, or if they did, they never told the police about it, because despite the extensive search that followed discovery of the murders, despite the obsessive soliciting of witnesses, no descriptions of anyone like me, tentative or otherwise, ever appeared in the papers. I don't remember what story I told Mum and Patrick. Certainly it didn't involve either Cronulla or Wanda Sands. Wherever I'd been, nothing had happened there, nothing terrible. My T-shirt was torn, I had a nasty knife cut across my chest and my thigh was bleeding — but there was a normal explanation, a fight between friends, dares and rough sport. An accident. I don't know what I said, but whatever it was they believed it — or pretended to. Perhaps they thought I was the Wanda Beach killer. Perhaps I was. Nothing was clear for a while. My mind was in torment. I stayed out of their way and tried to act normally.

I began reading the newspapers. The mutilated bodies of Marianne Schmidt and Christine Sharrock were found by someone called Peter Smith on the Tuesday, buried in shallow graves in the sand. The community was outraged. Cops swarmed over the beach. They searched it for clues, finding nothing. Not the knife. Not the pipe. Not even my wallet. It must have been lost too far from the crime scene, in the scrub rather than on the beach. Wouldn't have mattered much if they did find it. There were initials on it — mine — but what sort of a lead was that? Unless they already knew about me, they'd never put a name to them. There was nothing to help in the wallet either. Two pounds. Some coins. A picture of Hayley Mills, who I'd fancied for a while. No pictures of me or my family. No driver's licence. No credit cards. That was in the days before every kid over twelve had the magic plastic of capitalist wish-fulfilment in his pocket. So, nothing to connect with me.

The days go by. Bushfires rip through the bushland surrounding Sydney. BOY SAW YOUTH WALK INTO SANDHILLS WITH SCHOOLGIRLS. A man who worked on the railways shot during an attempted holdup. DEATH CAME ON A DIRTY BEACH. DUNES TO BE SIFTED IN MURDER CLUE HUNT. APPEAL BY POLICE. Dawn Fraser declared "Australian of the Year". Finally CLUES HUNT ABANDONED AT MURDER BEACH. The leader of the Opposition, Mr Robert Askin, says that the police force must be strengthened to prevent such outrages in future...But the state Opposition was attempting to "gain political capital at any price" in its criticism of the strength of the New South Wales Police Force, the Premier Mr Renshaw, said yesterday. POLICE SEEK VITAL CLUE FROM EIGHT ON WANDA BEACH. The election date still isn't set. APPEAL TO PUBLIC BY POLICE. Fourteen Liberals fight it out in a party pre-selection for Vaucluse. Timothy Evans, hanged in London in 1950, is posthumously pardoned. Dawn Fraser performs a schoolgirl prank with a flag. Jeanette McDonald dies, of a heart attack, 57. A man in Amsterdam drills a hole in his skull "To achieve the effect of smoking marihuana cigarettes"...I experience reality much more intensely, he says. The Stones play in Sydney. Winston Churchill is sick.

By 25 January Churchill was dead and the Wanda Beach murders had disappeared from the papers. No clues. No one in custody. Nothing.

Nightmares plagued my sleep. And what of Dean? Maybe I wanted to find him. Maybe I didn't. I don't know. I took to wandering along the beach, once the cops had stopped keeping an eye on the place. I skirted around the murder scene itself, looking at it through sun and the blustery autumn weather, feeling my mortality and seeing the violence again and again. Anger welled in me. I thrashed at the sand, tore at the bushes. I cursed my parents, broke things, stole a car and went for a joy ride. I beat up a bloke down the street because he looked at me in a way I didn't like. I got drunk whenever I could.

By late April the State election had usurped the headlines. "HOW TO VOTE LIBERAL AND GET THINGS RIGHT. WITH ASKIN YOU'LL GET ACTION". My father went out to vote on 1 May. He reckoned Askin was "a good bloke". "Likes a bit of a flutter," he said. He should have been voting Labor; that's where his roots were. But the ALP was moribund and mistrusted by the Church. That night the count was indecisive. Renshaw's government was in trouble and, though it would take a while before the final count was in, once it was done Askin would be premier, opening the gate on an era of organised crime such as Australia hadn't known before.

"I voted for him," said Patrick proudly. "He's going to be premier."

"Long live King Robin!" snarled my uncle George, who was a Labor voter and, at that moment, slightly drunk.

"Robin?"

"Sure," said George. "That's his given name. But he doesn't like it. Prefers Robert. A damn snob."

Suddenly memory tossed up its flotsam and I knew.

"Hates gettin' called that," Dean said, laughing.

"Called what?"

"Robin Hood, you dick...Wants to be called Robert."

Dean was a bagman for someone with the identical name problem. A gambler.

"What the hell do you think you're doing, Dean?"

"I'm big-time, man. Boss'll be king in May."

When I could, I visited State parliament, sometimes sitting in the public gallery, sometimes hanging around outside in Macquarie Street. I was there when Askin entered the House as

Premier, and I watched the MPs with their grey and brown suits and their folders and briefcases, scanned the faces of passers-by, took mental snapshots of assistants and lackeys and visitors. There was no sign of Dean, not during those scattered days. And why, I asked myself, should I expect to see a thug like him in that high place of rule?

At home, in bed, darkness roared in my ears; I saw parting flesh, blood, sun sparking off a bracelet, twitching fingers; heard screams; felt the knife in my back. Crawling in the sand. Always crawling.

"What's the matter with you, boy?" asked Patrick. "You on drugs?"

My investigation, such that it was, ended on a cloudy day in July as I walked away from the parliamentary gates toward St James' station, intending to catch the train home. I glanced across at the statue of a dribbling pig in front of Sydney Hospital, and from the corner of my eye I spotted him. Dean. He was coming along in the opposite direction, dressed in dark slacks and a sports coat. His hair was shorter, but still strawy. His lips were pouting, as though he was thinking about some slight done to him. He was carrying a briefcase. I didn't move.

"Do I know you?" he said.

In his eyes I suddenly saw recognition and my own death. Up until that moment I'd been nobody, forgotten. He hadn't known who I was and hadn't bothered finding out because I was just some arsehole kid, some ghost of a memory of that day, made insignificant by the razor-sharpness of the passion and the bloodletting.

"Hey," he said, reaching toward me, "Mike, wasn't it? You come to dance?"

I stepped back and he grabbed at me, pulling at my shirt. I struck his hand, making him let go with a yelp, and took off down the street, dodging a few pedestrians while trying to glance back to see what he was doing. He hesitated for a moment, then came after me.

I've participated in my fair share of chases, shoot-outs and confrontations, and most of them are just a blurred memory of violence; but that one remains crystal clear in every detail. Padding down Macquarie Street toward the park, fear like nausea in my chest, the air hot and oppressive on my face; nearly running into a woman with flaming red hair, who stumbled out of my way, cursing; men in suits and a group of kids, one of whom tried to trip me; a bus roaring past unexpectedly, against the curb, so that I was almost pulled under the wheels by its gravity. I glanced back and realised I'd gained distance but that I'd just lost it again by looking. Stumbled against someone — I remember a blue jumper — and ran on as Dean approached. He yelled, but I couldn't hear words, only the threat in his voice.

Pedestrian lights changed to DON'T WALK ahead and I sprinted across the road in front of the just-moving cars. The traffic thickened up behind me. If it stopped Dean at all, it didn't do so for long; there was a screech of brakes, horns blasting, and then I could hear the thumping of his feet on the concrete path. I glanced ahead: the Archibald Fountain, its waters glistening as the sun broke from behind a cloud, trees and open grass, the footpath, the road, cars, St Mary's, more cars...

Faced with a multitude of choices, I found myself leaping downstairs toward the underground, into shadow, into obscurity. Even as I turned toward the moving footway that led to the Domain carpark, I knew it was a mistake, a narrowing of options and a retreat from the busyness above-ground that might have at least hindered Dean from acting. Stupid, I thought, really stupid. But there was no time for regret. I fled down the narrow rubberised path, gaining speed from its movement, pushed past an old bloke and stumbled, clutching at the rail. Tripped against an angle, fell. "You okay, son?" the man asked. I didn't waste breath on an answer, but was up again, running as hard as I could. I nearly lost it at the bottom, where the moving footpath came to an end; momentum made me stumble, falling headlong. But I regained my balance and ran on, ducking out of my pursuer's line of sight as soon as possible by turning through a gap in the wall.

A low concrete roof and rows of cars seemed to close up around me, despite the vastness of the area. I hid behind a Vanguard and peered across the black curve of its hood, looking toward the gap through which Dean would have to come if he chose the right way. I was sure he wouldn't have seen which way I took. A minute went by, then another. Dean hadn't appeared. I waited while my breath echoed through the car park and tried desperately to calm myself, to limit the sound. Nobody came. After a few minutes more, I edged away from the Vanguard, keeping low, flitting from car to pillar in a zigzag motion toward the exit ramp which led down the outside of the building, and the pedestrian stairwell I guessed would be in that direction somewhere. My eyes remained fixed on the receding entrance.

It was chance that I heard a scuffing noise in the stairwell I'd been about to enter, and froze against the wall. Dean's head appeared. He'd got behind me, by going down to the lower level. I tried to duck away, but he'd seen me, or heard my feet on the concrete floor. He was right behind me.

I don't think I've been as afraid since as I was then. The horror of what I'd seen on the beach, the mortal truth of it, came from Dean like a shadow, and it seemed inevitable that he'd get me, sooner or later. Mingled with the fear, making it sharp and harder to limit, was a buried fury, a desire to gain some sort of revenge and by doing so to escape both Dean and his shadow.

But I couldn't stop, couldn't face him. I raced down the ramp, leapt up onto the wall at the bottom and flung myself toward the ground. Impact jarred my legs. I tumbled, rolled and, glancing back, saw Dean climbing onto the wall above, planning to follow but hesitating because he wasn't blinded to other dangers by fear and found himself more daunted by the drop. I didn't wait to see what he chose to do; I turned and ran toward the traffic, then up the hill in the direction of the city centre.

Behind me a horn blared; this was followed by a screech of brakes. I thought I heard a shriek. Despite myself I stopped and looked. Dean wasn't racing after me. Instead there was a figure sprawled brokenly on the ground, half under the wheels of a Ford panel van. The driver was just emerging from the car; a pedestrian gestured and yelled, while others gathered. Apparently Dean had decided to jump after all — right in front of a car that was starting to accelerate away from the concrete edifice after having paid the parking attendant at the gates. He hadn't seen it, hadn't heard it, fooled by the overhang. I'd jumped down to the same spot, but I'd been luckier.

I waited some distance away while an ambulance and the cops came, and they scraped Dean off the road and took statements. One of the witnesses — the attendant — pointed in my direction, though he surely didn't know I was there. But I understood he was describing me and where I'd run to and I decided that was my cue to get lost.

I felt like I'd had a reprieve. Though the nightmares of Wanda Beach continued, as the days passed I became more and more convinced that Dean was dead and that somehow I was safe, not just from him, but from other threats as well. Soon memory matched the conviction and I slept in peace, at least for a while.

"What're you staring at?" The drunk was narrowing his eyes at me, suspiciously. I realised I hadn't said anything for some minutes.

"You remind me of someone I knew once," I said. "What's your name?"

"Tony. Tony Gibson. Why?"

I shrugged. "It doesn't matter." For a moment my pulses had been racing, surprise and anticipation rising like a fever. I let them settle, emptying my glass in one swallow.

"Another drink?" he said.

"You offering to shout?" I asked with a sardonic smirk.

He looked hurt and indignant. He took an old wallet out of his coat and waved it at me. This time the shock of recognition was like a knife thrust.

"I got some money," he said. "I got some dignity."

It was my wallet. The one I'd lost on Wanda Beach so long ago. The initials 'MC' were inscribed on it in worn gold-embossed lettering. Gibson saw me staring at it.

"This belonged to...to someone I knew," he said, flipping it open. "From the old days. I keep it to remind me. Still got his stuff in it." He took out a faded, crumpled photo that had been cut out of a *TV Times*. "He liked Hayley Mills. You remember her? Dunno where he is now, but I wonder, I always wonder. He feels close, you know. Close. I keep expecting him to turn up," he glanced around in a haunted fashion.

"You scared of him?"

He looked at me. "Scared?" He laughed nervously, weakly. "Funny thing is, all along I've waited. For twenty years I've waited. That's somethin', eh? That you can let someone, some fuckin' kid..." He didn't finish. He closed the wallet and shoved it into his dirty coat. Showing himself like that had disturbed him. It had disturbed me, too. Dean was alive after all. Both the accident and the name had been a lie.

I became aware of the gun in the shoulder-holster under my arm. Fingered it mentally. For twenty years I'd wanted to kill him myself. The accident that had rescued me from him had always seemed like a cheat and the pressure of the remaining memories had demanded release.

Now he was there in front of me. Given to me. All I needed to do was get him out of the bar, to somewhere far from the light...

"I hate that kid," he said.

It wasn't anger. I looked into his eyes, and understood the depth of his fear — an ingrained fear that had lasted twenty years and become a way of life. There was nothing I could do to him that would be worse than that fear. I didn't want to do him any favours.

"Gotta be off," he said, dispirited. He stood, tried to smile, and failed. I didn't help him. He nodded, as though replying to some unspoken statement, and limped away.

He stumbled through the door and disappeared into the darkness beyond it.

Robert Hood

I let him go.

the beast
without

tatsu

Reece Notley

Don knew the first time he saw Tsukoi, that he'd met the man who would fulfil his desires.

He'd heard of the party through other people, deciding to crash it before he went home. It was in an area used to being cool; sprawling urban lofts filled with expensive liquor and women and the streets bristled with flashy imports, their paint jobs gleaming under the street lamps.

The guys standing outside nonchalantly gestured with burning cigarettes, saying hello to one another with silent upward jerks of their heads. A trail of women eyed the men up as they chattered past, their eyes meeting to pick off favourites like selecting a choice fruit at the market.

Don wondered what it was like to be one of those guys; mulling over which ripe, succulent peach to bite into before the night was over.

Wandering through the labyrinth of rooms, he stumbled from dancing to games of quarters, rounding a pool table where a group of solemn faced Japanese watched him back out slowly from the door. If he had to swear to it, Don would have said he'd spotted the dull gleam of a gun on the table's polished wood rim.

He looked for someplace to be. Any place would be preferable to a room filled with flat-eyed stares. What he found down the hall made him swallow his soul.

An almost nude woman lay on a flat chaise, her face hidden from Don's view. Her legs were endless and a towel draped over her hips, providing the barest hint of modesty. The white fabric tucked up against her mons, a darkened sliver hinted at her sex, a shadowed promise behind the cloth.

She'd be a bitch, he thought. She had that air about her, like the women coming through his work place. The skank would look right through him, passing by as if he weren't in front of her. He knew her kind all too well.

Don couldn't hear her speaking above the noise of the machine and the music pounding through the house but he imagined her husky whispers tickling the ear of the Asian man leaning over her. One bare hand rested intimately on her hip, the other working the rattling machine back and forth, filling in fractures, scales of an uncompleted dragon.

As the man moved back, the twisting shape revealed itself, powerful and fierce in its stark state. A Japanese dragon reached over her back - its front claw piercing one plum-tipped breast - and moved down her length, wrapping its frilled tail around her upper thigh. She seemed uninvolved in the inking, even as blood ran down her hip, pooling between the man's fingers as he stretched the skin to work. Stopping briefly to tap the needle head into a well of blue ink, he continued to shade in the lines of the dragon, going over a scale with skilled precision.

It was not what Don expected to find in the back room of a house party but sometimes destiny had a strange way about it.

"What's up?" Don choked briefly over his own tongue. It dried against the roof of his mouth, clutching to his palate when the artist stopped and looked up at him. Don skittered, took another look, a harder look at the slender man balanced on the edge of his stool. The red vinyl creaked and the machine stuttered to a stop as the artist's foot eased off of the pedal.

He could have been the woman's twin, barely masculine and too beautiful. Don could break this man in two if he wanted. He immediately stopped that thought, seeing the strength in the other's hands, the stains of ink under his fingernails. Here was someone who ground out the weakness in those who lay under him, turning the cast off grit of a man's skin into stained glass. Here was someone Don needed.

"What do you want, *howaido*?" The artist dipped the tip of his finger into the murky tea of blood and ink pooling on the woman's thigh. Sucking the liquid from his finger, he lapped at the granules clinging to his upper lip.

"He's turning green, Tsukoi," The name had an intimate sound to it and she yawned as she stretched back. "*Fugainai*."

"Did Heng tell you to come back here?" Tsukoi looked up, the dimness of the room masking his face. "What do you want?"

"That." Don jerked a thumb at the tattoo, keeping his eyes on the man's face. "I want what you're doing to her…on me."

"Why?" The artist moved and his eyes flared amber from the light bounced into the tiny room from the open door. "What do you think it will give you?"

Don's answer came easily, rising off of his tongue. "Power," He said with a long smile. "And respect."

Banks of rolling fog caught on the bay's orange lace bridge, pouring around its slender metal threading and stretching over the shore line. The low keen of a ferry echoed around the scattered islands dotting San Francisco's cold waters, the chilly bay now a stark black ooze pushing up against the bleached sky.

The City by the Bay took advantage of its coy veil, hiding behind thick white mists. Long trails of BART line wound through tangled streets, their cars bloated with warm, drunken human bodies. The trains smelled of puke, sweat and beer, the evening's riders adding to the pungent aroma with various degrees of dedication.

Grumbling under his breath, Don bumped shoulders with the tall blonde woman he'd been eyeing for the last few miles. When the train hissed to a stop, he jerked against her body, nearly knocking her to her knees. She slanted him a hard look and teetered off the car on unsteady feet, grabbing at the door as she stepped off. Don watched the plump flesh of her ass jiggle just above the hemline of her short nylon dress, its horizontal stripes widening over her curves.

"No time to chase some tail," He mumbled and stepped off onto the curb. The foreignness of it caught at him, a cling of earthy spice tickling his nose as he walked through the streets. He hated the oppressive feeling of secrets lying beneath the surface of San Francisco's winding roads. The signs offended him sometimes, a straggle of lines and dips he couldn't make out. There weren't enough real words on them for his liking.

A florescent walled dim sum restaurant nearly hid the place's entrance. Don spotted a small white sign over a slender doorway, its English added in a handwritten scrawl beneath bold black kanji. The addresses seemed to be a jumble of numbers, like the puzzles Don's mother did in the middle of the night. The foreign lettering looked the same to his eyes, aggressive black slashes against crackled white paint.

He knocked at the red door and it opened while he stood uneasily as people passed by, their dark eyes slanting curious looks at him. Tsukoi was as he remembered him, pretty faced and slender, someone Don normally would have pushed down. The man's black hair fell forward as he bowed his head and Don stepped in, unsure as to whether the nod was mocking or welcoming.

The door opened to a long hallway, squares of light from high set windows barely denting the shadows. Tsukoi stepped in front of Don after closing the door, taking the lead. His shirt rode up, exposing his back and colour glittered on his pale skin, rising from the waistband of his jeans to curve towards his spine.

The tattoo was of hues found between slices of a rainbow and parts nearly shimmered as the man walked. A pair of koi danced through stylized waves, bubbles and cherry blossoms floating on the sheer surface of painted skin. The tattoo... moved, breathing as if it had a life of its own and the Asian only served to carry it. Each scale of the fish fanned out, darker lines of colour scalloping every edge. Dappled with white and orange gold, the koi swam amid wrinkled folds of water, curls of fins splashing up to nudge away pink petals fallen down from an unseen tree above.

Don wanted to touch it...very badly.

This was what he ached for; wearing something that exquisite on his skin would make him *someone*…someone to be reckoned with.

"That's nice." His voice came out breathy, like a girl's and Don cleared his throat, hearing himself echoing in his ears. "Who did it?"

"My father." He left it at that, no other mention of the art or his family. Disappointed, Don followed Tsukoi closely, nearly slamming into him when the artist stopped abruptly at an open door. "In here. We can figure out what you want."

"I need something large. On my back and over my arms and legs." Don's eyes adjusted to the brighter light in the small room. Its walls were devoid of any decoration, a plain vanilla cream colour and the wooden floor was dull, dark wood run rough in spots from furniture legs. A long massage table lay in the centre, its folding sides flat and at the ready. Nearby, a stool on casters abutted a low table, an electrical cord from the tattoo machine under it stretching over to the outlet in a sinuous black trail. "I want it to be memorable. I want it to look like… important."

"Something like that is expensive. A life of work." Tsukoi played with a bottle of unopened red, swirling the ink around the plastic container. "Do you think you can pay that price?"

"I'll pay." Don thought of how much spare money he had at the end of each pay check. He'd have to play fast and loose with a few things while he had the word done but it was something he was willing to sacrifice for. "I want this. I don't care what it costs. Do you want money up front?"

"You don't pay me until we're finished. It will take a long time," The Asian nodded thoughtfully then his eyes flicked up, catching Don in their amber. "And it will have to be something that tells a story. Something that goes on a man's entire body should be complete. It should be a legend."

"Good," Don replied. "Because I want to be one."

It hurt.

There was no other word for the pain other than...hurt.

The thin black lines Tsukoi sketched over his right arm would take an eternity to fill in, Don knew that in his bones. He hissed and spat when the needle touched him for the first time and then wept when the buzzing grew to a climatic sting on the bone of his shoulder. More than once, he wanted to beg the man to stop but the steady grind of Tsukoi's concentration didn't seem like something he would dare to interrupt. Especially as the Asian swept back to refill his needle tips and turned back to daub away the blood pouring from Don's flesh.

His bare fingers stretched and played with his living canvas, seemingly immune to the sounds of displeasure pouring from Don's throat. Another burning touch came and then Don's nerves jumped, arcing towards the digging steel. The pain worked down from his skin and into his marrow until he felt sure it would crack apart and spill into his blood.

"Shouldn't you...be wearing gloves?" He remembered asking at one point, needing to talk to ease the silky, thick saliva in his mouth.

"I need to feel you under me. If I wear gloves, I can't feel you enough." Tsukoi stopped and angled his stare through the jet black hair fringe covering his eyes. "Do you want me to stop? You can get someone else to do this for you."

"No," Don said, shaking his head. "I want you to do this." Tsukoi didn't look convinced, giving Don a cocked eyebrow and a beestung pout that wouldn't look out of place on one of the Japanese school girls Don lusted after. "Please."

That one word was enough to bring the needles back down and Don bit the inside of his cheek to keep his screams in.

The tattoo itched and burned. Don rubbed at the scratchy fabric of his work shirt, hoping to ease the discomfort. The lotion Tsukoi gave him made the ache of his nerves subside for a few hours but then the crawling sensation was back in full force. He didn't put it on while at work because the green slime clung to everything but the stunning hues beneath the foamy gel were breathtaking. He could only dream of when the ink spread over his whole body.

Climbing the stairs to the apartment he shared with his mother, Don stopped at the third floor landing, irritated at the clutter blocking his path. Old Virgil sat on a metal chair amid the mess, his fingers marbled from cigarette smoke. The bent man once terrified Don, his shape menacing when he walked by and the hall shook with his footsteps. Ten years and a cancer later, the monster now huddled in his own doorway, spitting out chew or dropping almost empty cans of protein drinks that leaked onto the hall's industrial linoleum.

"Went down to get yourself some poon?" Virgil burbled, spit flecking his mouth. "You sure spending a lot of time with those gooks, boy. Bringing your mama home some of your banana babies to raise?"

The words didn't get to him, not like he'd thought they would. Hell, he'd said the same thing to a friend of his once when the guy sniffed around one of the FOB girls in their high school but Virgil's words...cheapened him, made what he was doing for himself...less.

Don wasn't certain what drove him on but one thing was for certain, bathing in Virgil's hot blood soothed his inked skin a lot more than Tsukoi's salve.

His back was on fire. If not for the constant buzz and whine of the machine working over his body, he could swear Tsukoi instead dripped acid on him from the head of a pin. The singing needles sang bass when the other man worked in a length of black in, going over the same spot until he was satisfied with its saturation.

Reaching up, Don grabbed what he could to steady himself, letting his fingers dig down deep into Tsukoi's calf. Panting, he fought the waves of sick coming over him and inhaled sharply when the needles stopped their descent down his spine.

"Let go of my leg," Tsukoi said, his voice a dark purr.

"You're hurting me." The solidness of the other man's leg felt good under his hand and Don was reluctant to withdraw. With Tsukoi under his hand, the pain lessened and he was anchored to something other than himself.

"You asked me to hurt you," He said softly, still under the throb of Don's palm. "Remember you asked for this. You're the one in control. I am only giving it to you because you asked for it."

Don let go and the needles began again, fiercer and deeper. His skin wept blood but his eyes were dry. He'd take what Tsukoi gave him without complaint. He would bleed out before he fed the pain any more of his whimpers.

She walked by him. Every night the blond woman he saw on the BART looked through him and stepped away as if Don were nothing. After a few weeks, he'd taken to wearing a tank top, showing off the exquisite ink he'd bled for but she continued to pass through his life as if he were nothing.

One day she brushed up against his shoulder and flicked a glance at his face before turning away, not before he spotted the sourness in her mouth and eyes.

No matter, Don thought as he worked a knife through the tendons of her shoulders, popping the joints as her screams bounced against the underpass, unheard over the Bay traffic. He'd make certain that she saw him. He would be the last person her cold blue eyes would ever see.

Catching her limp body up, he held her as the life gushed out of her chest, heart pumping to a furious beat as it tried to resuscitate its dying host. An upturned hubcap from an old Pontiac gave him the receptacle he needed to catch her fluids. His back hurt too much and reaching around to smooth ointment only crinkled the skin, rumpling the healing ink.

He'd found creased skin on newly inked tattoos made for unsightly lines that had to be filled in and Tsukoi had already hissed at a line in the dragon claw reaching over his ribs. That was not an experience he wanted again.

Don's fingers shook as he held them up to the gibbous moon. Her life dripped from his hand, inky red and lush. Her mouth held nothing for him now. It lay open and slack, her prettiness faded under his knife. Bringing his fingers to his lips, he sucked at them, pulling her into his body.

He spent himself washing with her blood, watching her limbs sink down into the cold blackness of the Bay.

Tsukoi was waiting for him outside the next time he came. Smoke wafted around the man's face, an ethereal fog that reminded Don of the mists on Alcatraz. Exhaling out, the Asian released a clove-scented ring, following it up with his eyes until it was lost in the pearled dimness of a lit San Francisco night.

"You're here too soon," He said, snubbing the butt out against the wall before flicking it into a street grate. "You should take more time. This kind of thing should take years to finish and you're rushing your life."

"I feel like I'm not...complete," Don leaned against the wall besides Tsukoi, catching a whiff of the man's spiced breath. "I want to feel it on me. It's like I can't do anything but think about how it is going to be when I'm done...when you're done."

"Come on then," Tsukoi replied softly, opening the door to let Don in. "Let's get to work."

He screamed this time. Don was ashamed to hear his own shrieks echo against the wall but when Tsukoi stretched his hand over the inside of his thigh and began to work close the fold of his leg, he nearly blacked out with the agony crawling with hooked talons into his tender nerves.

The story was told in inches, a brutal tale of a dragon and a man fighting over a treasure they'd die before having. Tsukoi murmured as he worked, soft rolling streams of Japanese that caught on Don's imagination until he dreamed in a language he didn't understand. Now came a battle of demons and a woman turned *oni*, the *hannya* Tsukoi told him. The long-nosed mask stretched on his thigh, turning it blue before it ran crimson as he bled out profusely, the thin skin giving in to the rapidly moving steel tips.

Don struggled for something to distract himself from fierce visage forming on his thigh. Gasping when the machine's clicking arm caught on a leg hair and yanked it free from its roots, Don's eyes grew blurry and he leaned forward, placing his hand on Tsukoi's shoulder.

"God, just talk or something." Don leaned back, letting his fingers trail off of the man's arm and flopping onto the padded table. "Get my mind off of this shit. Talk about anything. Chicks. Your dad. Anything."

The needles stopped singing, a blurring lull in the room but the pain increased as if the skin had memory of the tips moving in and out, leaving behind minute drops of ink and punctured welts. Canting his head, Tsukoi brushed his bloodied fingers through his hair, moving it off of his face.

Slowly, the Asian eased his lean body moving along Don's length until their faces were nearly touching and he shuddered at the coldness of Tsukoi's full mouth. The man's whisper tickled his cheek, hot and rolling like the pin tips he wielded.

"I am nothing to you but ink and pain, remember?" Tsukoi's lips hovered at the plump of Don's ear. He filled Don's world, until nothing existed but the ache along his thighs and the ivory and black blend of Tsukoi's features. "You are nothing to me but skin, something to work on. You come here because I can give this to you and I do this because you come for it. There is nothing else between us."

He lay there, mute as Tsukoi began again, steadily hooking ink under Don's pale, stretched skin. The pain rushed him anew, thickening in his mouth until all Don could taste was the sickly sweetness of his fear and the gurgle of bile rising from his throat.

When he's done, Don thought, *I'm going to have him on me. Just like the others*.

Nothing worked like it was supposed to. No matter how much he smeared blood over the length of his thigh, the ink burned before the liquid dried. Things were *moving* under his skin, Don was sure of it. Tsukoi had placed something inside of him that was hungry, ravenously evil and thirsty. It left trails of ache as it swam through his body, bringing pinpricks of agony along its wake.

His lashes were smarting and the back of his eyeballs were bleeding out. Don could feel the drip-drip-drip of his fluids leaking into the bowl of his skull.

There was a sea of blood washing over the kitchen floor, a cloud of flies swarming in its rich metallic scent. He stared down at his mother's broken form, her fingers crooked and twisted around a pencil. She'd fallen where he flung her, lifeless when her strings were cut from her.

It had been so easy to reach into her and yank her life out of her chest, digging in with a long kitchen knife she'd purchased from a shopping network she watched. Red splatters filled in the circles of her number puzzles, drops from the slice on her arm providing answers that she never seemed able to figure out. Some of the pages were rubbed through from her eraser, little holes of her stupidity.

Much like the ones dimpling her torso and arms.

Maybe, he needed the place he'd come from, Don reasoned, moving to her cooling flesh. It would stiffen then soften again, her body's spoils flushing from the relaxed orifices once it realised its death. Amid the gush, he excavated the worn floppy organ lying under her belly. Its intense redness was a surprise then the oddness of its shape struck him.

"Will it taste like bunny too, Ma?" He nudged her leg, avoiding the sharp nails on her stubby toes. Turning on the burner, Don placed it into the cast iron skillet they left on the stove and waited for his dinner to sizzle.

"I want it finished," Don said to Tsukoi when he opened the door.

Sheets of rain covered the city, obscuring buildings that were mere feet away. Don's jeans were soaked to the knee, the denim dripping water as he walked in. The squelch of his sneakers echoed in the hallway, its length now a dank grey from the watery light of its windows.

The room was as they'd left it, the machine lying inert and rows of ink bottles lining the cabriolet. Tsukoi waited for him, barefoot and lithe, his face an unreadable mask as Don stripped off his shirt, preparing himself for the final stretch of blank skin to be filled in, the curve of the dragon across his shoulder blades.

He knew the story by now, etched into his body and under his skin. He carried the legend of a warrior and the *tatsu* discovering a phoenix's treasure, battling one another over the smallest golden coin bearing the likeness of a beautiful woman. Armies of demons warred down his belly and across his thighs, rousted from the hells by a scorned princess, the warrior's former beloved. The roll of Tsukoi's voice accompanied each prick and dot of ink and Don flexed his broad shoulders, rippling the creatures fleeing the epic battle as the dragon descended from the heavens.

"You don't have to do this now," Tsukoi said, quietly. "You should have more time. At least to…be who you need to be before it is completed."

"No," Don hooked his leg up over the edge of the table and slid onto his belly, tucking his arms under his chin. "I won't be complete until it is."

"No," He whispered as he took up the machine, setting the safety off. "You won't be."

Don woke to find himself on his back, a pressing weight pushing down on his throat. Shining lights seared his eyes and he blinked, trying to find himself surcease from their burning glare. Grunting, he lifted his head and gasped helplessly when all he did was flop his head to the side. His limbs were unresponsive and the crawl of his tattoo burned distantly in the back of his brain.

Something was wrong. Something was horribly wrong.

"Good, you're awake," Tsukoi stepped out of the light, his pretty face swimming into view. The Asian brushed at Don's forehead then down over his face, resting his hand on the other man's shoulder. "It's better when you're awake."

"Whhaaa?" His tongue didn't move and Don choked as the fleshy tube slithered back down his throat. Alarmed, he fought to regain control of the limp muscle but it merely folded back over and closed off the airway tighter. Tsukoi nodded, calm and knowing, before sliding his fingers into Don's mouth, pulling out his tongue before he lost consciousness.

"Don't worry. I've seen that happen before. I won't let you go like that," He said, fitting a small white waffle ball into Don's mouth, closing his jaw over its spongy form. It trapped his tongue against his teeth, cutting down into the muscle.

Frantic, Don looked around him, hoping to see someone, anyone, who could help him. His eyes strained with the effort, the muscles slowly fading under the press of whatever Tsukoi had injected into him. Struggling did him little good, his body refused to move and he could hear the Asian move about, connecting something and sliding items around.

"I know you're scared," Tsukoi came back into eyesight and Don was relieved, despite his fear. This was the man who spent a year carving out a story onto his skin. There had to be a reason for this, Don thought. Something happened and Tsukoi would soon sort it out.

Or so he thought until he spotted the fleshy scrolls hanging around them, the stiff husks of people's hides hanging from wooden Ts set behind glass.

There seemed to be...at least a hundred of them, each as brilliant as his own tattoos. Those closest were vivid, the skins' limbs sporting creatures and people, the wide swath of chests or backs ripened with court scenes or even mountains bristling with pines and layered with the soft white of snow.

"I know. You see them," Tsukoi glanced back behind him, a smile curling his full mouth. "Those are the others, the stories that have come before you. We keep them so we don't tell the same one again. The dragon beneath us is fickle. It's not right for him to hear something twice."

"This is hard for me, you know. You've rushed things forward. You've not had much time," He continued, unrolling a length of plastic tube. Its end dully gleamed with a spigot tip that reminded Don of an oil punch. "But you're the only one who could make that decision."

"The *tatsu* hears the legends every time we let the blood drain into the grate. My father says he suckles at the walls, looking for each word that is whispered over the tattoo," Tsukoi prattled on, above the pain covering Don's body. An acrid smell rose from under him and then a gush of fluids poured from his body. Tsukoi stepped back, keeping his bare feet out of the stream. "Don't worry about that. Everyone pisses themselves. He doesn't mind."

"He'll eat your blood and meat...I'll cut out small pieces as I go. They have to fit down the grate but I'll keep your story safe with the others. That's why I'm lifting up your skin." Tsukoi worked the metal end under Don's skin, lifting up the flesh on the inside of his elbow. Despite the numbness of his limbs, Don winced at the thick sharp bulb sliding into him. He choked again, trying to pull more air in with hisses through the plastic ball. "I'm sorry but it's better if the blood is spiced with pain. We know what the *tatsu* likes. We've been feeding him for years."

Another tube then another slid under his skin, tunnelling under the inked story until Don's body sprouted clear tentacles, each leading to the pump. With a delicate ease, Tsukoi took a scalpel and sliced vents into Don's back and thighs. He stepped out of Don's eyesight and then the chitter of a pump began, churning out long streams of something richly plum scented into Don's raised skin.

"Thank you for paying me so soon. I appreciate your dedication to my duty," Tsukoi rested his chin on his fists, his mouth brushing on Don's cheek with a gentle kiss as the *umeshu* surged into Don's body, lifting the skin up in long patches and draining wine-soaked blood through the slivered cuts along his torso. "I shall keep you here with the others...and remember you always. You have my word. I promise."

wayang kulit
L. J. Hayward

It was a relief to get out of the hot, humid air of Jakarta in summer. Scott's raw silk shirt clung to his back, his damp hair curled around his ears and neck. He ran his hand back across his scalp, trying to rearrange the sweat slicked mess into something less horrific. Not that it seemed it would matter here.

The theatre was dark and dingy, smelling of damp rot and something else, something sickly sweet. Smoke coiled around the ceiling, shifting on sluggish eddies of air. Locals scurried through the rows of seats in search of the best position, as tourists mingled in the aisles, exclaiming loudly about the 'quaintness' and 'atmosphere' and demanding enough seats in one row for their entire party.

In comparison, Ramelan lead Scott and Kerri straight to the front of the theatre and through sublime luck found three seats together. Squeezing in between Kerri and an old Indonesian woman wearing a sarong and an AC/DC t-shirt, Scott sank into the chair. Only when his arse touched the worn, thin vinyl and lumpy stuffing did he wonder just what he might be sitting in. And these were his new Cavalli jeans.

"Isn't this exciting?" Kerri's blue eyes glimmered in the hazy dark of the theatre.

"Yeah, exciting."

"Oh, come on, Scott. Just try to enjoy something for once. Don't be such an arsehole."

Shifting so the spring jutting out of the chair wasn't jabbing anything vital, Scott grimaced. "All I'm saying is that we could have seen this puppet show in more comfort. I'm sure I saw something about it on the entertainment list at the hotel." A drip of sweat clung tenaciously to the end of his nose. He swiped it away. "At the very least we could have caught a taxi to this place. My shirt's going to be ruined. Not to mention the any number of questionable things embedded in the grooves of this chair."

Kerri, comfortable looking in her white t-shirt and newly purchased batik sarong, pursed her lips. "If you had your way, the only part of Indonesia we'd ever see was the inside of that ridiculously expensive hotel! You need to learn to live a little, Scott. Get out there and see the world, experience some culture for once." She leaned closer, lowered her voice. "*It* means so much to Ramelan that he can show us his home and *culture*. Be nice. Or you can just go home and leave us alone to have fun."

On Kerri's other side, Ramelan stared fixedly at the stage, showing no signs of having heard any of their conversation. With his thick black hair and easy smile, Ramelan had gathered many admiring looks from locals and tourists alike, yet he'd shown little interest. Instead, he'd been more concerned with pointing out landmarks and sharing jokes with Kerri.

It means so much to Ramelan that he can show you his home and culture.

Leave his girl with this pretty boy? Hell no!

Scott settled deeper into his seat, already writing off the Cavalli's as an expense in the war to keep Kerri from her *best friend's* clutches.

"So you're staying." Kerri didn't look at him, but her lips twitched into an almost smile.

"You'll be pleased you stayed," Ramelan said. "The very best of the dalangs don't just tell the story. They become the medium through which the spirits talk to mortals. The dalang performing today is one of the best. His skill is extraordinary. Some people say watching him perform is a spiritual experience. They say it's as if he gives the shadows a life of their own."

"I can't wait." Kerri's voice held that breathy quality that meant she really was excited. "What did you call it again?"

"Wayang Kulit," Ramelan answered, his tone just as eager. "It's a shadow puppet play. The puppeteer, the dalang, sits behind the screen and performs all the roles in the story. He sings and narrates and keeps the beat for the musicians. It's a highly skilled art."

Kerri and Ramelan turned to each other as Ramelan continued to prattle about the mechanics of the play. Kerri 'oohed' and 'aahed' far too earnestly for Scott's comfort. Friends? Right…

There were far better places to go for a holiday: Rome, Hong Kong, New York, Dubai. Places where Kerri could have shopped for a better pedigree of fashion than ludicrously coloured sarongs from a vendor in a flea market. He didn't see why he had to be dragged into the near-third world just so Kerri could appease her *friend's* need to *reconnect* to his *heritage*. Who cared where a snotty-nosed kid played when he was little or about the old woman who used to weave baskets and tell stories? Ramelan had moved to Australia to make a better life for himself. Why come back? Scott had managed to escape his childhood horrors and he would be damned before he ever went back.

Scott ignored their happy prattle and tried not to think about things he could be doing if he wasn't stuffed into this cramped, hot little stink-pot of a theatre. At the very least, he could be back in his hotel room, making sure his software company wasn't going bankrupt without his constant supervision.

The seats Ramelan had found them were right at the front. Scott's knees threatened to knock against the boards of the stage. He glared at the screen set across the front edge, incompletely hiding the men behind it as they set up for the show. Just how spiritual could fucking *puppets* get?

Three resonant taps sounded from behind the screen and a quiet settled on the audience, leaving the air saturated with expectation.

Ramelan sat up. "It's about to begin. The dalang taps three times on the box which contains his puppets to wake them up." His voice was quiet, reverent.

"It's a puppet show," Scott muttered. "How great can it be?"

"Scott," Kerri hissed, jabbing him in the side.

"I think you might be surprised," Ramelan said calmly.

I'll be surprised if I'm not dead from boredom by the end of it, Scott thought but said, "We'll see."

Kerri looked between them, repressed a sigh and let her chin drop into her hand, staring at the stage morosely. Guts twinging with guilt, Scott slipped an arm around her shoulders.

"Sorry," he whispered in her ear. "I'll be good."

It earned him a bright smile that, as usual, pulled a genuine smile out of Scott. A small, quiet voice buried somewhere deep inside tried to tell him that she was too good for him, but he quashed it.

Light blossomed behind the screen on the stage. It was orange and flickered in hypnotic, magical patterns. It cast a circle of light onto the centre of the screen, an intense flame at its heart, fading to shadows at the edges. From behind the screen, a steady beat started: to this a deep, throaty chanting was added. It rose and dropped in rhythmic measure, mesmerizing in its simplicity. To the left of the screen, the shadows moved and, slow and stately, a figure grew from the darkness. It stretched up, cutting its shape out of the light.

The figure was a stylised human with an elongated neck, forward jutting head and exaggerated nose. It hobbled from the shadows, movements jerky. Music began, using the steady beat as a base and adding to it with resonant gongs and chiming xylophones. The chanting died away and as the shadow raised a long arm to beckon to something, a voice called out in Indonesian.

Ramelan leaned close to Kerri. "It is a mother calling to her son. She tells him he must go fishing or they will starve."

A second puppet joins the first, scampering from the shadows. He stands before his mother, smaller but more vibrant, dancing for the pleasure of the audience. The good child puppet sets off in his boat crafted of shadow and light.

"This is the story of Malin Kundang," Ramelan said softly. "It is an old folklore."

"What happens?" Kerri asked, her attention on the shifting patterns of light and dark.

Ramelan chuckled. "Watch and find out. I'll translate for you." He flicked a look at Scott. "Both of you."

"Gee, thanks." Scott couldn't hide the sarcasm in his voice. Thankfully, Kerri seemed too entranced to notice.

On the stage, the good child Malin Kundang fishes for his mother. Malin Kundang fades from sight and is replaced by a larger ship. On its deck, two shadow puppets fight. Their battle is fast and furious, blurred and indistinct. The music rises in tempo to match the action.

Scott couldn't look away. The shadows jerked and jumped across the screen, as fascinating as an over the top action movie. Perhaps this wouldn't be so corny after all.

The fight ends with one figure triumphing over the other. Arms rising into the air, the victor calls out .

"He is a pirate, and he's just defeated a merchant."

The small shape of Malin Kundang appears on the deck. Another fight ensues and this time it is the good child who wins, tossing the pirate from the ship. The defeated merchant stands once more.

"The merchant is thanking Malin Kundang for saving his ship. He asks the boy to join his crew and sail with him."

Kerri's lips pursed. "But his mother…"

"He's got a chance to make something of his life if he goes with the merchant," Scott said.

"Without her son, the mother will starve."

"A son can't stay shackled to his mother his whole life. Why should he stay poor when he has a chance to become something better?"

Her expression softened as she touched Scott's arm. "I know you're thinking about her and—"

"Shh." Ramelan pointed to the stage. "The show is still going on."

Scott moved his arm from under Kerri's hand and looked resolutely at the screen. He'd be damned if he was going to talk about this shit here and now. There was a better time for conversations like the one Kerri wanted to have — never.

On the screen, Malin Kundang agrees to sail with the merchant and Scott celebrated quietly to himself. When Malin Kundang's choice led him to a life as a rich merchant and marriage to a princess, it was all Scott could do to keep from snickering. Kerri, however, seemed to be aware of his glee and dared him with sidelong glances to gloat out loud. He settled for a superior smile.

Rich and famous, Malin Kundang eventually finds himself back on his home island. There the folk recognise him and from the crowd, comes his mother. She is old and slow, staggering toward her good son, arms wide in greeting.

"She is so pleased to see her son again," Ramelan murmured. "She is calling to him, reminding him of their bond."

Malin Kundang holds up his arms against his mother. He backs away.

"Three times she begs him to recognise her, three times she calls to him. Finally, he cries, 'Enough, old woman. I have never had a mother like you, a dirty and ugly peasant.' Then he orders his crew to set sail."

"Oh, that's cruel," Kerri said.

Scott stared at the shadows and beyond them, to the flickering, intense flame that gave them life. There was something like that flame inside his chest, burning hot.

Rejected by her good son, the mother raises her arms and shouts after the retreating ship.

"She shouts, 'Apologise, my son. Admit the truth, or you shall be turned to stone.'"

On the ship, Malin Kundang laughs and sails on. From the calm sky comes a sudden thunderstorm. The music rises in a threatening crescendo. Dark clouds roil at the top of the screen, waves toss the ship this way and that, dashing it upon the rocks of an island. Malin Kundang is thrown from the ship. He stands, arms flailing for balance. The music thrashes to a chaotic and sudden halt, silence ringing in the stuffy air, and Malin Kundang freezes in place — turned to stone.

Sudden cold whipped through Scott, dousing the flame that had moments before burned inside him. He felt as stiff as the shadow of Malin Kundang. Kerri clapped loudly with the rest of the audience.

"I'm so glad he got his comeuppance," Kerri said to Ramelan. "He was just nasty." She turned to Scott. "Not so happy now, are you?"

There was teasing in her tone, but Scott ignored it. He chewed his lips and stared at the screen, still lit by the flame, but lifeless now that the shadows had gone.

"What kind of mother turns her only son into stone?"

"It's just a story," Kerri said, no teasing now.

Scott scowled. "Fucking stupid story."

"Here comes the dalang," Ramelan said.

A slender man emerged from behind the screen and bowed to the appreciative crowd. He looked around the audience and for a moment his gaze settled on Scott. A shiver rattled Scott's shoulders. The dalang nodded to him and then retreated behind the screen again.

"What happens now?" Kerri asked Ramelan.

"The performance will continue. The dalang will tell many more tales tonight. Wayang Kulit may sometimes last until dawn."

Scott's stomach churned. "I don't feel so good."

"What's wrong?" Kerri put her hand on his arm.

"I think I ate something that didn't agree with me." Scott pressed a hand to his gut, swallowing against the urge to retch as his innards squirmed.

"We've all eaten the same things today," Ramelan said. "I feel fine. Kerri?"

"Yeah, I'm okay. Scott, are you sure?"

Scott staggered to his feet, swayed and caught himself on the back of the seat. "I just need to lie down." He ploughed his way past the old woman's knees, heading for the aisle and escape.

"Where are you going?" Kerri asked, half out of her chair to follow.

"Back to the hotel."

Kerri gathered up her backpack. "I'll come with you. Ramelan, I'm so sorry. You stay, keep watching. Maybe we can catch another performance tomorrow."

Scott reached the relatively clear space of the aisle. He bent over, grabbed his knees and concentrated on breathing.

"No, I'll come with you." Ramelan too began to push past the old woman, who muttered darkly under her breath.

"I'm so sorry," Kerri repeated. "We don't want to ruin your holiday."

Ruin *his* holiday? Scott straightened, even though it felt like his stomach would erupt from his mouth.

"You know what," he managed to get out. "Don't come with me, Kerri. Stay here with your *friend*. I would hate to ruin his holiday by being violently sick all over him. I'll catch a taxi. I'll be fine on my own. Stay, watch your little shadow play."

Kerri's jaw dropped. "Don't be ridiculous. You need help. I'm coming with you."

"We're both coming." Ramelan reached for Scott's arm.

Scott pulled away so fast he lost balance and crashed into the next row of seats. A British voice rose in protest. Kerri and Ramelan rushed forward to help him up. He shoved them away and hauled himself to his feet.

"Get off me. I'm going home alone. I don't need either of you."

"Oh, for cryin' out loud," an American called from the crowd. "Either go or stay. Just make up your freakin' minds. Some of us want to enjoy the show."

Scott whirled to face the general direction of the speaker. "Fuck you, yank."

"Scott!" Kerri glared at him. "What's gotten into you?"

Wobbling, Scott stalked for the exit. "Reason, at last. Don't follow me. I want to be alone."

Certain that if he risked looking behind he would fall over and not get up again, Scott stared ahead. Teeth clenched to keep his guts on the inside, he pushed through the doors of the theatre. Intense sunlight slashed into his eyes. Blinded, he lurched for the gutter and caught himself on a streetlamp. Holding on for dear life, he squinted through watering eyes, searching for a taxi. The traffic was heavy but moved at a steady pace. Horns honked and drivers shouted at each other. Motorcycles buzzed in and out of the lines of cars. People hurried by on the footpath.

A white taxi appeared in the traffic. Scott leaned forward, arm outstretched to signal the driver. The car began to ease over to him.

Something dark moved beside Scott and he jerked away, stumbling onto the road. The taxi screeched to a stop mere inches from him. Spinning, Scott looked for the prick who'd tried to hit him. Several locals had stopped to watch him standing in the middle of the road. None looked malicious, just curious and alarmed.

"Hey!" The taxi driver leaned out of his window. "You got a death wish? Get in or get off the road."

A few more people had stopped to watch. The sun cast their shadows onto the wall of the tiny, run down theatre, creating a many headed, bulbous creature. As Scott watched, the shadow moved upward, moulded into a new shape by the angles of the walls and awnings. It crawled from the mass of darkness, long arms reaching up and out toward him.

Cold snapped through Scott's guts. What the fuck was this? He had food poisoning. It was affecting his head. He wasn't seeing this. A shadow was not hauling itself off the surface on which it was cast, it was not reaching across the gulf between them and reaching for him. It was not. Was not!

The shadow touched his head.

Scott threw himself backwards, away from its cold, hungry touch. He slammed into a car, rolling along its side as it continued driving on. Darting behind it, he barely missed a collision with another car. With his field of vision narrowing to the opposite side of the street, he scrambled between the slowed traffic, barely aware of the horns and verbal abuse in both English and Indonesian following him.

He made it to the footpath, latched onto another pole for support and spun to see what the shadow was doing.

It wasn't there. At least, not as it had become — alive and hungry. It was just as it should be: a hazy impression of the objects that blocked the light. There was nothing unusual, nothing scary.

Heart racing so fast he couldn't feel individual beats, Scott leaned over and tried to catch his breath. "Oh fuck, I think I'm having a heart attack."

It would round off the day perfectly: watching Kerri slowly leave him for Ramelan, food poisoning and a fucking heart attack. This wasn't right. Things like this didn't happen to people like him.

After several minutes of deep breathing, and scowling at any do-gooders who got too close, Scott managed to get his heart under control. Even the nausea eased. The day, winding down into evening, was still blasted hot and sweat made his shirt cling to his skin. Getting his bearings, he guessed at which direction the hotel lay and set out on foot, keeping an eye out for a taxi.

Towering over the surrounding buildings, the Wisma 46 skyscraper was his guiding point. Their hotel was south of it, with a view of the concrete and glass construction. Ramelan had dragged them almost to the harbour in order to find the dingiest, smelliest theatre he could. It would be a long walk if he had to go all the way on foot, but he was certain he'd find another taxi before too long.

The sun sank as he walked. Shadows stretched across the footpath. Streetlamps and sign posts striped the streets, bars on a prison window — bars that moved as if alive.

Scott blinked and focused on them again. They writhed under more influence than the shifting surface they fell across. One curled back toward the footpath, snaked toward Scott's feet.

"What the fuck?" He jumped out of its path.

Another shadow whipped backwards and struck. It hit with an icy punch. Scott reeled amidst the other pedestrians. They shoved back, swore at him and stepped with casual arrogance on and over the shifting shadows. Buffeted through the crowd, Scott fell into the opening of a narrow side street. No sunlight reached the ground here at this time of the afternoon. It was dark and muggy, shrouded in shadows.

A chill rippled down Scott's spine. Encased in grey, he clambered back to his feet.

Blackness crawled along the wall. Hand shaped, it scuttled toward Scott. He raced away, fleeing further into the alley. It reared off the wall and galloped after him, silent and cold.

From behind a dumpster, another dark shadow came. It slinked across the dirty ground, flowing over rubble and boxes and broken bottles, tendrils reaching ahead of its bulk, eager for him.

Scott hurdled it, coming down on its rear edge. His Bunkers absorbed the impact but didn't stop the shadow from flipping up and curling around his shoe. Shouting incoherently, Scott shoved, pulled and pushed until his foot came out of the leather Bunker. Staggering away, he watched dumbly as the shadow consumed his very expensive shoe.

The two shadows merged into one large mass. It pulled up off the ground, rearing over him, blocking out what light there was.

"Fuck you," he screamed, all too aware of the hysteria bubbling through his voice.

He turned and ran, his shoe-less foot unerringly finding each and every puddle of stagnant, putrid water. Light bloomed at the end of the alley. He raced for it, wanting nothing more than to stand in the brutally hot sun of Indonesia, sweat himself into dehydration and never see another shadow again for as long as he lived.

Scott barrelled out of the alley into an only slightly wider street. A bajaj swerved around him, both driver and passenger rocking back and forth. The motorised rickshaw rumbled on, trailing curses from the driver. But all Scott cared for was the narrow river of sunlight coursing down the centre of the street. He drowned himself in the light, soaked up the heat.

Careful to remain in the light, Scott followed the street. He didn't know where it would take him and, at this moment, didn't care. He just wanted to keep out of the shadows, stay warm and pretend he wasn't going insane.

The street widened and Scott recognised the flea market where he, Kerri and Ramelan had spent the morning. Kerri had gotten her sarong and Ramelan had coaxed them into sampling food Scott couldn't pronounce the names of, let alone recognise the ingredients. His stomach squirmed: it *was* food poisoning. That bastard had made him ingest some exotic toxin that was fucking with his brain, making him hallucinate.

The market was over for the day. The vendors had gathered up their 'native artwork' and moved on. Striped awnings that had provided cherished shelter from the sun in the morning now harboured dark shadows. Black shapes moved in the depths of the shade.

"It's not real. It's just a hallucination."

Still, Scott's feet moved faster and faster until he was running down the middle of the street. There was no traffic beyond a few bajaj. A smattering of late vendors watched him with mild curiosity.

He followed the street, vaguely aware that he was not heading toward his hotel. He was as far from it as he could be and still be in this crazy, stinking hot, overcrowded city. The buildings on either side reduced in size and quality as he ran. Brick became scarce as a building material, replaced by weathered wood, corrugated iron and tin. Even though the height of the buildings dropped, his path of light narrowed as the sun continued its downward spiral. The shadows crept closer.

The street came to an abrupt end in an arching, narrow bridge. Scott slowed to a stagger and climbed its gentle curve. The sharp tang of salt water hit his nose. He'd reached the water, a small harbour surrounded by ramshackle slums and filled with battered fishing boats. Children played on the far side of the bridge, stopping their game to look at him with wide, dark eyes. An old man half buried by a net called them away.

Gasping for breath, Scott leaned on the railing, head hanging over the murky brown water. A weak swathe of sunlight washed over him and the water, but the shadow of the bridge held the dark hints of his pursuer — whatever it was.

Pressure intensified in his chest, twisting and turning. Heat sparked between his lungs, behind his sternum. It seared through his chest and spread out into his limbs.

"Scott!" Kerri raced up the bridge, slammed into him, almost knocked him over. "Oh my God, I thought I'd never find you. What the hell are you doing here? What's going on?" She sobbed into his aching chest.

It was starting to get hard to pull air into his lungs. He'd had heartburn before but it had never, *ever*, felt like this before. This was like a true fire burning inside.

Kerri pulled back, put a hand to his cheek. "You're burning up. How did you get a fever so fast?"

Ramelan jogged up. "It must be food poisoning." He hardly looked out of breath, though he did seem concerned.

Scott tried to push away from Kerri, but couldn't get free of her hold. Everything turned into a bright blur, a dancing, flickering landscape of orange light. Kerri and Ramelan were dark blurs on the edges of his vision.

"Scott? Scott, can you hear me?"

Kerri's voice was an arrhythmic counterpoint to the tympanic beat of blood through his veins. It was if the dalang of the shadow play had set up inside his head and pounded out the bass beat on his skull.

"Ramelan, what if he's having an anaphylactic reaction to something?"

Scott opened his mouth to tell them it wasn't an allergy. It was something else, something inside that burned. But nothing came out of his mouth.

"Sit here. Ramelan's gone to get some help. Scott? Please say something. Can you hear me?"

Scott nodded and she sobbed with relief, pressing her ice cold face against his cheek. He wanted to push her away; he would melt her if she stayed too close. Yet, like his mouth, his arms would not work. He wondered if he still had arms or had they burned to ash and cinders? All he could see was the frantic wavering of the orange light.

Tap. Tap. Tap.

Where had that come from? It sounded — it felt — as if it had come from inside him.

Darkness grew on the edge of his flame coloured world. A shadow bulged and grew and unfolded itself. A tall, slender figure with an elongated neck, forward thrust head with an exaggerated nose.

The shadow puppet clambered across his vision, beckoning to something behind it. Chanting rose as a dull throb. A voice sounded, hollow and empty.

"Come," it said. "See what you have done."

Another shadow appeared on the edge of his flickering flame, more recognisable. A man of normal features, he strode across the stage that was Scott's world, arms manipulated by rods held by some unseen puppeteer. He gathered objects to himself as he walked — a big car, a house far too large for one person, a boat that sat idle in the canal by his too big house. Other shadows came to him — countless, nameless girls, drawn by the big things he owned, that he took so much pride in. On and on he walked, the accumulated junk of his life building up around his legs, holding him in one place while he believed he was moving.

The first puppet returned, skittering over the piles of possessions. "And what is the worth of this?"

From the deep shadows around the man's legs the puppet pulled a new shape of darkness. It tumbled from the heap and stood. A woman separate from the girls.

"What am I worth?" Kerri's voice demanded.

"You are worth more than all this." The man attempted to reach the woman, but was hampered by the gathered detritus of his life, the things he thought so precious, so important. His legs were trapped and he couldn't break free.

"And what is the worth of this?"

Again, the shadow puppet pulled something from the pile. It too tumbled down and stood. Another woman who danced on her rods to music only she could hear, a woman who dressed far too gaudily for someone her age and who laughed too loud. A woman who told anyone who would listen that she and her son lived in a caravan, moving from caravan park to caravan park whenever the fancy took her, or whenever she couldn't pay the rent any longer. A woman who sang off tune at the top of her voice in public, who danced with her son's classmates and told them about her last orgasm. A woman who spent the rent money on cheap booze and picked fights with the neighbours.

"What is the worth of this?" the hollow voice asked again.

The man floundered in his pile of wealth, his unseen puppeteer losing control of the rods that directed his actions. He flailed about and fell, his shadow melding with those of the big things he'd bought with his life. They consumed him and darkness enfolded Scott. The flame that he was faded and he became the shadow.

A shape moved in the shadows. Darker than the rest, it defined itself in movement — a thin neck and long nose.

"Will you apologise?"

"For what? I have done nothing wrong."

"You have denied her the right to be your mother."

"No. She's the one who denied herself that. She wasn't a mother, she was a child who refused to grow up, a drunk who wasted her life instead of making something of herself."

"Like you made something of yourself. Are you happy with your house and boat and expensive clothes? Do they help you forget where you came from?"

"Yes, they help me forget. They're very good at helping me forget."

"Will you apologise?"

"To her? Never."

The puppet bowed its strange head and vanished.

"Scott?"

"Kerri."

Kerri sobbed. "Oh my God, you scared me so much. What happened? I thought you were going to die. Scott, what happened?"

Relieved that he could again talk, Scott said, "I don't know."

A cool hand brushed his forehead and cheeks. "Your fever's going down. I don't understand. You must have had a reaction to something."

"I think I'm better now."

Yet even as he spoke, Scott's feet became numb. He tried to wriggle his toes, but they wouldn't move. He could feel them as a weight on the ends of his legs, but they wouldn't respond. Then the numbness moved up his calves.

"Something's wrong," he muttered, swinging his legs. It was hard. It suddenly felt as if his legs weighed a tonne.

"What's wrong now?"

There was panic in Kerri's voice, matching the rising fear in Scott. It bubbled through him a split second faster than the rapidly growing numbness. The strange sensation hit his knees and crawled so fast up his thighs he couldn't comprehend it. Then his guts froze and his hands.

"Kerri." He didn't care that his voice cracked with terror.

"Scott!"

He faced her, eyes wide, mouth gaping. It reached his heart, stopped it. For a moment more he was aware of the solidity rushing up his neck and into his face. The abrupt weight of his body rocked him forward. Kerri reached for him, but he fell too fast, hit the water and sank.

contaminator
Rebecca Lloyd

There's a fine balance to be struck between consideration and self-preservation in the vast underground complexes deep beneath London. The fast moving crowd practises a knowing blindness; looking without seeing, touching without feeling, and by this crude but long established etiquette it supposes to disperse into daylight again unharmed.

On Friday nights in particular, the crowd does not tolerate a slowing of the pace. It does not care about the beggar woman and her wan-faced child, the musician who cannot play, or the bewildered foreigner. It aims only to reach the surface undisturbed by peculiar incidents.

The fear of accidental burial is never far away; the heavy air is sharp with slivers of anxiety. When a warm gritty wind signals the coming of a train, we scramble rudely forward and pack ourselves intimately into the carriages rather than linger down there in the tunnels longer than we have to. We pretend composure; only the smallest signs of agitation appear when someone, done with the harshness of life, jumps onto the track and halts our train in a black tunnel. In those stationary moments women pick at their ringed fingers, men clear their throats, and somebody sneezes and reminds us of disease.

For some months I have tried to find my way back into the surging blindness of the people I move with every morning and evening, but Monument's clinical white tunnels and grey floors flecked with yellow, unnerve me. I am in the crowd, but not part of it; I falter and stare, and no longer move with the flow. At the base of a great metal escalator the crowd divides, one half pushing onwards for the Northern Line and a sweaty journey beneath the old plague pits, the other takes me with it to Docklands Railway where trains go quickly towards East London through a sooty wormhole.

There are old underground stations beneath London that have never been renovated - Oval, Baker Street, Borough - sombre halls heavy with tiny ceramic tiles in black, oily green and brown, more fitting places to have encountered the woman who filled me with fear than at Monument.

Each time I descend, I am alert in my hunt for her, each evening I hesitate for a second at the place she stood. I'm glad of the swiftness of the Docklands train and the lightening of mood as we reach our own territory along weed-strewn tracks, orange with rust. The allotments at Cable Street are busy now, the black poisoned soil turned over, the first seeds in. The clouds above St George's Church are suicide grey with pearly rims, and along the river beyond Wapping, the sun slides like a new plate into the Thames.

I do not think about her in the day while I'm at work, I do not think of her at all before I reach the first escalator. As I descend, her wide face comes to me again and I remember her size, her clothes, the way she stood, although nothing about any of it was remarkable. I look at the heads in front of me for her dark hair, and search the up escalator just in case she's travelling the other way.

There were no forewarning signs, nothing that registered as peculiar. The worst of the matter is that I was merely a bystander caught up in a freakish and improbable moment. It was not me she singled out; chance alone brought me into close proximity with her, and my unsought for witnessing has left me with a memory I can't get rid of, one as persistent as the foulest of stains.

She'd know me instantly if I came upon her again, and just as on that Friday night, the crowd down there would no longer exist; my attention would be hers alone. I don't want to see her basilisk face a second time, but I would re-live the moment in the hope that I could shroud it in innocence, assign its strangeness to some freaky shunt in my own thinking, then, the vividness of the experience might fade.

I think about the second girl often. I wouldn't recognise her again, a tired-faced blonde, anonymous, hurting. I imagine her at home, in a flat in north London, somewhere small perhaps, with scatter cushions on a deep sofa. She lives with her boyfriend; a restless man, impatient of her feelings. She dyed her hair blonde to please him, and it didn't in particular. He's tired of her and tired of living in London, although he's not ready to admit it yet. She's still hopeful that there's something of value in the grimy city for them. They're pleasant to people, they work hard and live quietly. Nothing they see in the newspapers, no knifings, no muggings, have anything to do with them.

Nothing should be remarkable in a city like London, nothing, or perhaps everything. The dark haired woman was standing just at the curve of the tunnel before the second down escalator comes into view. Her back was to me, her left shoulder close to the wall. I saw her as an obstacle to negotiate, saw the crowd in front of me swarm past her like water around a rock. I was irritated by her unusual stillness; it was a stupid place to stop. I took her to be a foreigner confused in the crowd and watched her as I approached.

I saw the blonde young woman in front of me pass close by her. I never sensed that anybody behind me saw what happened; I was aware of no sudden intake of breath except my own.

The dark woman's head swivelled. Her black hair swung across her shoulders. I saw her profile; her neck stretched outwards, her jaw slightly open. She jutted her head towards the blonde, and opening her mouth wide, coughed twice with huge vigour, straight into the girl's nose and eyes, a barking hideous noise, a twisted and queer manifestation of violence. I saw the jugular vein in her neck bulge with the effort.

The blonde, not changing pace looked round at her attacker and scuttled sideways. I saw her face contort fleetingly with revulsion that within a single heartbeat had changed to fear. She stumbled slightly, turned away, and moved quickly onto the escalator.

I'd never seen a random act of violence before and felt the horror it evokes. The idea of a cough as a weapon startled and revolted me. If the standing woman had clawed the face of the blonde in one vicious movement it could not have been more aggressive, more predatory.

The queer act, the more perverted for its randomness, contaminated only a moment in the blonde girl's life, and yet I knew she would fail utterly, as I would, to ever describe its impact. *On the Underground a woman coughed at me*, she might say.

How rude, never mind, you're home now.

You don't understand. It was intimate, deliberate, violent.

That's London life, for you.

As I stepped onto the escalator behind them, the blonde, running hard on the metal steps, was about three-quarters of the way down. With a dainty and repulsive little kick of her booted foot, the dark woman began to hurry to shrink the distance between them. I knew she was not yet finished with her prey. I hurried too, determined to reach the victim before she disappeared into the crowds beyond. I'd touch her arm, tell her I'd seen it, tell her I'd felt it. Then I'd melt away, a stranger in the underground again, but having left her with a tiny thread of comfort in knowing she hadn't imagined it, should he sneer at her story.

As I drew level with the attacker, I had a strong compulsion to look right into her eyes, but I feared I'd see Medusa or something worse. And she, knowing by my face I'd witnessed the thing, would vomit the psychotic maelstrom she carried with her over me. I held my breath as I moved past her.

The fleeing woman was still in my view, but by the time I'd stepped off the escalator she was far ahead of me in the Northern Line crowd. I stopped; I had to turn right for Docklands. This was not my business; I needed to forget it. Things happen in London.

The Northern Line crowd surged around me carrying the dark creature with it. I didn't move. About twenty yards in front of me, she stopped too. I found myself unconscious of the crowd, the guardsmen, the noise. I knew before she ever turned her head to find me that she'd sensed I'd tried to come between her and the blonde.

On turning, she found me instantly, the only other traveller unmoving in the swarm, and as I gazed at her, I was glad I hadn't looked at her close up minutes before on the escalator.

Her beautiful face was broad and strong boned, but across it, as she glowered at me, a ripple of seething anger moved in a visible wave from her forehead to her mouth. There was something occult-like and compelling about the moment. I saw her mouth twist in contempt, I saw her register my face, hesitate, and look back quickly to locate the blonde. She turned to stare at me again, her eyes brimming with something baleful far past hatred, then she turned away and moved on quickly.

"You all right?" a guard asked. "You look ill."

I pointed, and before I spoke, I sensed the uselessness of any words. I could still see them both, now on the up escalator towards the northern line. "That dark headed woman..."

"Where?"

"That one," I stabbed the air with my finger repeatedly, and sensed the guard move away a pace. "She's following the blonde about three quarters of the way up, the one with the light coat. She mustn't catch her." I sounded ridiculous. "She's hunting her."

"Nothing will happen, there's cameras up there, you know."
I turned to look at the guard then, and found him smiling.

I think now the few seconds of my own encounter with the dark contaminator gave the blonde enough time to escape. I hope so. I imagine her walking into the light and warmth of her flat. She throws her bag and coat on the floor, puts her trembling hands to her face and sobs. She feels fouled. *A woman*, she begins, and then stops. Hellish images come to her, as they still do to me - demons from some arcane region in the human psyche quicken and take shape in her mind. The encounter cannot be told, and her journey through the bowels of London is tainted from that day forward, like mine is.

the dead must die

Ramsey Campbell

As soon as I push the doors open I know I am in the presence of evil. The lobby walls are white as innocence, but the place stinks of deceit. It is crowded with lost souls who wander aimlessly or talk to one another in low voices as though they are in church. Sensitivity to atmospheres is yet another gift which the mass of mankind has abandoned. I breathe a prayer and cross the threshold, steeling myself against the unhealthy heat which refutes the pretence of healing, the disinfectant stench bespeaking the presence of corruption, the closeness of so much unredeemed flesh.

Except I single myself out I may pass unnoticed. I silently intone the Twenty third Psalm, and am halfway through the fifth verse when I reach the lifts. I step into the nearest, thumbing the number of the floor to which I have been called. The doors are closing when they spring back as if possessed, and two men dressed like choirboys push in a trolley laden with a draped form that is sucking up blood.

The doors shut, embracing the heat which now I understand is meant to dull the senses, and the lift shudders as though revolted by the burden it is being made to carry. But the cage rises, humming smugly to itself, and I close my eyes and attempt not to breathe in the stink of devil's incense that reminds me I am in a place which might be a chapel of rest if it were not teeming with unholy corrupt life.

"Aren't you well?" one of the surpliced attendants says.

His clammy breath in my ear is like a shameful kiss. I step back from him and shake one finger at the thing on the trolley, mumbling "Can't stand..."

"You get used to it," he says with a laugh which I gather is intended to express sympathy but which shows me that he sees no deeper into me than I desire. I pray God that all his kind here will be as gullible, as indeed their employment in this place suggests.

The lift stops, and I button the doors open, resisting the instinct to let them close and burst the dangling sac of blood. The temptation to perform good works in haste, at the expense of the greater good, is one of the Adversary's subtlest tricks. As the attendants rush the trolley away the other lift releases a stream of visitors in the direction I am pointed by an arrow on the wall. I let them pass so as to move more swiftly to my goal; but when I emerge I see the way is guarded.

A uniformed woman sits at a desk in the corridor like a wicked child cast out of a schoolroom. She is playing the scribe, noting on a clipboard the names of all who pass. Some she appears to have turned back, for they are slumped against the walls, their faces sagging with the heat. I grip my case more firmly and stride forwards, silently repeating the psalm, and the woman raises first her face and then her eyebrows. "Visiting?"

"As you see."

She shakes her head like a beast that has been struck across the face. "Whom?"

"Paul Vincent."

"Relative?"

"A *caring* relative."

She lowers her gaze to her list as though my emphasis has crushed her. "Name?"

"George Saint."

Presumably this is as nothing to her, for she merely grunts and sets it down. When I make to pass, however, she emits a more bestial grunt and bars my way with a hand luxurious with fat and jewellery. "Two visitors maximum even in the private rooms. You'll have to wait."

I see myself driving a nail through her outstretched palm, and I press my free hand against my thigh. "I have come a long way to be here."

"Then I imagine you'll be staying for a while." When I refrain from contradicting her she says, "You needn't be afraid you won't see Mr Vincent again. He's our star patient, getting better every day."

That is a taunt even if she is unaware the Adversary is using her voice. "When his wife wrote to me," I say loudly, "she said he was not expected to live."

"These days we can perform miracles."

Perhaps the triumph in her voice means only that she suspects I would have profited by my brother's death. I retreat for fear of venting my wrath upon her, and I am beyond the lolling visitors when the door of Paul's room opens and my niece Mary looks around for me.

"Yes, it was him," she calls into the room. "Hello, Uncle "

I interrupt before she can arouse suspicion by pronouncing my name from my former life. "Mary. I must wait until someone makes way for me."

"I'll stay out here if you want to see dad."

The guardian of the corridor turns to ensure that she doesn't re-enter the room, and I wait until Mary comes forward. I have not set eyes on her for fifteen years — not since she would sit on my lap while I told her about Our Lord — and if I had any doubts about my mission they vanish at the sight of her. She is paler and thinner than she ought to be, and I believe I glimpse a knowing look in her eyes before she says, "Dad will be pleased you've come to see him."

I detect no guile in this, and pray that her knowingness is only a facade which she feels bound to present to the world. "I hope he can find it in his heart to welcome me."

"He says it's up to the individual what they believe."

For a moment I assume she is defending her father out of misplaced loyalty, and then I grasp that she thinks I was apologising for my faith, though she has no idea of its strength. I must surmise that she is not beyond redemption, however insidious are the influences which surround her. When she says "I'll wait here" I stride past the desk of the false scribe, repeating the fourth verse of the psalm under my breath, and enter the room.

My brother is lying in a bed, his eyes upturned to Heaven. His wife Penelope sits beside him, holding his hand. Their stillness almost persuades me that I am not needed here, and I succumb to a craven feeling of relief. Then my brother's head wavers up from the pillow, and his eyes, which are watery and veinous, light up with a blasphemous parody of intelligence and life. "Thomas," he whispers.

I want to proclaim my outrage with all my voice, but instead I advance to the foot of the bed and gaze solemnly at him. That appears to satisfy him, and his head sinks back. "Thank you for coming, Thomas," says his wife.

Her gratitude is as bogus as everything else in this evil chamber. She must have felt bound to contact me when my brother was at death's door. His eyes close, and he expels a long slow breath. "He waited for you," Penelope tells me.

Though that sounds as if she is holding me responsible for the unnatural prolongation of his life, I am filled with a hope that it has come to an end. His wide, pasty face has collapsed as though it is no longer anything but a mask, and he has folded his hands on his chest. Then his hands stir, betraying their mockery of piety, as his chest rises and falls. He is dead, yet he breathes. He has joined the Undead.

How can God's daylight allow such a thing to be? When I attempt to recall how long it has been since I last saw the sun, it seems to me that the sky has been overcast for weeks before I was called to my brother. And the sun and the air were darkened by reason of the smoke of the pit, and there is no sunlight to combat the room's Godless light, which celebrates the flush of my brother's cheeks that gives him the appearance of a whore rouged with the blood of her victims. I turn away in revulsion and confront his wife, who says "I didn't know if you would come. I wasn't even sure we had your right address."

Nor have they, God be thanked. "I felt I had to," I confess.

"You're still born again, then. You're still of the same mind."

"We are all of His mind, however we regard ourselves. There is no birth nor death but proceeds from Him."

At least she has the grace to look embarrassed, though only because in these faithless days God is the dirtiest of words. "We've become quite friendly with the Beynons," she says defensively. "The donor's family."

The heat and stink coagulate in my throat, and for some seconds I cannot swallow for the thought of my brother with part of a corpse sewn up inside him. "Have you visited the grave?" I croak.

"Whose?"

"What you call the donor."

"Why, no," she says as though it is I who am in the wrong. "We don't want to intrude."

"Where is he buried?"

"She. Kidneys don't have a sex, you know. She's in the churchyard near where you used to have your flat."

"A short walk from where I am staying. If there is no objection I shall pay my respects."

"I expect you'll do whatever you think is right," she says in a tone which suggests I ought to be ashamed of doing so. "I hope you don't mind staying in a hotel, by the way. I've my hands full getting the house ready for Paul to come home."

She must take me for a fool if she imagines I assume that otherwise I would be welcome in her house, when everything about myself is a reproach. I succeed in sounding casual. "When is that to be?"

"The doctors say Sunday."

The word should choke them. "I shall be in church."

"Come over afterwards to say goodbye to Paul if you have time."

She clearly hopes the opposite, and I may let her think her wish is granted. Sometimes a venial sin is justified in the prosecution of His work. "I have troubled you enough for the nonce," I tell her. "Beynon, you said. What Christian name?"

She seems reluctant to answer, but perhaps she senses that I am prepared to demand the information of my brother, for she replies "Bernadette."

It is indeed Christian — the name of the saint to whom His Blessed Mother chose to appear — which makes the mutilation yet more blasphemous. "May God watch over you and Paul," I curse, and retreat into the corridor.

Only Mary and the guard remain. The guard is studying her clipboard as though it holds a sacred text, while Mary leans against the wall. As I approach, her eyes open and her pale, undernourished face attempts to counterfeit a smile. "How was dad?"

I needn't lie. "I am more concerned with how you are, Mary."

"I'm all right. I'm fine," she says, failing to conceal her evasiveness.

I raise my case against my chest so that neither she nor the guard can see what I am carrying, and reach in. "Will you wear this to please me?" I say, and hand Mary the twin of the cross which I never remove.

She hesitates, and I feel as if the Adversary has seized me by the throat. If she is unable to take hold of the cross I shall know she is already a victim of the Undead. Then she holds out a hand palm upwards and suffers me to lay the cross on it. "It's a bit heavy," she complains.

The childishness of her protest convinces me that she is still fundamentally innocent, and I offer up a silent prayer of thanks. "Wear it always," I exhort her. "If anyone tries to dissuade you, do not hesitate to contact me."

"I like wearing pretty things."

I am taken unawares by a wave of grief for her. "I'll buy you a pretty cross if you promise to wear this one at night until I do, and say your prayers."

"Do I really have to, Unc—?"

I interrupt her, though the guard appears to be trying not to overhear, by taking the cross from her hand and touching it to her lips before lifting the cord over her head. "Wear it until you get home at least, for His sake."

She looks rebellious, as children can be. I walk quickly to the lifts and step into the nearest before she has time to argue. Perhaps if my brother or his wife attempts to influence her not to wear the cross she will turn her rebelliousness against them. I say another prayer for her as I pass through the lobby and out of that place.

As I entered it had seemed an anteroom to Hell, but now I find it little different from its surroundings. In less time than it takes me to repeat the psalm, I am in the shadow of chemical factories discharging their poisons into a sky the colour of sin. Behind them, on the bank of a filthy river, chimneys spout flames that dance and struggle, and I think of machines that begin to consume souls at the hour of death. Opposite the tract of factories gaunt terraces like cellblocks extend as far as the eye can see face one another across pinched streets with narrow pavements unrelieved except by tainted plots of grass. Broken glass surrounds every streetlamp, and I see that the denizens of these streets abhor the light. How many of them may be Undead, freed by the shrouding of the sun to walk by day?

It takes me half an hour's unbroken march to come in sight of the hotel near the factories. I comfort myself by repeating the psalm aloud, and whenever anyone approaches within earshot they pass by on the other side. I raise my voice to let them know they have betrayed themselves. Their dull self absorbed faces are pale as tissue paper — a tissue of lies.

A few cheap shops huddle opposite the hotel, and I buy vegetables from a greengrocer whose hands are calloused with toil and who wears a small cross at her throat. As I enter the hotel's dim and dismal hall, where the walls are a mass of advertisements for gluttony and other forms of self indulgence, the landlady accosts me. "I'm afraid cooking isn't allowed in the rooms, Mr

Saint," she says, slowly wringing her colourless hands in a pretence of regret.

"Nor do I propose it, Mrs *Trollope*."

"And I still have to charge for meals even if you don't take them."

"We must all be guided by our consciences, Mrs Trollope." Since she has no answer to this I say "If I may have my key I need trouble you no further."

She thrusts at me the cudgel to which the key is attached, and I climb the shabby stairs to my cheerless room, which smells of must and stale smoke and nights of solitary lechery. I hang my overcoat in the nondescript wardrobe and fall to my knees between the sink and the bed. When I feel I have prayed out the evils of the day I eat half a cabbage and two raw potatoes, savouring the taste of God's earth and the gritting of it between my teeth. The vegetables are as wholesome as can be expected in this place, and at least they were sold to me by a believer. Anything that is served in the hotel will have been touched by blood.

Night has fallen. The factories howl and glare with evil light. Hordes who have squandered their day in the factories shuffle into the narrow streets as if their shadows are dragging them home, while their neighbours swarm to take their places in the workshops of pollution. Then the land is quiet until the young begin to prowl, quaffing wine and smashing bottles in the roadways, if indeed the wine has not undergone some sacrilegious transubstantiation. After a time the corpse lights of the factories show only lost souls fleeing after their shadows through a lurid icy rain, and I have prayed enough that I crave sleep.

I use the communal bathroom, which is full of warm fog and a suggestive smell of perfumed soap, and then I set about defending my room. I rub garlic around the inside of the door and windows, and employ the cloves to plug the taps and the sink. I hang a cross above the bed and another at its foot, and lay a cross on the frayed carpet at each side. Though thus protected, I am reluctant to switch off the lamp while I sense the land is teeming with corruption. Even the miserly light of the room seems preferable to the unholy glow outside the faded curtains. I kneel to recite Psalm 130, pummelling my breasts and temples as I raise my voice, and when I feel Him answer me in my depths I lay me down to sleep.

But the Adversary has sent his minions to beset me. As I cried out, my left hand neighbour buffeted the wall in a vain attempt to interrupt my supplication, and now I hear Mrs Trollope's voice, first beneath my window and then much closer. I think that she has scaled the outer wall, as the Undead are known to do, until I realise that she is at my door. "I hope you won't be keeping that light on much longer, Mr Saint," she says.

I hold my peace, hoping that she will conclude I am not to be awakened by trifles. Then she begins to smite the door with a clumsiness which suggests to me that she is the worse, if such is possible, for drink. "I know you're in there, Mr Saint," she bawls. "Put that light out or I'll put you out."

When I tire of her blustering I grasp the cord above the bed. As I pull it, darkness descends like the outpouring of a cloaca. A muffled discussion ensues in the corridor outside my room; no doubt the Adversary's minions are plotting further ways to disturb me. Let them seek to enter — they will find me armed. But nothing transpires except the closing of several doors, and so I lie on my back and take a cross in each hand.

In the fullness of time I slumber, as best I can while maintaining a vigil over my hands for fear that the Adversary may endeavour to loosen their grasp and trick them into repudiating the cross. When the sky begins to pale with the dawn I rise and pray that the sun may sear away the pall which darkens the land. Hours later only an enfeebled glow has seeped through the shroud, which I see is the colour of the corpse lights, as though some poisonous exhalation has grown solid overnight to snuff out the day.

I venture to the bathroom in order to do the penance of voiding myself, then I scour my body at the sink in my room. I plan to spend the greater portion of the day in prayer. The

Adversary will have none of this, however. I have scarcely fallen to my knees when he sends his trollop to besiege me. "I want a word with you, Mr Saint," she shouts.

"Have it, then."

"I can't hear you. I won't talk through a door."

"I thought that was a favourite pastime of yours," I say, and fling the door open. "Now you see me, madam."

I have revealed only my right hand side when she falls back and shields her eyes like Eve after eating the apple. "For God's sake, Mr Saint, cover yourself up."

"We are all naked before Him." Smirking at her hypocrisy, I hold a cross in front of myself. "Now I am as clothed as any man need be."

She stays out of sight and raises her voice. "I'm afraid I must ask you to leave at once."

"May I ask who requires it of you?"

She stamps her foot, shaking the floor. "Let me remind you this is my house."

"It's worthy of your name."

"I don't know what this room smells of, but I want it out, and you. I've had complaints about the row you made all night, snoring and carrying on like I don't know what."

"Why, madam, I took you as my model."

She stamps so hard that the crosses on the floor spring up. "I'm giving you ten minutes to pay up and get out and then I'm calling the police."

So the scheme is to have me cast out before I can fulfil my mission. It would be the work of moments to pursue her and cut her down, but how many of her creatures might I have to put an end to, thereby perhaps drawing unwelcome attention to myself? Shall I abase myself and plead to be allowed to stay two further nights? The notion sticks in my gullet, and then I know that He has not forsaken me, for all at once I see where I may take refuge. My cases are packed in five minutes, and in less than ten I am downstairs, jangling the bell of ill repute which stands on the counter. When Mrs Trollope pokes her face through the hole in the wall above it I cast my coins before her. "I think you will find that fits the bill."

"Haven't you any notes?"

"I thought silver more appropriate. Please count it."

She glowers and with a Jew's gesture scoops the coins together so as to pick them up with both thumbs and forefingers and drop them onto two piles. "That seems to be right," she grudgingly admits.

Can she really not have noticed there are thirty coins? "Wholly," I assure her, and depart out of that house, shaking off the dust of my feet.

The railway station where I arrived is five minutes' forced march distant, up a steep hill between extravagant windows choked with finery. The flesh of the crowds around me seems no less discoloured and artificial than that of the cheap sculptures modelling luxury in the stores which steep the pavements in alluring light. In the station the voice of a false oracle echoes through the vault, sending the lost fleeing hither and thither. As I slide my suitcase into a locker I am reminded of the ungodly practice of cremation. The thought fuels my anger as I set out on the first stage of my task.

The churchyard crowns a hill ribbed with mean streets. While the spire still points to Heaven, many of the gravestones have been overturned, perhaps by the revels of the Undead. Stone angels display mutilated wrists, as thieves in heathen countries do, so that I wonder if this may be yet another symptom of the undermining of our Christian ways by the influx of the heathen. Let it never be forgotten that the Undead originated in lands less Christian than ours.

A few mourners, if that is what they are, loiter morosely near wreaths, and a pair of silent workmen are spading out a grave. Rather than draw attention to myself by enquiring of the labourers where I should go I play the aimless visitor, wandering the stone rows, at whose junctions wire baskets are piled with empty bottles and withered flowers. I am halfway across the churchyard when a funeral arrives at the new grave, and I watch the mourners weep more copiously than is Christian. By the time I reach my goal, a family grave near the top of the churchyard, a vicious wind has cleared the place except for myself.

The Beynon plot is marked by a granite obelisk. Gilded names and dates are etched on the shaft, and the lowest name is Bernadette. As I would expect of a family which allowed her helpless body to be violated, no prayer has been inscribed on her behalf. Her yearning to be hallowed is as clear to me as though she is murmuring a plea in my ear. I kick the pharisaical wreath away from the obelisk and grind the flowers underfoot before falling to my knees on her mound. "The Day of Judgment shall find thee whole," I vow, and immediately I sense her gratitude. I grub her mound open with my hands and bury a cross as deep as I can to keep her safe.

I stay at prayer until the hellish lights of the town begin to waken; then I make for the church. I know that tonight the Undead must exert all their powers against me. I pass through the porch and open my flask to collect holy water from the font, and my heart quails within me. The church is starkly furnished with thin pews and an altar. How shall I go unnoticed when the priest locks the church for the night?

As I stopper the flask I hear footsteps on the gravel path outside the porch. I run to the sole refuge the place affords and crouch behind the altar. The inner door opens, and footsteps approach. Should I not declare myself and my mission, and crave sanctuary against the Undead? If the priest doubts my mission he is no priest, and I must strike him down before the altar he has desecrated. Yet I have little stomach for such an act in God's house, and breathe a prayer as the footsteps halt at the altar.

In a very few minutes the priest, having presumably breathed a perfunctory prayer, retreats along the aisle; then I hear him stop at the font and mutter what sounds all too like profanity. How can a man of the cloth let slip such a word, above all in church? I prepare to follow him and cut him down like the fig tree that beareth no fruit but cumbereth the ground. But darkness falls inside the church, the inner door closes, and I hear the false priest lock the outer door.

At once the church is no longer dark. A faint evil glow rises from the town, transforming the saints in the window above me into swarthy heathens and encrusting the pews with a dimness that appears to crawl. I should be safest where I am, guarded by the altar. I grasp two crosses and lie down on stone with my case for a pillow, and try to pray myself to sleep in order to be ready for the morrow's task. Out of the depths have I cr

A crash of glass! I leap up, brandishing the crosses, and stumble against the altar. The sainted window is intact. I have slumbered; was the sound only in my dream? No, for there comes an outburst of bestial yelling beyond the window, and the thump of gravestones on the earth. The Undead are abroad to trouble my sleep.

When I begin to pronounce an exorcism with all my voice the clamour falters momentarily, then redoubles. The Undead dance and jeer while their hands, if hands they are, belabour the wall of the church. More glass shatters, and I replace the cross in my right hand with my blade. If anything enters the building I shall shed its foul gore.

Perhaps the church is secure against evil, however, because the Undead content themselves with lupine baying in a vain bid to blot out my exorcism. When I grow so hoarse that I can barely whisper, their uproar subsides. I hear them shambling away, toppling gravestones as perhaps they seep back into their graves. I am seized by a fit of coughing, and when at last I am able to contain myself I strain my ears, distrusting the silence. Much later I sink to the floor behind the alt

"Who's there? Is someone there?"

The voice is in the church. The door has been unlocked. I have slept longer than I meant to, until a snore wakened me. Too late I understand that the Undead have achieved their purpose after all. I try to remain absolutely still, praying silently that I need not use my blade, as the priest comes up the aisle. He is almost at the altar — he has only to lean over it to see me. Then he turns on his heel and trots away, and I hear him on the gravel that surrounds the church.

I drop the blade into my case as I run on tiptoe to the porch. The priest has yet to reappear around the building; he must be searching among the graves beyond the far end of the church for the sleeper he overheard. I dart over the grass and crouch behind an angel, only to be overwhelmed by the sense that I am in a position for my bowels to betray me. I hear the priest marching over the gravel, muttering and rubbing his hands together, having presumably righted the gravestones. As he arrives at the porch, a loud and lengthy noisome wind escapes me. The pollution of the land must have inured him, for without hesitation he re-enters the church.

I compose myself and follow him. I mean to spend my time in prayer and fasting until I must be about my mission. The priest is replenishing the font, and gives me a sharp glance. "God be with you," I bid him as I cross myself.

Perhaps he recognises that I feel it to be more appropriate that I should wish him this than the reverse; he can hardly bring himself to respond, "And with you." I make my way to the foremost pew and kneel, scorning the luxury of the kneeler. I shall pray silently until the priest says Mass, and th

Something is thrust between my ribs. The Undead have invaded the church and turned my weapons against me. "Retro me, Satanas!" I scream, and find myself surrounded by churchgoers, one of whom has elbowed me. All of them, and the priest in the pulpit, are staring at me. If his sermon and his celebration of the Mass had been sincere I would not have slumbered. "Pray continue," I say with a wave of my hand.

When he tires of striving to force me to avert my gaze he recommences prating to the congregation on the subjects of forgiveness and tolerance. In this land there is far too much of both, and almost all of it misdirected. I keep myself awake by gripping crosses so that their corners dig into my palms, though the false priest appears to frown on crosses. The Mass ends and the congregation straggles out while I remain on my knees. I have by no means done praying when the priest sidles up to me. "Are you in need of help, my son?"

"Psalm Twenty eight, verse seven."

"I'm sorry, I'm not too familiar— "

"The Lord is my strength and my shield. My heart trusted in him, and I am helped."

He scowls at the rebuff or at having revealed his ignorance, and stalks off to gather prayer books; then he loiters about the church until I finish praying although I continue until it is almost dark. It seems that, like the landlady, he is being used to drive me out and rob me of a day's grace, and there are moments when I have to struggle to contain my wrath. When at last I succeed in relaxing my grip on the crosses and return them to my case I perform a solemn obeisance before the altar; then I glare so fiercely at the priest that he feigns a sudden interest in the contents of a hymnal as I stride out of the church.

The grubby light is draining into the vile landscape. As I make my way downhill through the blackened furtive terraces the tethered flames jerk above the soiled roofs, and I see I am descending into Hell. The sight of a telephone box diverts me along a terrace whose windows are shrouded with net curtains like the dusty webs of a dozen or more enormous spiders. The box is derelict; holes gape where its instrument and light should be. No doubt the denizens of the land are anxious to prevent anyone less irredeemable than themselves from communicating with the outside world, though surely I saw telephones in use when I arrived at the railway station.

As I enter its vault the voice of the oracle proclaims the name of the town where I live. This is so transparently intended as a temptation that I scoff aloud. Few are there to hear me, and most of them are supine on benches after some debauch. I walk to the nearest telephone and dial the number of my brother's house before turning my back to the wall.

The bell ceases its measured tolling. "Vincent," says Paul's wife.

"It is I."

"Oh, yes," she says discouragingly. "Calling to say goodbye?"

"That is what I understand you wanted me to do."

"Did I? Paul's home, but he's in bed resting. I'll tell him you rang."

"Perhaps," I suggest after mouthing a prayer, "I could say goodbye to Mary."

"She isn't here. She's at a friend's, watching videos."

My prayer is answered. I need not wait until tomorrow, when Mary will be at college. Nevertheless Penelope's tone is too defiant for me to allow it to pass unreproved. "On a Sunday?" I rebuke her.

"She's been working hard all day helping me to get the house ready for her father."

"Working on the Sabbath is a poor excuse for self indulgence," I declare, and am abruptly overwhelmed by the panic I experienced on Mary's behalf at the hospital. "Besides, when I last saw her she hardly looked fit for work."

"I suppose you think that's funny."

"I assure you I am not smiling."

"Do you ever?" Penelope says, and with a sudden weariness which I suspect is counterfeit "This sort of conversation's why I'm glad Paul's in bed. I don't want you upsetting him, or Mary either."

"I fail to see how one can upset somebody by enquiring after their health."

"You know perfectly well what I mean. Or if you don't I'll tell you, because I'm proud of her. She's become a lot more responsible since she nearly lost her father. When you saw her she'd just given a pint of blood."

I shudder so violently that I almost kick my case away, and my knees scrape together. Even worse than the revelation is my sense that I ought to have known — that only my fears on Mary's behalf had prevented me from realising the Undead were already battening on her. I sway against the wall, and the oracle names my home again. "It sounds as if it's time to go," Penelope says in my ear.

If there is one thing the Father of Lies can be trusted sooner or later to do, it is to contradict himself. The attempt to lure me home has rebounded on my enemies. I hang up the receiver as a response to her and, snatching my case, leave the station at a run.

My brother's house is hidden among the terraces opposite the factories. As I stride up the street which leads to it, my shadow lengthens ahead of me. I will not allow myself to feel that it is leading me into darkness; rather am I forcing it onwards between windows black as the pit or flickering with light from screens around which pallid faces cluster. Some of the faces rise as though from feeding and gaze dead eyed at me. Each step I take brings me closer to a black panic which, it appears, I can fend off only by outrunning it. I force myself to slow down and intone the psalms until their rhythm imparts discipline to my walk.

My brother lives in our parents' old house. It, and the square of which it is a part, seemed like a haven to me until I began to perceive the errors of my life. Now I see it is an unhallowed sepulchre concealed deep in a monstrous graveyard. I unlatch the gate and venture past the willow into the garden, where the cloying scent of flowers cannot disguise the tell tale smell of turned earth. I have taken out my largest cross, and I hammer with it on the front door.

In a moment my brother's voice, feeble when it should be mute, calls out "Who's that, love?"

"I'll see. You rest," Penelope says beyond the door. At once it is flung open, and her frown multiplies at the sight of me. "I thought you— "

"Is Mary home yet?"

"No, I told you—"

I need hear no more. I raise the cross above my head. If I had any doubts, the fear which immediately fills her eyes would show me what she is. I bring the cross down with all my force, and one arm of it strikes her left temple, which splinters and begins to leak. A second blow shatters her throat as she attempts to cry out. She is already falling to her knees like a slaughtered beast, making obeisance too late, and I slam the door as I step into the hall. I am raising the cross to deliver a final blow when her eyes go out, and she topples over backwards, still kneeling, so that I hear her knees creak and then snap like pistol shots. If she were alive I am sure she would scream.

I stoop to wipe the bloodied cross on her breast, and then I hear the voice of my dead brother. "Penelope? Penelope?"

The sound infects me with terror, but also rekindles my wrath. As I straighten my back I repeat the Twenty third Psalm aloud. I have just reached the foot of the stairs when my brother's walking corpse gropes out of his room and advances to the banister on legs that should no longer move. Grotesquely, it is wearing pyjamas instead of a shroud. "Thomas, what are you—?" it says in a voice like a wind in a churchyard, and its eyes focus, though they must be rotting from within, on what is left of Paul's wife. "My God, what's happened to — Thomas, what have you —
"

I am not interrupting. Its brain must be rotting too, and able to recall only fragments of living speech. The thing is no longer my brother, although I may be right to have heard a plea when it took His name in vain? "God help you, Paul, if you can understand me. I'll save you," I cry, and spring up the stairs.

The suffused remains of its eyes turn to me as if they can hardly focus. I hope it will welcome the end, or else I expect it to recoil before the advance of the cross in my hand. The Adversary has clouded my thoughts, so that I am unprepared when the face of the thing that was once my brother darkens as though all the blood it has consumed is rushing to its brain, and it flies at me, snarling like a wild beast, seeking whom it may devour.

My case is open. I drop it beside me on the stair and snatch out the flask of holy water. I barely have time to unscrew the cap when the Undead thing is upon me. I retreat a step and dash holy water into its eyes. It staggers, moaning, and falls on its back on the stairs. Before it can recover I seize my blade from the case and plunge the point deep between the thing's ribs.

The stolen blood gushes high as though grateful for release. I lean all my weight on the blade, and feel it penetrate the stair beneath as the Undead corpse writhes like an impaled insect, fluttering its hands. When at last it ceases moving I withdraw the blade and hammer the stake in its place, hearing ribs splinter.

The foul but necessary work is not yet done. I unbutton the thing's jacket and, cutting open the flesh beneath the lower ribs, widen the incision with my hands. By digging with the blade I am able to lay bare the kidneys. One is slightly smaller, and my instincts tell me this belongs to the victim of the Undead. I hack it free and prise it out of its raw nest and pray over it before wrapping it in the bag which contained the potatoes. I place the bag in my case and trudge downstairs, bearing the cross before me.

I am almost at the front door when I catch sight of the directory beside the telephone. I leave my gory fingerprints on the page that lists Blood. Long before the prints can be identified my task will be done. The key to a mortice lock protrudes from a keyhole inside the front door, and I lock the door behind me as I leave, then I break off the shaft of the key in the lock. Now Mary must seek help with entering the house, and I pray she will not be the first to see how my brother and his wife have been redeemed. I should like to be with her when she sees them, but there is still much to do. In the morning I shall ask the greengrocer where I can buy a pretty cross to have sent to my niece.

My shadow follows me out of the dead terraces and turns ahead of me. It leads me past the station and uphill to the church. It seems to me that the shadow is my own black soul, urging me to redeem it with further good works. For the moment the churchyard is silent; the Undead must be elsewhere. I make my way swiftly to the Beynon grave and, withdrawing the cross from the mound, place the stolen organ in the hole before covering it with the cross and with earth.

Now I shall keep watch here until the morning. I could go now and destroy the house of vampirism, but I mean to strike down those who administer this iniquity. Whatsoever soul it shall be that eateth any manner of blood, even that soul shall be cut off. The victims such as Mary I shall spare, and the town of the Undead shall rise up against me, nor shall I escape. Let my exploit and my martyrdom act as a sign to the righteous, that they may destroy the false healers, the vampires whose uniforms mock sanctity, the halls of intensive care which are factories of mutilation. I am not alone. Our time has come.

the ringing sound of death in the water tank

Stephanie Campisi

The driveway to the Platts' farmhouse is narrow and crunchy, and the haggard wire fences that line the paddocks sag and sigh, a loose garrote. They are too close to the sides of our car, which is old and wheezing, and has deep cracks from the sun in its light brown vinyl upholstery. Stuffing oozes out from my seat like guts, and I try to stick it back in, but it doesn't want to go, like when you get a paper cut and the skin separates like a zip.

The driveway is less of a driveway and more of an avenue, and it stretches far behind us and far ahead of us like a dusty piece of string. Gum trees stretch overhead, on their tiptoes like ballerinas en pointe, but they are not elegant. Their branches are twisted and writhing like old crones, and their bark is peeling off in dark brown sections like snakeskin. They interlock in a leafy roof, making me think of what it might be like inside a church, particularly as the farmhouse up ahead juts steeple-like out of a hill.

It takes a long time to drive up to that house, but we are going very slowly, avoiding potholes and blue-tongued lizards that look like patchy clay riddled with fingernails. I think I could probably run down to the main road in maybe five minutes, although very few cars pass down that way, so I would have to make sure there was somewhere to hide. You have to think of these things when you visit the Platts.

When we reach the house, Simon is waiting for us, with his stocky Jack Russell straining against its red harness. Simon keeps it reined in tight, the skin around his fingers spotted with white from the effort, and the dog tugs so hard it spins around. The dog has a saddle of brown fur, and a tail tipped with white that stands up like a paintbrush or a flag. My mother smiles, and I smile, too, but only because we have talked about this in the car.

My mother says that Simon is fragile, like an egg, but I think that he is cracked, or rotten.

She unclasps the dog's harness, and the dog leaps up against her legs, scrabbling at her knees and leaving a trail of flower-like paw prints down her trousers. She leans forward to take my hand, her eyes avoiding Simon's, focused instead on the faded pink and grey of the dozens of galahs that are gathered around a damp hollow in the ground, preening and puffing out their bearded jowls and bobbing their mohawked heads. They seem so insipid, like pale clothes stained by darker ones, but maybe it is the light, which makes everything against the dark red earth seem only half there. Her attention on the birds, who barely resemble their fairy-floss, Technicolor-vibrant relatives in the city, she ends up groping air, as Simon is already pulling me along to the corrugated tin shed that houses the tractor, the header, and two old, green cars that scare me because their bonnets and grilles and lights and the metal tusks that once held their license plates seem to all merge together to make a face.

Simon pulls down a rust-rotten oil can with a spout riddled with holes like a doily from splintery shelf, and he tips it so that a few drops fall on to one of the cars, where they sit, shimmering like a rolled-up ball of snail muck. He sticks out two of his fingers, the way that smokers do, and he rubs the oil into the chipped paint, so that the smeary rainbow of the fluid mixes with the grit of dust until there are sticky, muddy bits, and smooth, shining areas resembling stretched-out tears.

"But look what else," he says, and he leaps over a metal bar and some coiled chain that sits there with the malevolent quiet of a king brown. His shoes, scuffed runners with frayed, filthy laces full of burrs and bindi-eye that and have no labels, crunch over the crisp autumnal leaves eddied in by a willy-willy. He stomps on the leaves, gouges the toes of his shoes into them and shreds them. They make a sound of old newspaper tearing.

"Over here", he says, as he lifts a piece of ragged blue tarp, fringed at the edges like a plastic fern. Red dust like shattered bricks, and thicker sandy granules, trickle down the slope he has created like it is an hourglass. "Here. Birds. Chicks."

They look feral, deformed, the way baby birds look: their thickly-lidded eyes freeze-dried peas, and their down wispy old-man hair. Their beaks are stretched gramophone mouths, or bursting succulent flowers: the brightest red ringed with yellow. Their crops dance up and down, minute corn cobs, as they scream at us. Simon picks one up, cradling its pathetic form, cupping his hands around it, blocking out all light save for a tiny sliver from the gap between his thumbs. He puts his eye up to the crescent moon-shaped space, and peers in at the chick, which shivers in his grip, a quick sound, the fanning of a deck of cards.

The remaining two chicks writhe over each other, groping blindly at each other with dwarf-like wing-stubs and wobbling heads.

"You should put it back," I say, watching as Simon presses his thumbs together so that no light shines through. "You'll scare it."

"I can't put it back. It's got my smell now. Its mother won't want it."

He steps over the metal bar, swinging one leg wide and grazing the tarp with the side of his ratty shoe. The air is crisp and has a sharp clean edge, even with the obese sun that swelters in the sky, but Simon steps out onto the dusty track, with its kerb of flattened spiny feathers of wheat and fallen pine cones leaking sticky blood. There is a wind, a low, cold wind, that seems to sing as it flees like a fugitive down from the pigsty at the end of the paddock closest to us.

I lift up the two tiny birds still huddling beneath the tarp, and nestle them into the folded lip of the bottom of my shirt with a few peeling bits of straw and some shit-covered clumps of grain. The birds wriggle against me like fish, like my baby brother against the swollen and yellow freckly flesh—like an overripe mango — of my mother's belly, only days before she lay crying on the cold bathroom tiles, the ones I pretended were a Scrabble board, her fingers red as though she had been painting.

I clutch at my little birds, feel them burring about in the dark space I have made for them, and I smile a little as I think about saving them, and how I will hide them in the bedroom where I will be staying, with its two beds pointing at each other and with their blue floofy covers that have not changed since the eldest Platt son moved out of home. His name is still on the door, painted on a felt flag with crumbling thick paint. There are also two thumb-tacks stuck in the wood, and it's impossible to prise them out.

I stumble over a fallen branch from one of the few oak trees that can be found on the farm: they exist only in a small section between farmhouse and the tractor shed, but their leaves, gummy, spiny dog hairs, are everywhere. This is the only dark place on the farm, even in autumn, when the trees are going bald, their rain-spattered pates looking oily like hairless men. The white-painted wire fence of the farmhouse can be seen at certain points, but mostly the dirt is deep and loose and thick beneath my feet, and it sticks to my dew-damp legs where my jeans have ridden up. There are white rocks clustered about like giant mushrooms or pulled teeth beneath a pillow of pine needles and fallen plumage from cockatoos and the two plump frilly-knickered chooks that dart about here hiding from the hawks that swing by overhead. Old bottles and tins, lined up according size and likeness, lay together in a clearing, reminding me of the tombs in the cemetery half an hour out of town. They are encrusted with sap and mud, and some of them are broken, with vicious edges like tiaras of glass.

Beyond them, back out in the rust-red open with its rough stubble of scraggly weeds and native grasses, the rain water tank, bleached and with peeling paint from sunburn, teeters on the stiletto points of its scaffolding. Simon stands near it, scuffing a foot around in half-circles, the same way my mother folds in cake mixture, and I see that he is teasing the taut, rusted maw of a rabbit trap, whose plate is the only thing about it polished enough to catch the light. The ground around it is stained, even darker than everywhere else. There are soft piles of fur trimming the claws of the trap, an old-fashioned stole, the sort my great grandmother would have worn.

"Lots of times", Simon says, "they don't die straight away. Usually their leg just gets snapped, like foxes. And Dad comes out in the morning to kill them — he just snaps their necks like that. Sometimes he goes out in the ute. And sometimes their heads just come off in your hands, if you pull too hard. And their spine just looks like a long white straw. But they're pests. I don't think we should waste good man hours putting them out of their misery."

And he draws apart his hands, which have been pressed together against the chick as though in prayer, and very slowly he draws back his right arm, and throws the bird against the tin ribs of the water tank, so hard that the tendon of his elbow clicks over the bone.

The bird slaps into the side of the tank, making a tiny burst of applause; then falls on to the wooden platform at the base of the tank, which is high above me, and looks like a raft.

There is a sound in the air, a humming, a ringing, a sound that pounds through your chest and then needles its way up to your eardrums, where it holds on, tenacious and cruel and desperate. And I think I can hear a crying, too, an arrhythmic sobbing that jabs at me worse than that terrible sound, and then I realise that it's me, and with the tiny birds pouring over each other in my shirt like congealing liquid, I run back to the farmhouse, dirt spiralling out behind me in a dusty parachute.

For lunch we have sauce and cheese sandwiches on fat white bread. The cheese is that sort that when you put it in the oven, it bubbles and shrinks like hot tar, or like chip packets over a fire.

251

We eat at the breakfast bar, which is used for every meal, not just breakfast. There are fly-flecked bunches of fake grapes hanging from the walls and sitting in baskets. They have lurid leaves that are similar to the plastic green wall of grass you get with sushi. Some of their ends are squished in like wasting dates from where we used to stand beneath them on our tiptoes and strain to grasp the bottom grape, squeezing it so that you could feel the slippery fabric of its insides grazing over itself.

Mrs Platt starts telling us a story as I walk across the patched, peeling lino on the floor, dragging my toes against the rough patches where the pattern has been gouged out by falling crockery or heavy crates. I go into the pantry, looking for a bottle of cordial, gently drawing aside the clinking green plastic beads that hang like seaweed from a row of nails across the top of the door.

"So I'm in the pantry," she says, taking long sips from the cup of tea she twirls around and around on its coaster. "I'm cleaning it out because Myra's coming over, and you know what she's like, and I don't want to give her something to tell people down at the club. And I've moved aside all the tins and preserves and what have you, and I'm rooting around in that plastic ice-cream container I keep all me rubber bands in, and I'm trying to knot all the loose pieces of string together. So I tug on this bit of string, and it tugs back!" She laughs, and I can hear her bottom lip and her tongue slurping over her false teeth, which she pops in and out, in and out. My mother is giggling, too, saying incredulous things, but she is slightly hesitant, as she always is when the Platts discuss animals.

I find the bottle of cordial, but take off the lid and sniff it first, because there is a dusty bottle of vinegar that looks exactly the same sitting next to it. It smells like blackcurrant, and I take it back to the table.

"Now," says Mrs. Platt, slapping the brown chequerboard tiles that march up and down the breakfast bar, "God knows I can handle any animal 'cept spiders. Give me the heebies, they do. So Simon offers to go in, and he gets it in his bare hands, this bloody huge huntsman spider, and takes it outside, just like that. No fuss, no fluff-arsing around."

My mother doesn't respond this time: she just chews for a very long time on a piece of her open-faced sandwich. I know she is thinking, like I am, of that spider in Simon's hands.

I excuse myself, saying that I want to play with the totem tennis pole that creaks when the wind bustles by and where a willy wag-tail perches sometimes, waiting for Mrs. Platt to hand-feed it a moth. Simon follows me: I know that he wants to see where I have hidden the baby birds, so instead I sit on the old bench swing on the broad, high verandah. The verandah is a massive block of cement that has been painted with thick green paint, as though it is pretending to be grass, but it does a poor job of blending in with the crumbling tree that sits in the lap of its L-shape, drowning under heavy garments of ageing, browning ivy. It shades us from the heavy autumn sun, which darts between overlong trembling branches and creeping burnt tendrils.

Stink beetles clamber up the rusted arms of the swing and over the floral-patterned vinyl, darting beneath the sharp plastic findings and down the gaps between the cushions. Simon is eating Smarties, licking them and then running them over his lips and tongue and chin so that his face turns various garish colours. A scaly skink tumbles down the verandah and darts over the sun-warmed brick paving and into the bowels of the suffocating ivy-covered tree that waves above us like Medusa.

I realise that there are too many small, innocent things here around us, and every time I see one, my heart beats a little faster.

Up close, the dam smells putridly of fish guts and decaying yabbies. The drought means that the water levels have dropped, and on its inclined banks are several metres worth of salt, sudsy bubbles on a drained bathtub. Yabby holes like vague freckles hide at the very edges of the water, and a necklace of blue and orange pincers and shells rings the dam.

A few metres out, far enough away that the rank water seeps over the tops of my gumboots before I get a quarter of the way there, on a notched yardstick, sits a crow, its scaly, reptilian feet gouging into the mud-flecked skull of a ram that Mr. Platt set out there like a voodoo totem as a joke years ago. The bird is glossy and fat, and it huffily puffs out its plumage to make itself look bigger, like Simon's brothers when they bicker.

I run my fingers, which are cross-hatched with shallow grazes from dancing between briars and reaching for plump fruit, over the surface of the water, which breaks and shivers, like a dog when you pat it. The crow cries out once, throaty and harsh, the voice of the art teacher at school who has laryngitis. It must know that it is out of place here amongst the dusty greens and pinks and browns. It is stark, a stain, and it watches me sometimes in between snatches of staring at the sluggish fish.

The sun goes dizzily behind a cloud, and when it comes back out, something shiny catches my eye. I wade through the water over to the other side of the dam, yanking my clay-heavy gumboots up with each step and watching the water rush to fill in the holes I've made. I wonder if there are leeches in the water, hiding amongst the shimmering cellophane ribbons of drowning grass beneath the surface.

At the edge of the other side of the dam, there are seven carp hanging by the gashes in their necks. They aren't very big, and they are the colour of a smoky day in the city. The sticks propping them up sag a little, even though they have been driven deep into the mud. They have sharp little arms that stick out in awkward places, and if you squint, you could almost think that they are seven people standing at the edge of the dam, waiting.

The crow is watching me again, and I look away, looking instead over at the rickety barn that stands on legs of sand-filled oil tins.

The next day is cool but humid, and the sky is fatly pregnant. It sags under the weight of a broad doona of rain clouds, which crack together like marbles every half hour or so.

"Like breaking bones," says Simon, staring out of the window. We are in what used to be his grandmother's bedroom, and the room smells of mothballs and talcum powder. There is a long clothes rail on one side of the room, and it is loaded with padded pink coat hangers that are cloyingly sweet with hanging bags of crunchy potpourri. Simon takes one off and sits on the bed, where he slashes the hanger down its belly with a pocketknife, as calm as a surgeon wielding a scalpel. It makes me think of the time Mrs. Platt made me go outside to pat the still-writhing body of a king brown she had peppered with sparrow shot. I was surprised to find that the snake was muscular and solid, not slimy and cold like I had expected. Simon's curiosity had gone beyond my own, of course, and I had gone out to the chook shed later that day to find him staring on in fascination as a black carpet of ants storming the long red scarf that was the opened snake.

Simon shreds the wadding inside the coat hanger, pulling it out and scattering it so that there is a small pile of fuzzy snow near his crossed legs. It makes me sneeze.

"Wonder when Mum'll be back," he says, running his pocketknife over the callused skin of his thumb.

"They'll be another half hour or so," I say. "We can get them on the wireless if you want."

He digs his thumb into the wadding, kneading it with his hand as though it is a lump of soft dough. Then his other arm flashes out and back so quickly that I'm not sure that it actually has, until I see a small thread of blood unravelling itself across my leg, and I think of the snake, sliced open, of the bird he clutched in those praying hands, before those opened...and I think of myself, opened.

I am barefoot, and the broad loops of the burgundy carpet are spongy beneath me. A multi-stringed orange plastic necklace slithers around on its hook as I slam the door on Simon. I want to open the flywire door closest to me, but it shrieks when it opens as though it is being slaughtered. There are four battered armchairs in the lounge room, and a ribbed orange recliner, but he would find me within moments.

I sprint down the passageway, throwing closed the door behind me, trying to keep my footsteps as light as possible. I can hear him behind me, his breath harsh and cruel, just like him. I think of him being fragile, and I think again of breaking eggs, like when Mr. Platt taught us how to blow out the yolk from swallows' speckled eggs, and Simon had an obscene grin on his face when a long string of red poured out.

The front door swings closed behind me, making a hissing sound, and I interrupt a gathering of sparrows that are picking at the lawn with seizure-like stiffness. They flee past me, as though I am the one wielding the knife, and I skid a little as I try to decide where to turn. My arm blooms with blood from a trimmed-back branch of the pomegranate shrub.

I end up sprinting past the concrete podium of the old drop-down dunny, with its bouquets of flowering weeds and pulsing black lines of ants. It is getting darker, with the sun surrendering to the oily clouds that bully their way across the sky. Something hits my face, and I think it is Simon until I realise that it is only rain. I run with my arms outstretched so that the back gate swings open as I slam into it, and then I am in the dusty area that butts onto the house. Succulents and cacti clamour at my feet, their plump green forms deceptively soft. The pine needles and brittle fallen leaves are light but noisy against my tread, and to my hazy eyes they are mottled snowflakes, unfamiliar and confusing.

One of the chooks darts across my path, its head bobbing back and forth. It seems unnerved by the bursts of thunder that roll by in slowed down bursts of static, and I'm not surprised, because the air is so heavy that it presses at my face like cling wrap.

When I get to the graveyard of bottles and tins, I scoop one up, but when I swing it against the knotted, piebald trunk of a tree, it does not smash, but clunks dully, the way that the middle C key on the piano in the music room does.

A few seconds later, I am at the base of the water tank, and I scramble, spider-like, up the web of rusted scaffolding, my leg still weeping blood. The rain mingles with it, diluting it like cordial, and it runs down the inside of my calf like piss. I clamber up on to the dilapidated wooden platform, which is a series of splinters and leaf-filled holes, and try to avoid the caked-on birdlime. I shuffle my foot to the left, and I kick something soft and hollow. When I look down, I have to clamp my hands tightly over my mouth as though I am suffocating myself so that I don't cry out.

It is the baby bird, dehydrated already like the hanging ducks in the windows of Chinese restaurants. It is an old man, sagging skin on needle-like bones, and its beak has shrunken into its eyeless skull. It is riddled with ants, so many of them that it seems to be moving, and all I can hear is the ringing sound of its death on the water tank, a sound that for all I know might never have stopped.

I hear Simon approaching, and even with my eyes closed I can see the feral look on his face, and I pray, standing above the church-roof of leaning gum trees that line the driveway, that he will pass. And if he does, I will climb down from here and run, for as long as it takes, until I reach that main road.

june
Paul Finch

The first video was in grainy black-and-white, and started with an elderly man seated in a car at traffic lights. It was broad daylight, but that didn't stop another man, in a leather jacket and khaki trousers, appear from a side-alley and smash a claw-hammer through the driver's window. It was unclear how badly the driver was injured, but the attacker struck him a further six times before casually reaching in, unlocking the rear door, opening it and walking away with a briefcase.

The second video had been taken from high vantage, and showed a narrow alley. Two workmen were painting a ground-floor window. As they got on with the job, a youth, no more than 13 years old, walked past and idly kicked over a tin of emulsion. One of the decorators made a comment, for the youth turned and confronted him. There was an exchange of words before the youth sauntered away. Two minutes later, he returned with several other youths of varying ages. Before the two decorators realised what was happening, they were being bombarded with bricks. When they dropped to the floor, they were set about with bats. The beating, which included their heads as well as their bodies, was savage and prolonged, and left the two men lying motionless in pools of blood.

The video-tape clicked off and someone turned the light on. Nick Brooker looked across to where Superintendent Wentyard and Detective Chief Inspector Knox were watching him. The Super was a tall, elegant man with an immaculate uniform and a shock of white hair. He spoke impeccable English. The DCI, on the other hand, was a dour Scot, squat and paunchy, with a pale, rugged face and thick red-grey beard. His suit was scruffy, crumpled.

"Pretty grim," Nick finally said.

"Pretty senseless, too," Knox replied. "I mean, there are inner-cities and inner-cities, but this level of violence is unprecedented even for the twenty-first century."

Nick glanced at the empty TV screen. He was in his late thirties, but had hard blue eyes and a sharp, badly scarred face. His dark, unruly hair hung down past his collar.

"It's the same pattern as last year?" he asked.

Knox nodded. "More or less. Underwood is a busy sub-division all year round, even by Birmingham standards, but things *really* get going about now."

"Summer's always been bad for disorder, sir," Nick said. "Long, warm evenings, outdoor drinking, that sort of thing."

Wentyard leaned forward. "I think, Detective Sergeant Brooker, there's a little bit more to this than that." He steepled his fingers. "Incidents of reported violent offences in Underwood have gone up steadily since the end of April. Last week alone was a ten per cent increase on the previous week."

Even Nick was surprised to hear that. "And you expect the showdown at the end of June?"

"That's when it happened last year," Knox said. "And the year before. And the year before that. We're talking serious rioting. Officers badly hurt...the whole place barricaded off. Took us weeks to get it under control."

"This time we intend to nip it in the bud," Wentyard added. "There are no such things as no-go zones in this country."

"I wish I believed that, sir," Nick replied.

"Whatever you believe, just do the job you've been given to the best of your ability and we shall all be a lot happier. Personally, I'm not sure I buy into this Un-Crime business, or whatever your unit is supposed to call itself. I don't buy into this special unit ethos full stop, especially when it's something as fanciful and money-wasting as yours. As far as I'm concerned, this job is a serious one and it belongs in the real world. It starts and finishes on real streets, with real men and women in real uniforms confronting real criminals and hooligans. Still... as DCI Knox is impressed by your record, I'm prepared to give you the benefit of the doubt. For the time being."

Nick nodded and smiled to himself. This was no less than he got in whichever force area he was sent to; what else could he expect? A Scotland Yard department formed specifically to target strange and bizarre crimes — 'unconventional crimes' for want of a better phrase (hence 'Un-Crime') — was always going to generate hostility in a conservative body like the police. That was why it still only boasted a staff of one — him.

Underwood was on the fringe of Birmingham society. Geographically, it was located close to the city centre, but it was still on the fringe.

Thirty faceless blocks of concrete maisonettes, linked together by rubble-strewn underpasses and vandalised walkways, comprised its central area. Many units were boarded-up, a few just gutted shells. The parking areas underneath were seas of litter and broken glass, burned hulks of vehicles jammed into every narrow space. Even the playgrounds, once fenced off and secure, were bleak patches of wasteland with only rusted iron bones remaining of their equipment. Obscene graffiti ran wild over everything.

June, such a joyous month in much of Britain, made little difference here. In fact, it made things worse. Flies swarmed in the alleys. Rubbish festered and stank. The shadowy places where people lived grew hot and thick and stifling.

Nick didn't wonder there was scope for riots in this place, though that didn't excuse it. Not to his mind. He'd seen enough decency emerge from poverty to know that there was no hard and fast rule about crime and its causes; and anyway, who did the hoodlums punish when they went on their lawless rampage? Those who lived alongside them: timid householders, frightened pensioners. Not the rich and powerful, not the establishment. Long-term sociological solutions were fine, but in the meantime the scumbags needed locking up.

He arrived on the evening of 20th June, dressed in oily denims and rotted trainers. He hadn't shaved in three days and carried all his worldly goods in two plastic bags. The flat was on a balcony overlooking a litter-strewn plaza, and consisted of a kitchen, bedroom, lounge and bathroom. It contained only the most basic furnishings. He settled in quickly, unpacking the few belongings he'd brought with him: tins of food and booze, which he left in the kitchen; his phone and his 'burglary kit' — pliers, crowbar, screwdriver, brace-and-bit. Courtesy of the West Midlands Drugs Squad, he also had a few wraps of speed, a bottle of amphetamines and ten cubes of resin — just enough for a small-time dealer. He placed that on the bedroom window-sill, where intruders could easily find it.

His money he slid into a plastic wallet and taped to the underside of the wardrobe. There was strictly no warrant-card or paperwork. This was what Hollywood might refer to as 'deep cover'. Anything he needed to know, he'd already memorised: names and addresses for local hoods and trouble-makers; anarchist groups active in the area; known heavies doing time in local jails, just in case anyone wanted to test him on his cover-story.

He ventured out onto the estate that evening and the first thing that struck his experienced eye was how physically menacing it was; all narrow corners, dark doorways and precipitous drops to concrete lots. There were ambush-points every twenty yards. Nick had grown up in a town in the south Lancashire coal-field, which by the mid-1970s was severely deprived and unemployed, but thanks to its residential layout — rows of crumbling but neighbourly terraced houses — had managed to retain some community spirit. What possible community could exist in Underwood?

He strolled idly. Music was throbbing, but he couldn't locate its source. Ragged children played on the wrecks of cars, jumping up and down on metal, smashing glass; older youths hung about in silent, watchful groups — they looked as if they would kick you to death as soon as spit. More disturbing was the graffiti. Every type of mindless drivel was scrawled or sprayed on the walls and floors, but one particular symbol repeated itself again and again; a horned-head with no facial features. Nick wasn't sure how or where, but he felt he'd seen that distinctive image before.

He was on a street-corner, puzzling over one large example of this when a car suddenly screeched up and two men leaped out. They had him against a wall in seconds, and were patting him down. He didn't know either one, but made them for local plain-clothes. They wore casual suits and hard frowns.

"Mr. Waldron," one of them said loudly. "A rare pleasure. Carrying, are you?"

Nick sensed the faces appearing at windows and balustrades. "You bastards are harassing me," he protested. "I've not done anything."

They rousted him anyway, pushing him face-first into the brickwork, telling him he could have it easy or rough, and that it would be better for all concerned if he went back where he'd come from. Things were bad enough round here without scum like him lowering the tone even more. They then left, but only after warning him at the tops of their voices to piss off or expect the most miserable time of his life.

He glared after them, before hurrying back to his flat. As he closed the door, his phone rang.

He lifted it to his ear. "Brooker!"

"How are you?" came a Glaswegian voice.

"You might've told me. Scared the crap out of me for a minute."

"Got to keep up appearances," Knox replied.

"There's nothing else I don't know about, is there?"

"You're probably wiser than us already. What's it like in there?"

"Like a castle ready to close its doors. Whoever designed these places really knew what they were doing."

"That thought's crossed my mind a couple of times," Knox said. "Almost like it was pre-planned. Take care, Nick." And he hung up.

The Sleeping Prince was a pub that had actually been built into one of the residential blocks. Its inn-sign showed a knight in armour reclining under a leafy tree, though years ago someone had spattered it with scarlet paint. The front door was set in a metal frame and its windows covered with wire-mesh grilles.

Inside it was a little more wholesome. Air-conditioning hummed gently. The upholstery was of plush blue velvet, the brasses and woods all polished and shining. Aside from Nick, only two other customers were present; two scruffy men shooting pool. A young woman was mopping the bar-top; a shapely, rather handsome young woman. Her long red hair was tied in a neat pony-tail, her lithe figure clad in jeans and a t-shirt.

"Evening," he said, approaching. "Bitter, please."

She nodded and began to draw a pint.

"How's business?" he asked.

She glanced at him suspiciously; up close, her eyes were forest-green. "Who wants to know?"

Nick shrugged. "Sorry. Just trying to be friendly."

He paid for his drink, and sat down in a corner. The seat-cushions, he noticed, had been repeatedly slashed but fastidiously re-stitched. Above them, a chunk of plaster had been knocked from the wall and later repaired with Pollyfilla. He didn't doubt that similar patch-up jobs had been carried out all over the establishment. Suddenly the barmaid's lack of welcome was understandable.

Five minutes later, he went back to the counter and ordered the same again, fixing her with his best 'average-kind-of-guy' smile.

"I'm sorry about before," she said, refilling his glass. "I didn't mean to seem rude."

By her accent, she was local but educated. She seemed an unlikely employee for a place like this.

He leaned on the bar. "Must get a few tough-nuts in here from time to time."

She moved empties to the sink. "I wish it was only time to time. What brings a northerner like you to this neck of the woods?"

He smiled sheepishly. "Been here for a while...at Her Majesty's convenience."

She didn't seem surprised. "Well you'll be right at home in Underwood."

"What keeps you here?" he asked.

"Work. But it won't for much longer."

"Oh?"

"Brewery closes this place down in a couple of days."

He sipped his beer. "Pity."

"Only temporarily," she added. "Until autumn. Things get a bit too hot around here in summer."

He watched her over the rim of his glass, but she didn't elaborate. A moment later, she'd moved away to serve somebody else. He drank up and left; better not to press things too hard at this early stage.

On his way back to the flat, he spotted several more of the horned-head symbols. It was clearly an insignia, but whether denoting a gang or an individual artist he couldn't be sure. He'd definitely seen it before.

It was late-evening, warm and very sultry, the sun glaring orange from the blank faces of the buildings. Additional people now seemed to be hanging around. The teenage gangs haunting the walkways and underpasses had been supplemented by characters in their twenties and thirties. Most were smoking and drinking from bottles of cider, talking and laughing in loud guttural voices. Nick passed few without drawing curious stares. One bunch was particularly menacing; they hung around a bench at one end of the plaza in front of his block. One had a fully shaved head and cobwebs tattooed on his face and neck. As Nick passed, the Cobweb Man directed a big grin at him, as if in response to some quietly whispered joke. Nick didn't bother to ask what it was. He was sure he'd find out in good time.

That night he had a nightmare. He was lying in bed when someone beat on the frosted glass panel of the front door. Approaching it, dressed only in underpants, he saw a fearsome silhouette on the other side. It was vaguely humanoid, but low, hunched and of abnormal breadth, with a wide, flat head. A terrible stench of fish seeped in from it. Nick shouted at the monstrosity to go away, to take its fat ugly bastard face back to Hell, but it beat on the door again, this time with the flat of its hand, which was huge and had webbed fingers.

He woke up shuddering, his body damp with sweat. For a few seconds as he lay there, he fancied he could still smell it. The memory alone put him off breakfast, so he got dressed and went for a walk. He'd made some headway with the barmaid from *The Sleeping Prince*, he decided. Later on, he'd see if they served lunches there, and try to make a little more. For the time being, he'd scout the estate properly — if nothing else, he'd be able to provide the tactical support groups with detailed reconnaissance.

The bench where the gang had hung out the previous night was deserted, though surrounded by empty bottles and cans. The flagstones around it had been heavily inscribed with the horned-head symbol. Nick stared at it, wondering.

Then someone cried out.

He looked up sharply. The plaza was deserted, morning sunlight bright on its cracked paving. The cry came again; now there was pain in it. He pivoted round, looking for the source, and spotted movement in a shadowy entry — *violent* movement. He hurried towards it. It was a narrow passage, and, thirty yards down it, an old woman cowered against a wall as a youngster kicked her. A second child emptied her shopping bags.

"Hey!" Nick shouted, sprinting.

They glanced in his direction, unconcerned. Nick continued to run at them. If he'd learned anything in dealing with criminals, especially urban Apaches like these, it was that positive, aggressive action always got the best results. No matter how tough they thought they were, they were essentially animals of instinct, and would run if they sensed danger. He was right. The young hoodlums — they couldn't have been a day over ten — looked surprised that someone was actively intervening. They backed away, turned and fled around a corner.

Nick kept up the chase. He couldn't afford to arrest them, of course, but he wanted to make damn sure they were scared enough to think twice before casually committing day-time robbery again. He ran round the corner and found himself in another back-street, this one lined down either side with bins. The youngsters had made it to the far end, stopped and were now staring back at him. They began to catcall, throwing him the V-sign. He hesitated before walking towards them. Suddenly there was something about this he didn't like. He halted — and sensed figures emerging from behind the bins.

He swung around, hands balled into fists, but someone he hadn't seen smashed a bottle across the back of his head. There was a hollow explosion in his skull, and his legs turned to rubber. He had a vague impression of dark shapes closing in, and then the concrete floor hit him in the face.

The next thing Nick knew, his hands had been cuffed behind his back and he was seated at a wooden table, the surface crusted with drying bloodstains. It took a second for him to realise that the blood was his own; his hair was thick and sticky with it.

Someone was leaning on him from behind, forcing him forward. Someone else shone a bright torch into his face. He fleetingly glimpsed a black leather rapist-mask with zippers on the eyes and mouth, before his head was shoved down again.

"So...who the fuck are you?" a voice asked, in nasal Scouse.

"Who the fuck are you?" Nick replied.

Someone punched him in the kidneys. "What are you doing here?"

The blow sent shivers of nausea through him. A moment passed before Nick could say anything. "Name's...name's Todd Waldron. I got out of Blakenhurst six weeks ago. I've been looking for somewhere to live and they dumped me here. I wish they hadn't!"

A gloved fist with steel knuckle-rings on it appeared next to his face. "You'll wish they hadn't if you're fucking lying to us!"

"Who are you people?" he said, struggling. "I've not done anything to you!"

More weight was applied from behind. "Not done anything? You interfered in our business!"

"Knocking an old girl about! What kind of business is that?"

Again he was punched — with sickening force.

"We're asking the questions! Reckon yourself a hero, eh?"

"I just...I just reacted." He tried his best to sound frightened, which wasn't hard. "I didn't mean to screw anything up for you. Look...I'll leave the area. I'll just go."

"You're going nowhere." Now the guy with the Scouse voice leaned fully into view. The rapist-mask was diabolical, but it didn't conceal the cobweb tattoos on his neck. "What did you do time in Blakenhurst for?"

"I got pissed, battered a couple of coppers."

"How long?"

"Year and a half."

"Sawney!"

A burly, thickly muscled figure, also masked, stepped forward. His eyes were like lumps of broken glass in the gleaming leather.

"Sawney here gets around," the Cobweb Man said. "I'm sure he must know someone in Blakenhurst."

"As it happens, I do," Sawney replied. He gazed down at Nick with a fierce intensity. "Sam Duggan. You heard of him?"

"Yeah," Nick said. "I knew Sam Duggan."

"What was his line?"

"Burglary. He was doing ten for aggravated."

"Alec Fageline."

Nick shook his head. "I think you're making a mistake there, but I'm sure it's an honest one. Alec Fageline was never in Blakenhurst — least, not while I was there. Far as I know, he was in Brockhill. And before you ask, he was doing six for knocking over a building society."

Sawney stepped back. "Seems to know what he's talking about."

Nick struggled to free himself, but again they leaned on him.

"Look...I didn't get sent down because I'm a nice bloke," he said, "but I couldn't stand by and let those little bastards work that old woman over. Listen, if it's fucked anything up for you, I'm sorry. It won't happen again."

"Bloody right it won't," the Cobweb Man said. "Make a habit of battering folk, do you?"

"Been known to."

"That might be useful to us."

"I don't do old women, though. You'd better get that straight!"

The Scouse voice laughed. "You'll do whoever the Dead Names demand."

Then the knuckle-dustered fist re-appeared, and smashed into the side of Nick's face. Again and again and again.

When he came round, someone was dabbing his cheek. He reached up and felt gingerly at his jaw. The inside of his mouth tasted coppery. Loose teeth waggled under his probing tongue.

"Welcome back," said a friendly voice. "Someone gave you quite a kicking."

Through bleary eyes, he spied the barmaid of *The Sleeping Prince*. She was sitting in front of him, delicately touching his cheek with a ball of wet cotton wool. Behind her lay the pub's interior; a hefty man watched from over the pumps.

Nick groaned. His neck was stiff, his head and face throbbing. Several strips of Elastoplast had already been applied to his various cuts and bruises. A roll of bandages and a bowl of bloody water sat on the table in front of him.

"How did I get here?"

She dabbed at his swollen cheek. "Bill found you. He's the landlord." She nodded towards the man behind the bar. "You were lying in the alley at the back, with your jacket thrown over you. You've been unconscious ten minutes at least."

"You didn't think to call an ambulance?" he asked.

"Nope," she said simply. "The emergency services aren't too popular round here, and it isn't just the police. I've seen fire engines torched, ambulances stoned. We can't have that at the pub. If you want to go to hospital, you'll have to make your own way."

"I think I'll pass."

She shook her head. "I thought you might have fitted in here, being a jailbird and all. Seems I was wrong."

He sat up painfully. "I don't go looking for trouble, if that's what you mean."

"Generally speaking, you don't have to in this neighbourhood." She gathered her first-aid gear together and took it back behind the bar.

"Want a drink or something, mate?" the landlord asked him. "It's on the house while you've probably been robbed."

Nick checked his pockets — the money and key he'd taken out with him had indeed been lifted. "Er yeah...I'll have a whiskey. Might help."

A moment later, the barmaid re-appeared, placed his drink in front of him and began to mop the table with a cloth.

"Thanks anyway," Nick said. "Er...I don't know your name."

"Valda." She smiled.

"I'm Todd."

"Hi Todd."

He couldn't help ogling her as she leaned in front of him. Her light summer dress showed her generous cleavage to perfection. Her flaming hair, now loose, hung in lustrous waves about her shoulders.

"Surely someone like you could find something better than this?" he said.

"It's only part time. Paying my way through uni."

"What you studying?"

"History and folklore, would you believe. In particular the Midlands region. That's one reason I hang out here all summer. Not that there's much potential for field-trips."

"I can imagine."

She folded the cloth. "It's always been a rough place though, this. Lots of killings."

He wasn't sure if he'd heard right. "Killings?"

"In the past. Back in 1768 there was serious rioting. I mean, there was trouble all over the country — John Wilkes and all that — but nowhere worse than round here. A lot of troops got killed. During the Civil War, this place was a village and a centre of Royalist sentiment. Its population got wiped out by Roundheads. Literally butchered. Even Oliver Cromwell was shocked."

"Never been boring, then?"

"Oh, it's never been boring. Historically it's very interesting. Sometime between 60 and 70 AD, there were mass executions on this site. Thousands got the chop apparently. Probably Roman prisoners captured by Boadicea's rebels. They say the ground ran red for days."

She moved onto the subject of excavation rights in built-up areas, and the many obstacles archaeologists routinely faced. But Nick was hardly listening. Something she'd just said — about the ground running red. As with the horned-head symbol, it seemed weirdly familiar.

"Everything alright?" she suddenly asked.

"What? Oh yeah...thanks."

"Sorry...I get boring about history. My pet-subject. It's just...well, there aren't many people I can chat to during the summer, if you know what I mean."

"Well," he said, seizing the opportunity, "why not pop round this side of the bar sometime and have a chat with me? I'll even buy you a drink or two."

She laughed, and moved back behind the counter.

He got up, somewhat unsteadily, and followed. "I'm serious. I mean, I know I've looked better than this, but bruises fade. Besides, I *like* history."

"Yeah, right." She started washing glasses.

"I'm serious...honest. Even if it's just to thank you for patching me up. When do you get off tonight?"

She appraised him warily. "Ten. You're not really thinking of bringing me *here*?"

He smiled. "I'll *meet* you here. You can choose."

Valda didn't seem convinced she'd made the right decision, but she finally nodded. "Okay. Ten."

On his way back to the flat, Nick wondered how much she really knew about Underwood. She might be an outsider, but she was obviously a fixture at *The Sleeping Prince* and some locals might occasionally confide in her. One thing was certain — he wouldn't get many better chances.

When he got back to the flat, he found — as he'd expected — that it had been broken into and trashed. His stolen key stood in the lock. What little furniture there was had been smashed, while his tools, drugs-stash and phone had been taken. He could have done with hanging onto the phone, but it wasn't a disaster — by prior arrangement, Knox had only called it from an unlisted number, to it wouldn't be traceable back to the police. Thankfully, the wallet and cash he'd hidden on the underside of the wardrobe had not been found. He stood in the wreckage, thinking. This was more or less 'Phase One' of the operation complete. Time to start 'Phase Two'.

That evening he showered, locked up the apartment early and headed off the estate on foot, making sure to pass the bench where the Cobweb Man and his cronies hung out. As before, they were gathered to while away another pointless evening. So far there were six of them, including Cobweb. As Nick hobbled past, someone made a comment and they laughed loudly.

On the edge of the district, he found a pay-phone.

"It's me," he said, when Knox answered.

"Go ahead."

"Strike the contact number. The phone's gone west. I've also had my fucking face kicked in, but I reckon I'm getting somewhere."

"Good. You alright?"

"Fine. But listen...something *is* going down. I'm not sure what, but I can sense it. There hasn't been much gathering of the clans, as I can see, but you never know in a place like this. There doesn't seem to be anyone normal here at all, apart from a couple of beleaguered bar-staff. Check out any references you can to the 'Dead Names'. I don't know who they are, but I suspect we're talking people who've died in police custody. It'll probably be the motive for this year's disturbance, or at least the excuse when their apologists start coming on telly. I'll call you the first inkling I get that it's about to kick off."

"Just watch yourself, Nick."

Nick hung up and crossed the road to a service-station, where he bought two plastic buckets from the forecourt shop and, much to the shop clerk's consternation, filled them with petrol.

He was back on the estate and walking up to the Cobweb Man's gang before they'd noticed him. The first they knew was when a bucket of petrol sloshed over their heads. They rounded furiously, shouting and swearing, only to get the second one full in their faces. Curses became coughs and gasps. All six were sodden, t-shirts, hair, jeans, trainers. They looked up, eyes blazing, only to see Nick holding a cigarette-lighter, a long tongue of flame flickering from it. Rage turned instantly to shock, then terror. They froze, eyes wide in their dripping faces.

"I want my stuff back," he said quietly. "I want it back now, or you're burnt meat."

"Look..." Cobweb stammered. "Just take it easy. What's your fucking problem?"

"Now." Nick repeated calmly. "No shit. No arguments. My tools, my draw, everything."

Cobweb glanced nervously at his compatriots.

"My my," a different voice said, "you really *can* kick arse."

Nick looked slowly round and saw another man leaning against a street-light. His complexion was ice-pale, his hair, which he wore in matted dread-locks, a dirty blonde colour. His eyes were grey, a distinctive jagged scar running beneath the left one. His clothes were garish in the extreme: a designer running-suit of shiny red material, and an ankle-length raincoat, which might or might not be concealing a weapon. Nick suspected the former, because though he hadn't met this person before, he'd seen his evil visage many times — on police bulletins all over the country.

Mickey Speranza might not be Public Enemy Number One in the old sense, but he was very much wanted. Aside from his Manson-type connections with an oddball community up in west London, where child-abuse was alleged and heavy drugs-use reported, he was also suspected of at least four armed robberies and two shooting incidents. He was 'Category A'; his file on the PNC carried every conceivable warning.

Nick was under no illusion about how dangerous this guy was, but pretended otherwise. "Who are you?"

Speranza grinned. "The only person who can get you what you want. So put that lighter out...right now."

"Try anything, and I torch these bastards!" Nick warned him.

"No-one's going to try anything. I just want to talk."

The others were watching Nick intently, some shaking, some with teeth clenched. Suddenly, crazily, he wanted to put the flame to them anyway. To see these small-time terrorists melt like so many candles. It was a mad notion, but it was a nice one. He had no idea where it came from, but for a bizarre moment he genuinely *was* going to drop the lighter into the fuel.

"Don't get any stupid ideas, Mr. Waldron," Speranza said carefully. "These are associates of mine. They were only doing what I told them."

Nick stepped back and closed up the lighter. "I guessed they were puppets. Okay, what can I do for *you*?"

Speranza beckoned him down an entry. Nick followed cautiously. At the end there was a steel door, now open. Blackness lay beyond it.

"In here," Speranza said.

Nick held back. "You must be joking."

Speranza glanced over Nick's shoulder. Nick turned and saw the passage behind blocked by a squat, hunched figure in a cowl and cloak. Its breadth was immense — it filled the entry from wall to wall. For a second he was paralysed. Was it his imagination, or was there a fish-like odour in the air?

"I really don't want to have to keep forcing you to do things," Speranza said.

"What's this about?" Nick stammered, now shuffling after him down a steep, wet stair. He couldn't believe what he'd just seen.

"Just a little chat." Despite the sensation that a perilous drop lay just to the side of them, Speranza moved freely and easily as if the darkness was his home. "You're not from this part of the country are you, Mr. Waldron. Yet you're here. And that can't be coincidence."

"I don't know what you're talking about."

A flickering light was visible below.

"You're also a man of violence," Speranza added. "You've just proved that. Your prison credentials check out too...two pigs Section-Eighteened in Birmingham. Nice."

Nick could only thank God, and DCI Knox, that the cover story had held. The real Todd Waldron had been released from Blakenhurst six months ago and was now back on his home patch in Wolverhampton.

Speranza was still talking. "As I say, none of this is coincidence."

They entered a cavernous chamber with lit candles dotted all over its floor but deep shadows in its corners. Despite the June temperatures outside, their breath smoked in the dank atmosphere.

"Of course, the final choice is yours, Waldron. You can go on making a few bob committing two-bit crimes. Or you can be part of something a lot bigger."

"What's this place?" Nick asked.

It was the size of an underground car park, but it was clearly derelict. Their voices echoed. Water dripped everywhere.

"You might call this my church," Speranza said. "A place where dreams are made. Or nightmares, depending on your view."

The vast room had been covered with bizarre, red-brown handwriting. It was all over the walls, the floor, the ceiling. Every scrap of space had been invaded by loops and whirls of apparently meaningless script, all tangled together in a senseless mass. Some parts spiralled into wild, psychedelic patterns or deranged imagery: staring eyes, severed limbs, the plucked wings of flies, crawling foetuses. And here and there, in the midst of the madness, was that familiar horned-head symbol.

But the real shock came when Nick suddenly realised that the scrawl had been made in body substances — blood or excrement, or maybe both.

"Jesus Christ!" he exhaled.

"Does this upset you?" Speranza asked.

"What's it all for?"

"Discord."

Nick gazed at him. "What?"

"Look around you...it is pain, confusion. The food of Chaos."

"I don't understand."

Speranza walked past him. "Look down here, Waldron."

There was an aperture in the far wall, like the entrance to a broken lift. A rusted grille was folded back on it. He approached, and peered down a brick shaft into a blackness so foul it was almost mesmerising.

"Can you smash the rule of law?" Speranza wondered.

Nick wanted to pull away, to tear his eyes from that cancerous hole, but he couldn't. His hair prickled as he realised that something was moving down there, throbbing, pulsing — like a huge, disgusting heart.

"Can you kill when there is no purpose to kill?" Speranza asked him. "Can you maim and torture, burn and desecrate?"

Something was now ascending the shaft, rising slowly towards the surface — like a giant squid emerging from the murky depths.

Still Speranza's insane rambling went on. "Can you degrade the innocent? Defile the holy?"

Nick was frozen. A scream that was not his own filled his chest.

"Can you mock the old and sick, Waldron? Can you stamp on the graves of saints? Can you spunk and piss into the mouths and cunts of virgins..."

"Christ's sake!" Nick threw himself back, clattering to the ground in a heap.

Minutes seemed to pass as he lay half-insensible. When he finally looked up, Speranza was grinning by candlelight. "The time of Infusion is near, Waldron. Very near. It was no coincidence you came to us. You...and so many like you."

And only then did Nick notice the various groups of people watching from the shadows; countless numbers of them standing in rigid silence. He didn't need to see them properly to know who they were: the disturbed, the lost, the despised. They'd found themselves a place after all. And a voice. A voice that soon would be heard again.

He glanced back at Speranza. "When?"

Speranza's grin broadened. "When do you think?"

Nick didn't need to be told, not *he* — a member of Un-Crime, and thus a student of lore. Would it not be at the traditional time of strength and celebration, when all bad weeds are pulled, when all powers reach their zenith?

Would it not be 23rd June...better known as Midsummer Eve?

 "You look a little peaky," Valda said, when he met her in the pub that night.

"Yeah," he replied. He laughed. "Hah...yeah, I'll bet."

He'd spent the last hour sleeping, and when he'd come round he'd tried to write the incident off as a hallucination brought on by drugs. The more he thought about it, the more likely that seemed; possibly a hallucinogen in the candle-wax. Something simple like drugs or looting would be at the centre of all this. Money was reason enough to manufacture a riot. The Midsummer Eve lark would be the cover-story to get as many freaks and crazies involved as possible. Whatever the reason, it still gave him a couple of days' breathing space.

"It's nothing," he added.

Valda eyed him critically. "Glad you didn't bother dressing up. That would have been superficial."

Nick glanced down and realised that he was still in the scruffy denims and stained white t-shirt he'd been wearing all along. "Oh shit, sorry."

"It doesn't matter." She shouldered her bag and headed out of the pub. She was now in tight jeans and a loose cheese-cloth top, which looked a little hippyish but did a lot for her fulsome figure. Her hair shimmered in fiery waves. Only now did it occur to him how lucky he'd been to secure a date with her at all.

"I'll nip off and get changed," he said. "It'll not take long."

"Forget it." She turned down the first alley they came to. "There's no dress-code where we're going." At the end of the alley, a flight of unlit steps led upwards.

"Where's that?"

"My flat." She started up. "You don't need to worry. I've got plenty of stuff in. By the way...can you smell petrol?"

"Yeah," he said, following her. "Wonder where it's coming from?"

Valda's apartment was directly over the pub. Like so many others, its windows were grilled, its door and walls spattered with paint. But inside it was a different story; clean and neatly ordered, with plump comfortable furniture and a variety of potted plants. Surrealist pictures adorned the walls; the air was scented with pot-pourri.

She showed Nick to an over-stuffed sofa, then breezed through into the kitchen. He glanced left to where several DIY shelves were stacked with what looked like reference books, big thick hard-backs. He selected one and began to flip through it.

"Now this is interesting," he called.

"What's that?"

"*Ancient Mysteries of the Western World.*"

Beneath the printed title, a West Indian devil-mask was portrayed. It had been carved from red clay, with a long tongue and flaring nostrils.

Valda reappeared, closing the kitchen door behind her. She held two bottles of Bud, both opened. "Part of my course," she said. "Rubbish, most of it. Occult gibberish. Only bought it for research. Beer okay?"

"Great."

He continued to glance through the tome, even as she sat beside him. The first section dealt with the Americas, the second with Europe, the fourth with the Middle East, the fifth with Africa. All manner of subject matter was covered, from arcane lore to UFOs to monster sightings. The reference to monsters set him thinking again about the events of earlier. Nothing bothered Nick more than the unexplainable. He sipped his Bud and turned another page.

"Did you come here to read?" Valda wondered. "Or to take me to bed?"

He looked at her, surprised. A look she returned boldly, her hair tousled, her lips glinting.

"Well?" she asked.

"Seeing as you put it that way..."

She leaned forward and pressed her mouth to his, all but swallowing his tongue. He was stunned by her force and passion, but responded by tearing off his jacket. They tangled wildly, falling onto the sofa. Valda unbuttoned her jeans and began to wriggle them down. Nick ran a hand over her smooth thigh as he kissed her, shoving the book out of the way. It fell to the carpet, bouncing open on a page of photographic illustrations — one of which caught his eye.

He immediately pulled back from her and stared at the page. "That's where it's from!"

"What?" She sounded bewildered. "*Where what's from?*"

He climbed off her and picked up the book. "That symbol! That's it!"

The black-and-white image showed a mass of hieroglyphics on some ancient Middle-Eastern obelisk, and in the centre the carved shape of the horned-head.

"That's the one," Nick said.

Valda sat up and glanced at it. "What are you talking about?"

"It's all over the place...surely you've noticed?"

She shrugged. "Can't say I have."

He tapped the picture with his finger. "The thing is, I knew I recognised it. And I do. It's carved on one of the monoliths in a stone-circle in Cornwall. It's on the coastal moors near Tintagel Head."

She peered at the picture. "This symbol represents Bael-or, the god of the Philistines. He stood for storms and darkness."

"Chaos," Nick said slowly.

"Why the interest?" she asked.

"Bael-or. Not the same as Baal, by any chance?"

"That was the name given to him by the Egyptians. It's the one scholars generally use in the West."

Nick felt a creeping numbness down his spine. "They still have a party in his honour."

"Who does?"

"Down in Cornwall again. I was involved in an invest... I mean, I heard about a police enquiry into the druids who gather there. Most of them are acid-heads and that, not too serious about it. But there's a big bonfire and piss-up at the stone-circle. The 'Baal-fire', they call it. They roll burning cart-wheels into the sea, to simulate human sacrifices. One year, someone really did get murdered. And that was the other thing — you said the ground here once ran red with blood?"

She nodded.

Nick paled. "They said that about that place in Cornwall. The ground there was once red with the blood of human offerings. *Jesus Christ!*" He stood up. "I thought it was going to be Midsummer Eve, but it isn't! The Baal-fire's held on the summer solstice...21st June. Jesus H. Christ, Valda...that's tonight!"

He grabbed for his jacket and scrambled to the door, only to find it locked.

"You're leaving now?" she asked, astounded.

"I've got to," he said. "Look, I'm sorry Valda. I'll explain later. Have you got a key?"

She shook her head with disbelief, but began a slow search around the room. Nick watched her on tenterhooks. "You must have a key. What about a phone? Have you got a phone?"

"No!" She stopped searching to zip up her jeans.

"Well what about the key? Christ, I can't be stuck in here now!"

She turned and stared at him — very intently. And then, quite unexpectedly, she smiled. "You keep invoking the Nazarene, but it won't do you any good. Not if you haven't got faith."

Her voice had changed. It was deeper, throatier. Emerald flames suddenly burned in her eyes. Her lips curved into a vampiric grin. "You poor unfortunate. You think we didn't know you were coming? We who comprise all knowledge of the Old Ones, of the Herd, of the Dead Names who will live again: Peor, Othan, A-Ciliz, Nyarlathotep, our slumbering lord Bael-or!"

Nick heard glass shattering somewhere on the estate, and a woman start to scream. Hideous laughter roared down one of the alleys.

"You bitch," he said quietly. "You tried to keep me here!"

"Just how keen on doing your duty are you, Sergeant Brooker?" she asked. "You don't have to go out and risk your life. You could stay here instead, and fuck my brains out."

An agonised shriek rose from somewhere below. A detonation, like a head-on car crash, echoed from the next court.

"No thanks," he said, picking up her coffee-table and heaving it at the window.

Incredibly, it bounced back — and Valda leaped onto him, sinking her claws into his shoulders. Nick staggered under her weight. Fingernails raked his neck and cheeks, drawing blood. She bit his scalp with wolf-like teeth. He slammed an elbow into her midriff, sending her reeling away, whirled around and, catching her with a left hook on the point of the chin, dropping her to the carpet.

As she fell, the kitchen door creaked open — and a vile stink of rotted fish rolled out. Nick gagged and backed away. The thing in the cloak and hood was there; broad as an ox, yet low, squat. Under its cowl, he saw green, blubbery lips bloated with warts. It raised its hands as it advanced — long, hooked fingers, webbed together with brown translucent flesh. Nick remembered that old movie, *Creature From The Black Lagoon*, but knew this was something far older and far more terrible.

He grabbed the coffee-table again and hurled it back at the window, which this time ribbed with cracks. He darted towards it, but, in a single frog-like bound, the cloaked abomination had beaten him to it. Nick aimed a blow at its head, but it caught his wrist, twisted him round and hurled him across the room, slamming him into the bookshelves.

He looked up weakly, his previous wounds now open again and bleeding. The horror ghosted through the wreckage towards him. He slung ornaments at it, but they made no impact. It snatched him by the lapels and flung him again. He crashed through the kitchen door and over the sink and draining-board, before landing heavily on the linoleum floor.

It lurched after him. He grabbed two kitchen-devils from a wooden block next to the oven, and slashed at it, but it knocked them from his grasp and seized him in a massive bear-hug. Nick's bladder weakened as the creature began to crush the life out of him. He grabbed pans and pots from shelves and rained them on its broad head, smashing them into all sorts of shapes, but its resistance to pain was superhuman. This time it flung him clear across the kitchen, straight through the closet door.

Nick found himself lying among mops, buckets and bottles. Knowing he had less than a second, he searched frantically through them, and found what he wanted just as a misshapen shadow fell across him — a jar of white-spirit. As he was dragged bodily out, he unscrewed the top and splashed the liquid onto the monster's cloak and hood. It continued to grapple with him, bending and twisting him until he screamed in agony. It hurled him again over the work-tops, sending cutlery and crockery to the floor.

He jumped to his feet and threw himself at the gas oven, hitting the ignition switch. As the thing swept him up in its arms, it failed to notice the blue flames come roaring to life. Nick kicked and punched, desperate to force it back against the live appliance. Instead, it drove him the other way, pressing him into the tiled wall, trying to flatten his rib-cage. Half-blinded with agony, Nick clawed along the shelves, and his right hand closed on something cylindrical and hard — a pepper-pot. He jammed it against the wall, breaking it open, then flung its contents into the monster's face.

The creature grunted and backed away, letting Nick fall. Its shoulders jerked as it doubled forward and sneezed, ropes of green mucus stringing to the floor. Nick leaped up and barrelled into it, finally thrusting it against the oven. The spirit-soaked cloak went up like touch-paper. It took several seconds for the creature to react, but when it did it literally ran amok, dashing itself from wall to wall. It barged into the lounge, falling over furniture, tearing down wall-hangings.

The entire garment was now ablaze. Nick appeared in the kitchen doorway watching in fascination. The monster's hands were on fire as well, twisting and melting before its eyes. The hood was burning away at the back, revealing a flat warty head, now popping and blistering. An appalling stink of burn added itself to the already repugnant fish odour. With a daemonic, gelatinous bellow, the thing sprang at the window, hitting broken glass, woodwork and metal grille in one battering-ram blow, and erupting through onto the outside walkway. Nick dashed across the room and gazed after it as it fled into the darkness, a fiery, cavorting shape.

Other sounds of violence now distracted him. He vaulted through the window and ran to the concrete balustrade, peering down. Dark figures were dashing past below, brandishing weapons; bottles, machetes, axes. A wild shouting and banging could be heard all over the estate.

He climbed back inside and surveyed the wrecked apartment — there had to be a phone. A sideboard had been overturned in the fight, and spilling out from it were some tools — his own, the ones he'd had stolen. It didn't surprise him. He kneeled down and sorted through them. His phone was in there too. He punched out Knox's number.

It was answered almost immediately. "Hallo?" said a sleepy Scottish voice.

Knox was playing it carefully in case whoever had pinched the phone was making a re-call on the last number dialled.

"It's me," Nick said. "Hit 'em now! Quickly. No questions. It's started."

The line went dead.

Nick stood up — and noticed that Valda was no longer lying on the carpet. He spun around, but if she hadn't shrieked madly before swiping at him with the kitchen-devil, he would still have been slaughtered where he stood.

He was able to dodge back at the last second, and instead of severing his jugular, the blade ploughed into his left shoulder. It bit deep, sending spears of pain down his arm. Valda shrieked again, produced the second devil and took another wild swing. But Nick swerved around the blow and caught her on the side of the neck with a hard backhand chop.

This time she hit the floor dead.

He fell to his knees, gasping. A crimson stain was spreading down his T-shirt; his left arm had filled with pins and needles — he could hardly move the fingers. Had the bitch cut a ligament or an artery? Just probing the wound was agony. He'd need masses of stitches, possibly surgery. But right now there were more important things.

He heard the sound of helicopters, and, when he gazed from the window, saw search-lights blazing down onto the estate. Someone was shouting orders through a loudspeaker. The familiar bedlam of the riot-zone was rising to full crescendo. There were screams of rage, profanities. Burning rubbish was being hurled from roof-tops, deluging onto the roads and pavements.

Despite what he knew about their operation, Nick was astonished at the speed of the WMP response. They might not have nipped the trouble in the bud, but they were meeting it face-on, straight from the outset. They should easily be in time to prevent it spreading to other districts. He climbed out onto the balcony and looked down. Armoured vans were thundering through the plaza, riot-men clad in helmets and fireproof suits following in organised lines. Dogs barked furiously. Snatch-squads had already rounded up individual trouble-makers and were frog-marching them away. Several bodies littered the scene, and for once it didn't look as if any of them were policemen.

Nick went quickly down the steps, right hand clasped to his shoulder. He ran past the pub and turned down an alley into his own plaza, where yet more riot-officers were busy reclaiming the streets. It was the same everywhere. Most of Speranza's troops seemed to be running or trying to hide. Vast numbers were being cuffed. Nowhere was there sign of an organised missile-barrage or barricade.

Round the next corner, he found Superintendent Wentyard, also in riot-gear, his visor raised. The senior officer was standing by a heap of confiscated weapons, a glittering array of nailed and bladed implements, terrifying to behold but mostly unused. He'd just thrown a home-made sword onto the pile, and was beating his gloved hands together with more than a little satisfaction.

"You didn't waste any time, sir," Nick said.

"We didn't," Wentyard agreed. "We've had a task-force on standby for the past week. Hurt, Brooker?"

Nick's T-shirt was now sopping crimson, and he was feeling nauseous through blood-loss. But he had more work to do before he could declare himself unfit for duty.

"I'm okay, sir."

Despite all visible evidence to the contrary, Wentyard seemed happy with that. He nodded. "Hope you've got a few names and addresses for us...so we can have some show-trials, then some exemplary prison-sentencing."

Nick glanced down the fire-lit plaza. "I haven't got their addresses. But I know where we can find them." And he stumbled away.

"Brooker!" Wentyard shouted. "Brooker, wait!"

Nick ignored him, sidling past another phalanx of armoured riot-cops marching behind their shields like a Roman cohort, turning a corner and entering the passage leading to Speranza's 'church'. Half way down it, a figure was crawling towards the open basement door. Nick approached from behind. It was the Cobweb Man — he was slithering weakly on his belly, his features broken and bloody from repeated baton-blows.

"People like you always back the wrong horse, don't you," Nick said, hunkering down in front of him.

Cobweb regarded him with bruised, hate-filled eyes, but said nothing.

"Who do you think's going to protect you down there? You've screwed up, you've bolloxed it. They'll spread you around this housing estate like strawberry jam."

"Better than what you're offering," Cobweb croaked.

"I'm not offering you anything, son. Nor any of your mates. That time's passed. You've lived by your own decision-making. And soon — pretty soon, I think — you're going to die by it."

Nick strode on to the basement entrance, leaving Cobweb behind, and started down the stair. The chasm below was as ghastly as before; lit by unearthly flames, written all over with blood and excreta. It throbbed to the sounds of the battle above. Dust eddied from its dingy ceilings. Muffled shouting could be heard, even at this depth.

Speranza was standing at the far end, by the shaft-opening. His back was turned, but as soon as Nick appeared he whirled around, his pale eyes glittering. Nick limped forwards; his left arm now felt numb, lifeless. But he still had time for this. He *had* to have. Defiant to the last, Speranza drew a gun from under his coat; a shiny black Mauser. It was a hideous-looking weapon, with a huge magazine fitted under its stock. He levelled it at Nick and grinned.

"That's far enough, pig. Your boys can hammer skulls all they want up there, it only adds to the energy."

"But it'll be brief," Nick replied. "Briefer than you want it. Your army's finished. Your troops are already being rounded up There'll be no long, drawn-out siege here, Speranza, no simmering resentment with endless violent undercurrents that will last well into the autumn. No infusion."

Speranza's finger tightened on the trigger. "You, at least, are dead."

"No Mickey, you're dead! That's the price of failure, isn't it? For the cult-leader?"

Speranza curled his lip in a feral snarl. He took careful aim at Nick's face — and then his legs were swept from under him. The Mauser went off as he hit the deck, bouncing lead from wall to wall. Nick dived to avoid the ricochets, rolling over and over before looking up again. Speranza was now writhing on the floor, kicking at something that was dragging him towards the mouth of the shaft.

Nick kneeled up, ice running down his spine. Speranza was howling dementedly, triggering bullets everywhere. It made no difference. Whatever had him was remorseless. Nick climbed to his feet, took a tentative step forward to get a better view. Speranza was now on the brink, clawing for a hand-hold. A tenuous, tentacle-like thing, something milky-white, more wraith than flesh, was wrapped around his left leg.

The Mauser's magazine was now spent, but still Speranza pumped its trigger. He only cast it aside in the last second, before peering helplessly back at Nick, reaching out with an imploring hand. And vanishing from sight.

A nightmarish scream hung on the air behind him.

It took almost a minute for the echoes to fade. Nick fell to one knee, breathless, stunned by what he had seen. He didn't notice the flobbering, frog-hopping shape approach through the shadows until it was almost upon him. As soon as he heard its agonised wheezing, he glanced around — and, despite himself, gasped. The monstrosity now truly was something from Hell. Its cloak was burnt tatters, its face a puffy, pustulant mass, its webbed hands blackened claws. A single red eye flamed with malignant hatred. It reared over him like a deformed gorilla.

And then — flashing light and deafening automatic-fire.

The creature was flung to the ground, squirming horribly. Another prolonged burst ripped chunks from its head and torso. The third and final volley was just for good measure, raking it head to toe, jerking it about like a marionette.

After that it lay still. Nick looked slowly to his left. Through a pall of cordite-smoke, a cop in helmet and armoured suit, carrying a sub-machine gun, approached. He stopped and lifted his visor. The wan, bearded features of DCI Knox lay beneath.

He stared at Nick, then down at the thing he'd shot. It was dissolving — like butter in a pan, breaking itself down into constituent chemicals, all solid parts liquefying. Section by section, the tattered cloak caved in on itself, until at last it lay flat and sodden in a lake of oily fluids; fluids now running away down cracks and faults in the floor, trickling over the edge of the shaft, evaporating. The reek was unbearable, but it was dissipating quickly; more quickly than anything in nature had a right to.

At last they found themselves gazing only at a heap of filthy cloth and a drying blotch on the floor, which, among all the other stains in that grisly chapel of blasphemy, was virtually indistinguishable.

"I think you were right," the DCI said, his voice shaking.

Nick glanced back at the mouth of the shaft and imagined the roiling blackness beneath it, which almost certainly — for the moment at least — was subsiding again. "About what?"

"About no-go zones. Maybe it's time we all started believing in them."

a shade of yellow

Gary McMahon

Brett came home from the war a changed man; in many ways he was a slender shadow of his former substantial self. It didn't particularly matter which war he'd fought in, or where it had been located, for as far as he was concerned all wars were, inevitably, a smaller part of the same war that continued throughout history, consuming lives like some huge infernal machine that worked away behind the scenes. Anyway, this one was considered a mere conflict — a *skirmish* — by the media and the politicians and the man-in-the-street. Not a real war at all.

Like so many broken and unappreciated men before him, Brett returned not to poems and parades but to an empty house and an absent wife and infant daughter. His family had deserted, just as he wished he'd done on that far-flung sandy battlefield where he'd received his injury.

His leg was ruined, a flaccid dead thing that trailed behind him where once there had hung healthy apparatus meant for kicking footballs, running races and stretching out in quick karate kicks during sparring sessions at his local dojo. This injury, he realised, was simply another war — a form of psychological warfare; a war of attrition. A fight that he could never win because he was not equipped with the correct weapons. Rather than guns and tanks, this conflict required patience.

He struggled through the empty rooms of his house, touching the familiar objects, the touchstones (and heart stones) of his former existence: framed photographs, awards, sporting trophies, the very real memories of a life lived in *extremis*. After five months in an army hospital, it was good to be back with his possessions — however little they now meant to him. Still, the familiarity was good, a bonus. So much else in his world had been rendered alien.

The period after he'd been flown back to the UK was nothing but a blur: his memories were sketchy at best; at worst they depicted yellowish crimson-stained nightmares, like sketches on scraps of burnt and bloodied paper. Brett's mind retained images of the walking dead staggering through green-tinted hospital corridors, and wards whose floors were soaked in blood and greyish matter through which the staff would wade in high rubber boots. His mind filled the gaps in his memory with stock footage, random clips from every horror movie he had ever seen.

And his time before entering the hospital *was* filled with horrors: of that much at least he was certain.

He lurched into the living room, driven by nervous energy and unable to settle, to sit down and rest. His hand drifted to the telephone as he neared the little waist-high table upon which it rested. He flicked the switch on the answering machine, and waited for the message to begin.

His wife's voice, light and seemingly carefree, the hint of a smile coming through in the familiar words:

"Hi, you've reached the home of Cathy and Brett Jones. We can't take your call right now, but if you leave a message after the beep we'll get back to you." She ended on a slight giggle; she always did when her mood was good, her humour light.

He would change the message eventually, but for now, her tinny voice could stay. It was all that remained of her presence in the house.

That night, as usual, Brett drank himself to sleep. His whisky-fuelled dreams, were as dry as the desert he'd left behind and filled with images of casual violence and bloodshed. Ruined bodies lay stacked across each other like discarded uniforms in a whorehouse foyer, and sick-bright flashes of yellow dotted this corpse-strewn landscape, moving among the dead: a ragged cloak rippling in the warm, still air, or a sickly-coloured carrion bird dipping and rising between snacks…

"Excuse me," said the woman as she barged her trolley into Brett's withered limb. When she glanced down below his waist, her gaze passing from the aluminium walking stick to the thin appendage that hung below the hem of his army jacket like a cloth-covered tapeworm, the woman's eyes went dead. She hurried on, looking back only once with a look of disgust on her face. Brett did not know if the expression was born of the sight of his injury or his shabby soldier's apparel. Or perhaps a fear far deeper and less easy to define had prompted her hasty exit.

He reached the end of the supermarket aisle and turned right, heading for the refrigerator section and the frozen pre-packed meals for one. Just as he emerged into the main shopping area, he caught a glimpse of the tail end of something yellow and fluttering as it disappeared past the edge of a free-standing stack of cereal boxes.

Brett's heart raced; his good leg went rigid. Surely all he'd seen was the hem of some housewife's yellow dress, or the trailing hood of a child's parka. Nothing more. Nothing out of the ordinary.

The wire basket in his hand clattered against his stick as he hobbled around the corner. He peered along the suddenly telescoping perspective of the aisle: it was empty but for some stocky pensioner struggling gamely with a bargain-sized sack of basmati rice. The old geezer's sweater was a pale shade of mustard: not quite yellow, but close enough to ease Brett's frayed nerves and put to rest his stirring terror.

At the cash register, a pockmarked young man listening to music through tiny headphones served him reluctantly, as if he'd rather be somewhere else. The kid's eyes were heavy-lidded, as if he needed far more sleep than he actually got, and as he passed Brett's purchases through the barcode-scanner he inspected them with a look of distaste on his slack features.

Restless and none too impressed with the shop-boy's dismissive attitude, Brett turned his head and looked around the store for a distraction. It was a small place located on a quiet corner of town, with untidily packed rows of cheap produce leaning from slanted shelves in aisles that were too narrow for comfort. A sudden patch of yellow moved quickly between aisle ends, appearing and disappearing like something viewed from a bad angle.

Brett glared at the boy, silently urging him to hurry up and register his purchases.

When he looked back at the small shopping area, he eventually saw the swathe of misplaced colour pressed up against the glass lid of one of the big horizontal freezer units, an unnaturally elongated face leering at him from a bed of frozen peas and broccoli.

"No," he said, fingers clenching around the handle of his stick. "Get away from me!"

The boy paused in his scanning, and stared at Brett. His hand strayed to the security button located beneath the till and a nervous twitch jerked at the corner of his mouth.

Brett back-pedalled furiously, his eyes roaming the open spaces, then the shelves and nooks and crannies where anything might easily hide. Where was it now? A hand fell on his shoulder from behind, and Brett struggled to free himself from its grip, raising his arm in a defensive gesture.

"Sir? Can I help?" said a distant voice.

When he turned, the security guard's face looked puzzled for a moment before Brett landed the punch, snapping the man's nose in a clean horizontal break. The guard went down heavily and Brett hurried to the automatic sliding doors. Once outside on the busy street, he crossed the road and headed home, leaving his provisions behind. It didn't matter: he had not paid for them. Everything had happened in such a rush that he'd acted purely out of instinct.

Alone in his house, sitting by the window and watching the quiet suburban street, Brett felt the Fear descending upon him; the cold, unstoppable terror that gripped a man during battle. The thing in yellow had followed him here, stalking him out of the desert and onto a military plane, where it sat on the wing and waited for landing; hanging on his coattails like a voodoo curse from a paperback thriller, then waiting, waiting for its chance to strike.

Everything had seemed so uncomplicated in the dry desert heat: the choices one made during warfare were black and white, straight down the middle. Fight or flight: kill or be killed: stay or go.

The memories, however, were not so simple…

The old man must have had something to do with it. Brett had discovered him there, squatting in a shallow excavation beneath shattered concrete foundations, lighting votive candles and arranging edible offerings on a cracked stone plinth altar that held a dusty glass bottle filled with some kind of yellow vapour. The old man wore dirty yellow robes, and one side of his face looked like molten plastic. Wounds caused by a fire, or perhaps the result of another botched allied assault. The flesh below his eyes had run like liquid before setting in an abstract pattern. The old man glanced up at Brett from his kneeling position at the altar, edging in front of the bottle and hiding it from view, and when he pulled the large dagger out of the folds of his robes Brett was so afraid, so out of it, that he opened fire without even thinking about the possible consequences.

The old man's head fragmented into jagged chunks and blood misted like a fine powdery residue: it still happened now, in Brett's mind. It happened all the time, like a film stuck on a loop. That crimson mist was like a stain on his life, a discoloration, a tattoo on his soul. It settled slowly, like discoloured water vapour, coating the altar and the shattered remains of the bottle.

That was the exact moment when the roaring choir of gunfire struck up outside the shrine entrance. The men were under attack, and all that

Brett could think to do was run. Just as he turned and headed for the exit, he saw a flash of muddy yellow stirring in a corner; then he was moving, fast and low, panic taking control of his tired body.

Brett sat at the window rocking like a senile old man, his eyes not straying from the street outside, his hands gripping the arms of the chair on which he sat perched, back held ramrod straight. Remembering.

When the rapid gunfire became the sound of the world and his men started dropping like flies, Brett panicked and ran out into the ruined village they'd discovered during what was supposed to be a routine patrol through a depopulated zone somewhere to the west of Baghdad. His feet sent up puffs of dust and his legs ached from the God-knew-how-many days they'd spent marching deep into hostile territory; his eyes scanned for snipers and other hidden assassins.

The outpost must have been empty for years, and ancient ruins poked up like abandoned grave markers through the pale crust of sand. Brett remembered reading somewhere that the ancient Mesopotamian city of Babylon had possibly stood somewhere near this site, but lately there were rumours of pockets of resistance in the nearby hills and dunes — guerrilla cells who were willing to fight to the death.

Blood. Screams. The wind-whip of bullets tracing through the dead air and the unforgettable sound of grown men screaming. So he ran for open ground, praying to find safer cover, perhaps even an elevated vantage point from which to take stock of the situation. But all he'd done was run into a minefield, and when his legs were blown from under him, he took to the air like an Olympic diver from a high board.

He sat weeping in the chair, seeing it all play out behind his eyes. He could never stop remembering; never turn off the movie. An endless repetition of cowardice.

Fleeing out into the open desert that surrounded the village, leaping a low barbed wire fence. Not even realising that he had strayed into a minefield until the explosion rang in his ears and he felt suddenly and shockingly elevated, as if the hand of God hand swooped down out of the sky to scoop him up.

Sprawled in the sticky-sand mess of his own pooling blood, feeling nothing, not even the pain. Ears ringing like he was in a church on Christmas day, eyes running with tears and blinking from the grit of displaced sand. A vague yellow shape approaching across the dunes, eating up the distance, flitting ever nearer. A figure, but seen through the prickly haze of settling sand and eyes that were loosened in their sockets by the force of the unexpected blast.

Then the figure was upon him, lowering over his body like a scabrous angel. Long nicotine-yellow hands, rail-thin arms; a narrow cadaverous face as yellow as the head of a sunflower. Sad amber eyes. Black gaping mouth. Leaning over him, moving closer to the mangled ruin of his injured leg. A sense of great hunger. Then: feeding. Eating.
Darkness. Huge yellow wings flapping in the long night of his mind, and then…

He'd woken on a stretcher in the back of a speeding military Humvee, phasing in and out of consciousness as the vehicle headed back to a safe US military compound. Everything was choppy after that, like small pieces of an unstable picture rather than entire experiences. He only managed to communicate properly when he was back in the UK, after being sewn together and patched up by an already exhausted army medical crew out in the field.

His right leg was ruined, the left one merely crippled, and he was informed that he would spend the rest of his life walking with the aid of a stick. The psychologists had done all they could, so they sent him home to rot. It could have been a lot worse: some of his friends had not returned at all from the Middle East; others had left entire pieces of themselves over there in the hot desert, body parts left behind to take root and flower like strange foreign plants. Most of the time Brett considered himself lucky. The rest of the time he thought of himself as finished.

By the time morning came he had slept little, dozing only fitfully and in an upright position. His back and neck ached; his leg throbbed like distant explosions. He lurched awake to inspect the empty street for quick snatches of yellow, but saw nothing of his phantom pursuer.

He pushed himself to his feet and went to the bathroom. Struggling to balance on the one good leg while he urinated, Brett watched as splashes of yellow soon decorated the white toilet seat. A strange panicked terror gripped him as he washed away the stains, and he hurried from the house to pay a visit that he had put off for too long already.

He caught a bus at the end of the street; the journey took a little over an hour, but he didn't mind. Once-familiar streets blurred past the bus window, but all Brett could see around him was a vast ocean of yellow.

Pausing outside the front door, Brett took a quiet moment to summon his strength. He knew now that he was a coward — his actions during combat proved this beyond any doubt. It was all he could do not to turn back and go to ground in the first pub he saw, whittling away his remaining self-esteem in a pint glass.

A pale face appeared briefly at a ground floor window: it was her, peering out to see who stood at the door. Brett smiled, but the expression felt like a protective mask. Cathy's mournful, tight-lipped face, framed by an aura of jet-black hair, ducked away behind the curtains.

Half a minute later the door opened.

"What do you want, Brett?" said Thomas, his face stern, arms loose at his sides, ready to strike.

"I want to speak to my wife. To see my daughter."

The sound of a baby crying drifted through the open front door, and Brett felt his good leg buckle under the strain of confronting all that he had lost.

"They don't want to see you, mate. Not ever again." Thomas' tone softened at the sound of baby Carrie's baleful weeping; he was finally attempting to be human, to show some compassion. It was the least an old friend could do.

"I need to see them. To tell them..." but he didn't know what he wanted to say. How could he? Everything felt so confusing, so strange. Lemon-yellow wallpaper hung on the corridor walls behind Thomas; his shirt beneath the cardigan was the colour of butter. Brett closed his eyes, squeezing them shut as hard as he could, but the darkness behind them held a subtle yellow hue.

"Just go, Brett. Leave them in peace. Haven't you caused them enough pain? Seeing your face all over the newspapers...hearing about what you did on the television. It almost killed them. You're a fucking coward. You're nothing but yellow."

Brett turned away, almost smiling at his rival's choice of insult. He hobbled along the path to the steel gate at the front of the three-storey townhouse, feeling his entire life speed up to pass him by.

A decision was made; a bridge burned. He didn't look back, but he hoped at least that Cathy watched from the window, Carrie cradled in her arms, and perhaps shedding a quiet tear for all they'd once shared. His dead leg ached, the pain nothing more than a phantom of the agonies he'd once known.

Deciding on a sadistic impulse to walk home, Brett felt hunted by the yellow shadow of his cowardice. He could remember nothing of what they claimed he had done, but of course he'd read the official report. Had even been told the details during his dishonourable discharge from the armed forces.

What Brett remembered most was the horror in yellow: its saliva-dripping teeth and haunted eyes. But the platoon of US Marines that found him claimed that he was alone, gnawing on the bones of his flayed right leg and with dead men's possessions spilling from the pockets of his bloodied fatigue jacket. They said that he had plundered corpses, and even taken valuable artefacts from the vandalised underground shrine before fleeing and leaving his men to die. Rumours of cannibalism persisted despite no official charges being brought.

Brett knew that the thing in yellow had placed the booty on his person; it was the carrion wind of cowardice, a ghoul that stole the coins from dead men's eyes, and somehow Brett was marked out for this treatment. Perhaps because he'd murdered the strange Muslim priest and desecrated his secret place of worship; or perhaps because he'd run from battle, leaving his squad to be slaughtered. In reality, he was nothing but a lowly Sergeant, but the untimely death of his Colonel had meant that he had assumed command of the company until he could lead them back to the nearest allied position.

Brett had never been a natural leader of men. Nor had he possessed any of the assets necessary to guide them to safety. Even his rank of Sergeant was awarded out of nepotism, at the request of his late father, a man whose name was legendary in military circles. Brett was a buffoon, a danger to everyone around him. So they had done the only sensible thing, and sent him to war.

He limped along dirty back streets and quiet leafy avenues, hiding away from the world. As late afternoon stretched into early evening, and a deep shadow fell upon him, Brett felt the dreaded yellow presence nearing. He glimpsed its reflection in a cake shop window, and hovering in a doorway across the street. Heard its scrabbling bare feet in the mouth of an alley as he passed clumsily by. Sensed the hunger, the overpowering desire to finish what it had started in the boiling wasteland from which it had emerged.

In Islamic culture, didn't the colour yellow symbolise air? He knew for certain that Muslim brides wore yellow robes. In the rest of the world it represented the colour of treachery and cowardice, of age, pestilence and decay. In some western religious paintings, the pale horse of death was also depicted in a watery, pusillanimous variant of yellow.

But no malefic jinn or vengeful ghost of Islam stalked him; this was something older than faith or tradition, more secret than organised religion. It was a sensation, a whisper of an act. A cold yellow thing born from somewhere deep inside his own psychology — a sharpened facet of his own damaged soul beaten into cantankerous life.

When Brett finally arrived home twilight was falling; long shadows scraped the ground like fingers and doors and windows were sensibly locked up against the slowly encroaching night. His body ached; the atrophied muscles were no longer accustomed to so much exercise. Knowing that he should sleep, Brett instead took out the kit bag festooned with a military crest that lay hidden under his bed. He unlocked the clasp and took out the folded uniform, laying it out on the bed. When he handled the gun he felt stronger than he had in months.

Then he whispered a prayer to whatever might be listening.

Once he'd managed to dress himself, he stood before a full-length mirror. He looked the part: like a real soldier, despite his discharge, despite his reputation being in tatters. Straightening his hat and flattening his collar, Brett stepped awkwardly back towards the bed and hefted the firearm. It was an old pre-2000 military issue SA80 assault rifle, small and trim and easy to smuggle aboard a plane in a bag supposedly checked and sealed by military police. Brett could never understand why the weapon was almost universally vilified; he had always been fond of the design, and he found its accuracy a comfort.

Brett ejected the magazine. A full clip: 30 rounds. Enough to last him quite some time if he picked his shots carefully; and he would have to do just that, because he remembered from folklore that a ghoul must be struck only once — a second blow would invest it with new life rather than killing it.

Darkness descended like cascading black waters beyond the bedroom windows, and Sergeant Brett Jones did his best to march out of the room and into the upstairs study. The room provided an excellent view of the front street, and the main road beyond. It was ideal for a siege situation.

The thing in yellow appeared as a smudge in the distance, flapping closer as he watched, billowing in the restless air. Within minutes it stood in the road outside his house, one wasted arm held straight up and out in a mock salute.

By the time he raised the gun and took a bead on it, the figure was gone. But he knew it would be back. It would never leave him: it was his personal phantom, and no amount of belated valour could ever release him from its subtle grasp. Its eyes were the colour of swamp gas, or sickly sodium light; and when it smiled its teeth were a leprous yellow, too, sitting in ruinous gums. He had seen its zombie face in the lifeless countenance of every soldier shot in the back by a hidden sniper or vaporised by a suicide bomber; every General who sat behind a desk at a distant command post while his troops dropped like flies on the front line; each single squaddie shredded by an assassin's blade on a lonely street long after curfew.

Not long after, he let off the first round.

Spying a smattering of yellow reflected in a patio door across the street, he took out the glass and whatever stood behind it. He barely had time to register that the crumpling reddened shape was that of a neighbour in a yellow dressing gown before he was shooting at a child's yellow bicycle parked against a crooked concrete gatepost. The child beside wore a yellow hat: it was enough to convince him that his actions were just.

When the sound of police sirens reached his ears, he hoped that he could keep them at bay at least long enough to take down his enemy. Flashes of yellow appeared everywhere, tugging at his attention, causing his aim to suffer. Brett took deep breaths and tried to remain calm; if he panicked, he would use up his supply of ammo before making a direct hit.

The street was cordoned off before he even realised the sirens had stopped. Flashing lights distracted him, clouding the sight of yellow. He shot them out, watching with enthusiasm as the annoying sounds exploded into multicoloured showers of glass on the roofs of stationary police vehicles. Uniformed police officers ran for cover, and produced handheld lighting units from the boots of their cars.

A fat man in a tight-fitting suit spoke loudly into a yellow bullhorn, and Brett caught him with a round to the face. Blood and bone flew like shrapnel and the man's voice was silenced. Another poor chap fell because he wore a bright yellow safety jacket as he ran crouched and on his tiptoes behind a parked van. Red flowed around the wheels of the van, channelling into the gutter, but all Brett saw was a vivid vision of yellow.

The thing in yellow. *A shade of yellow*. It was everywhere, and in every thing. Mocking him.

Pausing in his private war, Brett turned and caught sight of his own sallow face in the mirror that hung on the wall above a framed photograph of his smiling family. Yellowish eyes glared back at him from the dull yellow mask that had stalked him across continents. In the dead yellow glow from temporary emergency lights and the few streetlamps he had not yet shot out, the tears on his face shone a diseased shade of yellow. Yellow. *Yellow...*

then...

the blue stream

Kaaron Warren

My brother will be home soon. Home from the cool Blue Stream where he has been floating for seven years now, since I was four, and where I will soon be floating; but you sink first, a cold, fresh shock, and as you rise you begin to float. It's just like being back in Mum's womb, apparently, only you're there for longer. I don't see how anyone can actually know that. My brother will be amongst the first Streamers to emerge, so how can they know? It's like saying if you dream you're dead then you're dead. How could anyone know that?

"Streamers Stream-Line the Future" we see everywhere. So my brother's going to be some sort of hero. They all are. Coming back to do all the jobs the adults don't want to do. Hopefully some of them will be teachers. The ones we've got now are so stupid. We have whole classes about How To Welcome a Streamer:

1. Smile pleasantly at them. If I used to smile at my brother he'd snarl. But I suppose that's the whole point, isn't it? The whole idea of the Blue Stream?

2. Speak to them in a friendly fashion. About what, though? What've you been up to, big brother? Learning how to swim?

3. Invite them to join you and your friends for lunch. But they're OLD. They're all twenty. Why would we want to eat with them?

Thanksgiving Day today. So much to be grateful for.

We are thankful for peace that exists in our homes, on our streets. We study riot behaviour at school — I had to memorise what a riot was because I kept forgetting. We watch old news, funny, jerky-looking pictures of big-eared teenagers. They smash and run, run over each other sometimes. We saw one, it was supposed to be a celebration of the New Year (how weird! To be happy that another year had passed!) but it looked terrible to me. Thousands of teenagers crammed together, drunk on alcohol, smoking cigarettes and burning each other with the red end. Then we heard a clock ringing twelve times and they all went mad. They poured beer on each other, threw bottles. They started to fight! They ran in fear, pushing, squeezing and when some fell over, others just jumped on them like they were rubbish. We would never treat people like that. Then there was the next day, all the teenagers (except the dead ones) were gone, and there were the adults to clean up the mess as usual. They showed us the face of one of the dead kids, before an adult lifted a sheet over his head. His face was calm. We give thanks for there being no more riots.

Since the Streamers were set afloat, our world has been far more peaceful. Not on a global scale; we still have wars and terrorism, that sort of thing. But that stuff will go too, we thanked, when the Streamers begin to emerge to grow older and take their place in the world. Soon everyone will have a position, and know their limitations, be accepting of their situation and be able to face the reality of it. We are thankful for that. We are thankful for no teenage pregnancies. And we are glad that those bad habits, like cigarettes, alcohol and drugs, are not formed at an early age, only later when a person can cope.

We give thanks for the safety of our belongings. Vandalism is gone, and our houses are safer. Not totally safe, but safer. The teenagers can't reach us from the Blue Stream, and we are thankful for that.

Before the Blue Stream there were more suicides than road deaths. Now there are far less of both. For this we are thankful.

Some of the adults are getting worried. There was a meeting at the hall, which everyone had to go to. Mum and Dad took me because I was too young to be trusted at home alone. Not everyone was a parent there. A lot of them had never had a child and didn't care if they never saw a young person again. There was a big group of them who shouted louder than the rest,

"Why take the risk? We've waited this long." That sort of thing. My parents wanted Jim back, so they were on the side of letting them out.

My Dad said, "We can't leave them in the Stream forever," and most people had to agree.

I was pleased with my father that day. All those other adults don't think the teenagers have grown enough. They think another year will do it, or two, maybe. They are just scared of their own plan. It's been easy to talk, the last seven years, of how the world will be, how wonderful. Now the proof will appear, or the evidence. I can't remember the difference. There was a survey in one paper, "Should we release the children?" They're just scared of what they've done. None of the questions matter, though. They have to stick with what they said. They have to. I do twenty sit-ups every day so that they won't leave my brother in there any longer.

And then there he was, climbing carefully out of the back seat and staring. He is a stranger to me. He has been gone from sight, floating through the country for seven years and now he is back. I don't recognise his face, I don't remember his smell.

How To Welcome a Screamer more like. He hasn't shut up — though his throat's getting sore so it's a bit quieter now. He'll stop eventually. He's started to look around and notice things, his gaze flicking about while his mouth still screams. They're all doing it, and everyone thought at the same time to call them Screamers. The PR company quickly sent out ads saying, "The Water Babies are here," as if they'd never called them Streamers, never thought of it. But Water-Babies is almost as bad, because they're like new-born, full-grown babies, not wanting to leave the safety of the

Stream for the big world where they are told what sort of person they will be.

"It's important to know who you are," my father said, the family sitting around him as he spoke of the perfect world we were helping to create. "Teenagers were troubled by their lack of identity, by the great nothingness which faced them in the mirror. We are simply supplying the identity to fill the nothingness."

"Nothingness," my brother said, "that's what it was."

"You see what society has saved you from?" my father said, nodding like it was his idea.

"The Blue Stream was the nothingness," Jim said, aping my father's nod because he is still learning and can't always connect action to meaning.

Jim has been home for nine days. He hasn't screamed since two days ago, only his wake up scream. He carries a little satchel, which he was given as a welcome present. In it, papers grow; he receives them in the mail, pinned to his pillow, under his plate. If he sees something written on the ground, he is to write it down.

"*As a Mature Person, you will Look Your Best*" (found on the bathroom mirror)

"*As a Mature Person you will Perform Disagreeable Tasks Without Undue Delay*" (Stapled to an invitation to a job interview)

"*As a Mature Person you will Be a Good Family Member*" (In the bar under Dad's favourite glass)

Some of Jim's Friends came to visit and they all sat in the lounge room with the same frightened smile on their faces.

"What's wrong?" I asked him. I was helping him get drinks from the bar.

"I don't know who they are," he said. "Were they Friends of mine before?"

"I was only four. How would I know? Why don't you ask them?"

"I don't think they know either."

There was silence as we sat. I sat close to him. It was nice to be able to do so.

"Haven't been out today?" one of the girls asked him. She has these big boobs she barely knows are there; pinned to one was a badge. Everyone in the room had them except my brother.

"*Minimise Daydreaming*," she read, twisting the badge so she could see it. The others read theirs aloud, too;

"*Overcome Anger and Fear*"

"*Avoid Complaining*"

"You'll get one if you go up the street" the girl said kindly.

My brother was staring at her chest. I pinched his elbow.

"Don't be rude," I said.

They know as much as me, these Screamers. No more. After primary school they went straight into the Stream. Some, now, will go to high school, but not many. There are too many urgent jobs to be done. Some will go to Uni if they have to be doctors or something. My brother won't. He has to be a gardener.

"Happy Birthday," Mum said to me. She was the only one excited. She brought out a cake with twelve candles on it. Jim stared at the flame like he didn't know what it was, just stared and upset me so I couldn't blow out the candles.

"Blow out the candles," Mum said, "then we'll have some cake in the back yard."

We didn't go anywhere else. Jim still gets nervous when we go out anywhere, if it isn't part of some stupid Screamer instruction.

Sometimes I really hate him being a Screamer. He's supposed to involve his parents in his activities, but they're my parents too, and they hardly ever leave me alone. So I have to go. Today Jim had to go to the beach so we all had to go. People I knew were there and saw me with my parents. Jim would have gone purple with embarrassment if he wasn't a Screamer. The whole time we had the radio on, it played only one song, which happens to be Jim's favourite — same with all the Screamers. It's like a chant, slow and boring, and it just sings about what a great time you can have with your family.

Go to the beach
Read a sto-ry
Watch TV
or TELL a sto-ry
Take some lessons
Try a square dance
Do some sewing
Maybe some pants
Work on puzzles
Play a Game

Blah blah blah. I don't want to do any of that stuff. I think Jim is supposed to go all the way through the song, doing one of everything. I can't wait till he gets to square dancing.

I saw a terrible accident today, and it's all because of that boring Sara from school. She couldn't learn her rationale and the teacher said that I had to help, because I was smart and we both had a sibling home from the Stream. So I had to go to her house to help her. I made her try to remember on the way home.

"Teenagers have identity crises."
"Teenagers have identity crises."
"They develop negative personalities."
"They develop negative personalities."
"They join gangs."
"They join gangs."
"They rape."
"They rape."
"They riot."
"They riot."
"Once the physical changes have occurred, they will take their places as confident members of our society."
"I can't remember that."
She's a stupid girl.

We got to her house and her mum was crying.

"There's been a terrible accident," she said, "in the bathroom."

There was Sara's sister, empty pill bottles around her, vomit in her hair, a note clutched in her hand.

"It doesn't look like an accident," Sara said. Not so dumb.

But it was. The police said so. And in the newspapers, underneath the advertisements that said, "*Be tolerant of other peoples opinions*" was a headline:

"Screamer accident rate alarming." Sara brought the article to show me.

"Mum wouldn't let me read the note. She said I shouldn't have any new ideas before my birthday next week."

"You're lucky. I've got months to go."

"Yes, I can't wait. The peace, the rest, the water lapping my ears, cooling my forehead, washing me so I don't have to have a shower for seven years. I hate showers. And I won't commit suicide due to the confusion of my loyalties."

She has finally learnt the rationale.

Jim got a note today he didn't understand so I had to explain. He found it pinned to his towel in the bathroom.

"*Be not dominated by other's opinions nor in constant revolt against social conventions.*"

"It's just that you're not supposed to listen to what your Friends tell you, only what the adults tell you."

"And what's revolt? Like that casserole Dad made?"

It's good being smarter than your older brother.

"You're not supposed to argue when they tell you what to do."

"But if they tell me everything, I might get sick of it."

"Well, if you do, don't tell anyone. You'll get into trouble."

He could understand trouble. It meant the withholding of the nothingness which comes at the end of the lives of people who have been good. I don't like the thought of nothingness, myself, but then I'm not a Screamer.

My brother keeps telling me stuff that I'm not meant to know till I'm a Screamer, and he lets me watch stuff that's meant to be private.

He feels sorry for me because most of my friends have gone into the Stream. I was smart and they put me up a grade, but now all my friends are early into the Stream. He feels sorry for me because I'm lonely, and he's been given so many Friends.

I hid behind the couch so I could only hear what was going on. It was called a *"Give deserved credit or praise to other people"* party, and it is the only party they are allowed to have. They are getting very good at them.

Jim sat on the couch, and kept dropping soft lollies for me to chew quiet as I could. His friend Barry was there; I could tell his deep voice and the way he felt so unused to it — he has only just emerged. And there was June; she has a lovely soft voice. Andrea, who kissed everyone (you're not meant to do that). Beryl, Big Beryl I call her, though my father says, *"Nicknames Breed Contempt."* And Mark, who is nearly as nice as my brother and wouldn't tell if he saw me behind the couch.

"Who wants to start?" June said.

"Me," Barry said. "Andrea, I admire your friendly nature and the way you make people feel comfortable."

"Thank you," Andrea said. "June, you are a gentle and kind person and you will make a marvellous instructor."

"Thank you," June said. She's got that lovely voice; I wish she was one of my teachers. "Jim, I think it's admirable the way you helped me prepare my college application even though you won't be going yourself."

"Thank you," my brother said. "Beryl, you are a most marvellous cook, and the lunch you prepared today was a great accomplishment. Thank you for bringing it to my parent's house."

"Thank you," Beryl said. "Mark, I think you are very handsome."

"You can't say that," June said. "That's a compliment for something he has no control over. Think of another thing."

"I'm not very good at this," Beryl said. There was a bit of a silence. If the others were anything like me, they would have been thinking, "Useless." But then they're not like me. They're Screamers.

Beryl finally said, "I think you're very good being nice to Jim's little sister."

My ears burned.

"Thank you. Barry, I appreciate the fact that you are very generous with your car and don't mind picking us all up to bring us here."

"Thank you," Barry said. They all stood up then, all saying thank you, thank you. The party was over. What a rage.

Jim and I went walking to get out of the house. It was hot, he had taken his shirt off and tied it around his waist. I thought he looked nice, such a big chest, hardly hairy at all, still smooth and soft from being in the Stream. Better than Dad's wrinkled and greying old thing, which luckily I only see if we go swimming.

A man with a whole pile of purple pieces came up. He shuffled through them and handed my brother one, smiling. Like a teacher does when he knows you're going to get the answer wrong.

"*Behave acceptably in public.*" it said.

"But it's hot! This is acceptable!" Jim said. He knew what he was supposed to have done wrong.

"Put your shirt on, son. None of us want to witness your naked body," the man said. It was Mr Thompson from down the road. His two teenagers are in the Stream, and he has a Screamer back and his wife is quiet and ugly. I could imagine his chest; worse than Dad's, not even any muscles and probably covered with pimples. He has them on his face and neck; why would they stop there? I stared at this ugly man who was trying to cover up my beautiful brother.

"It's rude to stare," he said, and after my brother had put his shirt on, Mr Thompson left.

I found Jim lying in the back yard, amongst the grass he had just mown.

"I don't get it about daydreaming," he said. "I was just trying to see if I could daydream at all, and I can't. I've got nothing to think about."

"What about when you were a kid?" I said. I always daydream nice memories, from when I was five or six.

"I can't remember my childhood," he said. That sounded terrible.

"What about what you want to be? Or who you'll meet?"

"I'm supposed to be a gardener and I've already been introduced to June," he said. I moved closer and, the smell of cut grass filling my throat like sugar, I whispered, "But what do you *want* to be?"

He looked at me and there was a little smile on his mouth. "Nothing. I want to be nothing. I want to assume my duties as a citizen."

The sky-writer had smoked that into the blue sky earlier.

"Yes," he said. He went indoors and made good Friends with Dad. Dad gave him alcohol.

At least it isn't hard for him to assume his duties. He is told exactly what his duties are. At least he doesn't have to figure it out for himself.

Jim often went to the pictures with his Friends. In the morning I would ask him, "What was the movie like?"

"What movie?" he would say. He wouldn't remember. He smelt before he had his shower. He smelt like nothing I've ever smelt before.

"Is there a Stroking Party today, Jim?" I asked. I felt really cool, calling it what the Screamers did.

"What do you reckon?" he said, in a nasty voice. "Has there been a Thursday since I've been back when there hasn't been one?"

I hate it when he talks to me like that. I don't know what's wrong with him today. Something's up. Something's upset him. He won't even look at Mum and Dad, let alone get close enough for them to boss him around. Dad hasn't noticed, but Mum has. She keeps looking at me. Not as if I know what's going on, but in a thoughtful way, like she's trying to figure something out, something about me. It's confusing with the whole family gone weird.

I got into my spot behind the couch, but there were no lollies coming over. Five Screamers, my grouchy brother included, sat there saying nothing.

"Who'd like to start?" Beryl said. She must have thought it was her big chance.

"Mark's not here yet," June said. "Didn't you notice?"

"I thought he wasn't coming," Beryl said, "I thought he might be sick."

"He's not sick, he's in hospital," Jim said. There was this big noise, yelling and shouting and that. I couldn't tell who was who.

My dad slammed the door open and came into the room.

"Why was this door closed?" he shouted. "What's all this teenage rubbish?" That was a bad insult. He'd never called Jim a teenager before.

"We're just worried about Mark," Jim said. He is getting smarter and smarter.

"Mark will be released in the morning, Jim, you know that. He's learning his lesson early, he's lucky." There was quiet. My father left, without shutting the door.

"Arsehole," my brother said. I couldn't believe it. I didn't think he even knew a word like that. The others laughed, nervous but excited, it sounded.

"I can't think of anything nice to say," Beryl said, and that was the party finished with.

I never got to go to parties when I was growing. No one had them, no one had a big brother or sister to tell us what parties were like.

There was no one but our parents and teachers to tell us anything. Things like, when I wanted to go out late one night, to stay over at the twins' and sit up all night, my mum said NO, and I couldn't say but Jim is allowed. He wasn't there for me to say it about. I had to learn it all myself.

He won't come out of his room, only to do his chores and eat then back to his room. Dad gave him a bottle of whisky and I heard him in the night, crying in the voice I remember before he went away.

When it was party time again, I took my own lollies and ducked behind the couch.

But I had to peek my head around when Mark came in.

He didn't look very good. He was all yellow around his eyes and his arm was in a sling.

"I bit my nails," he said.

"But I thought we only had to *avoid the mannerisms*," June said. "I didn't think you could get hurt for them."

"Arseholes," my brother said. I think it's the only swear word he knows. I hid back behind the couch in case he told me to get. I heard a paper, then his voice, his nasty voice:

"Mannerisms to avoid.

1. *Biting nails* — you already discovered that one, Mark.
2. *Sniffling*
3. *Playing with hair*
4. *Putting pencils in mouth*
5. *Drumming with fingers*
6. *Wiggling a leg back and forth*
7. *Twitching mouth*

8. Twisting nose or ear

9. Moistening finger to turn page

10. Eating noisily

11. Playing with jewellery

And there I was, making little plaits in my hair!

"I think it's a bit much," June said, "but I think Mark is showing remarkable strength of character."

"Thank you," Mark said. "I think Barry was very brave for volunteering to take the food tins we collected to the city."

"Thank you," Barry said. I couldn't hear the rest. I blocked my ears and cried into my tucked up knees.

We had dinner with the Thompsons tonight. It was really boring. I was the only young one there, plus the parents, plus Jim and the Thompson's Screamer Laura. I was sitting there and I wanted to tell everyone about school, because I got best in maths, I got everything right and the teacher made me go to the other classes and read out my answers. It was really embarrassing.

I was telling everyone about it, thinking they'd be interested because they're all so boring, when I noticed how uncomfortable everyone looked so I shut up.

"*Don't talk about yourself all the time,*" Laura said, in that voice the Screamers use when they've learnt something off the purple pieces.

"*Don't talk about operations or dental experiences,*" Jim said.

"I haven't had any," I said. I was really annoyed.

"*Don't talk about controversial subjects, unpleasant happenings, or death,*" Laura said.

"I thought death *was* an unpleasant happening," I said. My mother, I'm sure, winked at me.

"What should we discuss?" Mr Thompson said. He already knew the answer.

"*News items and the interests of others,*" Jim said. It was the most boring night of my life, *and* we had to eat chops.

Jim and Dad were drunk in the kitchen. Jim tried to tell Dad about some music he likes that Dad doesn't like. Jim said, "But it gets you, you're into it, it lifts you away."

"Sounds dangerous," Dad said, "Sounds like daydreaming. Where did you hear this stuff? Some backyard?"

"It was on the radio. They said music for all ages. You just don't understand," Jim said. He was lying. They don't play music like that on the radio.

"No, you're the one who's supposed to understand. You have to put yourself in *my* place and understand *my* point of view."

Dad pointed at the purple piece he had carefully stuck on the fridge.

"But it doesn't make sense," Jim said, and I got nervous. He was saying stuff like that now. "It's easier for you to understand me cos you've been my age. I've never been your age."

"Never mind, you will," Dad said. Jim said nothing, which made me even more nervous.

"I love you, Dad," Laura Thompson said. I was at their place, watching Mrs Thompson make a cake. I looked at Mr Thompson and wondered how anyone could love him, even if they were told to. Especially if they've been gone seven years and come back a Screamer.

I looked puberty up in the dictionary. No other rude words were there. It said, "From the Latin 'pubertas' meaning 'age of madness'" That seemed weird, but it was a brand new dictionary.

We went to a movie with June and her mother. I was depressed because the twins had gone into the Blue Stream, they were my last friends. Luckily, Jim didn't mind taking me. It wasn't really a movie, it was more like a lecture. It was about this really dumb woman who kept getting into trouble. There was one bit where she had a mental at her children, threw things at them.

Jim said, "My mother has such a good temper, you really have to try to make her angry."

June and her mother smiled at him. I was amazed. Didn't he hear her yelling at me this afternoon? Just because I was late home from saying goodbye to the twins? She won't leave me alone; she wants me there all the time.

Running along the bottom of the screen through the whole "bad mother" screen were the words, *Show Pride in your Parents in Front of your Friends*.

At the end, a man stood up and said, "Isn't it nice to know exactly how to behave, even in the most embarrassing of situations? This hasn't always been the way. At one stage of the Human Struggle, people ignored the rules. It was a terrible time." All the adults and lots of the Screamers clapped, but the kids, old enough like me to be there, and the rest of the Screamers, just watched the titles. If they were thinking the same as me, none of them showed it.

I was thinking, So you can break the rules. People have done it before. Funny to think of that.

There was trouble after the movie was over. The adults gathered in the foyer, leaving kids and Screamers in the cinema. Then they let the Screamers out one by one, and us kids had to wait for hours.

Jim said that the adults were angry at the Screamers who hadn't clapped after the man's speech. They said, "We know who you are. We know each and every face."

They pointed at the ones who had clapped and cheered. Those Screamers were allowed to go. They were given a prize. Money, Jim said, but he couldn't quite see.

We were sent home then. We filed past the bad Screamers, who were standing facing the wall. Some of them were crying, and the adults said, "Don't cry like a baby. *A Mature Person does not Indulge in Childish Emotions*."

The Screamers tried to stop, but that just makes crying worse. Jim told me they had to watch the movie five times. He got home at breakfast time, his eyes red and tired.

"Enjoy the movie?" Dad asked.

"It was educational," Jim said. Then he had a shower and went to work.

Jim received a purple piece with his pay cheque. "*Take Disappointment Gracefully.*" I was very disappointed myself; I thought if I met him on payday he might buy me something on the way home. But he just walked along, watching his feet, ignoring me.

"What's wrong?" I asked him. He looked up. He wasn't depressed at all, he was smiling.

"Found another one," he said.

In red chalk on the footpath, were the words, You are an individual.

"Is that a rule?" I asked.

"Doubt it," he said. He was really happy. "Yesterday I found one that said, Your parents are far from perfect!"

"Maybe you shouldn't read them," I said. "You don't know who wrote them."

"It doesn't matter. The words are there."

From then on I always walked looking at my feet but I never found as many as Jim did.

Three months now until I take the big dip. Sara has been gone for ages, but her mother still goes to school to pick her up every day.

"Sara is in the Blue Stream. When she emerges, you will have a beautiful adult child to share your home," the Principal has told her.

They don't say how Sara can be more successful at avoiding accidents than her sister was.

Mum caught me the other day; she has no understanding of privacy. Neither does my brother.

"Privacy is far from Godliness," he said, standing at the door, when he heard me shouting at Mum. Luckily I had put my clothes on by then or I would have died. Mum sat on the bed and we had a talk.

"You feel a bit funny?" she asked. It was vague, but there was no way I could describe it.

"Yes."

She made me stand in front of the mirror and we looked at each other. Clothes on, thank god.

"You enter the Stream looking like you do. In the next seven years, your breasts will grow, your hips round. Hair will grow, under your arms and there." She pointed.

"Vagina, Mum," I said. Once I realised how embarrassed she was, I felt better.

"Yes. Your sex organs will increase in size - your vagina, uterus, clitoris."

"Is that a clit? The boys at school ask to see it sometimes."

"Well, don't show them. You'll grow in height and weight, perfectly, because you'll receive the right diet. And there are hormonal changes which are happening already. That's why the boys want to see parts of you they don't have themselves. It's a very difficult time, darling, physically and mentally painful, and if you weren't in the Stream, you might do things you'll regret later on."

"Like what. What did you do to regret?"

"I'm not really supposed to tell you. You're not supposed to have any ideas when you begin."

"Please, Mum. " It was sounding worse and worse, to me. I didn't want to miss out on the pain, I wanted to regret things.

Mum said, "The changes in you create the unrest. If you float in the Stream till the changes are over, you'll be perfect. That's what they say."

"But is it true?"

"Yes, of course. It's mostly true...for most people."

"Do you think it's true for me, Mum? What do you think?"

"We'll see," she said. She said we'll see. Maybe I'll stay here, maybe I won't have to go into the Blue Stream.

Something terrible has happened, something scary. A woman was walking along and four kids like me grabbed her, they hurt her, raped her, and they killed her. Kids! Some were eleven, some were twelve. One was ten. And there were girls there, as well as boys. They told us only teenagers committed gang-killings. So what are these kids then? It's really scary. The newspaper thinks that thirteen is too old now. But they can't drop us in the Stream earlier than that. There'd be no kids. We've been told we aren't allowed to hang around in big groups, just one or two. Too bad at school where we all used to sit on the oval and just talk about stuff. Too bad about going anywhere you might see someone you know.

My mother told my father she was taking me to the dentist, because I couldn't enter the Stream with cavities.

"I'm proud of you," he said, his eyes unfocused. He is drunk a lot these days.

"Nother drink, Dad?" my brother said, "nothing drink?" They laughed, the two men. Mother and I went to the station.

"I want to ask some questions about the Blue Stream," she told the man.

He made us watch a video about teenagers and then the office was closed.

Jim still screams when he wakes up. He keeps thinking he's emerging from the nothingness.

Jim and his Friends had to go to a meeting with the new Screamers and the old. It was for their twenty-first, instead of having a party. Barry couldn't go, because all the toilets he looks after were flooded, and they needed them for a conference.

When Jim came back he took my hand. He pressed something there. Red chalk. He went to his room. I didn't see him again.

June told me about the meeting, how all these Screamers from their year got up and said how wonderful the world was, and the new Screamers screamed and stared, and some of the old Screamers cried. She said Jim cried. She said she didn't cry, because she knew it was reality and that is how it is.

There was no scream this morning and I knew. My mother knew too. She left my father snoring in their bed and got in with me. We pulled the covers up and she held my hand and told me a long, long story, each story started another, and I helped. We told stories for three hours until my father woke up. He opened his door, walked into the hall, saw us sitting up in bed. Saw Jim's closed door. Made me love him by understanding. He closed my door.

We heard Jim's bed being dragged and had a sudden hope — perhaps he was asleep and Dad was trying to wake him. But we heard something heavy land on the bed.

Dad opened the door.

He came to us, took my hand and Mum's, and said, "I think you should look at his peaceful face," and we did. He was Real Jim on the bed with the marks of his own socks around his neck.

All his grief was with us now.

In the papers that day, the meeting was called a triumph of the human spirit.

Great moment in the human race, it said, all things taken into due consideration. Good adults greet new adults.

The number of Screamer accidents was not reported. Mr and Mrs Thompson came over to discuss Jim and the meeting.

"Terrible thing," Mr Thompson said. "Such a shame for Jim to suffer his accident so close to the success of the Program."

Laura said, "Funny how those socks knotted themselves." Her father, without turning to face her, pointed a finger directly at her. She stared. She said nothing else.

"All in all, a good birthday party," Mr Thompson. said "All things taken into due consideration."

It will be my birthday soon.

I can't tell you what will happen in my future; and once I'm there, I may not remember my past. From witnessing Jim's year of Screamers, I fear for my own life; I only hope I can conform. The only ones alive are the ones who are conforming now, and will do forever. The others have accidents. Screamer suicide does not exist. Why would they kill themselves when their lives are plotted for them, their behaviour planned and ordered? They have no worries. The adults say the strong human beings are left, but I say they are gone.

Dad's really angry with Mum. She won't share her drug.

"No one'll know, unless you tell them," he snarled, all angry and red-faced, standing over her as she sat on the couch watching the TV that wasn't on.

"Everyone will know," she said. She doesn't seem to mind the drug, but I don't want them to give her any more. She looks like Mrs Thompson now, like a photograph, barely moving, barely anything on her face. If I could steal her drug to give to Dad I would.

I woke up early this morning, excited because it was my birthday, but worried about the Blue Stream, no matter what the beautiful lady said.

Mum and Dad came into my room with a big tray of cake and lollies. For breakfast! Other years I couldn't have those till after eggs. There were two presents.

"One for now, one for later," Mum said. Her eyes were clear; I could tell she hadn't taken her drug. Dad sat on the bed and grinned stupidly. I thought maybe she had a plan.

I opened the present for now. It was some old record I can't even play because we don't have a record player.

"Thanks Mum," I said anyway. The other present I saved for later. Then I had to get ready for the Stream.

The guilt in my mother's eyes was the worst. Seeing it, I knew she didn't have a plan; other than to say goodbye. She had tried hard to keep me, and she had failed. So I suppose that's the end of me not going into the Blue Stream.

Mum did her best.

We went to many places, even the headquarters of these people called "Freedom Stream". But they had no plans of action — they talked a lot, that's all. They still sent their kids to the Stream.

Finally we caused a bit of fuss at the Minister's office. We got taken away by police. Mum got taken away and I got a talking to, by the beautiful lady with her hair in a bun, soft and fluffy around her face like a princess.

"The Stream is a place of beauty," she said. It made sense that she would know, she was so lovely.

When Mum picked me up she looked beautiful, too.

She didn't take her drug because she wanted to know, to experience the farewell, feel the pain.

I wept for an hour in her arms, saying goodbye. I didn't know if she would be there when I returned. It would depend. If she had a moment's selfish thought, she would have an accident. She wouldn't want to see me. But I would want her, need her to be there as I emerged from the womb so unlike hers.

I couldn't say I love you.

I always thought the Blue Stream would be out in the country, in the open, just covered with a perspex bubble to protect the floating, growing children inside. Where else would you find such a Stream? They even showed us pictures from a plane of the Blue line stealing across the land. But they took us to this big old building; there were heaps of them, all these huge old buildings I'd never noticed before.

There were no signs. We shuffled in the gloom. Barely able to see each other. The adults smiling, being kind, making jokes, saying, "See you real soon," as if we were supposed to laugh. The other kids were mucking around, excited, because it was their birthday, just like me. All born on the same day. They all shouted about the Blue Stream. I could only think of red chalk, and I wanted to remember it.

We entered through a small door, one at a time, so the ones outside had no idea what was inside. We expected a bus or something, an underground rail link to take us out to the country and the Blue Stream.

But inside, it was a huge room, even bigger than the cinema, a roof so high the rafters faded into a Blue. The whole lot of us fitted side by side, and there must have been a hundred. It was dark, at ground level, you could hardly see the next person, only the adults in their luminous suits, marching up and down, taking the roll about fifty times and refusing to answer questions. The only light came in a Blue glow from the plastic rectangular boxes held suspended above us. Ten wide, ten long, ten deep — one chained under another, a whole warehouse filled with a piece of art no one would like. The walls Blue and glowing.

The kids all shut up and gazed; the boxes way above were filled, the ones below were empty, inviting.

"What is it?" one kid asked, "Where's the Stream?"

"This is the transport there," one of the adults said and the rest laughed. I would have screamed but wanted my calm. Panic would remove control of my mind; my memory.

The perspex boxes above us moved, whispering slightly as they settled lower. It was like a ride at the fair (*Fun Activities to share with the family, number six*) or like a game where you had to end with the boxes in the right place.

Around me, kids were crying and trying to run away, but there were too many adults. They began a soft song,

"You sink first,
A cold, fresh shock,
And as you rise,
You begin to float,
And float, and float, and float."

Over and over they sang it, as we waited for our box to reach the floor and each kid was picked up and laid down and the next box moved along.

They called my name, and I climbed into my box as it was lowered to the ground.

They didn't have to lift me.

I lay down and breathed deeply like they told me.

Waited for the Blue Stream

Waited for nothingness.

I wake up screaming.

But I remember.

bios

Mark S. Deniz

A novelist and short fiction writer, Mark S. Deniz recently turned his hand to screenwriting for a short film Silverudden, which was screened at festivals worldwide in 2007. His published short stories (under the nom-de-plume Sin Deniz) can be found in the Big Finish anthologies: *A Life Worth Living*, *Something Changed*, and *Collected Works*. He also features in *FlashSpec: Volume Two*, and the *Black Box* anthology will have poetry featured in Doorways Magazine in 2009.

After a successful year at Eneit Press, Mark started his own company, Morrígan Books, closely followed by its imprint Gilgamesh Press, which is to focus on Assyrian topics. More can be found regarding Mark on his Live Journal account: http://mark.deniz.livejournal.com.

Mark S. Deniz lives in Norrköping, on the south east coast of Sweden, with his wife and their two children.

Bernie Mojzes – The Collector

Bernie Mojzes has, at various times in his life, framed pictures, taught college courses, practiced martial arts, and designed and built computer networks. He has also been accused of committing public acts of Music and Philosophy. Bernie has short stories published or forthcoming in the anthologies *Bad-Ass Faeries 2*, *Dragon Lure*, and *Barbarians at the Jumpgate*. His illustrated book, *The Evil Gazebo*, will be available from Dark Quest Books. He can be found at www.kappamaki.com.

T.A. Moore – Licwiglunga

T.A. Moore is a speculative fiction writer from Northern Ireland. Her prose is elegant, surreal and disturbing, generally eliciting the response of 'but you seem so nice!' from readers. She takes this as a compliment. Her first novel, *The Even*, was published by Morrígan Books in 2008 and the second, *Shadows Bloom*, will be published in 2010.

T.A. Moore writes, edits magazines, designs websites and teaches Creative Writing. Her advice to any aspiring young author is to cultivate a taste for coffee early. Strong coffee. The sort of coffee that would scare a Turkish man into drinking warm milky tea for the rest of his life.

Carole Johnstone – The Blind Man

Originally from Lanarkshire, Scotland, Carole Johnstone now lives in north Essex with her fiancé, Iain, and works part-time as a medical dosimetrist.

A relative newcomer to the world of published fiction, she was first featured in *Black Static Magazine* in early 2008. Her short stories have appeared, or are due to appear, in several anthologies and magazines including *Voices*, *In Bad Dreams Vol. 2*, *Grants Pass*, *Dead Souls*, and PS Publishing's post-apocalyptic anthology, *Catastrophia*.

Her first novella, *Frenzy*, was published by Eternal Press in August 2009. Her website can be found at www.carolejohnstone.com.

Tom English – Dry Places

Tom English is an environmental chemist for a U.S. defence contractor. For therapy, he runs Dead Letter Press and writes strange tales of the supernatural. His recent fiction can be found in *Horror: The Best of the Year, 2008* (Wildside Press), and issues of *All Hallows (The Journal of the Ghost Story Society)*.

Tom also edited the mammoth anthology *Bound for Evil: Curious Tales of Books Gone Bad*, which was a Shirley Jackson

Award finalist for 2008. Tom resides with his wife, Wilma, and their Sheltie, Misty, deep in the woods of New Kent, Virginia.

Visit him at http://literaryalchemist.blogspot.com.

Sharon Irwin – Begin with Water

Sharon Irwin lives in northwestern Ireland. She has been published in *Flash Me Magazine*, *The Sword Review*, *Beyond Centauri*, and others. Her work has been short listed for the Hennessy Literary Awards and for the Francis Mac Manus Short Story Award. Her blog can be found at http://theladywolf.livejournal.com/, but it's sadly neglected as she is writing a novel.

Robert Holt – In the Name

Robert Holt lives in the Midwest of the USA where he graduated from business school and now manages a grocery store. He eliminates all his rage towards his fellow man, a by-product of any customer service job, by writing horror stories in his free time (much to the bafflement of his beautiful wife, Jessica).

He has only just begun submitting his writings for publication, but watch for his other stories to start popping up in anthologies and on websites everywhere. He also has two full-length novels that are being dissected and stitched back together.

When not working, Robert enjoys escaping from the society in which he lives. This could mean flying to Europe for weeks at a time, cruising the South Pacific, or hiking through the Mark Twain National Forest for an hour with his hound dog. He also loves escaping into a good book, as any writer should.

His personal favourites include Clive Barker, Chuck Palahniuk, Richard Adams, Orson Scott Card, and Kurt Vonnegut.

Bill Ward – When They Come to Murder Me

Bill Ward is a freelance writer out of Baltimore, Maryland. He has sold fiction to *Murky Depths*, *Flashing Swords*, *Every Day Fiction*,

Darwin's Evolutions, Kaleidotrope, and the anthologies, *The Return of the Sword* and *Desolate Places.* In addition, Bill has written background material and serial fiction for fantasy and science fiction games, has done editing for small press ventures, and is co-editor of the *Magic & Mechanica Anthology* from Ricasso Press. To read his fiction or check out his weekly book reviews, please visit billwardwriter.com.

Christopher Johnstone – The Unbedreamed

Christopher Johnstone is usually found in Melbourne.

Elizabeth Barrette – Goldenthread

Elizabeth Barrette writes fiction, non-fiction, and poetry in the fields of speculative fiction, gender studies, and alternative spirituality. Previous credits include the short stories *Peacock Hour* in *Triangulations: Taking Flight* and *Pvaga and the Censor* in *The Lorelei Signal*; the articles *Appreciating Speculative Poetry* in Internet Review of Science Fiction and *Cyberfunded Creativity* in EMG-zine; the book *Composing Magic: How to Write Rituals, Spells, and Magical Poetry*; and the poems *Artifacts of Intelligent Design* in The 3rd Annual SFPA Poetry Contest 2008: Energy and *Ansel's Army* in Heroic Fantasy Quarterly.

She hosts a monthly Poetry Fishbowl on her blog, The Wordsmith's Forge (http://ysabetwordsmith.livejournal.com), writing poems based on prompts from her audience. She also reviews books and music on Reviews from Hypatia's Hoard (http://reviewarchive.iblog.my/). At science fiction conventions and other events, she presents panels on various topics. She enjoys suspension-of-disbelief, bungee-jumping and spelunking in other people's reality tunnels.

Catherine J. Gardner – When the Cloak Falls

Catherine J. Gardner's stories have appeared in Fantasy Magazine, Necrotic Tissue, and Arkham Tales. She has stories forthcoming in

Postscripts, Space and Time, and the chapbook *The Sour Aftertaste of Olive Lemon,* which is to be published by Bucket 'O' Guts press. She also writes MG and YA dark fantasy books and is currently searching for an agent. Though she has been told she won't find one under her desk or behind the cupboard, she insists on checking both places daily.

Anna M. Lowther – The Price of Peace

Anna M. Lowther resides in a small Ohio town where her great-great-great grandfather settled after the American Revolutionary War. Though she holds a degree in Elementary Education she is also a history buff, which shows in many of her stories. She believes her work often takes a dark turn of its own making and may be influenced by her close proximity to both the spot where Pretty Boy Floyd was killed and the road where George Romero filmed the opening sequence for the original Night of the Living Dead.

She has been published in Sinister Tales Magazine, Theaker's Quarterly Fiction, and Necrotic Tissue. Her stories appear in the following anthologies: *Damned in Dixie* by Tenoka Press, *Abominations* by Shroud Publishing, and *Black Dragon, White Dragon* by Ricasso Press.

Look for upcoming stories in *The Scroll of Anubis* by The Library of Horror Press and *Dark Distortions II* by Scotopia Press.

James R. Stratton – Your Duty to Your Lord

James R. Stratton is a chameleon. By day, he is a mild-mannered government lawyer specializing in the field of child abuse prosecutions, and lives with his wife and children in southern Delaware. But he has been an avid fan of speculative fiction all his life, and began writing genre fiction over ten years ago.

In recent years, he's been forging his dark alter ego as a genre fiction author through publication of his tales in venues like Dragons, Knights & Angels Magazine, Ennea (published in Athens, Greece) & Nth Degree Magazine. The appearance of his first foray into the world of poetry in The Broadkill Review is but another step in his master plan.

Soon, he will step into the light as his stories appear in 2008 & 2009 in Tower of Light Online Magazine, Big Pulp e-zine and Paper Blossoms, Sharpened Steel: Tales of Fantasy from the Far East from Fantasist Enterprises. His appearance in Dead Souls is yet another step in his master plan. His final reveal, the novel *Loki's Gambit*, is under review for possible publication in 2010.

Kenneth C. Goldman – Mercy Hathaway is a Witch

Ken Goldman taught English and Film Studies at George Washington High School until 1999 when he left to pursue a writing career, fortune, and fame. (So far he has managed to achieve the first of those goals.)

His stories have been seen in over 500 publications in the U.S., Australia, The U. K., Ireland, and Canada, and have received honourable mentions in Ellen Datlow and Terry Windling's The Year's Best Fantasy and Horror 7th, 9th, 16th, and 17th Annual Collections, and in Datlow and Kelly Link & Gavin J. Grant's 20th and 21st editions.

A book of his short stories, *You Had Me at ARRGH!!: Five Uneasy Pieces* by Ken Goldman has been published by Sam's Dot Publishing, and (shameless plug alert) it can be purchased online at The Genre Mall where it has remained among its all-time top ten best sellers since its publication in October 2007.

A film of his short story, *The Keeper*, has been contracted by Australia's Precision Pictures. Ken lives in two homes, one on the Main Line in Pennsylvania, and one on the beach on the South Jersey shore... so he must be doing something right.

Lisa Kessler – Immortal Beloved and Subito Piano

Lisa Kessler's short stories have been published in print anthologies and seen on the web in eZines like Sinisteria, Horrorfind, Twilight Times, The Writers Hood, Savage Night, The Murder Hole, Behold and Shadowkeepzine. Her story, *The Third*

King, won second-place in Behold's short story contest, and her story, *Immortal Beloved* was a finalist for a Bram Stoker award. She was also selected to be one of the authors in the 2009 Ladies of Horror anthology.

She is currently searching for a publisher for her *Night Trilogy* novels, and working on two additional novels. For more updates, check out her MySpace page at: http://myspace.com/Lisas_Lair.

When she's not writing, Lisa is also a professional vocalist performing with the San Diego Opera, as well as other musical theatre companies. She lives in southern California with her husband and two teens.

Michael Stone – The Migrant

Michael Stone was born in 1966 in Stoke-on-Trent, England. Since losing most of his eyesight to Usher Syndrome, he has retreated from your world to travel the dark corners of inner space. To put it more prosaically, he daydreams a lot.

Mike's work has appeared in numerous publications, most recently Dunesteef, Pseudopod, Everyday Weirdness, TQR, The Fleas they Carried and The Beast Within. In 2008, Baysgarth Publications published *Fourtold*, a collection of his novellas with a foreword by award-winning fantasist Garry Kilworth. His vanity has a name: www.mylefteye.net

Robert Hood – Sandcrawlers

Robert Hood is a card-carrying psychopath whose stories are blatantly autobiographical. He knows where you live and he's got a bus timetable so he can get there. If you doubt the power of his mojo, check out the story collections *Day-Dreaming on Company Time* (1988), *Immaterial: Ghost Stories (2002)* and *Creeping in Reptile Flesh (2008)* or his novel *Backstreets (2000)* and his *Shades* series.

He's also got a story sequence titled *Remainders* in the Morrígan Books' anthology *Voices* (2008), edited by Mark S. Deniz and Amanda Pillar. A novel, *Robot War Espresso*, is coming out from Twelfth Planet Press in 2010, so make sure you look out for it… or he'll be coming for you.

Sandcrawlers was written by invitation for the anthology Case Re-Opened, edited by Stuart Coupe and Julie Ogden (1993), for which authors were asked to fictionally solve an unsolved true-life Australian crime. Hood cheated. He was there.

Reece Notley – Tatsu and Cover Art

Reece Notley was born and lived in Hawai'i until her late teens when her feet grew itchy, and she wandered off to see the world. After chewing through a pile of books, a lot of odd food and a stray boyfriend or two, she eventually landed in Southern California which she believes to be a very nice place but seriously needs more rain.

She has a day job herding pixels for the marketing department of a nice company with a fantastic view of the San Diego seashore from many floors up and fits in editing Three Crow Press, a sci-fi, horror, fantasy, and speculative fiction e-zine (www.threecrowpress.com) in her not-so-spare time.

As of this moment, she admits to sharing the house with three cats, a black Pomeranian puffball, a bonsai Wolfhound and a ginger Cairn terrorist and is enslaved to the upkeep of a 1969 Ford Mustang Grand Coupe, a 1979 Pontiac Firebird and a Toshiba laptop.

L.J. Hayward – Wayang Kulit

L.J. Hayward lives in southeast Queensland. Well, she works there and sometimes makes an attempt at this thing called life. She's had stories published with Eneit Press, Aurealis and Morrígan Books and is still working toward that editor-eye-catching novel. Like Robert A. Heinlein, she feels that writing isn't something to be ashamed of, but she does do it in private and washes her hands thoroughly afterward. You can read her idle prattle at Plot Happens (l-j-hayward.livejournal.com).

Rebecca Lloyd – Contaminator

Rebecca Lloyd has been writing fiction since 1999. Her short stories have been published in journals, magazines and e-zines in Canada, USA, New Zealand, and the UK. She is a group host and creative writing teacher for Writewords, an online writers' community, and in Bristol, she teaches creative writing at the Grant Bradley Gallery and at Borders Bookshop.

In 2008, she won the Bristol Short Story Prize for a story called *The River*. She has recently begun writing novels for young people, the first of which will be published by Walker Books in Spring 2011. She is a member of the Society of Authors.

Ramsey Campbell – The Dead Must Die

The Oxford Companion to English Literature describes Ramsey Campbell as "Britain's most respected living horror writer". He has been given more awards than any other writer in the field, including the Grand Master Award of the World Horror Convention, the Lifetime Achievement Award of the Horror Writers Association and the Living Legend Award of the International Horror Guild.

Among his novels are *The Face That Must Die*, *Incarnate*, *Midnight Sun*, *The Count of Eleven*, *Silent Children*, *The Darkest Part of the Woods*, *The Overnight*, *Secret Story*, *The Grin of the Dark*, *Thieving Fear*, and *Creatures of the Pool*. Forthcoming is *The Seven Days of Cain*. His collections include *Waking Nightmares*, *Alone with the Horrors*, *Ghosts and Grisly Things*, *Told by the Dead* and *Just Behind You*, and his non-fiction is collected as *Ramsey Campbell, Probably*. His novels, *The Nameless* and *Pact of the Fathers*, have been filmed in Spain. His regular columns appear in Prism, All Hallows, Dead Reckonings, and Video Watchdog. He is the President of the British Fantasy Society and of the Society of Fantastic Films.

Ramsey Campbell lives on Merseyside with his wife Jenny. His pleasures include classical music, good food and wine, and whatever's in that pipe. His web site is at www.ramseycampbell.com.

Stephanie Campisi – The Ringing Sound of Death on the Water Tank

Stephanie Campisi is an Australian writer of the weird and sometimes wonderful. Her work has appeared in magazines and anthologies worldwide. Her full and current bibliography can be found at www.stephaniecampisi.com.

Paul Finch – June

Paul Finch is a former cop and journalist, now turned full time writer. He first cut his literary teeth penning episodes of the British TV crime drama, *The Bill*, and has written extensively in the field of animation. However, he is probably best known for his work in horror.

To date, he's had ten books and nearly 300 stories and novellas published on both sides of the Atlantic. His first collection, *Aftershocks*, won the British Fantasy Award in 2002, while he won the award again in 2007 for his novella, *Kid*. Later in 2007, he won the International Horror Guild Award for his mid-length story, *The Old North Road*. He is currently working on the scripts for three movie adaptations of his own novellas, *Cape Wrath*, *Charnel House*, and *Hunting Ground*.

Paul lives in northern England with his wife, Cathy, and his children, Eleanor and Harry.

Gary McMahon – A Shade of Yellow

Gary McMahon's fiction has appeared in magazines and anthologies in the U.K. and U.S and has been reprinted in both *The Mammoth Book of Best New Horror* and *The Year's Best Fantasy & Horror*. He is the British-Fantasy-Award-nominated author of *Rough Cut, All Your Gods Are Dead, Dirty Prayers, How to Make*

Monsters, Rain Dogs, and has edited an anthology of original novelettes titled *We Fade to Grey.*

Forthcoming are the collections *Different Skins, Pieces of Midnight* and *To Usher, the Dead,* and his first mass market novel *Hungry Hearts* will be published by Abaddon Books in late 2009. Website: www.garymcmahon.com

Kaaron Warren – The Blue Stream

Kaaron Warren's first novel, *Slights* was launched at WorldCon in 2009 by Angry Robot Books, an imprint of Harper Collins. Two more novels, *Mistification* and *Walking the Tree* will be published over the next year.

Her short story collection *The Glass Woman* (*The Grinding House* in Australia) contained the story *The Blue Stream.* She still gets readers approaching her to say that the story made them angry, or that they can relate to it in some way.

Kaaron lives in Canberra with her family and the ghost of their cat, Zephyr.

acknowledgments

'Mercy Hathaway is a Witch', © Ken Goldman, first published in The Witching Hour, Silver Lake Publishing (print and e-zine), January 2001. Reprinted by permission of the author.

'Immortal Beloved', © Lisa Kessler, first published at HorrorFind.com in 2002

'The Migrant', © Michael Stone, first published at TQR (www.tqrstories.com), January 2008. Reprinted by permission of the author.

'Sandcrawlers', © Robert Hood, first published in Case Re-Opened, 1993, edited by Stuart Coupe and Julie Ogden, Allen & Unwin. Reprinted by permission of the author.

'Contaminator', © Rebecca Lloyd, first published (as 'Dark Contaminator') at Theatre of Decay, 2004. Reprinted by permission of the author.

'The Dead Must Die', ©1992 Ramsey Campbell, First published in Narrow Houses, edited by Peter Crowther. Reprinted by permission of the author.

'The Ringing Sound of Death on the Water Tank', © Stephanie Campisi, first published in In Bad Dreams, Eneit Press, 2007. Reprinted by permission of the author.

'June', © Paul Finch, first published at Sci-Fright 6, 2000. Reprinted by permission of the author.

'The Blue Stream', © Kaaron Warren, first published in Aurealis Magazine #14, 1993. Reprinted by permission of the author.

The following stories were originally submitted for an alternate Morrígan Books' title and were selected by Skadi meic Beorh:

The Collector
Licwiglunga
Dry Places
Begin with Water
In the Name
When they Come to Murder Me
The Unbedreamed

Goldenthread
When the Cloak Falls
The Price of Peace
Your Duty to your Lord
Mercy Hathaway is a Witch
Immortal
Beloved

All other stories were selected by Mark S. Deniz.
All stories in this anthology were edited by Mark S. Deniz.

Available Now
THE EVEN
by T.A. MOORE

*"In this grim fable, the stakes are suicide by Apocalypse, and
the question is what can endure, and what refuses to end."*
— Elaine Cunningham

In the Even — a city built in the intersection between the real and
the not — ruled by the iron whim of the demon Yekum where
treachery brewed amidst the ever-changing streets. Ancients
dwell in the city who have out-lived their purpose and grown
jaded with their immortality. They want only to die and they will
take the whole world with them if they have to: suicide by
Apocalypse.

Only Faceless Lenith, goddess, cynic and gambler, stands in their
way. The fate of the world rests on her shoulders and mankind
did not conceive her to be wise.

www.morriganbooks.com

Three Crow Press
Morrígan Books E-Zone

Editors
J. LEE. MOFFATT, T.A. MOORE & REECE NOTLEY

Three Crow Press is an online magazine specializing in quality speculative fiction, fantasy (urban, dark and gothic), horror and steampunk as well as non-fiction pieces and articles.

We are prepared to consider all forms of dark fiction works and are looking for stories that capture the imagination of the Three Crow staff. Please check submissions guides prior to submitting.

www.threecrowpress.com
www.morríganbooks.com